Kenneth John Atchity w
Occidental College in I
chairman of the comparat
MW00458796
Fulbright Professor to the University of Bologna. Aside from
his novels, his academic career saw the publication of dozens of
books, papers, lectures, and scholarly articles on Greek,
Roman, and Italian literature.

In a second career he represented writers of both fiction and
non-fiction, accounting for numerous bestsellers and movies he
produced for both television and big screen. He was nominated
in 2011 for an Emmy Award for producing "The Kennedy
Detail." He has drawn on his expert knowledge of Christian
history and his classical training to write *The Messiah Matrix*.

Other books by Kenneth John Atchity:

Eterne in Mutabilitie: The Unity of the Faerie Queene
Homer's Iliad: The Shield of Memory
Homer: Critical Essays
A Writer's Time
*Seven Ways to Die**
The Renaissance Reader
The Classical Greek Reader
The Classical Roman Reader

**With William Diehl*

THE MESSIAH MATRIX

KENNETH JOHN ATCHITY

The Messiah Matrix
By Kenneth John Atchity

Published by: Imprimatur Britannia (UK)
and Story Merchant Books,
9601 Wilshire Boulevard #1202
Beverly Hills CA 90210.

ISBN: 978-095721-890-1

A catalogue record for this book is available from
The Library of Congress.
Cover design and artwork: BakerComarsh

First Edition. Released in the United States of America.

www.messiahmatrix.com

For unto us a Child is born,
Unto us a Son is given,
And the government shall be upon His shoulder.
And His Name shall be called:
Wonderful, Counselor, the Mighty God,
The Everlasting Father, the Prince of Peace.

—Isaiah 9:6

We should always be disposed to believe that which appears to us to be white is really black, if the hierarchy of the church so decides.

—St. Ignatius Loyola, founder of the Society
of Jesus (commonly known as the Jesuits)

Emperor Marcus Aurelius: We should not say I am an Athenian or I am a Roman but I am a citizen of the Universe...For there is only one universe, one God, one truth.

—Lucius Annaeus Seneca

To All Seekers of Truth

Prologue

The three-wheeled truck, having weathered World War II and every day after, carried its battle scars proudly as it hovered on the curb of Via del Plebiscito. Its V-shaped bumper was as jagged as a saw. Behind the wheel its latest owner, Zbysek Bailin, waited patiently, as though he were long accustomed to assassination on a rainy Wednesday evening.

A red umbrella rounded the corner from the Piazza del Gesù. Zbysek took in a breath and turned the ignition key. The engine coughed to an idle, purred raggedly awaiting further command from its driver. The silver-haired man ambled toward the intersection of Via degli Astalli that flanked the rear of the massive church. Purposely leaving his headlight off, Zbysek shifted into gear and bounced into the street. His foot pressed on the reluctant accelerator, the ancient vehicle climbing all too slowly up to speed.

The man had reached the intersection, and as he passed beneath the streetlight Zbysek thought he might well be deaf—he was so lost in thought he didn't seem to hear the rumbling truck, even as it barreled toward him at full speed.

Clutching tight to the shaky steering wheel, Zbysek was hunched forward in the cab, eyes intent on his target. All he could see was the man's bent back, crawling up Via Astalli like a praying mantis.

In seconds the truck had jumped the curb and was upon him.

The man swung around with his books and umbrella, a

look of sudden shock on his face—the smile erased. His coat fell open.

For the first time, Zbysek saw his victim clearly in the light of the street lamp—the crisp white collar and the purple piping on his black vest.

His target was a monsignor!

Zbysek hauled at the wheel—but it was too late. His head struck the roof as the vehicle jerked over the body and slammed straight into the lamppost, thrusting Zbysek into the windshield and cracking his head on the glass. He climbed clumsily out of the cab and fell to his knees beside his victim. "Forgive me, father," Zbysek finally choked out.

The old man's face was twisted with pain. His narrowed eyes were glistening, blood trickling from his lips. He reached his hand toward his Angel of Death. He seemed to want to speak. Zbysek lowered his head to hear. The monsignor's final whispered words confused and frightened him, and he leapt for the three-wheeler and fled from the scene.

I / 1
Unholy Thursday

Father Ryan McKeown's mood was less than reverential as he headed for the confessional where he was to perform his priestly duties. The lines of penitents in Gesù were short today. Perhaps because there'd been no major holidays recently or any coming soon, the "occasions of sin" were easier to avoid. Just as Ryan was about to step into the polished mahogany cubicle, a bedraggled man burst into the nave. The man headed for the first confessional, and knelt briefly. Moments later he unceremoniously leapt to his feet to join a short line at the next confessional booth, causing bowed heads to look up in curiosity. Ryan was bemused. *Could a man's sins be so grave he feels the need to come clean of them to several confessors?*

Ryan settled himself behind the ivory baffle and listened, in turn, to an old man cursing God because his arthritis no longer allowed him to play *bocce*; to a teenager who abused himself fourteen times in the past seven days, using the image of his teacher, a nun, as inspiration—Father Ryan, doing his best to repress a smile, told him to say the rosary and promise never to sin again; and to a seminarian barely out of high school who asked if having concerns about his faith meant he should quit the seminary.

"Doubts are not in themselves a sin," he told the young

man. "Thomas, though he doubted, went on to become a great apostle and martyr. Not to mention Mother Teresa, whose troublesome doubts dogged at her heels even more persistently than Calcutta's poor. I can tell you, it's what you do with doubt that matters." He questioned whether his comments had been of any service, or whether he should have simply referred the seminarian to a therapist. He'd often wondered where he'd be today if he himself hadn't rejected psychotherapy as an option.

He was removing his stole to leave when a tardy penitent thumped down on the kneeler and activated the tiny red light. Ryan slid open the grate. In the obscure light he could see only enough to determine that his supplicant was a male. "Yes, my son?"

"Are you Father Ryan?" the man asked.

"Yes," Ryan answered, before he could consider how the penitent could know his name.

"Thank God I've found you."

Ryan realized he was speaking with the lost soul who'd been playing musical confessionals. "How long has it been since your last confession?"

"I killed a priest." Ignoring the sacramental protocol, the man blurted it out in a coarse accent that Ryan had never heard before. Then, remembering the ritual formalities, the man added, "I don't remember my last Confession. Many years ago, in Tirana."

So the accent was Albanian. "What do you mean you killed a priest?"

"I hit him with my truck. He was a monsignor. I tried to help him. His eyes...oh my God! I got scared and drove away."

Ryan's heart went out to the man on the other side of the grate. The anguish in the man's voice was dreadful. "An accident, no matter how grievous, is not a sin," he said. "You simply have to—"

"It wasn't an accident," the immigrant interrupted. "I was paid to run him down."

Ryan fell silent. What fate had led this man to *his* confessional today among so many hundreds in the Holy City?

"They didn't tell me he was a monsignor." Now the man was choking, the guttural sound poignantly wretched. "Oh, my God, I am damned to hell for all eternity."

"Why would you accept payment for such an act?"

"I was desperate—I am desperate. My family has no money, my children need doctors—" The man's explanations gave way to wrenching sobs. Then he regained control. "He looked at me. He told me words I didn't understand. But I will hear them for the rest of my life."

Reflexively Ryan slipped into his persona as an investigative scholar. "What were his words, my son?"

The poor man's scream echoed in the hollowness of the empty church. "No!"

"It's all right to tell me," Ryan said. "You're protected by the Seal of the Confessional, Holy Mother Church's—"

"You don't understand! It was Holy Mother Church...that paid me!"

II/2
Emily Scelba

24 hours earlier

With a growing sense of dread Emily Scelba scanned the skies from the cluttered deck of the diving barge. A storm was fast approaching from the northern horizon, its emissary gusts already whipping her red hair around her slim, freckled shoulders, as though she were a latter-day Botticelli Venus completely oblivious to the stunning figure she cast.

She fought to contain the fear that was steadily rising in her throat as the waves around her rose higher. Her graduate-school divers were still sixty feet down in the sea. She was angry the two rascals hadn't returned the moment their radio quit. Surely they knew the procedure. What could be keeping them down there?

The unexpected storm heading south from Haifa was moving faster than usual for this time of year. In seconds the waves had doubled in size, and the turbulence had knocked their communications out. Now the waves were crashing hard against the barge, blasting the oil drums under the timber frame, throwing a cold spray up over the deck.

Suddenly the air felt frigid. Emily pulled a windbreaker over her weathered khaki bikini, concealing the bronze musculature she'd developed from years toiling through springs and summers under the harsh Palestinian sun. *Keep calm,* she reminded herself.

The tragic loss of her mother surged to the forefront of her mind. She was thirteen years old when the person she admired most in the world, the eminent archaeologist Valentina Carlisle-Scelba, had disappeared into the murky sea in an underwater diving expedition. Her body was never recovered. Emily had vowed to herself that she would carry on in the footsteps of the woman she idolized and make iconic archaeology her profession.

Except for the responsibility etched in her striking gray eyes, and the worry that now furrowed her brow, no one would ever have guessed this youthful woman was one of the world's leading experts in archaeological iconography—and that she bore the title "Director of the Caesarea Ancient Harbor Excavation Project." Emily was proud to have been part of these excavations as an undergraduate at the University of Maryland. Back in her student days, while studying Latin in Jesuit high school in Kansas City, she'd first read Flavius Josephus' description of this ancient harbor which had been the capital of Judea at the time of Jesus Christ. At the age of fourteen she'd known that she'd somehow find her way to the ruins of Caesarea Maritima, with its long-buried Temple of Augustus Caesar overlooking the Mediterranean Sea—which she learned the Romans of the early empire had jovially referred to as *mare nostrum,* "our lake."

A few years later it was Emily's team that penetrated beneath the ninth-century mosque and the sixth-century martyr-shrine of the Holy Procopius to unearth three leaf-topped capitals that clearly belonged to the imperial cult temple constructed by King Herod the Great. It was Emily's hand that had brushed away the dust of centuries to uncover the first of the capitals, with its unexpected cross-like emblem carved in bas-relief. *Was it some sort of extraordinarily early Christian symbol?*

She could never forget the rush of euphoria that swept through her at that moment when she knew she had validated the profession to which she'd dedicated the last fifteen years of her career. Her only regret is that she could not share her achievements with her mother.

The important question was this: What was a cross doing on a Roman capital, from a temple consecrated in 10 B.C.? Pursuing the answer to this question and many others had led Emily to a Rhodes scholarship and a postgraduate degree in ancient iconography from Oxford and enabled her to mold life to her heart's desire. The publication of her doctoral thesis on "Early Romano-Christian iconography," tracing the evolution of the cross from the ankh of ancient Egypt through the shamanic world tree to the Buddhist swastika to the cross of Jesus, had toppled the long-unchallenged interpretations of Irwin Panofsky and rocketed her to a precocious associate professorship of archaeology at Yale. She concluded that the cross, from time immemorial, was universally symbolic of the intersection between earth and heaven, matter and spirit, the one and the many, human and divine.

By the end of each rugged six months in the field, she had to admit she was ready again to return to telling adventure tales in her Georgian classroom, complete with musty books, in Yale's elm-lined Timothy Dwight College. She would have gladly stepped into that dull routine now.

The sudden storm now whipping the waves wildly rocked the deck, making it almost impossible to maintain her footing. The rest of the team had already headed to shore in the larger of the two Zodiacs tethered to the barge. Emily was to follow them the moment the two divers surfaced.

But twenty minutes later they still remained below. Emily

fought to tie down the equipment, flipped on the night-warning beacon, and scanned the turbulent water. A pair of sandals left on deck was washed away in a torrent. A scuba tank broke loose from the bin and rolled across the slippery surface. Emily grabbed it and started to carry it back, but then found herself hooking on a regulator and strapping it onto her back. *I must be as crazy as they are,* she thought, and cursed herself as she pulled out her mask and fins and buckled on her weight belt.

Graduate students.

David wouldn't stay down this long on his own—it must be Harel, she thought. David was clearly the smarter of the two, but he always seemed to follow his brash roommate's lead. The big Israeli from Haifa University was always pushing the limits. Harel was crass and loud and unfailingly obnoxious, but he had a good deal of charisma as well—and the luck that always seems to go with it. *What was he up to now? What has he found down there?*

III/3

Ego te absolvo...
I absolve you.

The Albanian penitent's cry was punctuated by the thump of the kneeler as he stood up and lurched from the confessional box.

Father Ryan had slid his Dutch door open in time to see the emaciated man running for the front of the church. "Wait!" he shouted. "The Sacrament isn't complete." But the man was gone.

By the time Ryan reached the entrance and descended the few marble steps into the Piazza del Gesù, the man was opening the door to a three-wheel truck with a cracked windshield—the truck, Ryan realized, that must have been the lethal weapon.

What happened next was so unexpected Ryan would not have believed it had he not witnessed it with his own eyes. A stoplight turned green, the roar of the traffic circling the Piazza instantly resumed, and a red Vespa darted from behind a bus and headed straight for the three-wheeler. The motorcycle backfired so loudly that Ryan flinched—until he realized it wasn't backfire but gunfire.

Ryan ran for the falling penitent, his green stole flapping behind him in the wind. Blood was everywhere, spurting from the man's polyester jacket, and it didn't take a medic to realize the wound was accurate and fatal.

"*Ego te absolvo a peccatis tuis, in nomine Patris, et Filii, et Spiritus Sancti,*" "I absolve you of your sins, in the name of the Father, and of the Son, and of the Holy Spirit." Ryan made the sign of the cross as he spoke the ancient words of sacramental absolution.

Cradling the dying man in one arm, he signed the cross with his thumb on the sinner's bleeding forehead. As the light in his eyes began to fade, Ryan was startled to see the man's lips opening.

"*The monsignor said,*" he gasped, "'*Find Father Ryan...memory in the ashes of Jasius...in the Gesù.*'" Then the man's eyes closed as he breathed his last and made his way to the eternal gates that Ryan's absolution may or may not have opened for him.

IV/4
De Profundis
Out of the depths

Over the past dozen years of diving on-site in the ancient harbor in Israel, Emily had explored and uncovered many of Caesarea's underwater ruins.

But the Roman shipwreck into which her crew was now diving lay farther out in the open water of the south bay. Out here they were exposed to the strong offshore currents of the eastern Mediterranean. These far-reaching flows, reinforced by winds from the mountains in Sinai, carried huge quantities of sand and mud that severely clouded the water.

Emily was now cutting through these currents as she finned her way toward the bottom. With the storm moving in, the water was more turbulent than ever. Visibility was little more than six feet. She followed the snaking tube of the vacuum pump, which led from the barge to the bottom and could be relied upon to guide her to her divers.

Today it didn't. When she reached the bottom at sixty feet, there was no sign of divers—just the open end of the dangling tube.

Emily scanned the area around her. The water was thick with swirls of silt. With the sun obscured by gathering clouds, the light was unusually dim for this depth. Below her, a deeply rotted timber protruded from the sand. It was one of the many surviving ribs of the ancient Roman merchant ship, a 130-foot-long vessel from the first century A.D. The ship, like so many before and after it, had crashed into offshore rocks and never made it out of the harbor. Emily now wondered if it had run into a sudden storm like the one that was closing in on her team. If a squall in these seas could destroy a Roman trader, what havoc would it wreak on her ramshackle barge? Had circumstances like these sealed the fate of her mother? She could only hope the barge would still be there when they returned to the surface.

Emily had to locate her students quickly. Gliding over the skeletal remains of the wreck, she moved through the murky water as if through a kind of fog, her eyes straining to make out any specific semblance of form—the burst of bubbles from a regulator, the shiny glint of a tank. She saw nothing. Beyond the ribbed rows of the shipwreck's hull passing like railroad ties beneath her, she could make out only the occasional thresher shark flitting past, and the bright orange gridline cords that marked the extent of their excavation.

In the few weeks they'd been working on the wreck, Emily and her team had uncovered a variety of artifacts: hundreds of amphora shards encrusted by coral and corrosion, various scraps of the ship's iron fittings, and several more unusual pieces, including an olive oil lamp with a bas-relief eagle, a bronze key worn as a ring, even a number of small bronze coins, produced by the famous mint in ancient Caesarea. Loaded by the hundreds into the belly of the ship and carried to and from all corners of the empire, the amphorae had been filled with oil, wine, and grains.

Every scrap of pottery the diving team recovered, every bit of bronze and iron they might find, would be cleaned and recorded, photographed and catalogued, then sent on to the University of Haifa for further study and research. The excavating, though laborious and difficult, was easily the most exciting part of the archaeological process: it quickly became addictive. Emily was not surprised her students were progressively obsessed. It was easy, when absorbed in the hunt, to forget about dwindling air, or changes in the current, or the weather up top. Prying loose another prize became the only thing that mattered.

The water toward the stern of the wreck was thick with a nearly impenetrable murk. Emily moved slowly through it, feeling her way over the timbers and the grid. The oldest artifact they'd found in the bay was a stone anchor dating from the Bronze Age, some 3200 years ago. In the thirty-two centuries that had passed since then, hundreds of ships had sunk in these seas, thousands of sailors had drowned. She was now swimming through the murky sea dust of their bones.

Emily felt claustrophobic. Her breathing rate increased. The raucous babble of bubbles kept bursting past her ears. What had happened to Harel and David? Why hadn't they surfaced? How could they be working in this swirling stew of silt?

A fin smacked her face. Emily pulled back as water leaked into her mask. She quickly readjusted it and blew the water out. The salt stung her eyes. She blinked until they cleared.

David was staring at her wide-eyed through his mask. He held up his hands and shrugged an innocent apology. She wanted to throttle him. Instead she pointed angrily at her watch and jerked a thumbs-up toward the surface. David pointed his thumb over his shoulder and shrugged again. "Not my fault," he seemed to be saying.

She could have guessed as much. Harel was indeed the problem. He was the one keeping them down.

Emily pushed David aside and looked to see what Harel was doing. Difficult to tell in the murk, but he appeared to be down under the ribs of the wreck, stirring up a muddy mess. She could just make out the back of his tank and a rising burst of bubbles. She swam down into the storm of silt and tugged his buoyancy vest. Harel turned his bearded face up, looked at her a moment, then turned back to his work.

Emily fumed. She glanced across at David, who simply waited and watched, wondering what she would do.

She grabbed hold of Harel's vest and tried to pull him out of the pit. Finally he swam up and confronted her. He had a chisel in one hand and a pry bar in the other. His size was daunting. He was built like an American football lineman, with a hairy chest, strong broad shoulders, a long heavy frame, and meaty arms and hands. Although he was a few years younger than Emily, somehow he always seemed older.

But certainly not wiser, despite his inflated opinion of himself. She waved her thumb toward the surface, made a gesture with her hand indicating stormy seas above, then pointed her index finger at his chest and again jerked her thumb toward the surface.

Harel shook his head.

She couldn't believe it. Was he going to defy her order? Did he intend to drown in the storm?

She took hold of his vest again as if to haul him up. Harel pulled her hand away and started back into the pit. Emily grabbed the top of his tank. He continued pulling away, nearly taking her down with him.

Finally he came back to her again. Still holding the chisel and pry bar, he held her shoulders between his hands and looked at her intently. Then he shifted his tools to one hand, formed a fist with the other and clutched it to his chest. He seemed to be saying he must continue, that whatever it was he'd found down there, he couldn't go up without.

No artifact, no matter how rare or precious, was worth risking their lives. That was standard operating procedure. If they didn't ascend to the platform now, they might well end up drowning. She shook her head, repeated the wavy gesture. She looked to David and back to Harel, and pointed insistently to the surface.

David put a hand on Harel's shoulder and nodded his agreement. Harel looked at him, and then back at Emily. Finally, he gave in. He handed her the chisel and pry bar. "It's your decision," he seemed to say, and then started up toward the surface. David followed after him.

Emily looked at the tools in her hands. What had he been working on? What was it that couldn't wait? Was he afraid it would be lost again in all this effluvium? Was it possible the storm currents would wash the find away?

It would take the two students several minutes to prepare for their departure and to load the Zodiac. Enough time, Emily decided, for her to take a quick look.

She swam down into the pit. The light in here was dimmer and the water even murkier. She felt her way down along the rib of the hull until she reached the bottom. Harel had left his underwater light half-buried in the sand. Its beam was pointed at a crack in the hull frame, where the encrusted shell of a bronze krater vase had deeply embedded itself.

Emily examined it closely.

The krater was coarse with corrosion and covered with a

thin veneer of copper carbonates known as verdigris—the result of centuries of reaction to sea salt. The corrosion had almost eaten through the metal in places, but other than that there seemed to be nothing unusual about the oversized wine urn. She picked up the flashlight and aimed it more directly into the vase, moving her face within inches of its surface. The light was flickering—low battery—and it took her several seconds of study before she finally saw the source of Harel's obsession.

A coin.

Encased in the lime deposits on the exterior surface of the krater like some sort of flagrantly tasteless ornament, it was partly disguised, like the bronze itself, under the patina of verdigris. The coin was not bronze, not silver, not even copper or a copper alloy.

It was gold.

Her pulse was racing. She could barely contain herself. All thoughts of the oncoming storm, of her ascending companions, of the terrible danger they were in—all of it vanished.

All she could see was the coin, cleverly mounted in an envelope of bronze—as though to conceal it for safekeeping.

The Augustan *aureus.*

Never released for common circulation, used only by administrators, or bankers, or the wealthiest Roman merchants, *aurei* were the rarest of the rare even in their own time. Supposedly only one thousand were struck in the Judean mint, most of those sent in tribute to Augustus Caesar in Rome.

Never seen by a human being alive today. The stuff of legends. The stuff of her mother's dreams as well as her own. *I dedicate this find to you, Mom,* she thought. It wasn't the elemental gold that bewitched her, though that was certainly a part of it. Nor was it the fame of the coin itself. Rather it was the coin's imprint, the bas-relief profile of a man's head where the emperor's portrait should be.

Emily couldn't take her eyes from it.

This ruler was bearded—and was wearing a crown of thorns.

She stared hard at the golden disc and willed it to tell her its story.

V / 5
Flavius Josephus the Historian

70 A.D.

Josephus stood at the prow, his face wet with spray as his vessel approached the new harbor of Caesarea from the west. King Herod the Great's magnificent palace came into view, where the monarch of Judea had lived his happiest days—and died, some seventy years ago, in diseased misery. Josephus would later report that the grandeur of Herod the Great's legacy was imprinted in the semi-circular seawall, the tower, the palace, the public baths, and of course in the Temple of Sebastos that overlooked it all. He would *not* report that he was viewing this scene through eyes blurred with angry tears.

Herod the Great built the Temple of Sebastos—the Greek word for Augustus—to honor the Roman emperor who'd had the wisdom to *reward* Herod, who had once supported Augustus' rival, Antony, rather than *executing* the Judean king which by all rights and precedents he might well have done. Loyalty, like everything else among the hugely practical Romans, was a fully barterable commodity. To that imperial principle, King Herod the Great owed his life.

Now, in this year 70 A.D., a much lesser descendant of the Herodian line, Herod Agrippa II, had summoned Josephus to this unhappy meeting. As far as his eyes could see, the itinerant historian noted ships, most of them bearing Roman, Greek, or

Egyptian sails, some with banks over banks of rowers, seeking welcome refuge from the relentless southeast wind that dashed the wine-dark waves against the cliffs. The harbor was indeed larger than Athens' Piraeus or even Rome's Ostia, worthy of its reputation as one of the world's great engineering marvels. The solidity of the monumental masonry defied the turbulent sea, while its magnificence soared above the waves to proclaim that no obstacle of nature was too great for human imagination to overcome.

But today Josephus' imagination was more troubled than it had ever been, and he had a hard time concentrating on the careful observation that was his pride both as a general and as a historian.

A guide sent from the king met him as he disembarked and led him from the wharves. Preferring to find his own way, Josephus tried to dismiss his black-skinned escort. But protesting in rapid-fire Aramaic, the guide would hear nothing of it; he had been ordered to escort this honored guest to the rendezvous with the *alabarch,* the tax official, and must do so on penalty of a lashing.

Slowly following the nervous guide, Josephus made his way along the broad mosaic-paved promenade between groups of passengers arriving from all nations of the empire. He wished he could join them as an anonymous layman in marveling at the colossal statues flanking the harbor's mouth. White marble villas bordered the walls, and on their high balconies the historian could make out the wealthy merchants and senators of Caesarea reclining with their cronies under the shade of potted palms.

The bustling streets of the port city all fanned out from the harbor. Today they teemed with ox carts and chariots and veiled women at market, with sellers hawking resin wine from Greece, flax and grain from Egypt, flamboyantly colorful cotton cloth, and peppery spices caravanned in from far-off India.

His guide led him to a sidewalk cafe and retreated to a watchful distance. Josephus sat and awaited his assignation, sipping pomegranate juice in the light breeze of the promenade.

His eyes were fixed not on the women or the soldiers or the shouting sellers around him, but on the eminent feature facing the harbor mouth—the wonder that had brought so many pilgrims from throughout the empire to Caesarea. Though Herod's temple of Caesar Augustus was indeed remarkable for its beauty and grand proportions, it was the gigantic bearded statue of the first emperor of Rome that now compelled the visitor's imagination and captured his entire attention. The statue stood beneath a bold inscription carved in massive letters on the cult temple's façade:

JASIO AUGUSTO DIVUS FILIUS DIVI CAESAR
IMPERATOR PONTIFEX MAXIMUS.
TO JASIUS AUGUSTUS, GOD AND SON OF GOD,
CAESAR, EMPEROR, HIGHEST PRIEST

Indeed the rumor was accurate: The statue was not inferior to that which had served as its model—Zeus at Olympia—and was intentionally slightly larger even than the statue of Roma that stood at the opposite entrance.

Following twelve years of arduous construction, King Herod the Great had dedicated the harbor to the navigators who had braved these treacherous waters since the time of the Phoenicians. The palace he consigned to the exhausting task of satisfying his own earthly pleasures. But to his imperial benefactor, the divine Emperor Caesar Augustus, "son of god and god himself," Herod pledged the eternal glory of this new capital, christening the city "Caesarea." And so it had been called to this day.

Lost in his thoughts, Josephus failed to notice the quiet

man with the cropped hair and serious dark eyes who now stood across from him. The tax collector's simple brown tunic was embroidered with a single imperial eagle. He stood waiting respectfully for the historian's attention to return to the present, then dropped a heavy coin into Josephus' palm and looked at him. *"Salve, atque vale,* hail and be well, I am Alexander," he said.

He picked up the single sheaf of papyrus Josephus had copied in his own trembling hand for today's unspeakable rendezvous. "You have made the right decision," he said. "The King will be pleased. The survival of your histories is now assured; they will become known throughout the world."

Without bothering to read the papyrus, Alexander turned on his heel and moved in the direction of the temple, where he would personally oversee the copying of the new, slightly expanded, edition of *Josephus' Antiquities of the Jews.*

Not daring to breathe, Josephus watched the man recede until he had become a speck among specks on the crowded walkway. He noticed his guide had departed as well. Then he opened his hand, blinking his eyes as the rays of the sun caught the golden coin.

He squinted to read its denomination, then, at recognizing what it was, smiled widely and laughed so loud he attracted the stares of the merchants haggling at the next table.

The dread that had filled his heart since he'd received the royal summons was instantly lifted.

This wasn't the first time that the historian had been asked to add or subtract something from his narratives. But it was the first time he had complied. The threat that, otherwise, his work would be banned, indeed *burned!* had been worse than a sentence of death. When he learned that the order had come not from Herod Agrippa but from Rome itself, Josephus realized the die had been cast at a level far above his power to oppose.

But in his wildest imagination, Josephus had never dreamed of being rewarded with such a treasure for adding a mere one hundred words to his history. Nor could he have dreamed that those one hundred words would later, when they resurfaced three hundred years from now, become known and celebrated as the *Testimonium Flavianum*—and would be considered the unique evidence that the relatively new cult of Jesus Christ was, unaccountably, based on a simple man who roamed the Galilean countryside.

Eyeing the merchants who were still watching his every move, Josephus' only question was how to keep this golden disc safe on his outward passage in a world full of thieves.

That was when he noticed the bronze smith in his workshop beneath the temple balustrade, packing a krater vase for shipment. A few steps, a whispered order, small monies exchanged, and security was assured following the adage of old Hesiod: "Hide it in plain sight." The invaluable coin would masquerade as a medallion.

Hours later, the enormous vase stowed safely below, Josephus was relieved to be boarding the vessel that would carry him home. As the grandeur of Caesarea faded in the distance, he allowed himself to dream of how he would invest his new fortune.

His reverie came to an abrupt end with the shouts, "Storm from the southeast! Secure the ship!"

The next hour was a frenzied blur of smashing timbers and raging sea.

Nearly exhausted, his clothing in shreds, Josephus allowed himself to be hauled onto the small rescue boat that had saved him from drowning when the ship foundered just outside the breakwater of the great harbor. A few members of the merchant ship's crew survived, but he was the lone passenger to make it to land.

Was he the most fortunate man alive, or had he been spared only to live a cursed existence? If he had risked carrying the coin on his person, it might still be in his possession, a testament to his perfidy and proof of his dishonor to the profession that would be his only claim to dignity and honorable fame. Because of his fear, because of his bright idea of purchasing the bronze vase and paying the smith to "decorate" it with the golden medallion, Josephus now had nothing at all to show for his self-betrayal.

VI/6
Absolute Uncertainty

Anyone passing Ryan McKeown, S.J., on his morning walk down Rome's Janiculum, would have witnessed a worried-looking young man with dark shadows under his eyes. His usual composed countenance had disappeared and his furrowed brow revealed the burden he now bore. Images of the penitent's death plagued him, more so because of the man's extraordinary confession and enigmatic last words, "*Find Father Ryan...memory in ashes of Jasius...in the Gesù.*" *Why did this mysterious monsignor use his last breath to deliver this strange message to his killer? What was he trying to tell me?*

It was appalling even to entertain the thought that Holy Mother Church might have ordered the killing of a monsignor. It was just too horrible to contemplate. *Surely the Albanian was mistaken?*

Not only was he wrestling with the shock of dual murders but Ryan's doubts about his faith now consumed his every waking moment and haunted his nights. It was mind versus spirit, and the mind threatened to destroy every feeling his spirit flourished on. Ryan's mind was filled with a jumble of questions in a jumble of languages—English, commendably fluent Italian, and an ancient dialect insiders would readily identify as the vulgar Latin spoken almost exclusively at the highest ecclesiastical levels in Vatican City.

The names flashing through his brain—Eusebius, Philo

Judaeus, Lactantius, Origen, Tertullian—were an esoteric litany of historians, poets, biblical scholars, and philosophers—all from the infancy of Christianity. Ryan's obsession with tracking down the origins of the Catholic faith permeated his consciousness.

The area spanned by Via Garibaldi was a living postcard of tiled roofs, bell towers, cupolas and gardens set off in breathtaking contrast against the cloudless turquoise sky. But this morning the young American priest, lost in ruminations about the fateful confession and his biblical doubts, had been oblivious to the spectacular view—and to the breeze ruffling his curly brown hair to more than usual disarray. It would be difficult to recognize Ryan as a recently ordained priest in his casual street clothes and comfortable black Reeboks, much less one enrolled in the pontifically authorized Society of Jesus, known to the world as "Jesuits."

Ryan's questions about troubling inconsistencies in traditional Catholic doctrine had only grown more confusing as he'd turned from his graduate studies of the Latin epic poet Virgil to a temporary stint teaching a course on early Christian theology at Georgetown University in Washington, D.C. At that time he was a Jesuit scholastic, getting in-the-classroom experience, and testing the demands of his calling. Now that his priesthood had been consecrated through the sacrament of Holy Orders and he had been dispatched to the Eternal City to study the New Testament and its commentaries, Father McKeown's personal doubts and scholarly perplexities were, he feared, all too close to becoming a neurotic disorder.

"How can I accept ordination with all this uncertainty?" he'd once asked his confessor, a functional octogenarian alcoholic, one of the cadre of emeriti that staffed the Woodstock seminary.

"How do you *feel* about your faith?" the old man asked.

"I *feel* wonderful," Ryan admitted. "When I smell the incense in the presence of the Holy Sacrament, I feel...holy...I feel *right.*"

"Then act as if you were certain," the old priest had advised. "It is a corollary of Pascal's wager. There's no such thing in this world as absolute certainty. So accept that and go forward acting toward the best outcome no matter what."

As the days before his ordination became cluttered with crucial commitments and endless ceremonies, Ryan found he had no more time to entertain his uncertainties. *The trouble with me,* he ruminated, *is that I've always had too little time—for everything. Things just keep happening before I've got them figured out.* He'd always wished there could be an off-calendar eighth day of the week to do nothing but consolidate what you actually think, hopefully believe, and truly feel.

It was all, to Ryan, a bit overwhelming—especially for a young man who was still intent on figuring out, one piece at a time, the immense puzzle that was the Roman Catholic Church, the religion into which he had been involuntarily baptized as an infant, willy-nilly confirmed as an adolescent, and hesitantly ordained as a priest of its most militant order.

Now it was too late, as far as the priesthood was concerned. He had been confirmed in that direction and, following his old confessor's advice, determined to make the best of it. To his grateful surprise, even after his ordination his immediate superiors not only encouraged him to continue following his scholarly nose investigating the origins of the Church, but had also mysteriously arranged the residency in Rome.

Whenever his scholarly path seemed to disappear before his eyes, he returned to the simple basic questions that had inspired this quest: *How could it be that Theophilus, one of the earliest Christian apologists, wrote nearly 30,000 words about Christianity without once mentioning Jesus Christ? How come the name "Jesus Christ," in fact, doesn't appear in any Greek or Latin author until after the Council of Nicaea? Why was it that the only near-contemporary account that mentioned Christ, a suspiciously precise paragraph known as the* Testimonium Flavianum, *in Josephus'* Antiquities of the Jews, *had been proved to be a patent insertion into that historical narrative? How could Jesus have been born in 1 A.D. when the Gospels say he was born before Herod the Great died—and King Herod's death could be pinpointed to 4 B.C.? Even Philip Cardinal Vasta, now known to the world as Pope Pius XIII, had lamented that the greatest obstacle for spreading the Catholic faith today was that the historical existence of Jesus could no longer be made credible.* If Ryan could somehow find a way to stamp a measure of documented authenticity on the career of the Church's founder, he would be serving the Holy Father as well as his own wavering vocation. If he could make that tangible contribution to the church, he might justify his own doubt-ridden existence and give himself a break.

If he could find evidence to prove objectively that Jesus really existed as a human being, he'd be able to reconcile all the contradictions. Without that proof certain—that had eluded scholars for some two thousand years—every thread of the tapestry of biblical scholarship became just another loose end and his profession based on an allegory at best, at worst, a phantom.

VII/7
Eye of the Storm

The first thing Harel wondered when he reached the surface was whether the anchors would hold. Six-foot rollers were lifting the platform, and the wind was catching under it, blowing the barge like a bucking kite. The anchor lines held taut through the waves, but they wouldn't hold for long. The wind was growing stronger and would eventually bust them loose. The barge should have been hauled back into the safety of the harbor long before the storm began. It was no wonder Emily had been so upset.

The platform was built of Scandinavian pine frames and plywood, with oil barrels lashed to the underside. It wasn't much more than an oversized raft—a long jump from Cousteau's *Calypso*, aboard which Harel had interned as a student one fiery Mediterranean summer.

But he wasn't going to complain. The undersea archaeological crew had been lucky so far in finding the funds to keep the excavation alive. It seemed, to make this all possible, that Emily had to spend half her time begging for government money. Such is the fate of those scholar-adventurers who track the spoors of the unprofitable past.

Harel didn't even make the attempt to climb aboard the raft. The barge would either hold or it wouldn't; at this point there was nothing he could do to save it. He headed instead for the Zodiac.

David was not far behind him, bobbing up and down on

the waves. David had made the mistake of inflating his vest, which kept him safely afloat but slowed his swim. Harel made a deliberate attempt not to worry about him. The important thing was for one of them to make it to the boat so they all had a chance for survival.

The Zodiac was tied to the platform by a twenty-foot length of hemp rope. If the barge broke free, the dinghy would go with it, and the three divers would be left, like their ancient maritime predecessors, to the dubious mercies of Poseidon.

It was difficult to hold a steady direction against the force of the oncoming rollers. They lifted him up, gave him a view, then dropped him down in a perilous well, a valley under mountains of water. With each gut-wrenching drop the undertow drew him farther off course. Harel considered jettisoning his cumbersome scuba tank, but decided to throw off his weight belt instead. This helped considerably, and after several minutes of hard swimming, he finally reached the boat.

Climbing over the pontoons was like wrestling a giant sea serpent—the waves kept sliding the boat away and Harel kept slipping off. Finally, he removed his tank and tried to heave it on board ahead of him, but a wave caught it and carried it off; he watched it float away just under the surface. He spat. The cost of the tank would no doubt be deducted from his meager monthly stipend.

Clawing his way to the stern, Harel managed to climb up the fins of the outboard. He slipped when a wave struck, and the metal fin cut his ankle. Since he could move his foot, he decided it wasn't a severed tendon, only a bloody slice of skin. He looked around for David, wondering why he wasn't in sight by now—and what had happened to Emily?

She must have taken the bait, he thought. He scanned the heaving waves. Harel finally spotted David floating a hundred yards away, carried along by the force of the storm. He saw him wave a hand at him as he reached the peak of a wave, and lost him entirely when he disappeared behind it.

Lightning flashed across the sky, followed by a loud peal of thunder. They had to get off the water. Harel started the outboard and headed for his friend. At every peak he went airborne. The waves were reaching to eight feet now. Fearing he'd lose control, he tried slowing down, but this made matters worse. It was a simple matter of momentum. Decrease the horizontal component, and the vertical component would take the propeller completely out of the water. Harel opened the throttle and held on for the ride.

The peaks still sent the boat flying. The troughs were bone-crunching, but when at last he reached his colleague, he was wild with exhilaration.

In the deep valley of a high wave he reached his arm out for David. David grabbed hold, and the big man swept him into the Zodiac like a dripping sack of beans.

"Where's Emily?" were the first words out of David's mouth.

"She's going for the coin," Harel shouted back. "I knew she couldn't leave it." He fought to turn the boat around. A wave struck them broadside, and the propeller growled out of the water.

David clung to his seat. "It would take her hours to free that krater. She hasn't the proper tools." The vase had been wedged between two ship timbers and fused, by the ages, with a large amphora adjacent to it. To remove the coin without damaging the other artifacts, all of them would have to come out at once—a challenging enterprise in the best of conditions, all but impossible now. "I don't think she'd even try," David's voice rose to compete with the storm.

"She calls me a stubborn mule," Harel hollered back. "She's the empress of stubborn."

Then David spotted Emily off the portside of the barge and signaled to Harel to steer the Zodiac toward her. *Must have given up on the coin,* he thought. "Hang on," Harel yelled.

David was shedding his scuba tank when Harel struck a wave the size of a semi truck. The boat rose up and the tank banged onto the floor and onto David's toe, still wedged into his fin. He let out a wail.

Harel laughed. He seemed to be taking pleasure in the chaos of the storm.

The two of them gave Emily a hand, lifting her into the rubber boat. Another huge wave rolled into the Zodiac and knocked the three to its trampoline deck. Emily crawled up onto a seat and peered out in awe at the waves.

"Your fucking tank nearly brained me," she screamed, the shrillness in her voice betraying the dark fear that enveloped her.

Lightning seared the sky above. The sea looked genuinely terrifying.

"Get us out of here, Harel. Now."

Harel took the wheel, gunned the throttle, and steered the boat toward shore. Riding with the waves was a wonderful relief—he'd had enough of the mad bouncing. They'd be ashore in a few minutes, and although they'd probably lose the platform, at least they'd all survive.

David noticed Emily eyeing a crusted clump in her hand. "What the hell is that?" he yelled.

Emily rubbed the encrusted coin. "I can hardly believe it— I'll tell you when I'm absolutely sure," she yelled back.

David looked alarmed. "What about the amphora? What about the krater?"

"There wasn't time," Emily shouted.

David's face registered disbelief. Emily was meticulous, a stickler for procedure. Had his young professor simply broken the artifact loose? "But what—"

A sudden screech and grind of timbers cut off David's question. They turned to see a giant wave lifting up the barge, tumbling it over onto the sea, setting free the oil drums and smashing the frame to pieces.

After watching a moment, Harel bellowed, "We'll be lucky to be able to salvage any of it."

David looked equally gloomy. "There goes the season, and there goes my graduate thesis."

"Don't be such a pessimist," Emily called out with a wry smile. She looked again at the crusted clump of metal in her hands. "This coin could be the answer to all our dreams."

VIII / 8

☧

The rain was still falling hard nearly two hours after the storm hit. Harel and David had gone back to the dormitory to shower and change before rejoining Emily in the warehouse that served as their research facility. They found her in the light of a flood lamp, bent over a portable worktable, still wearing her damp swimsuit. She was patiently grinding away at the corrosion that caked the coin. The wind outside was howling, and the rain made such a racket on the corrugated roof that she didn't even hear the men arrive. She was so absorbed with the age-marred coin that Harel's sudden greeting made her jump.

"Don't get excited—it's only us."

Emily sighed. "You scared the living shit out of me." A wave of embarrassment washed over her.

David suspected her overreaction was connected with the artifact. She had asked them to keep it a secret. "Have you figured out what it is?" he asked.

"If it's what I think it is, it's the biggest find at Caesarea since the unearthing of the Pilate Stone. I've spent my life hoping to discover something like this."

"No kidding," Harel said, looking quite pleased with himself. "Imagine that."

In 1961, near the ancient theater of Caesarea, a building

stone had been recovered with a four-line Latin inscription citing "Pontius Pilate, Prefect of Judea." It was one of the few references outside the Bible to the man responsible for giving the order that Christ be crucified. But was it authentic, or not? The jury was still out on the question.

Emily brushed off the aureus and reexamined it under a magnifying glass. "It's been cited by historians, legendary to numismatists, but the series of commemorative *aurei* had seemingly vanished from the face of the earth. The last one reported was in the nineteenth century. But it disappeared, along with the only drawing of it."

Emily continued grinding the crust off the coin, until David cautioned her to stop.

"Why here?" David asked. "Why here in Caesarea?"

She glanced up at him, and stopped grinding at the coin. "It was said to have been struck by King Herod the Great in honor of Augustus, years before he built the cult temple here as a tribute to him."

She handed the loupe to Harel. "The back is still indecipherable because of the encrustation. But look what I've managed to reveal on the front."

Harel took the loupe and examined the aureus. The old gold shone brightly under the beam of light, and the brilliance for a moment obscured the relief. He canted the angle of the coin. Now the light cast shadows from the edges of the bas-relief print. It showed the profile of a handsomely-bearded man wearing a peculiar crown.

"The crown on the bloke's head," Harel said. "It looks like a crown of thorns."

David took the loupe and squinted at the disc. Indeed, the crown on the head was spiked, like a ring of pointed thorns. "It almost looks like a halo of spikes," he said.

"The sun crown isn't just a Christian symbol," Emily said.

"In many cultures as far back as ancient Egyptian, and including Roman and Christian, crown of thorns and halo both derive from the tradition that identifies every newly-crowned king with the sun. The halo nimbus represents the rays of the rising sun. It's a sign that its wearer plays the life-giving role of the sun in his subjects' existence. The Greek sun god Apollo was driving his chariot across the heavens wearing the sun crown when Rome was just a huddle of huts."

"But I still don't get it," Harel said. "Every bust of Augustus I've ever seen shows him clean-shaven. If this is really Augustus, why would he be wearing a beard?"

"The beard is an honorific," Emily said. "Like the beard worn by Jupiter's statue in his famous temple in Olympia—and legend has it that the giant statue of Augustus in the temple of Herod here was bearded as well."

"What is this?" Harel asked. Etched directly beneath the head was what looked at first like a single letter. It took him a moment to realize that it was actually a combination of two letters seemingly merged into one. "It looks to me like a 'P'," he said, "a 'P' with an 'X' laid over it."

Harel stood upright. "It's the Greek letters *Chi* and *Rho*," he declared.

Emily struggled to maintain her composure.

David took the loupe from Harel and closely examined the coin. "It's the *Chi-Rho* ligature."

Emily looked at him with pride. His knowledge of iconographical trivia always surprised her, but of course reminded her of why she'd chosen him in the first place.

"It's impossible," David said. "This ligature is a Christian symbol. I thought it didn't appear until the early fourth century when Constantine the Great used it on the standards of his legions to win a battle where he was vastly outnumbered."

"Yeah," Harel said. "This ship we've been working on went down more than two hundred years before Constantine was born."

Emily interjected, "I'll admit it's strange. The two letters, X P, in Greek, are the first two letters of the word χρϊστος, *Christus,* 'Christ.' She was muttering to herself as she googled something on her laptop. "Remember, Constantine adopted Christianity as the religion of the Roman Empire and actually held the title Pontifex Maximus."

"I thought that title was reserved for the pope," David said.

Emily corrected him. "That's certainly true today. But Pontifex Maximus was originally the title of the high priest of the college of pontiffs in the pagan Roman religion. *Pontifex* is Latin for 'bridge-builder'—the one who forms a link between men and the gods. Only later was the title adopted by the Christian popes."

David looked genuinely confused. "So was Constantine pagan or Christian?"

"Most scholars think he was a little bit of both."

"So how come the coin has the XP?!" Harel's voice betrayed his impatience.

"I'm not absolutely positive yet," Emily replied. "But I know the man who can piece it altogether: crown, beard, *Chi-Rho,* all of it. I have a very strong hunch something else is going on here."

"Like what?" David asked, cracking open a beer and offering it to Harel who looked relieved to accept something so mundane.

Emily was pecking at her Droid. "It's a pretty outlandish theory, but I have to be certain before I'd even hint at it out loud. The man I know in Rome has been hunting most of his lifetime for this aureus. If anyone could make its past come alive, it's him."

The graduate students looked at each other. They knew who she was talking about, the mysterious mentor they'd caught her talking to more than once late at night when she thought they were out of earshot.

Emily waited for an answer to the land line she'd found listed next to his name in her address book, cursing him for being the last hold-out to not carry a mobile phone with him at all times. "Damn," she said, eyeing her watch. "I was hoping I'd get lucky and find him in."

Finally, after the odd clicking on the line she attributed to a bad connection, she left a message: "Monsignor Isaac, it's Emily. We've found something in Caesarea I know you'll be most interested in. I believe it to be the Rosetta Stone you've been searching for. Please call me back the minute you get this."

IX/9
Lucas Adashek

Considering the amount of debris on the beach, and the power of the storm that had scattered it there, the sea looked remarkably calm to Emily as she made her way along the shore. Timbers and planks from her crew's shattered barge lay scattered about pell-mell, washed and nudged by the gentle surf. Beside a strand of nylon rope attached to a bumper buoy, she recognized her red windbreaker half-buried in the sand. She pulled it out and shook it off, liberating a white sand crab that scuttled back toward the sea.

David and Harel were out in the Zodiac, along with the technical operations director and the local Israeli divers. For three days they'd been scouring the ocean floor to see what they could recover. Most of their equipment had been lost or damaged and the wreck had totally disappeared beneath the shifting ocean sands. If she had not risked extracting it, the coin might have taken years to rediscover or might even have vanished forever. Emily wondered how long it would be before they could get back to work. She was anxious to find out if any more treasures lay hidden in the depths of these treacherous waters.

Gazing down the shoreline, she spotted a figure walking toward her. The man's brown seersucker pants were rolled up above his bare ankles, and he'd removed the matching suit jacket and slung it over his shoulder. He was bent slightly forward. His pale shaved head glistened in the sunlight as he continuously wiped it dry with his pocket handkerchief, and glanced up every now and then to gauge his distance from her. She would have recognized that oddly crablike gait anywhere, as though the man were taking a step back for every one forward.

Emily absently stuffed her windbreaker into her canvas bag. She felt her pulse quicken and reprimanded herself. *He doesn't look much different,* she thought, feeling a little disappointed. Even from a distance, it was obvious that her ex-lover had gained a few pounds—but not more than a few, judging from his inefficient pace that used up twice the energy needed. He still had a sedentary-desk-job look to him, but maybe the bus bombings in Jerusalem had scared him into the regular schedule of walking she'd once tried to enforce.

Lucas Adashek trudged up and stood before her, squinting in the sun.

She waited for him to speak. He'd had plenty of time to prepare himself; she wondered what he would say.

"Damascus Gate."

Emily looked confused. "What?"

"The last place I saw you. I was just thinking about it. You were enchanting, just squatting there making pencil sketches of the ruins. Can't seem to remember what *I* was doing there."

"I remember," Emily said. "I was copying the inscriptions. You were haggling at the Arab bazaar. You'd purchased a *hookah.* A gift, you said, for your landlord. I didn't believe you for an instant."

Luke looked amused and pleased that she remembered. "I still have that pipe," he said. "Between us, it's had a lot of use. Helps me forget why I signed up for duty in this hell-hole of a country."

Emily smiled, and her eyebrows lifted. "Your landlord, as I

remember, was quite an attractive lady."

His grin broke into a look of surprise. "So I *did* manage to make you jealous!" He folded his arms proudly, then shrugged. "Truth is, she had kicked me out a month before. Didn't fancy my Coltrane."

Emily recalled how he'd play his sax in the courtyard behind her apartment. "As long as we're being honest," she said, "I have to tell you—I never liked it either."

Luke laughed. Emily laughed, too. For a moment it seemed as though they'd never been apart, that their brief affair had never ended, that three years hadn't passed since that last chance encounter in Jerusalem.

Emily broke away from his eyes and glanced out at the sea. The Zodiac was heading back to shore.

She turned again to Luke. "Thank you for coming," she told him.

"The pleasure's mine," he replied. "You know how I love field trips." He scanned the scattered wood and rubble littering the shoreline. "And now I see why you asked me to come quickly."

She noted the tone of disappointment in his voice, and waited until he looked at her again. "Luke...we need your help."

In a tribute to the ultimate triumph of commerce, an Israeli restaurant had been planted atop centuries of Caesarea's ruins to cater to the throngs of visiting tourists. From the table where she was sitting with Luke, Emily had a spectacular view to the east, and let her eyes drift over what remained of the Crusaders: stone walls, a moat, the vestiges of a cathedral, most of it laid bare by Israeli archeologists working in the 1960s.

Luke's view looked more toward the south, where it would be impossible not to notice the Roman amphitheater built by Herod the Great, and where the stone inscribed with a tribute to Pilate had originally been installed.

Their talk was intermittent throughout the meal, consisting mostly of Emily reliving the terror of the storm with Luke muttering obligatory sympathies as he picked through the bones of his grilled tilapia. She wanted desperately to talk about funding, but they'd gone through half the meal without Luke bringing it up. She didn't want him to feel that she was taking advantage of their relationship, but it had to be obvious that she was. Why else would he have been so quick to accept her invitation? It was part of his job, of course, as liaison between the British and American academic establishments and the Israel Antiquities Authority, but she couldn't help thinking there was more than civic duty on his mind. He seemed to be toying with her, his eyes flirtatious above the wine.

The inability to escape their past brought on a sudden flare of anger. *Why couldn't they,* she thought, *put their little escapade behind them after three long years?*

"We need money, Luke."

She blurted it out so abruptly that Adashek started to laugh. "Of course, Emily. Everyone needs money. That's what we all hear every day. It's the human condition."

"But this is more—" Emily stopped. *Take your time,* she told herself. *Maybe I should toy with him.* "We're on the verge of something...something extraordinary. I can feel it in my bones. Everything I've lived for, all the work I've done... It's all brought me to this moment. That storm that hit—it's like...I'm not sure how to say this without sounding crazy, but...it's as if that storm came along to stop us from what we were doing, to stop it from happening."

Adashek sipped his Yarden Sauvignon Blanc, savoring his

moment of power and peering at her steadily. "Bit dramatic, aren't we?"

"I'm serious, Luke."

He continued staring at her, openly admiring her body. "Yes, I can see you are."

She stopped herself from buttoning the top buttons of her shirt. "We need a grant to rebuild and extend this year's season. And I need to hire another diver."

"Not to mention a new diving platform."

"Yes, and we need to replace the equipment that's been lost. The siphon's in a shambles—"

"Emily?"

She paused, eyeing him. "What?"

"I'm sorry, luv. But you're talking roughly half a million dollars."

She paused again. "Yes. I mean, no. I mean...my guess actually would be a little higher."

Luke grinned. His eyes locked on hers. "You're going to have to show me."

"*Show* you? Show you what?"

His eyes drifted over her. "As your people from Missouri put it, show me what it is you've got."

Emily feigned a look of confusion. "I don't know what you mean. There's nothing in particular to—"

"Stop it. I know you too well. Just like you know me."

She looked at him in silence.

"What is it?" he asked. "What did you find?"

She continued looking at him. Trying to decide.

"Tell me," he said.

She looked out the window a moment. The vast, exposed spread of ruins, their secrets all revealed.

She looked back at Luke. "I'll show you."

The dormitory that housed the team was close enough to shore that you could hear the waves crashing. Emily shut the door to her cell-like room and bolted it behind her. This reduced the sound of the ocean down to a muffled rumble; she could hear herself breathing. When she turned back to face him, Luke was standing in the middle of the room, still wearing his seersucker jacket, hands hanging limp at his sides, waiting patiently.

Emily stepped forward, then stopped. "Promise me you won't tell anyone."

Luke's mouth started to open, but he hesitated.

"Swear it," she said.

He shrugged. "All right," he said. "I promise."

She continued staring at him, wondering if she could believe him.

No choice. She went to the drawer of the bedside table and found the flat-nosed screwdriver. She used it to pry open the board in the pine floor, revealing a small, draw-string cloth sack. She plucked it out and set it on top of the dresser.

It was clear to Luke from the sound it made that there was something heavy inside it. "Why in heaven's name don't you keep it in the safe with the other artifacts?"

She glanced at him as she opened the sack. "See for yourself," she said.

He took the coin from her. After looking at it briefly, and glancing at her, he carried it to the window for a closer look in the light.

The center of the side that bore the *Chi-Rho* symbol was clean; but the circumference and the other side of the coin were still largely obscured by a metallic-looking corrosion. Luke continued his examination.

"We found it attached to a bronze krater," Emily said. "The corrosion of the metal seems to have bled into the imprint. I plan to have it sent up to the Jaffa Museum for a proper cleaning. I've done all I can do with it here."

Luke looked at her. "You've done enough," he said. He looked at the coin again, turning the *Chi-Rho* symbol in the light. "You've done more than enough. I hope you haven't compromised its integrity."

Emily watched him without speaking.

Luke glanced up from the aureus again. "You're certain about the dating of that wreck?"

"Positive. M.I.T.'s accelerated testing battery verified our field estimates a week ago."

He turned the coin over again and looked at the bearded face and nimbus crown. "Who else knows about this?"

"Harel. David. That's it."

"You'll send it by courier?"

"Of course not. Soon as I make arrangements with the Institute I'll take it myself."

Luke nodded approvingly. Again he looked at the gold coin.

"So," Emily said, "what do you think?"

He walked over to her, looked at the coin one more time before handing it back.

"It's a solid gold imperial Roman coin," he said. "They're increasingly rare, in any denomination. If you think there's more where that came from, I think you'll get your funding."

She slipped the coin back into the sack. She looked up into his eyes. "Thank you," she said.

He held her stare. "Pleasure's mine," he said.

She lowered her eyes. "Will you be staying the night?"

He gazed down at her eyelashes: tiny, bronze feathers.

"Yes," he said.

X/10
R.I.P.

Ryan rubbed his eyes and, for a moment, even forgot he was in Rome. But the smell of the freshly baked *rosette,* and the red blood orange juice laid neatly on the little table by the door to his austere dormitory room brought him back. The events of the last few days were a blur.

After the Albanian immigrant died in his arms, Ryan had insisted in his most emphatic Italian on accompanying the body to *Ospedale Maggiore.* But the attending *carabinieri* would hear nothing of it. "This man doesn't need a hospital, Father," declared the lieutenant who'd taken charge of the assorted police arriving at the scene. "The body will be taken to the Questura morgue for identification and cause of death determination."

"The cause of death was a bullet through the heart," Ryan responded. "I heard the shot. I saw him fall."

"Did you see the shooter?"

Ryan shook his head. "No. It all happened too fast, just before I got to him. I only saw that the killer was driving a Vespa."

"Color?"

"Red."

The *carabinieri* shrugged. It seemed every Vespa in Rome was red. His voice turned gentle. "Thank you for your offer, Father. And thank God you got there in time to give him Last

Rites. We'll call you if we need you for further questioning."

It had felt like days rather than hours later that he'd found his way back to the American College—only to be shocked by the official news that the priest who had been murdered was none other than his revered mentor, Monsignor Oscar Isaac.

A solemn atmosphere permeated the once-lively offices and corridors. His colleagues spoke in hushed tones about the senior Jesuit scholar who had been killed in a hit-and-run accident on Via dei Plebiscito, next to the Gesù, a man whose ghost-like reputation was a legend at the College. Ryan himself was considered a prodigy for having had a one-on-one meeting with the man in his first few days in Rome.

Monsignor Oscar Isaac's reputation for being a mostly invisible phantom, visible anywhere in the world *other* than in his College quarters, had generated countless jokes. "They change his linens once a year," one of them went, "whether they need it or not."

Even before Ryan arrived in Rome, he had greatly admired Isaac's prolific analyses of the writings of early Christianity and the conflicting sources of the Gospels. It wasn't until after he was actually enrolled at the prestigious Pontifical Institute for Biblical Studies that Ryan became aware that Monsignor Isaac's recommendation had cinched his position. He had managed to communicate his desire to meet the scholar through the American College's grapevine and, a few weeks later, found himself face to face with the man himself at a tiny restaurant near Piazza Navona where the monsignor had asked Ryan to join him in a *digestivo,* an after-dinner drink.

"Thank you for giving me the opportunity to express my appreciation for your recommendation," Ryan had begun, noticing the impression of Isaac's dinner plate on the spotless tablecloth. The stately monsignor's eyes grew moist as he put his hand up to cut Ryan's gratitude short.

"You will learn," he said, "that sentiment is a counterproductive starting-point for the course you are about to embark on."

Ryan had no way to discern Isaac's meaning. "I am at your service," he said, "and would be honored to contribute to your work in any way you request."

Monsignor Isaac appeared to take his offer seriously. He took a sip of his liqueur, and savored it before making a reply that had startled Ryan to the depths of his soul. "Explore your doubts thoroughly," the older man said. "They are healthy, and on target. Nothing is as it seems. When you've come to a point where your soul is so troubled by what you've discovered that you are paralyzed, contact me. You will then be ready for my mentorship."

Isaac's current research, Ryan learned, had long been the subject of bitter contention between him and his Vatican colleagues. No layman knew exactly what it was, but it obviously threatened to unravel the very fabric of the ecclesiastical matrix. Words like "iconoclastic," "eccentric," and even "sacrilegious" had been thrown about freely in the most esoteric circles of academia both in and out of Vatican City. But Isaac's Jesuit superiors stolidly instructed the scholar to ignore the incendiary hubbub. Isaac had caused consternation for the Pope's administrators, the Curia, by blatantly stating, "Two dozen of the most famous Roman historians and chroniclers were alive during the time of Jesus Christ, *and yet not a single one mentions Him.* I have uncovered the reason for their silence."

Isaac refused to elaborate his declaration—turned on his heels and left the Vatican Library review committee without another word.

Ryan had planned to make Isaac's provocative statement the opening line of his doctoral thesis.

The taunting statement had dogged Ryan's consciousness from the moment, on Friday afternoon, he'd learned from the police the shocking, heart-wrenching identification of his Gesù penitent's victim with the dead man who had enabled his research in Rome.

That Isaac had finally been forbidden by the Curia to publish had deterred the intrepid monsignor not at all. Galileo had been treated worse, Giordano Bruno much worse. Under the protection of the Society of Jesus, who warned him to be more discreet, Isaac had simply continued his ghostly obsessions.

Finding out all he could about the mysterious scholar soon became Ryan's own mission—as though he felt responsible somehow, not for the old man's death, but for discovering in the ghostly trail of his research some wispy shade of meaning he could bring to his life.

His anonymous phone call had once again tipped Ryan's faith into question. To tell the Questura that the Albanian who died in his arms had just confessed to being hired to run down a monsignor in cold blood would be breaking the seal of the Confessional. He'd heard a Jesuit logician argue that, in the case of capital crimes, the seal's protection didn't extend to the deceased criminal. But was that liturgically correct, or mere "jesuitry"? Ryan had long ago trained himself to suspect all rationalizations, especially his own. In any case, his compromise was making the coin-call to the authorities to suggest that they test the front bumper of the Albanian's impounded three-wheeler.

As he returned from the corner phone booth, the young American priest was burning with curiosity. *What if the* carabinieri *took his advice, tested the truck, and discovered that it was indeed the vehicle that killed Monsignor Isaac? Then what? Would they follow a case this tenuous in a city of blatantly evidenced crimes begging for attention?* His head spun with the ramifications of this thinking. He was like a puppy chasing its tail; only there was nothing playful about it.

As the days passed he recognized that he had already embarked on a personal quest, his penance for the unproductive sin of confusion. For the past six months, his reading of the most ancient manuscripts of historians writing between A.D. 25 and A.D. 100 had produced only questions, and no answers, about their omission of any reference to the life and times of Jesus Christ. The learned Jewish philosopher and theologian Philo Judaeus, alive "at the time of Christ," never mentioned Jesus in any of his writings. Compared to Jesus' fame as laid out in the Gospels, this omission seemed strange. Similarly with the Latin author and moralist, Valerius Maximus, who flourished during the reign of Tiberius, and should have been intrigued by Jesus' teachings. Yet the book Maximus published around 30 A.D. is silent on the subject.

Even more puzzling was the play written by Roman philosopher and playwright Seneca, who lived from 4 B.C. to 65 A.D. He portrayed a son of God as appearing on earth to suffer for the sake of humankind, to overcome death, and to be raised to rejoin his father in heaven. How could the early church hold Seneca in such high esteem when the hero of his play was the pagan god Hercules—not Jesus Christ?

Although Ryan knew that it was common for early Christians to identify Christ with Apollo or Hercules or Prometheus, that didn't resolve his doubts but only made them more complicated. The historian Marcus Annaeus Lucan lived in Rome during the twenty-five years that tradition placed Peter and Paul there—and was himself persecuted by Nero—

—yet he never mentioned Jesus Christ by name.

Of course Ryan had known that Josephus was considered the main source for the history of Judea and, as a tireless historian, boldly proclaimed he would leave out nothing of consequence to Jewish history in his chronicles. He had served as governor of Galilee, and at the beginning of the Jewish war with Rome, 66 A.D., was a general of the Roman forces in Galilee. A few decades earlier, according to the Gospels, Jesus attracted great crowds to Judea. But Josephus' *Antiquities of the Jews* did not record the savior story we read in the Christian gospels. He did cover many major and minor details of the period, even reporting a number of deeds and decrees of Pontius Pilate, the Roman prefect that, according to the gospels, allowed the Sanhedrin to condemn Jesus to death.

Yet he failed to report Herod's alleged wholesale slaughter of male infants at the rumor of a "royal birth" that might upset his reign. He did not mention the very public spectacle of a slow, agonizing death of a famous condemned miracle worker and healer. Though he did find that Josephus referred to no less than twenty individuals by the name of Yeshua—the letter "J" not in existence until the fourteenth century—Ryan's investigation could turn up not even a single legitimate detail of the physical life of Christ in Josephus's entire opus.

Except, of course, the historian's one alleged mention of Jesus of Nazareth—a little over one hundred notorious words in all—that was considered by Josephus scholars as a later insertion by an unscrupulous Christian scribe. Some historians believed that Josephus himself must have inserted the passage upon threat of his book being banned, or that it was inserted by later forgers. Ryan didn't know what to believe about the famous *Testimonium Flavianum:*

> Now, there was about this time, Jesus, a wise man,
> if it be lawful to call him a man, for he was a doer of

wonderful works, a teacher of such men as receive the truth with pleasure. He drew over to him both many of the Jews, and many of the Gentiles. He was the Christ; and when Pilate, at the suggestion of the principal men amongst us, had condemned him to the cross, those that loved him at the first did not forsake him, for he appeared to them alive again the third day, as the divine prophets had foretold these and ten thousand other wonderful things concerning him; and the tribe of Christians, so named from him, are not extinct at this day.

The fourth-century church father Ambrose of Milan apparently possessed an early first-century manuscript of Josephus' *History* that did not contain the passage reporting on the activities of Christ the savior.

But for the time being Ryan found he could no longer concentrate on the jumbled puzzle of ancient Christian history. The present was tugging insistently on his shirtsleeves, demanding attention. Finally he made his decision: he would turn his full investigative energies into finding out as much as he could about why in heaven's name Holy Mother Church would supposedly hire someone to run down and kill Monsignor Oscar Isaac.

By the time he learned that there would be not even a memorial service for Isaac, Ryan had put together just enough pieces of the puzzle to form a partial image of the man's wraithlike life and mysterious death.

The monsignor had been frugal, walking everywhere rather than spending even a few euros on buses or the Metro. "Walking gave him time to think things through," someone commented to Ryan, who was quietly interviewing everyone he could find who knew anything of Isaac's habits.

They were austere habits. In Isaac's room they had found a dish of virgin olive oil, in which he dipped his morning's unleavened bread, washed down by a single cup of unsweetened, uncreamed espresso. Most days he hoarded two oranges from the morning delivery, to eat quietly for lunch on an ancient wall of his ruin de jour. Only at dinner, at a tiny trattoria, "just north of Campo di Fiori at the mouth of Piazza Navona," did the old man display anything that approached indulgence: a Cinzano-soda on the rocks sipped while munching the small hard olives he picked up once a week from the same vendor in Campo di Fiori; fettuccini, usually *à la puttanesca,* ordered from an ancient waiter with a knowing grin; and a small wedge of cheese—he preferred Pecorino romano— accompanied by a single glass of the cheapest Barbera on the list. Though he mostly dined alone, from time to time Isaac was joined by a fellow scholar. At least that's who the restaurant's management supposed Isaac's guests were. Ryan knew this to be accurate from his single encounter with the monsignor there.

Gradually Ryan learned other details as he traced Isaac's routes around the ancient streets of the Eternal City. Anyone the old man came into regular contact with spoke of him as though he were innocently mad—the ethereal insanity reserved for living saints. "He'd spend twenty minutes selecting his olives one by one," explained a reverential vendor, a Tuscan immigrant who sold his vari-colored fruit from a three-wheeler almost identical to the one that had ended his long-time customer's life.

The aged clockmaker Giovanni Riga, with whom Isaac stopped to discuss the absurd fanaticism with which humanity kept track of time, provided a verbal map of Isaac's absences from the city. The two old men would walk around the cobble-stoned Campo in circles discussing the evolution of the Vestal Virgins into modern nuns, the ins and outs of the Council of Nicaea, and Dante's brilliant borrowings from Virgil. Ryan deduced from Giovanni's reports of the last year of Isaac's life that the monsignor had invested what little time he spent in Rome almost entirely at the Cathedral of St. Paul's-Without-the-Walls.

This magnificent basilica stood in a squalid district of factories, gas-works, and tramlines outside the ancient walls of Rome at the site where St. Paul was reputedly buried, and upon which the original church had been built at the time of Constantine. Since his discovery, in 2005, of the Saint's actual sarcophagus, Isaac's laser-like attention had been aimed at St. Paul until just months before he died.

According to Giovanni, all of that had changed a few short months ago. Isaac's interest in Paul seemed to vanish. "Suddenly he was off to visit hell," the old clockmaker chuckled, and then laughed out loud at the frown on Ryan's earnest face. "*Facilis descensus Averno,*" he quoted from Virgil's *Aeneid.*

> Ryan found himself answering, by rote,
> *The gates of hell are open night and day;*
> *Smooth the descent, and easy is the way:*
> *But to return, and view the cheerful skies,*
> *In this the task and mighty labor lies.*

John Dryden's rhyming translation of *The Aeneid* had been Ryan's favorite, since the day he first picked it up at the Harvard Coop.

It hadn't taken Ryan long to guess that Isaac's visits to "hell" had been the cave at Cumae—"the poppy fields north of Naples"—identified by Virgil as the domicile of the Sibyl, the pagan oracle who had predicted a host of momentous events in the history of Rome including the birth of the Son of the Great God, the long-awaited Messiah. Aeneas, in Virgil's epic, had convinced the Sibyl to lead him through her cave straight into the underworld; just as Dante, writing his Divine Comedy thirteen hundred years later, would enlist Virgil as his guide to the same region—*that* was the easy part. The hard part was finding the way back.

Had Monsignor Isaac been escaping from some scholarly hell when the Albanian angel of death descended on him in his three-wheeled chariot? What could the old man have found in the Sibyl's cave? Ryan remembered him saying something about Augustus burning all the books attributed by ages past to the Sibyl— except the ones he ordered redacted to suit his image as the Awaited One, the Eternal Son of the Eternal Father, and Initiator of the Age of Gold.

At the Pontifical Institute Ryan got nowhere trying to locate Isaac's office, which was supposedly kept secret to avoid students descending on the monsignor and wasting his time. His questions were met with stony silence from every *assistente* he confronted.

He even tried asking a Sicilian housekeeper to let him into Isaac's cell at the College, only to confirm with his own eyes her prior assertion that the room had been stripped bare to make room for the next scholar. There was no trace of Isaac, much less of his computer. It was as if the man had never spent a night in this place he'd occupied officially for nearly forty years.

Finally Ryan submitted a formal request to the College Library, asking for access to hard copy notes of Monsignor Isaac's recent research. The response came summarily, delivered on his tray with next morning's *rosette* and oranges: "Isaac Notes Transferred to Jesuit Archives. Request cannot be granted."

He was surprised by the jolt of adrenaline, not at all in keeping with his vow of obedience, with which he received this impersonal and suspiciously prompt response. He wondered if the Vatican Curia was aware that the Jesuits had commandeered the notes.

That same night he decided to try his hand at hacking into the mainframe that was shared by the Gregorian University, the Pontifical Institute, the Vatican Library, and the American College. Despite all rumors to the contrary, he discovered that the security system was rather primitive. The various libraries, in order to share data freely among their scholars, had sacrificed internal firewalls. If you couldn't go through them, Ryan soon realized, you could go around them.

In an hour he came across a file marked OISJ and realized it was Oscar Isaac's user name. In another half hour, after trying every variation of Jesuit terminology in English and Latin that he could imagine, he used an old mnemonic trick he'd learned in high school. "I can't figure it out," he said out loud.

Sure enough, the answer came to him. Monsignor Isaac was a Jesuit, trained, like Ryan was, in habits that could stick with you for a lifetime. He typed in the initials A—M—D—G, *Ad majorem Dei gloriam,* "for the greater glory of God"—the initials found above the golden tomb of Ignatius Loyola in the Gesù, the initials every Jesuit student was taught to write at the top of every homework assignment, every essay, every test.

A file flashed before his eyes but he barely had time to read the words, "Paul = Poly—DNA—match?—Greek..." before the screen closed down with a message, "Fatal Error." And the desktop shut down.

No matter how many times he attempted to reboot it, the result was the same. The operating program would not come up. He faced a black screen that blinked the infuriating white message: "Fatal Error."

Another long contemplative walk on the Janiculum brought Ryan's logic into perfect confluence with his instincts and what he had learned in the confessional. It was an epiphany, a moment of unmistakable clarity. There could be no doubt in Father Ryan McKeown's mind that Monsignor Oscar Isaac's death was intentionally arranged by an ecclesiastical source, and that Isaac's last words to his assassin—*"Find Father Ryan...memory in the ashes of Jasius... in the Gesù"*—signified his will that Ryan continue his investigations until he ascertained what Isaac had been up to. And there was also no doubt that Ryan, no matter how many "fatal errors" he had to confront, would not rest until he discovered the thread that had unraveled the old scholar's life. That would be his own toil and trouble: *Hoc opus, hic labor est.*

XI / 11
Stolen Gold

"Harel, if you make one more remark about our 'sudden cash flow,'" Emily jibed, "I'll sneak into your tent at midnight and strangle you with your weight belt." She sipped her morning coffee and eyed him through its steam. He was ruining her good mood. The euphoria that began with the discovery of the invaluable coin had only accelerated with the receipt of "initial emergency restoration funding" from the Israeli authorities a few days after Lucas Adashek had returned to Jerusalem with the aureus.

Despite his barely expressed disappointment when she had gently changed her mind about revisiting their former relationship, Luke had been as good as his word. His dual citizenship once again had given him clout with both the English and Israeli governments.

Harel raised his dark visor and adjusted the flame on his welding torch. "Never seen government funding sprung loose so fast in my life," his coarse voice repeated.

"It's the power of the gold artifact we found," David said, trying to defuse the in-your-face Israeli before their American boss kicked both their asses off the project permanently.

"Are you sure it's not another treasure he found to his liking," Harel responded, eyeing Emily salaciously.

"That's enough," she finally interrupted. "One more word out of you, mister, and—"

"Okay, okay," he muttered, laughing as he returned to

welding the brackets that held the diving barge together.

"He's just jealous," David told her. Which didn't help her mood in the least.

"Nothing happened between us," she proclaimed, perfectly aware that she was under no obligation to explain herself to them. Even if she had allowed her instincts to prevail against her better judgment, a tryst with a former lover was in no way reprehensible. To be "accused" of having one when she had most definitely *not* was doubly infuriating.

She'd felt elated that night when Luke confirmed the importance of her find, but the elation brought on a hollow sensation, which Emily at first equated with feeling physically deprived—frisky. Yet with the first sip of wine she realized that inviting Luke to spend the night was a gesture she already regretted as being, at the very least, too stupid to justify even to herself, much less to her bawdy and envious young crew. After all, she wasn't deaf. She'd overheard the locker room banter that went on behind her back. Any one of them would have given a year of his life to bed her. Especially Harel, whose lewd suggestions she'd learned to tune out and ascribe to his kibbutz not having offered a course in elementary manners.

But the most important factor was her look into Luke's eyes. There she recognized the flat deep-down angst of a lost soul that had years before turned her away from him—fearing it might be contagious.

He had noticed, of course. It was the characteristic empathy of the insecure that allowed him to read her mood. Without her saying a word, he'd ended the evening with a jovial laugh and the statement, "I see I must regain your trust!" And looked at her oddly.

She said nothing on their walk back to the dormitory, where she led him to the guest room and gave him a quick peck on the cheek by way of good-night. She didn't bother to clarify that trust had nothing to do with it, neither now, nor then.

Or did it? The last few days, as the diving platform became near operational again—thanks to her students and the day laborers from Gaza provided by the emergency relief funding—edginess had dogged Emily's steps. She had a thought that she really didn't want to bring to conscious acceptance: She hadn't heard from Luke. Why was it taking him so long to contact her with the news that she could reclaim the coin? Surely they had authenticated it, which he'd explained was necessary before he could get the full authorization she'd requested. How else would the funds have begun to flow?

"So when are we going to hear about our little Augustus?" David asked, as though she'd been arguing with herself out loud. It had been ten days since the coin had been dispatched with Adashek to the Jaffa Museum of Antiquities. Emily had spent two years there as a resident scholar early in her career. Her twice-daily path downhill from Kikar to Mifratz Shlomo Street had haunted her dreams these last few nights, as though she could astral travel and keep her eye on her discovery.

The coin would put her name in the ranks of archaeology's great, all the way back to Heinrich Schliemann who discovered Mycenae and Troy, and Sir Arthur Evans who'd turned his discovery, Knossos, into "the Disneyland of Archaeology." Not to mention that it could validate Monsignor Oscar Isaac's lifetime quest, which he would now finally have to reveal to her in detail.

Before Emily could answer David's question, her cell phone rang.

David looked at her. "Maybe that's Luke now."

She could see from the display screen it was indeed a Jerusalem number. But it wasn't one she recognized.

Nor did she recognize the voice that greeted her "hello" in high-speed Hebrew. "This is Commander Jacob Kahane from the Israel Criminal Investigations Department in Jerusalem," she finally made out. "Who am I speaking with?" The voice was crisp and businesslike.

"I'm sorry," Emily said. "I understand Hebrew but don't speak it very well."

"Shall we speak in English?"

"That would be great," she said, feeling embarrassed for no reason. "Did you say you were with the Jerusalem police?"

"Yes, you may call me back if you'd like to verify that."

"That won't be necessary." She had a very bad feeling about this call.

"Nine days ago," Kahane began carefully, "you sent an artifact to the Jaffa Museum for cleaning and authentication by diplomatic pouch. Is that correct?"

Why was he using the word "artifact"? "Yes. It was a gold coin. A British cultural attaché named Lucas Adashek delivered it to the Museum for me."

Apparently she'd passed some kind of test. "Excuse me," Kahane said, "but I wanted to make sure who I was speaking with. I don't operate under assumptions," he added in a tone she somehow found scolding.

"Why are the police interested in my coin?"

"Because it's been reported missing by the curator."

Emily paused. "Okay, this is a joke, right? Who are you, really?"

"You're still welcome to phone me back at headquarters to verify," Kahane said.

Emily felt a sudden dizziness, and the coffee in her empty stomach seemed to rise up into her throat. "But... that's impossible."

"I'm afraid not."

"That coin is unique. Irreplaceable."

"So I've been told."

"What...when did this happen?"

"Sometime over the weekend, when the Museum restorer moved it to the safe in Mr. Rosenthal's office."

The curator was Haim Rosenthal. Emily thought of him as her Jewish uncle. During the time she spent at Jaffa, he'd insisted more than once on taking her to lunch because "you look like you're starving to death." When she refused, he brought her plastic bags full of food from his home. By the time her studies there were over, she'd become a member of the family, invited to the Rosenthals' noisy household every Sabbath.

"Why didn't Haim call me himself? Where is Adashek?"

"We ordered Mr. Rosenthal not to. We opened the investigation immediately, and insisted on making the call ourselves. We haven't been able to locate Mr. Adashek."

"That coin is everything to me," she stammered, near tears. If what she was hearing hadn't been so horrible, Emily might have laughed out loud, as she had more than once when Rosenthal tucked something into that damned box in her presence. The safe couldn't have weighed more than twenty pounds. It was a miniature replica of the Ark of the Covenant. "Are you telling me that someone broke into Mr. Rosenthal's safe and stole my coin?"

"No, I'm telling you that someone stole the safe."

XII / 12
The Golden City

Jerusalem is not just the Holy City of Jews, Christians, and Muslims, it's one of the world's universal Cities, ranking with Rome and Cairo and Benares and Beijing as places that have celebrated the ecstasies and borne the sorrow of humanity from the dusty dawn of history. Love. Promises. Betrayals. Deceit. Thievery. Murder. Wherever you walked, you walked on graves.

The past seemed to weigh down on Adashek as it always did in this city—a city familiar with his personal sins, and with the collective grief of his race.

He made his way through the labyrinth of shaded arcades and near-hidden passageways, so intent on his destination that nothing else fazed him. The vibrant and raucous crowds—Israelis in jeans, brown-robed monks, soldiers in camouflage, Arabs in *keffiyahs*—that swirled through every inch of the souk might as well have been ancient wraiths themselves. Here the past wore a thin veneer of the present that lied like the paint of a clown.

For the moment, he had no time to entertain such fancies. He wove his way tentatively through the foul-smelling crowd, oblivious to the muezzins' call to prayer rising above the shrill sounds of bartering, as well as to the stench of donkey shit mingled with the exotic odor of frankincense, spices from the orient, and pungent seafood being hustled to buyers before it could spoil in the relentless sun. The bustling bazaar held nothing of interest and Luke moved through it as though walking on contaminated eggshells. Since the Six-Day War, it had lost some of its allure to all but residents forced to be practical, or tourists paying to marvel.

Adashek's interest lay ahead, in retrieving the answer to the question he'd asked on his first expedition three days earlier.

His seersucker suit was now wilted in the sun and soiled; he'd worn nothing else for the last week. He'd decided to walk from the Damascus Gate rather than risk his life needlessly in one of the suicidal three-wheeler taxis that braved the narrow and congested streets of the Old City. Now, the Khan Ez-Zeit behind him, he was heading up from Abu Shukri and wending his way through the Muslim sector toward Via Dolorosa, where stalls of spicy hummus, exotic tobaccos, and aromatic flat bread gave way to embroidery, ceramics, and antiques.

He reached the door of Fatall, one of the antique shops, and grunted at the red fez hat—and the autographed photos of the late Moshe Dayan that lined its entrance. Jamil Fatall was Lebanese, and could give a shit whether Moshe Dayan lived or died. The pictures were there only to satisfy Fatall's combined need for vanity and camouflage.

Inside the shop, the tight-jeaned teenager whose dark eyes flashed in synch with her iPod® motioned him to the stairs with a sexy smile. Luke reminded himself he had no interest in flirtation today. Still smarting from the red-haired vixen's rebuff, he would continue his involuntary abstinence in that department—at least until his present mission was accomplished. *Yes, give me the* gelt *over the woman any day. Until I no longer have to choose,* he thought.

Conscious of the rare privilege he had been accorded by the

shop owner of entering the master's lair where amateurs were strictly unwelcome and transactions never recorded, he stopped mid-descent to allow his eyes to adjust to the dim light. The melodious voice of Jamil Fatall came to him. "Luke, Luke, come on down, my friend."

"How did you know it was me?" Adashek responded.

The shopkeeper laughed. "You're the only one I know who stops halfway in the middle of each step to think. It's your personality—"

"What have you got for me?" Adashek wasn't interested in the character analysis that his old friend never tired of offering him unasked for and for no extra price.

Fatall reached inside a Greek amphora and pulled from its depths a tiny jeweler's velvet envelope. "What do you think?" he said with pride, as he revealed the aureus to the man who'd consigned it to his good offices.

Thanks to the work of the museum restorer, the coin's patina was gone, as was the millennial encrustation that had covered the inscription. Even in the dark cellar, it shone with the undiminished splendor of pure twenty-two-karat gold alloy. From the moment Emily had revealed it to him, Adashek had fallen under the coin's spell no less than she had, though he'd done a better job of disguising it. Now without more than a confirming glance, he accepted the coin from Fatall and returned it to the envelope he'd found it in when he broke open the miniature Ark of the Covenant in a hidden alley near the museum. He'd overcome his initial reaction. He wasn't going to let an object, at least this object, possess him. Quite the opposite.

"May I at least offer you a coffee?" Fatall, who'd spent hours polishing the coin and as many hours simply admiring its beauty and its age, never understood the desperate and eager people who came to his shop to buy or sell. To him the thrill of life was to savor its artifacts, objects invested with value because the past had allowed them to survive its remorseless disintegration.

"No coffee." Adashek shook his head impatiently. "What did you find out for me?"

"Well, I've found the buyer who will pay you the best price for it," the old man said, now eager to have Adashek and this abducted coin out of his shop.

"Where is he? When can I meet him?"

"He's in Rome. He will come to you, or you can go to him."

"How do I know I can trust him?"

"He's a bishop."

"What price is he willing to pay?"

Fatall laughed. "When I read him the inscription, he said he will pay any price you ask."

XIII/13
St. Paul's

By a stroke of luck, Bishop Giuseppe Giammo, S.J. spotted the American the moment Ryan McKeown exited the Metro at the Basilica di San Paolo station. He tailed him up a graffiti-marred stairwell to the street, stopping to light a Gaulois in order to keep his distance. Why wasn't the young priest taking the more direct route Giammo wondered—the church's underground entrance? It wasn't until they reached the street that he realized the priest's intention. *He wants to see the exterior. Approach the edifice like a pilgrim.*

Instantly Giammo disliked him. The American naiveté, the sentimental intensity. *Look both ways before you cross! Ignore the pretty women!* His simplicity was apparent even from afar, in the boldness of his stride, in the sudden halt to appraise the facade. *Tilt head, drop jaw, savor brief enchantment.* This priest who'd been so ardently described as a threat was at heart a harmless American tourist. The physical description he'd been given was accurate: "tall, lean, pale-skinned, earnest;" but they'd left out the crucial character trait: the hunger that seemed to inhabit his body, the hunger for faith, of a priest in doubt.

This poor bastard wasn't a threat. He was a budding martyr. An inexperienced priest in hot pursuit of the truth, hoping the truth will save him—completely ignorant of truth's infinite facets. Lord knows, he'll probably pull out a camera and start taking photographs!

Almost as if he'd read Giammo's mind, Ryan looked

behind him. He scanned the crowd, and for a split second, his eyes locked on his stalker. Ryan's open face confirmed what the bishop had suspected: piety and skepticism, the fateful combination, just as the Procurator General had described it.

Giammo slowly lowered his eyes, as if absorbed in reverence, and the American turned back to resume his walk, striding on toward the basilica. He'd been right, Giammo thought, to wear lay garb today. The white *guayabera* was a stroke of genius. He could be Mexican, Argentine, Peruvian, or any one of many million God-fearing, fiesta-loving Hispanics. No one, least of all this unsuspecting American, would guess he was a ruthless soldier of the true Christ.

At one time pilgrims approached the Basilica of St. Paul through an awe-inspiring mile-long colonnade, 800 columns of marble. All that had vanished long ago. Now pilgrims arrived by the Metro.

Ryan turned to look at these moderns, visitors and tourists from around the world making their way toward the basilica of a 2,000-year-old saint. A Roman in a business suit, staring at the basilica, flicked his cigarette butt into a puddle at the curb. A young woman, dressed entirely in black, led by the hands two blonde-haired bickering boys. Ryan speculated she must be a widow. Three white-collared French nuns whispered their astonishments to one another and behind them the thin middle-aged man in a Mexican wedding shirt bowed his head solemnly in prayer. His dark eyes reminded Ryan of the new pope, Pius XIII, who had paid a visit to the tomb of the saint shortly after his coronation.

St. Paul, "the thirteenth apostle" whose legendary lightning conversion allegedly knocked him off his horse, was eventually beheaded for his outspoken and eloquent proclamation of faith in *Jasius Christus,* though for some unaccountable reason the author of the famous Epistles made not a single reference to the historical Jesus. Three fountains allegedly sprang up where the martyr's head hit the ground, a few miles from the Ostian Gate at a place then known as *Ad Aquas Salvas.*

The three fountains had long ago dried up, some say because the eucalyptus trees that thrived in the area sucked them into oblivion. Where the water once ran now stood three churches, their gift shops selling the Trappists' pharmaceutical-tasting *Liquore Eucaliptina,* distilled from the essence of the eucalyptus that had literally incorporated the sacred waters. According to oral tradition, a pious Roman widow named Lucina had claimed Paul's body for her family burial place near a vineyard on the Via Ostia where the basilica was later built.

Ryan followed the French nuns inside. He scanned the bronze doors' inlaid silver reliefs, scenes from the lives of Saints Peter and Paul, then turned his gaze on the interior. The vastness of the space was overwhelming. He compared the interior to the basilica of St. Peter's—the only one larger in Rome—and found St. Peter's wanting. The wide nave felt more expansive and grand, with double side aisles separated by what looked like a hundred granite columns. The columns reflected on the polished marble floor like trees at the edge of a lake. He wandered out onto the reflective marble surface and thought of the story of Christ walking on water. Surrounded by beauty like this, a person could believe in such miracles.

The nuns huddled and spoke in a hush. One of the twin boys shouted, and was quickly collared by his mother. Ryan continued past them all, floating down the nave toward the triumphal arch. The arch, supported by two colossal columns and inlaid with brilliant mosaics, was a relic of the original basilica. The high altar would be found beneath the glorious marble canopy.

Beneath the altar, Ryan knew, lay the tomb of St. Paul, in the very spot where it was uncovered at the time of Constantine.

Ryan stared at the place in silence. For a while his mind wandered, drifting back to childhood, overcome with nostalgia for a time of unquestioning faith. He recalled his brilliant father arguing doctrine with the pastor; his mother at the communion rail, stubbornly going to her knees while all the others stood. And his own hormone-fevered fantasies of naked demons and holy saints, a battle in his brain that had raged ever since.

A full minute might have passed. When Ryan finally checked his watch, it was exactly ten a.m.

He found his way outside to the cloisters. In this medieval courtyard, stacked with mounted stones and relics recovered from the original basilica, he was to meet with the church's living relic—*abbas et rector* Stefano Lanati, the aged Benedictine who ruled over St. Paul's in the name of the Holy See. Ryan found him sitting on a stone bench amid thorny, flowerless rose bushes, scribbling miniscule notes with a pencil in a small black unlined book. Ryan approached discreetly, his hands clasped behind his back. "Father Lanati?"

The old man lifted his gaze. His moist eyes were a bluish gray, peering over half-rimmed spectacles.

As Ryan introduced himself, he gave a subtle bow. "Excuse me if I'm interrupting."

"Not at all," said the aged monk, closing his tiny book. The top of his head was bald and shiny. It made him look masculine, despite his robe, Ryan thought. "Just jotting down my thoughts," he said. "Keeps me from bothering others with them."

"I'm sure they're worth preserving."

Lanati looked out over the garden. "In a place like this,

many things are worth preserving. But the dull musings of an old worker in the vineyard of the Lord can hardly be counted among them." He rose to his feet and offered Ryan his hand. "A pleasure to meet you, Father." The rims of his glasses caught the bright sunlight, adding a sparkle to the old man's eyes. But the eyes broke quickly away from Ryan's; and once again stared at the garden.

Ryan had many questions but when he arrived at the main question he'd come all this way to ask—what was Isaac's interest in the tomb of St. Paul?—the rector sidestepped the question.

"Monsignor Isaac was interested in all manner of things. His obsession with the tomb of St. Paul was really no different than his obsession with the sources of the Gospels, or the history of the Egyptian sun kings, or the ruins of the cave of the Sibyl—any number of ancient obscurities. He told me once he was a pilgrim, 'a pilgrim into the past, which we carry inside us. I seek the rebirth of the true Christ,' he said. As if he were one of the Wise Men."

They were walking slowly through the garden as he spoke, and now Ryan noticed that whenever he glanced at the monk, Lanati never met his look. He seemed to be carrying on a double-track of thought, as if only half his mind was present and engaged; the other half absorbed in silent worries of his own. Ryan grew impatient. He finally asked the abbot bluntly if he'd show him Paul's sarcophagus.

At the very least he should be allowed to see the famous tomb that Isaac had uncovered.

Lanati raised his gaze, but not to Father Ryan. He continued staring as he had been—at some vague point ahead, somewhere out in the honeysuckle-scented air. "Of course you may, Father." His head tilted slightly. "Though I must tell you, there's really not much to see. The sarcophagus cannot be opened."

"You mean it hasn't been opened since Monsignor Isaac discovered it?"

Lanati paused. Staring at the ground. "Even Monsignor Isaac was not allowed to open it."

Ryan was dumbfounded. "You mean...no one...?"

"Orders from the Holy Father," he said. He was staring across the courtyard at a figure seated on a bench in the shade of the colonnade. It was the thin man in the white wedding shirt, his face obscured in the shadows.

Lanati stared at the ground again. Then he gestured toward a doorway that led back into the church. "If you follow me I'll show you why."

The old priest led Ryan through the gate in the altar rail and behind the massive altar. "Monsignor Isaac discovered that by lifting up certain pavement stones in the basilica's floor, a series of underground chambers and tunnels became accessible—most of them unmapped and long forgotten."

They came to a place behind the altar where a large marble floor slab was partially dislodged. Lanati knelt down, and motioned for Ryan to help him lift one end of a heavy slab—to reveal an excavated chamber beneath the marble floor.

Allowing the slab to lean against his torso, Lanati nodded toward the opening and the rope ladder that was coiled nearby. "If you climb down into this chamber, you can get a look at the sarcophagus."

Ryan secured the rope ladder to the newly-installed eye ring and climbed down into the pit. It was carved through rock and tufa, and the air was cool and damp. While Ryan's eyes adjusted to the gloom, Lanati stared down at him from above, his head like a bust perched on the slab.

"The sarcophagus," Lanati explained, "lies several feet below the main altar, embedded in a platform of ancient concrete. Isaac managed to reach the back side of the sarcophagus, but the Commission of Sacred Archaeology decided that opening the tomb would be practically impossible without destroying the altar above. I left a candle and a box of matches in that metal box behind you."

Ryan opened the old biscuit tin on the packed clay floor, and found a partly used church candle and a matchbox with three matches. His first two attempts failed, the match heads disintegrating on the damp sandpaper. His last attempt was more successful; he held the match near the tip and let out a curse as the flame momentarily scorched his fingers, but the candle flaring into life cast an eerie glow on the sweating walls around him.

On the side nearest the altar he saw that a small opening had been carved through the stone wall. Holding up the candle, he could glimpse a ghostly block of marble inside a diminutive chamber.

Lanati's voice sounded from above. "The marble sarcophagus was apparently first placed there during reconstruction of the basilica in 390 A.D. Before that the bones of Paul had rested in a simple wooden box carved with doves and eagles—which had nearly disintegrated by the time his tomb was discovered."

Ryan, caught up in exhilaration, had to remind himself to breathe. To be so close to the bones of St. Paul! The saint credited with turning a Judaic cult into a world religion. The thought gave him gooseflesh.

"Did Isaac try to gain permission to examine the interior of the sarcophagus?"

"Yes, but from what I understand permission was denied

by the Holy Father himself."

Something brushed against Ryan's back. He turned to see the rope ladder disappearing, a flash of white above—and the marble slab crashing down.

The sudden draft extinguished the candle, to seal him in utter darkness.

XIV / 14
Judas

It was strange how uncomfortable she felt being dressed up. Emily tried to remember the last occasion she'd worn a dress or skirt, but all she could recall was an Institute fundraiser in Jerusalem with Luke. She couldn't remember the dress, exactly, but she did remember the look on his face when he saw her climbing out of the cab, her long legs sleek and bare. It never failed to surprise her how men reacted to the sight of her limbs. Sometimes Luke would just stare at her arms across the table until she had to snap him back to reality. Her attractiveness to the opposite sex was a power she always seemed at odds with.

On this trip—though she'd worn her everyday jeans and the mandatory helmet on the motorbike—she'd packed along her steel-gray silk business suit to change into in the ladies room. The lacey camisole she wore under the jacket and her clicking high heels drew admiring glances as she strolled into the drab waiting room of the Israel Police Division of Criminal Investigations. The occasion called for professional attire.

She gave her name, then took a seat and waited. Just when her nerves were about as jangled as they could get, she considered going to the ladies room and changing back to jeans. Her insecure thoughts came to an abrupt halt when a serious-looking assistant opened the door to the inner offices. "Ms. Scelba? Commander Kahane is waiting to see you."

Emily nodded at the others waiting, as though to tell them she was no longer part of their company. Only the hooker in the miniskirt acknowledged her. Emily straightened her hair self-consciously as she stood up and moved toward the door.

Jacob Kahane rose to greet her with a frown-like smile to indicate the gravity of her visit. "Thank you for coming so quickly."

The commander appeared younger in person than he'd sounded on the phone. He was trim and fit, with a square-shouldered military bearing, his thick black hair neatly combed, his taut face tanned and shaven. But his voice was as deep and gravelly as a bear's. When she saw him light a cigarette from the butt he was still smoking, she understood why.

"My entire career is riding on your success in recovering this artifact," she answered, then removed her jacket and accepted the chair he was holding for her. "I made the biggest mistake of my life trusting it to Adashek. I have a lot of questions."

His eyes seemed to twinkle beneath their squinted lids. "We both have questions."

Once Emily had satisfied Kahane with a recital of how and where she found the coin, how Adashek had come to know of it, how she had turned it over to him, and when she herself had last seen it, he was almost ready to answer her questions. The sticking point was the matter of her personal relationship with Luke. At first she refused to answer, but realized that just as her folly had caused her to lose focus, the investigator's inquiries proved that he wasn't about to lose his. He needed to understand.

She slumped in her chair. "He was an old boyfriend. He'd driven all the way from Jerusalem at my request for funding. It'd been a long time. I asked him to spend the night. He mistook the invitation for—" She paused.

Kahane's eyes betrayed nothing, neither understanding nor disapproval. He simply dragged on his Time cigarette and waited.

"It was a mistake." She reddened. "I knew that it was the moment I'd opened my mouth. We had dinner; then I made it clear nothing more was going to happen. I couldn't stand feeling like I was using him."

"I don't think it was a mistake." This time Kahane's smile was genial. "I can understand how disappointed he must have been."

He was looking at her arms, damn him.

"It turns out he was using *me*. That was his *modus operandi* the entire time we were together. Over and over, I watched him use people and walk away. One day I'd had it up to here, and walked away myself."

"Why did you trust him with the coin?"

Her blush was so deep it made her freckles disappear for a moment. "Because he's a British diplomat. He once told me that he was bonded. You could entrust him with anything at all and he was bound by law to protect it. He told me he had to show it to the authorities to expedite the immediate funding I needed." She imagined the commander was doing all he could to keep himself from bursting into laughter at her naiveté. She reassessed him, and her situation. "You don't—" she started.

Kahane didn't allow her to finish. "No, we don't suspect you. Certainly not after studying your remarkable curriculum vitae. And after meeting you in person." This time he looked directly in her eyes.

"Now that you're satisfied with the probe into my reckless private life," she said, "why isn't the son of a bitch in custody?"

"His apartment was empty by the time we got there." Kahane didn't look pleased to report this. "Apparently someone had called ahead to warn him."

"And the British Consulate?"

"He hasn't shown up there since Monday. They have no idea where he is. It seems he was somewhat of a recluse. No one seemed to know much about him."

"Yes, Luke was that way. Loved pretending to be mysterious, but I always suspected it was because he had nothing interesting going on—and he knew it."

"You must have found him interesting in some regards." Kahane let the jibe sit there.

She reddened again. "Need clouds judgment sometimes," she finally said, earning a sympathetic nod from her interrogator. "Never again," she added firmly. "I'll find him. And I'll deal with him for what he's done to me."

"That's our job now, Ms. Scelba. How do we know Adashek is the guilty one? How do we know that *he* wasn't being used? Or that he wasn't working with others? We were hoping you might have some idea—" But the commander's words were cut short by the entrance of his serious-looking assistant.

"Sorry to interrupt, sir," the woman said. "Thought you'd want to see this."

Kahane glanced at the information she handed him, then offered it to Emily. "You may be right after all. It appears our mutual friend left for Rome two days ago."

She pushed the piece of paper away. She didn't need to see it. The sickening feeling in her gut intensified. She knew it wasn't going away anytime soon.

XV / 15
Dark Night of the Soul

"Father Lanati!" He'd been shouting so long his voice was hoarse beyond recognition. It was futile. Sound couldn't penetrate the ancient stone, and he was only using up whatever oxygen lurked in the fetid air he shared with the sepulcher. Ryan forced himself to take a deep breath.

Nothing made sense. Why would Lanati seal him in the tomb? What was the flash of white he'd seen as the slab descended?

Hands outstretched, he began a Braille-like reconnaissance of his prison, moving to his left until his fingertips made contact with the rough-hewn wall. Lanati said there were other chambers. Maybe he could find a way out. He worked his way forward, feeling the shape of the wall, seeking a crack that might betray an exit. After what felt like four or five feet his fingers encountered the perpendicular wall. Tracing it in the same fashion, he estimated a full ten feet of seamless stone before he reached a point to his right where he felt the edges of an opening, perhaps a doorway sealed with stones. After half an hour or more of struggling and skinning his fingers raw, he failed to dislodge even one stone. Maybe Lanati had been lying about the other chambers and tunnels.

His mind raced—was this dank hellhole going to be his final resting place? What was the Pope so afraid of that he would forbid Isaac's investigations, even to the extreme of the Vatican Curia arranging for the Albanian to silence him? And—

—how was Ryan, a mere American Jesuit, a threat to anyone?

Quieting his fear, he went back to regulating his breathing.

Then he folded his legs into lotus position, his back against the tomb and shaped his breath into the rhythm of meditation he'd learned from Joseph Sebes, S.J. many years ago. His Jesuit instructor in comparative religions had spent a good part of his adult life in India and China, and had instilled in his students— including Ryan—a deep faith in the healing powers of mental serenity and the awakening of the divine within. Like the Hindu elephant god Ganesh, he would use the weight of his spirit to quiet the scurrying mouse mind that otherwise would overcome his entire being with fear.

He didn't know whether the calming white light that now filled his soul was the God he'd been ordained to serve, Socrates' *daemon*—"god within"—or a hint of the ultimate reality of Brahman, identical with the life of the universe itself. Knowing or not knowing was a function of the mind, and Ryan had turned his mind off to feel the serenity of pure being where time, with its concerns for functions of the body like hunger and thirst and pain, no longer exists; and where past and future give way to a now that reaches to eternity.

XVI / 16
Illegal Entry

Luke had told her about the history of the cobblestone square known as Ohel Moshe. They'd been making their way from the Foreign Ministry that spring day, admiring the purple irises and sweet-smelling narkis peeking up from nooks and crannies in the cobblestones. She remembered wondering if she really loved him even then.

Tonight, seething with the opposite of love, she was back in her jeans and on her motorbike, crossing the busy square. Ohel Moshe may have only been a hundred-some years old, but its houses looked as if they'd been there forever. She barely noticed the raucous Greek music blasting from the neighborhood as she indicated a turn into a narrow street below Agrippas and pulled over in front of one of the two-story stone houses covered with violet bougainvillea.

The full moon was obscured by clouds, giving her the cover she'd been hoping for as she approached the dimly lit square. Luke's lodging was on the upper floor, its balcony facing the square. She knew the balcony all too well; it was where she was standing, under a crescent moon, when she realized they had no future together. As she'd motored from Ruppin to Ben Joshi, Emily had been reviewing the layout of Luke's flat in her mind. She recalled that the balcony was graced by honeysuckle that nearly concealed an eminently climbable trellis. Seconds later, with hardly a skip in her heartbeat, she found herself on the balcony.

The French doors from the balcony were hardly an obstacle. Though they were locked, a shove of thigh and knee brought her into the muddle that Adashek called home. If there was furniture here, it had long been buried under the sheer weight of records—boxes and boxes of them, stuffed with receipts and lists and maps and scribbled notes.

If the coin was in this topsy-turvy room, she realized, it might take her the rest of her life to find it. But she hadn't come here to find the coin. She knew as well as Kahane had known that the coin would only be found when the man who had stolen it was found.

She had six hours to kill before her flight to Rome and began rummaging randomly through the endless accumulation of this eccentric man's life. Looking for something—anything that might tell her more about his intentions, how and why he had done what he'd done, and exactly where in the hell he'd disappeared to in the Eternal City.

In a Nike shoebox under his bed she found a stash of photographs. She tossed them onto the bed and spotted a snapshot of herself. She was wearing a black swimsuit on a beach near Tel Aviv and pushing her hair away from her face. She'd worn her hair below her shoulders then, as if defying the encroachment of time over her adolescent spirit.

Another memory. Another life. It made her unexpectedly furious. How could a woman so precise in her profession be so slipshod in her private life? She flicked the photo into the air and resumed her search.

There had to be a thousand books in the room; the shelves were overflowing. More were stacked in tottering piles, growing like mushrooms out of the refuse and debris. She crawled between them on hands and knees, clawing through the papers that were scattered on the floor. Drawings. Notes. Diagrams of archaeological digs. Beneath the mattress, a pornographic Arabic magazine apparently purchased in Beirut. More photographs.

Emily yelped.

A mouse scurried out from the pile, terrified by the human tornado that was upsetting its protected environment.

She picked up the folded paper shopping bag the beast had emerged from and discovered a cord underneath it—a telephone cord. Emily followed it through the debris, searching for its end. Surely that instrument, even in the midst of this chaos, might be the center for clues of some sort of organization.

She found the old-style phone on a broken shelf under what Luke must have thought of as a cocktail table—it was scarred with a thousand moisture rings caused apparently by the exact same glass. She searched the telephone's perimeter, all the way out and around the table. Just as she was about to give up, she found a crumpled piece of paper that had missed its intended target: a bachelor's wastebasket that looked as though it had never been emptied in the sixteen years he'd owned it. How could she ever have put up with sleeping in this room, with this man? The paper had been torn from a desk calendar, and the page was from two days ago.

Luke's scribble was meager, but it was enough for Emily Scelba.

"Fatall, 2 P.M."

How perversely anal of this reprobate to use a comma in a note to himself.

XVII/17
Lazarus, Come Forth!

How long Ryan remained lost in his yogic trance he had no idea. He was startled to alertness by the deep grumble of the slab being moved and piercing rays of light entering the chamber.

He peered up to see Lanati and a sacristan wrangling the heavy stone. Lanati's head was swaddled in what appeared to be altar linen. The look on his face made it clear he had nothing, voluntarily, to do with Ryan's entombment.

"Are you all right?" Lanati asked.

Ryan nodded. He felt light-headed and calm, the effect of the prolonged meditation. "How long was I down here?"

"Almost twenty-four hours," Lanati replied as the sacristan threw the rope ladder down. "Antonio here found me when he was making his morning rounds. I was still lying here covered in blood from the blow to my head. We've called the police," he added, answering Ryan's unspoken question, and offering him a glass of water.

Ryan climbed out of the grave-like hole. Accepting the water and drinking slowly and deeply, he looked from the sacristan to Lanati. "Are you all right?" he asked.

Lanati nodded. "I have a splitting headache, but nothing that a good cup of espresso won't cure."

The sacristan looked at him dubiously. "You need to go to the hospital, to have your head checked."

"What's wrong with my head," Lanati laughed, "can't be

cured at a hospital."

The rector and Ryan were still sipping coffee at the refectory table, and the American was devouring his third breakfast roll. The questions from the police had been brief and to the point. They'd left a few minutes earlier stating that if neither Lanati nor Ryan were interested in filing an official report there was nothing more they could do.

"It wasn't about you," Ryan commented, stirring an extra lump of sugar into his espresso. "I'm certain it was a warning— for me."

Lanati shrugged his shoulders. "I was—what is it you Americans call it—'collateral damage.'"

Ryan nodded. "I'm afraid so. Monsignor Isaac is dead and everything about his death makes me suspect he was on to something deeply troubling to the papal authorities. Are you absolutely certain he followed the orders of the Holy See not to probe further into the sepulcher?"

"Like yourself, Monsignor Isaac was a Jesuit. To a Jesuit, disobedience is not an option."

Ryan registered his assertion, but it troubled him because it sounded more like a warning than a statement. The two men stared at each other. Ryan realized it was the first time the old priest had looked directly into his eyes. Ryan found his look disturbing. There was a hint in it of something dreaded, of fear and apprehension. It was a look of deep foreboding.

The old priest's eyes finally disengaged, to notice something behind Ryan. Ryan turned, and through the wrought-iron grate of the sanctuary, for a fleeting second thought he saw the thin man in the white shirt, standing in the aisle. *But that was impossible. Twenty-four hours has passed.* He blinked and the man was no longer there.

When Ryan looked back at his host, Lanati's eyes again grew vague.

"I think you've learned all you can here," he said.

Ryan pushed his chair back from the table. "I wonder," he said. "I sincerely wonder."

He was halfway to the door when Lanati's voice followed him. "You take care of yourself," the abbot said. "Among your fellow Jesuits in Rome there are some who are literally soldiers of Christ. They don't shoot blanks."

Outside the air was bright, and after the hush of the silent basilica the sounds of passing traffic seemed annoyingly mundane. Ryan hurried to the front entrance, where the man in white would have made his exit. He scanned the green grounds with their towering royal palms. A group of giggling English teenage girls wearing backpacks was heading for the station. Squinting at the sunbeams that flickered through the breezy palms, Ryan spotted a man in a long-waisted white shirt climbing into a taxi. He continued walking toward the man but the taxi sped away. He shook his head. If indeed the man in white had dropped the slab, why would he still be around a day later?

XVIII / 18
Thirty Pieces of Silver

He hated dramatic ritual of any kind and was never amused when those he had to deal with insisted on it. "Why the Pantheon?" Luke asked the voice on the phone. "Why not the middle of the Coliseum under the full moon at midnight?"

The click at the other end of the phone indicated that his sarcasm had missed its mark.

And so it was that, after fortifying himself with an outrageously expensive gin and tonic, Lucas Adashek entered the ancient monument just as the slanting rays of the late afternoon sun pierced through the oculus that centered its perfectly arched ceiling. Some said the structural perfection was such that rain falling through the skylight would be dissipated even as it entered the building. Adashek could care less. What he cared about was the *gelt*, that mysterious substance that humans used to trade for the pleasures of the earth. Compared to the treasures he knew Emily would dig up thanks to the ongoing funding he had ensured for her, this one little coin was the least he deserved.

Lost in his self-justifications, he failed to notice the thin man in the expensive Hawaiian shirt until he was virtually at his elbow.

"Mr. Adashek?"

Adashek whirled to meet the stranger. "Yes," he said. "And you are—?"

"My identity is unimportant to the transaction at hand," the man answered. His breath smelled faintly of milk. He held out his hand. "May I see the coin?"

Did he detect a tremble in the man's open hand? Without ceremony Adashek withdrew the pouch and placed the coin on the proffered palm.

A beam of evening sun illuminated the crowned head on the surface of the polished aureus, flashing gold from the man's palm so bright it forced Adashek to look away momentarily. Gazing at the coin as if it were a consecrated host, the thin man turned it over reverently. What he saw on the obverse was enough. "All that matters to you," he turned to Adashek, "is that I represent a patron who must acquire this coin for his private collection. What is your price?"

Adashek felt perspiration announcing itself on his forehead. He hated to be in this position: if he asked less than what the buyer was willing to pay, he would never know. But Fatall had told him he would get his asking price. "One million euros," he answered, hoping his hesitation wasn't too apparent to the thin man whose eyes remained riveted on the shining coin.

"I assume you'll want that transferred to an account," the man said. "I will—"

"—no, as a matter of fact, I prefer cash." Adashek's voice betrayed elation mixed with anxiety that he had indeed set his sights too low. But one million euros, to a man of simple habits, was serene retirement on the bikini-laced Croatian island of Istria. He shouldn't be too greedy, after all. This was a gift from heaven. Then he thought of Emily Scelba, and realized his urgency. He needed to escape to Istria sooner rather than later before the cock-teasing minx caught up with him. If that happened, there would be hell to pay. With the sleight-of-hand of a gypsy, Adashek retrieved the coin from the man's palm and restored it to its velvet pouch.

The steely eyes registered no surprise. He nodded. "All right," he said. "You shall have it in cash. Meet me here tomorrow evening at the same time."

"Come alone," Adashek said.

"Don't worry."

Adashek moved toward the exit doors, but turned before he reached them. The man stood waiting for him to leave. "What would you have said if I'd asked for two million?"

"Count yourself fortunate that you will never know."

XIX/19
Christus Rex et Redemptor Mundi
Christ the King & Redeemer of the World

Ryan was surprised from his cot this morning by the summons to a meeting with Ramon Pimental, S.J., the Procurator General of the Society of Jesus whose job it was, as the Society's chief canon lawyer, to liaise between the Jesuit Curia and the various departments of the Roman Curia of the Vatican.

What have I done to deserve the Procurator General's attention? Could he have heard about the incident at St. Paul's already? Ryan hurriedly dressed and mechanically observed his morning rites.

To enter the Vatican museum on the famous *Mons Vaticanus,* the apex of the smallest nation in the world, the everyday pilgrim must first suffer the purgatory of lining up along the walls of the Palace of the Popes—sometimes for as many as six blocks and as long as four or five hours. A rainstorm like today's brought no exception to the waiting rule, and purgatory offered a soggy taste of hell. The less stalwart visitors, apologetically, drift out of line to the warm and dry pleasures of a café across the boulevard. There they witness the dreary file of more stolid sufferers waiting for a taste of heaven while they sip their *macchiati corretti*—mini-cappuccinos "corrected" with liqueur of choice.

Ryan had no need for this particular penance. The momentary flash of his College and Vatican identification to the orange-and-dark blue-garbed Swiss Guard manning the

V.I.P. turnstile was enough to earn him a wave through the crowd and toward the private entrance.

Rome was alive with rumors about who might succeed the outgoing head of the Jesuit order, Regis Schork, S.J., who had himself succeeded the controversial Pero Manuel. Schork had more or less set the Jesuits back on track as far as the Holy See was concerned, correcting a course of political activism and comparative religious scholarship that the Vatican considered errant—a course on which the Jesuits' dedication to "political justice, the rule of law, tolerance, and human rights" might have caused a detour from their militant loyalty to His Holiness, the Vicar of Christ on earth. *How did Pimental find time to summon me,* Ryan thought, *when he must be up to his eyeballs in the Synod to attend to Jesuits who had traveled from every Continent for the election?*

Ryan navigated his way through the maze of privileged passageways and paused in reverence at the strategically sculptured ribbon positioned on the staircase emblazoned with the slogan made famous by the Emperor Constantine whose reign led eventually to Christianity being declared the official religion of the Roman Empire: *In hoc signo vinces,* "In this sign you will conquer."Diplomatic audiences were arranged for that time of day when the sun's rays illuminated the slogan just as the visiting royalty passed the statue and started down the marble staircase.

Ryan increased his pace, taking two steps at a time down the Scalia, wondering if he were keeping the Procurator General waiting.

Pimental's office door was as modest as that of a university professor's. It took only a single rap for Ryan to receive an authoritative, *"Venga!"* He entered to find the Procurator General lifting barbells. The sleeves of the tall Spaniard's cassocks fell toward his shoulders, enough to reveal remarkably well-defined musculature for a man who must be in his mid-sixties. Pimental's hair was still thick, black with streaks of silver that made him look dashing. His sideburns were muttonchops, and the smile he gave to his visitor as he set the barbells down was both warm and devilish. "What am I gonna do with you, boy?" he said to Ryan, forming his spatulate fingers into the hand gesture of prayer, as though Ryan were a rebellious teenager in his sophomore Latin class.

The familiar tone took Ryan aback. "What do you mean, sir?" he asked.

"Call me Pimental," the man said, in what was clearly an Andalusian accent that made his English feel somehow sinister. "Monsignor Isaac was one of our favorites," he said, in a tone of admonishment. "His death was devastating enough. None of us are happy about it. Why can't you let him rest in peace as the Sacred Curia has asked you to do?"

"Why has his research been sequestered?"

"Why do you want to know? It's not your business. Did someone appoint you his scholarly executor?" Pimental snapped, all trace of playfulness gone. For an instant his eyes burned like those of a fanatic, but just as quickly returned to their flat slate of unreadable command.

"It's just that I knew him from the College—"

"You met him once." Pimental had done his homework, or someone had done it for him. "Your work at the College has nothing to do with his. Or are you tired of your assignment, and looking for something more challenging? Perhaps a ten-year epigraphic research project living in the dark like a mole would satisfy your investigative interests?" His tone was caustic, the question clearly a warning. "We could assign you as our resident epigrapher here in the catacombs." Pimental motioned in the direction of the door at the end of the corridor. "That way I could keep a close eye on you."

"No, *signore*, I have much work still to do here."

"Then remember your vows, and do as I say. Abandon your self-indulgent inquiry—and behave yourself!"

Beads of perspiration formed on Ryan's forehead as Pimental continued his tirade.

"I'll make sure none of this appears in your files," he mercifully concluded.

Ryan nodded. The interview was over. Pimental had already opened a folder on his desk, dismissing his visitor with a cursory sign of the cross.

As he reached the end of the corridor leading away from the office, something made Ryan glance back. A black-suited figure was entering Pimental's office, entering without pausing to knock. For a split second, the two men looked at each other; then both turned away.

But Ryan had no doubt. The face he saw was the thin man in the white shirt he'd caught sight of in St. Paul's. He recalled the flash of white that had preceded the fall of the marble slab, entombing him for an entire day and night. His gut told him instantly what his brain would spend the next few hours carefully piecing together.

Inside the Procurator General's office, Pimental's orders to Giammo were as brief and precise as his warning to the young American: "Complete the transaction tonight. The funds have been arranged by the Superior General himself." He handed Giammo what appeared to be two plastic cards, one silver, one gold. "Enter the *Banco* near the Pantheon at the steel door on the side away from the Piazza. That gives you the shortest possible distance to carry it. Make sure the *Gendarmeria* aren't following you when you leave here. I needn't point out the disaster it would be if the Papal Curia got wind of your mission. If you don't succeed, they will."

Giammo rose. "I've been alerted that the American woman is en route to Rome."

"Another goddamned American?" The vein on Pimental's forehead signaled his anger. "Why can't they stay home? If she tries to interfere, do what must be done."

"Ho capisco, monsignore," Giammo murmured.

Pimental sighed, and the two clerics dropped their eyes reverentially. Labor in the vineyard required tilling the dark side of the hill as well as the light.

XX/20
Pilgrimage

An hour after her entry into Luke's flat Emily Scelba had motored down Jerusalem's Via Dolorosa with an intensity equal to that of her nemesis as he walked along the same route days earlier. Fatall's face made it clear he wasn't thrilled to see her. Why would he be? Years ago he'd tried to sell her an artifact smuggled out of Palestine. Had it not been for Adashek's diplomatic persuasion, she would have turned the shameless Lebanese merchant over to the authorities.

Yes, Fatall admitted, he'd seen Luke. No, he had no idea about an ancient Roman coin. She'd interrupted the no-doubt fascinating tale he started to tell about why he and Luke were hobnobbing by reminding him that she could still make his life miserable. "I don't care about you, or what you do for a living, or where you get the antiquities in this shop," she said. "I just want to know where my aureus is and what features you found on it after it was cleaned." Her voice cracked. "I presume that Ramle Prison would not be your location of choice for your golden years?"

Fatall sighed. "The buyer's name is Giuseppe Giammo. I will write down his cell number for you. He's a creature of habit..." Fatall proceeded to give her all the details of the coin as well as Giammo's daily routine in Rome.

Emily looked him in the eye. "You'd better be telling me the truth. One way or the other, you'll be hearing from me. I'm on my way to the airport now so I can recover my stolen coin, no thanks to you."

She reached over the glass-topped counter, snatched the antique diamond and emerald necklace he had been working on, and slipped it into her shirt pocket.

"Don't worry; it will be safe with me until I get my coin back." Emily walked to the door, with a slight spring in her step.

"But, my dear," Fatall pleaded, "that necklace is worth 80,000 euros!"

Emily took a backward glance over her shoulder. "I am *not* your dear," she said, "and think of your necklace as a temporary gift of gratitude for not having your ass hauled off to Ramle for your sins."

XXI/21
The Bishop's Shadow

Ryan had intended to take a peek at Raphael's "Room of Constantine" before leaving the museum hoping to find a clue there why Isaac had imbued himself with the writings and records of this particular emperor in the last few years of his life. But the sight of White Shirt from St. Paul's changed his plans.

Ryan's curiosity about the man surpassed caution and he turned back toward Pimental's office and walked by its door, careful to control the squeak of his standard issue clerical loafers on the polished marble. Judging from the violet designer darts on his black suit, the thin man in the Roman collar was a bishop—which made no sense to Ryan at all.

As he suspected, there was an exit door at the far end of the corridor. It had to be the door the thin man used. The exit was marked *Riservato,* but he turned the doorknob and found it open. Stairs spiraled downward into darkness. Without hesitating, he followed them.

When the light vanished after a single turn, he used hands on the railing, and his feet, to find the way. Two more turns and he saw a ray of brightness—enough to reveal an ancient door on the right marked simply *Tesoro,* "Treasury." Now he could see the light leaking through the cracks of the stairwell's exit door, which opened into a narrow patio behind a trellis of dark ivy. Taking care to close the door firmly behind him, Ryan made his way around the trellis to find himself in the

Belvedere courtyard.

He positioned himself on a bench behind a remarkably Christ-like statue of Apollo. Ryan removed his Latin breviary from his pocket and began reading the prayers he knew by heart. Anyone noticing him on the bench wouldn't have given him a second thought—just another of the thousands of priests in Rome reciting his daily office. But his attention remained fixed on the ivy trellis that concealed the exit door.

His vigil was rewarded a few minutes later, just as the bells rang to signal the closing of the museum. The mysterious bishop moved out from behind the ivy and nearly faded into the shadows cast by the setting sun. But not before Ryan rose and, mingling with an exiting crowd of noisy German tourists, followed him.

Once outside the Vatican, the bishop hailed a taxi. Ryan was fortunate enough to find another and climbed inside, with a command to the driver to follow.

The drive down *Lungotevere* to *Centro Antico* took nearly twenty minutes in the heavy traffic. At Ponte Garibaldi, the taxi turned left to cross the Tiber River.

As it approached Largo Argentina, his quarry's car slowed and let the bishop out. Ryan thanked his driver for his persistence through the mad traffic of early evening by handing him a twenty euro bill and telling him to keep the change. The driver accepted the over-generous tip with the nonchalance characteristic of Romans, showing not the least surprise that a spendthrift American Catholic priest was tailing a bishop from the Vatican.

Without a glance at the illuminated ruins in the ancient Campus Martius, Ryan crossed toward Piazza Vidoni where his prey was striding purposefully like a man late for a speaking engagement. By now the shadows had turned to patches of darkness, intruded on sporadically by dim antiquated streetlamps and passing headlights. Ryan kept a half block behind the man, and wished he'd worn his Reeboks instead of the more formal loafers he'd chosen for his meeting with Pimental. He fell into matching the thin man's pace for three hundred meters or so—once looking down when the bishop turned his head as though to see if he were alone—once having the absurd feeling that he himself was being followed.

The black suit turned right at the Piazza di Panteleo, and continued straight onto the short block that provided the final link between Piazza Navona and Campo di Fiori. The place felt very familiar. When the man abruptly turned and entered a tiny restaurant, the familiar garlicky odor of artichokes *carciofi alla romana* assaulted Ryan's nostrils.

Ryan's pulse raced with excitement when he recognized the place as Monsignor Isaac's favorite eatery, where the two of them had shared a *limoncino* the first and only time he saw the monsignor alive.

Just as he was debating about whether he should walk in and confront Giammo or wait to see what the bishop would do next, Ryan felt a sudden push from behind.

Someone had indeed been following him—and had run into him at full force.

XXII/22
Intersection

Based on Fatall's meticulous description, it had been easy for her to spot Giammo as he alighted from a taxi at Largo Argentina and to dog along behind him once he crossed the avenue in the direction of Piazza Navona. Emily's eagerness to confront him was mitigated by her desire to size him up first. She dissected him like an artifact. He appeared to be determined, older and taller than she expected, of some refinement judging from his Armani ecclesiastical suit; steel-nerved, his purpose not easily set aside by something as trivial as a flight of motorcycles roaring directly across his path. Giammo did not even break his stride.

She followed him as he took a right past the newsstands on Corso Vittorio Emanuele and then turned her head to study the medieval throwback nestled in the flank of a Renaissance palace into which he disappeared. The little building, which she realized was a restaurant, like a mushroom at the base of a mighty oak, had somehow withstood the encroachment of the lofty edifices in whose shadow it managed to sustain its humble existence.

The light coming from the restaurant illuminated Giammo as he entered, and Emily took careful note of the violet piping on the elegant black suit. Lost in momentary contemplation, she failed to notice the tall American in front of her until she'd charged directly into him. "I'm so sorry!" she exclaimed, reaching for his hand to help him regain his balance.

"Was I in your way?" The twinkle in his eye confirmed he was joking. "Or are you mugging me?" She didn't bother to hide the confusion on her face. "I noticed you a block or two back on the Corso," Ryan said.

"I wasn't following you," she blurted out. I was-"

"Following someone else?"

The deep blush showed he'd guessed correctly.

"Don't feel bad," he continued. "I was following someone myself."

"Giuseppe Giammo? The man who just entered that restaurant?" she asked.

Ryan nodded. *So the bishop had a name.* "You know him?"

"I know who he is. And you?"

"I only know that he's a Jesuit bishop-"

Emily stepped on his words, "-who got raised to that office to give him proper credentials for a highly volatile mission to Venezuela."

"For some reason," Ryan said, "the good bishop tried to-" He stopped himself. *What in the world was he doing blabbing to a complete stranger?*

"Tried to do what?" Emily wasn't letting him get away with it. They had drifted toward the pub across from he little restaurant.

"Let me buy you an espresso, and you can tell me more," he said.

"You mean that the other way around, don't you?" She glanced back toward the restaurant to make sure her target was still in sight. "You didn't finish your sentence about the bishop." She frowned. "But I suppose we can stake him out from here as well as anywhere else." She made the comment sound like it was an everyday affair for them both to be tailing bishops through the streets of Rome. "I'm buying. It's the least I can do after nearly knocking you over."

Despite his full involvement in the delicate *carciofi*, Bishop Giuseppe Giammo, S.J. had studied the exchange between the impetuous American priest who'd just visited Pimental and the red-haired woman who fit Fatall's description perfectly. He'd known he could count on the greedy merchant to warn him of anything that might interfere with the five percent baksheesh he'd agreed to remit to Jerusalem if the clandestine transaction was completed satisfactorily; one soul could be bought for a million, another for fifty thousand.

He wiped his hands dry of olive oil, sipped his milk, lit a Gaulois and, oblivious to the disapproving stares of the Californians across the room, took a deep inhale. Then he flipped open his cell phone, dialed a number, and spoke a few terse orders in Italian. When he flipped it closed he returned the phone to the shoulder holster that also contained a customized Luger, made sure the holster's profile was not apparent beneath his jacket, and returned his attention to the artichokes and the veal that had been charred to perfection.

What the young man and woman were doing together he had no idea, and even less curiosity. They had followed him, and would no doubt continue to do so. This bright-eyed freckled woman and this over-curious American cleric that had ignored his superior's direct warning were no more than petty obstacles.

Giammo had risen to the heights of his Society by his deftness at eliminating obstacles—and by his uncanny ability to *survive*. He had fashioned his own peculiar conscience, one based on an observation by Mahatma Gandhi, without being the least bit affected by the man's non-violent philosophy: "I can see that in the midst of death life persists, in the midst of darkness, light persists. Hence I gather that God is Life, Truth,

Light." In his own way he would continue his pursuit of life, truth, and light until his dying breath. He had been told by Pimental on more than one occasion that the greater good of Holy Mother Church was worth the sacrifice of a single soul now and then—even if that soul happened to be his own.

XXIII/23
Cambio

Maybe it was the handsome Irish-American's collar that gave Emily the encouragement she needed to follow her instincts and to offer him a blow-by-blow account of what had brought her so unexpectedly from Israel to Rome. Withholding much detail, she told him she'd discovered an important coin in her excavations, and that it had been stolen from her by a perfidious friend who'd brought it here to sell it to Giammo. If she followed the bishop, she would find her coin.

Ryan, on his part, though he wasn't quite sure what to make of her account, was magnetized by the intensity in the woman's gray eyes as she described the events of her past week. He couldn't help feeling that, if he wasn't careful, it would be all too easy to be mesmerized by the sheer energy in her voice. For now he was secure in observing it from the safe distance of his celibate vows. He realized he hadn't been paying close enough attention. "Tell me again, what makes you think this Giammo will lead you to your...friend?" At his hesitation in choosing the correct designation for Adashek the same look of embarrassment he'd seen when he introduced himself as "Father Ryan McKeown, S.J." flashed again across her face.

"Giammo's planning to buy the coin," she said. "I don't know why. I also don't know where or how. What I do know is that Luke will meet with him to retrieve the money and turn the coin over to him. I will be there, and take it back."

He studied her physique as though assessing her military prowess. "Alone?"

"Of course." The intensity of her tone made it clear she had no doubts about her abilities.

He laughed, but stopped short when he saw the flash of indignation in her eyes. "So you're planning to stalk him until he meets your thief?" If the whole story she recited hadn't sounded so preposterous he might have dismissed it. But his own recent experience had reconfirmed what he learned long ago, that truth could be stranger than fiction.

She nodded. "I don't have a lot of options. My one trustworthy contact in Rome won't return my call. Oddly enough, he's the one I would have brought the coin to."

Ryan felt a chill of foreboding. "I find it hard to believe that anyone would fail to respond to you," he finally said.

Emily let the compliment slip without acknowledgment. For reasons she couldn't identify, she was still perplexed that the man sitting across from her was a priest. "Yes, his not responding is extremely disturbing. He's spent ten years searching for what I found."

"What was so important about this coin?"

"That's—"

He finished the sentence for her. "—none of my business? I've been getting that a lot these days."

"It's your turn," she said. "You still haven't told me why you're following the good bishop."

"Look," Ryan said.

Across the alley, Giammo was signaling for his bill.

The Jesuit bishop left the trattoria. Ryan and Emily kept their distance as they followed him across the brightly-lit Piazza

Navona, both of them feeling their blood racing. Fearing Giammo would turn to look their way, Ryan removed his collar and pulled her closer to him—as though they were one of a hundred tourist couples discovering the romance of Rome. After a few moments, he let her go but was a little unnerved to notice she was in no hurry to draw away. *Maybe she's not so brave after all,* he thought.

For the next few minutes, they shadowed Giammo through the ancient streets leading to the Pantheon. Unaccountably Giammo paused a few times, as though to make sure they wouldn't lose sight of him. Ryan spoke once or twice, but she didn't reply. Either she was lost in thought, he guessed, or was irked at him for not divulging more.

A light drizzle had made the streets treacherous. She slipped once on a broken cobblestone and allowed Ryan to steady her elbow. But her chemical reaction to his touch was interrupted when she turned her head back to their quarry, who had suddenly disappeared near a half-modern, half-ancient building directly across from the Pantheon; its portal bore the words *Istitute per le Opere de Religione.*

Ryan's eyes followed her gesture. "That's strange. He's vanished."

Across the piazza a shining silver door glared out of the darkness on the far side of the bank building. A cigarette glowed in the gutter, but Giammo was no longer in sight.

Emily peered into the shadows. "That son of a bitch," she said. "He's ditched us."

XXIV/24
Den of Thieves

"Maybe he went into the bank," Emily said. They perched on the edge of the dolphin fountain to wait. Several minutes later a tall, thin shadow appeared out of the gloom and headed toward the Pantheon, a metal Halliburton briefcase in hand. It was too murky to tell for certain, but the form resembled Giammo. Ryan felt the irony of witnessing a supposed holy man heading for a clandestine assignation with a shameless robber in a shrine honoring the gods of all nations. He thought of the Gospel story of the money changers that Jesus had expelled from the temple in Jerusalem: "This is my father's house, and you have turned it into a den of thieves."

"Should we wait here or follow him to make sure it's Giammo and that your man is in there?"

"I'm sure it's Giammo. Let's wait for him to leave, then make our move. I have no doubt Luke is in there. He's remarkably punctual when he stands to gain something." She remembered the promptness with which he'd arrived at her camp, and berated herself again at the lack of self-discipline that allowed her, even for a few hours, to toy with a possible distraction from her career goals.

Ryan said nothing as they waited by the fountain and watched the street merchants hawk their wares to the tourists' children. Luminescent whirligigs were being launched like flying saucers dueling in the misty air of the ancient square. The massive inscription above the giant columns of the Pantheon, paying tribute to Augustus' confidant, general, and son-in-law, caught Ryan's eye as it always did:

M·AGRIPPA·L·F·COS·TERTIUM·FECIT

"Marcus Agrippa, son of Lucius, consul for the third time, built this."

Emily's eyes darkened and Ryan turned to see what had changed her demeanor. A portly middle-aged man was walking out of the inner rotunda of the temple between the central columns of the portico.

"That's him!" Emily started to stand, then quickly thought better of it and slid closer to Ryan to make it appear they were a couple. She watched Adashek mingle with the crowd as he headed south in the direction from which they'd come. "I would love to go after him and kick the living daylights out of him."

"It must be torture to let him go."

"Not to mention I'm dying of curiosity to see how much cash is in that briefcase."

"Thirty pieces of silver," Ryan suggested—just as Giammo slipped from the giant door of the Pantheon and sought the cover of the deep shadows to glide unobtrusively back toward the bank.

Ryan and Emily stood up to follow. "Why in the world would he be going *back* to the bank?" she was asking—when the infernal roar of an unmuffled Fiat Cinquecento drowned her words.

Ryan flashed back to the scene of the "backfire" that took the life of the Albanian penitent in the piazza in front of Gesù. Acting instinctively just as the shots rang out, he pushed Emily to the base of the fountain and threw himself between her and the Cinquecento. Bullet holes appeared in the marble at their feet. The onslaught continued and steps at the pedestal of the fountain shattered, causing pellets of marble to fly in all directions around them.

Seeing them fall, a group of Austrian teenagers wearing soccer t-shirts yelled at the car and scattered in all directions. The group of Italian schoolgirls that had been flirting with the boys screamed and plunged for cover behind the fountain. Ryan, continuing to shield Emily, looked over at them and put a finger to his lips to gesture they stop screaming. One girl had become hysterical, her wails echoing shrilly off the ancient walls. Her friend reached over and put her hand over her mouth, holding her tightly until she calmed down.

When all was finally quiet, Ryan peered out and was relieved that the car had disappeared in one of the many narrow streets that led from the piazza.

"Are you all right?" Ryan was helping Emily to her feet while the girls ran for the cover of darkness in a side street.

She brushed off the shock of the attack with sheer will power. "I'm fine. But I'm furious. I think we've just been warned."

"I've already been warned. I'd say this time was for real," he said. "What the hell is it about this coin that's worth killing us for?" His voice became agitated. "Come on, let's make a run for it—they may be back."

Then she saw the blood.

Though protesting it was just a surface wound, Ryan slid his jacket off his shoulders long enough to allow her to use her silk scarf as a tourniquet as they paused to catch their breath in a dark alleyway. As far as he was concerned, they had more important things to deal with. "Let's not waste another second.

Those killers are probably still on the lookout for us."

He knew of a small hotel nearby where he stayed in his student days, and led the way as they ran through the narrow cobblestone streets. "We've got to disappear," he panted, "until we sort this out."

Emily didn't disagree, and kept pace behind him, a worried look on her face. "Are you sure you're okay?" she asked.

"Yeah, it's nothing," Ryan gasped. He was doing his best to ignore the sting where the bullet had grazed his upper arm. If he hadn't been diving to protect Emily, it might have been fatal. They looked up and down the street and, seeing no cars, slowed their pace to a fast walk.

Emily stopped abruptly and announced. "If you're sure you're okay, I could use a drink." She'd spotted a cantina on the other side of the dimly-lit street. She walked toward it with a sigh of relief.

Ryan followed. "It is probably to our advantage to get off the streets for awhile."

They settled into rickety chairs at a table in the back corner and simply stared at each other across the time-worn table while they waited for the *cameriere* to bring them a liter of the house *rosso*. The shock of their ordeal was only now fully registering.

Ryan took a gulp of wine and broke the silence. "You said you know Giammo's schedule, but you don't know who he works for."

"Do you?" Emily asked.

"I know only that he reports directly to the Procurator General. He tried to bury me alive two days ago, and I plan to find out why."

"So this attack was meant for both of us."

A brief flash of pain crossed Ryan's face as his wounded arm brushed against the wall. "Who is your contact here in

Rome that you mentioned at the pub?"

"A monsignor. Another Jesuit like yourself and Bishop Giammo. His name is Oscar Isaac."

Ryan's face went white. He reached across to place his other hand on her arm. "There's a good reason you haven't heard from him. Monsignor Isaac didn't return your call because..." Ryan's voice broke, "...he's dead."

Emily was too shaken to respond. Her whole body was trembling from the shock of his words.

Ryan summarized the unsettling events of the past few days and his unusual relationship with Monsignor Isaac, including their one and only meeting at the same restaurant in which they'd just observed Giammo dining. His tone was somber as he shared his knowledge of how Isaac met his death in the shadow of the Gesù.

As he finished, he could sense that she was reacting the same way he was: that their lives had strangely, but somehow fatefully, become entwined.

She lowered her voice to avoid prying ears. "Why would anyone kill Monsignor Isaac? I don't understand." Her question hung in the air between them. "It had to be just an accident."

"I know for certain that it wasn't an accident, anymore than that Cinquecento was just now. But the why of it is all I can think of too. It's the question that's been haunting me."

They finished the last of the *vino rosso* and as they rose to leave, Ryan felt strangely embarrassed when Emily insisted on paying the bill again. But his thorny thoughts soon passed as he became occupied with leading her through the maze of tiny streets and alleys toward their hiding place.

Their pace quickened at the sight of the hotel in the

distance.

Two men wearing black who had been standing outside the entrance were now rapidly walking in their direction. Ryan grabbed Emily's arm and pulled her into an unlit alley. "Keep quiet and put your arms around me," he whispered. Emily obeyed and could feel his heart pounding next to her own. *Of all the men in Rome I could be embracing right now,* she thought, *fate deals me a celibate priest.*

As they approached, the men's soft conversation became audible—it was Yiddish.

Ryan and Emily managed to suppress laughter when it became all too apparent that the men in black were Hasidic travelers wearing their traditional garb.

She hurriedly disengaged from Ryan, grateful that the color she could feel rising to her face couldn't be seen in the shadows.

XXV/25
Albergo Portoghesi

Emily left the bathroom and headed for Ryan with a steaming washcloth draped over her arm. He'd already removed his Roman collar on the street and now, at her insistence, slipped out of his white oxford shirt. Sitting on the edge of one of the twin beds, he obediently awaited her ministrations. She felt another stab of troubling chemistry as she scrubbed the blood from his arm. Without the collar, Ryan had become even more disconcerting than when they'd first bumped into each other. Not to mention attractive. "You're right, thank God. It *is* just a surface wound. Your clerical serge deflected the bullet."

"Holy man of steel," Ryan agreed.

"I'll bet they didn't prepare you for this in the seminary."

"They didn't prepare me for a lot of things in seminary," he joked. *Like spending the night shirtless in a hotel room with a beautiful woman.* Though he knew staying together was the best cover, he couldn't help but wonder what it would do to his equanimity; he made Emily's acquaintance only a few hours ago, and already she was rousing feelings in him that he didn't even know he was still capable of having.

He thought back with some consternation to a high school Saturday night long ago when he and Carrie Catherine Callahan had fogged the windows of his father's Buick Riviera after a dance. It was well past three a.m. when Carrie finally broke their clinch, and dashed inside the house.

Only hours later, at six forty-five Mass—that he attended because his parents would be attending the nine o'clock Mass, and he couldn't let them see him *not* receiving the Eucharist; which he could not receive in a state of unabsolved sin—he was stunned to see Carrie Catherine walk in with her parents.

Ryan was relieved she didn't see him, hidden as he was in a throng of strangers half way to the back of the church.

The Callahans marched to their usual front row pew. After the kissing and fondling that occurred in the Riviera, Ryan couldn't wait to see what Carrie would do when the time arrived for Communion.

To his astonishment, she not only approached the altar rail with her parents—she also received the Host in her hands.

On her way back to the pew, their eyes met. Carrie Catherine, like Emily, was a fair-skinned, highly-freckled redhead. But she didn't blush as she saw his darkly questioning eyes. She met his glance and smiled.

At that precise moment Ryan's doubts about the tortuous details of his Catholic faith were born. The doubts, growing into deep misgivings, had never stopped haunting him to this day.

Why hadn't Carrie been struck by lightning for the sin of receiving the Sacred Host in a state of mortal sin? Which meant she would go straight to hell should she die without confessing.

Was it possible that the F-E-A-R rule—that kisses were mortal sins when they were Frequent, Enduring, Ardent, or Repeated—could be bogus? How many more rules and regulations of Roman Catholicism should be taken with a grain of salt? Could it be that the strict rules and regulations of his Catholicism were man-made instead of issued by God himself?

They had checked in for three nights, taking the last available room of the glorified *pensione* called the Albergo Portoghesi, giving the desk clerk only Ryan's passport—which, fortunately, had been issued before he was ordained. Emily had gone along with Ryan's suggestion, deciding that her hotel was useless because they knew her too well. She was aware a hotel desk wouldn't need her passport if they registered as husband and wife.

Before they'd exchanged stories in the cantina, Emily had assumed that it was she not Ryan who'd been the intended target in the square. Giammo knew exactly where her interests lay. He had to have been tipped off by Fatall. Now, however, for better or for worse, the two of them were in this together. Ryan told her everything. The memory of his entombment was all too fresh, and Pimental's warning was still ringing in his ears. Neither had any doubt now that the Cinquecento gunman was in the employ of the man who bought Emily's coin—or of his superiors, Jesuit or otherwise.

Emily was lying on her back in her twin bed staring intently at the dimly-lit ornate ceiling. Her memory flashed to another ceiling in another place and time. She looked over at Ryan, the faint rays of an ancient street lamp outlining his body in the matching bed across the room and she began speaking softly as if confessing her deepest secrets in the dark.

A dozen years ago on a scorching afternoon when she was barely out of graduate school, she found herself flat on her back in Egypt examining the famous zodiac ceiling on the roof portico of the Temple of Hathor in the Dendera complex.

She was absorbed in her studies beneath the enigmatic astrological relief that had been the subject of intense scholarly debate since the time of Napoleon. She'd been oblivious to the curious stares of occasional tourists who had milled around her when suddenly she was startled by the sound of snoring—and discovered a man in a black robe and Roman collar propped against a wall ten feet away—sound asleep. She had no idea that this strange scholar-cleric would become her closest mentor.

Her reaction to his snoring was a burst of laughter so uncontrollable that she woke him up.

The priest looked at her intensely for a moment. "They say laughter is contagious, like yawning."

That only made her laugh the harder, causing him to join in.

The cleric got to his feet, and extended a hand to help her up. "Oscar Isaac," he introduced himself, adding, "S.J. What we both need is a strong Arabica." He reached into his backpack and removed an aluminum thermos.

Over the most fragrant coffee laced with brandy she could remember ever having tasted, Isaac gave her a vividly dramatic, and often quietly amusing, presentation that brought the artistry of the temple ceiling to life; and provided the scholarly angle she'd been seeking for the report her grant required. Isaac's lectures, she told Ryan, always took the form of stories. The images in the astrological ceiling stylistically memorialized the year 30 B.C. as the "return of the phoenix" to witness Caesar Augustus being crowned pharaoh of Egypt and commemorated his birth as a god.

Isaac explained he'd come to Dendera to corroborate his theory that the ceiling's cryptic iconography included certain details concerning Augustus' elevation to the rank of a god.

"He told me the circle enveloping the small figure represented Ra, the sun god. 'In my theory,' Isaac said, 'that figure stands for Horus-Augustus on the occasion of his ritual nativity, his transition from mere mortal to divine. The sun as a god found its way into every ancient religion; not only of the Mediterranean, but also of China, India, and the early Americas. And Augustus fully intended to be the greatest sun god in history.'"

Ryan's mind was racing. "I'd forgotten that Augustus became a pharaoh of Egypt. But what do you mean, 'Augustus' birth as a god?'"

"Let me finish my story. It'll all make sense in the end. I remember Isaac was pointing to an image of the baby Augustus with his thumb in his mouth near the center of the ceiling, identical to the image of the baby Horus, solar disc above his head, being held in the arms of Isis that I had noted in nearby monuments. His tone became conspiratorial when he told me, 'I've calculated that the date of 17 B.C. has been carefully embedded within the zodiac's iconography, that is, for initiates with the eyes to read it. It was the year when a conjunction of the planets Jupiter and Venus was predicted to occur.'

"I asked him to clarify. 'You mean when these planets would appear in the sky as if they were a single planetary body?'

"'Precisely,' he said. 'To the human eye they became one dazzling star.'

"'But wasn't Augustus' apotheosis in 15 B.C.?' I asked him, wondering if I'd found a glitch in Isaac's logic."

"'That's right,' Isaac agreed. 'But Augustus' Egyptian astrologers used the date of the conjunction to 'predict' the coming of the new Horus, the Anointed One, the Messiah, two years later. It was opportunistic strategic planning. Even more amazing, the table of planetary conjunctions formulated by Augustus' astrologers survives on papyrus to this day in a Berlin museum. Look it up sometime; it's called *The Berlin Table*.'"

☧

Emily smiled across at Ryan. "The Dendera zodiac had suddenly taken on a new life for me." She turned on her side to look over at Ryan and continued her story.

Isaac told her how Augustus put his scribes to work rewriting the ancient religious teachings of the kingdom, city-state, or empire that was about to fall to the Roman war machine. They incorporated into their Romanized transcripts the hints, clues, and foreshadowing that made his—or his lieutenant's—triumphal procession through the city gates one that had been "predicted as of old."

Egyptian artisans traced the bearded visage of the newly-crowned Augustus to imitate the direct line of stylized bearded images back to Ra, Amon-Ra, and Aten, the sun gods whose human embodiments were the rulers of the Egyptian nation.

Emily recalled being so rapt by Isaac's words that she had to be reminded to drink her coffee—only to find it cold. "Why are you so fascinated by Augustus?" she'd asked the Jesuit, remembering her second year Latin teacher's fascination with Augustus' great-uncle and adopted father, Julius Caesar.

Isaac had replied wryly, "That's a good question. Are you sure you really want to know?"

They walked down the ancient staircase from the roof chapel and into the Hall of Offerings. Isaac motioned to a wall relief covered in hieroglyphic writing.

"Let me show you something I discovered recently," Isaac said. "This hieroglyphic register is a song to Augustus, King of Egypt, heralding him as 'Lord of the Dance,' meaning 'Lord of Life.' I will translate:

> *The King of Egypt*
> *Pharaoh comes to dance*

He comes to sing
See how he dances
See how he sings...

"I remember Isaac looked at me to gauge my reaction. In truth I was spellbound. He went on to say, 'The song of Augustus eventually spread to Medieval England where a carol, called "Lord of the Dance," was sung at Christmas and is sung to this day.'"

"That's remarkable!" Ryan's eyebrows rose. "So, Augustus was Lord of Life? That means whenever that carol is sung, people are actually singing praises to Augustus!"

"I was just as shocked as you by Isaac's bombshell but he just smiled and started walking. That was when I first discovered the monsignor loved innuendos."

They'd entered the hypostyle hall; each of its columns surmounted by the face of Horus' consort the goddess of love, Hathor—all, unforgivably, defaced by early Christian fanatics. Isaac topped her cup with steaming brew from the thermos. Though they were alone in the shady courtyard north of the temple, he leaned toward her and spoke in a whisper.

"The astronomical conjunction I was referring to earlier was the sign in the heavens that led the three wise men from the east." He let his words sink in, waiting for her brain to put it together.

"But how could the wise men be following their 'star' so many years before the birth of Christ?"

Isaac chuckled. "The answer concerns Augustus' intention to restart history," he said enigmatically. "You've got some catching up to do, my friend. But that's a story for another day. I didn't mean to distract you from your work."

Her brain churned trying to fit the puzzle together before he revealed it all. But he'd been working on whatever his theory was for years, and this was her first encounter with the conundrum. "Wait a minute, did you say 're-start history'?" she asked. "You've given me goose bumps."

"Yes, Augustus actually had his poets and scribes rewrite his mythic biography to fit his own agenda that included changing calendar years in order to substantiate his divinity." His face crinkled into a smile. "I'm not completely certain what my findings add up to yet. I can tell you I've found convincing evidence that there's a fundamental identification between Octavius Caesar Augustus and Christianity as we call it today. I've studied comparative religions all my life, but only recently come to the conclusion that the Emperor Augustus was a comparatist extraordinaire, albeit a thoroughly pragmatic one. He was a master of turning the common themes in the religions of the cultures he conquered to the service of his empire, and of his personal reputation. He based his own spiritual practices on the moral principles he encountered in *all* religions," the priest added.

"If everyone in the world would do that," Emily responded, "we might eliminate war and terrorism once and for all."

"Amen," Isaac had sighed.

Emily tried to stifle a sob at the thought of her departed mentor.

"Did Isaac ever spell out to you this secret theory of his?" Ryan's voice was gentle.

"Well, he did admit that he was gathering evidence for a connection between Jesus Christ and Augustus Caesar that would 'turn the Christian world on end.'"

"It's curious," Ryan sympathized. "I met him only once, and I experienced a profound link to him."

"I only met him once myself," Emily admitted. "I was his virtual intern: we communicated only by email and telephone."

"And his telephone was probably tapped," Ryan said

quietly.

The room was suddenly silent.

XXVI/26
Dangerous Implications

Despite the wine they had sipped to sedate themselves in the cantina, neither had rested well. Ryan had been the first to fall asleep, respectfully with his back to her; but both of them tossed and turned almost in unison in their twin beds, their brains churning to digest and make sense of the events that had brought them together.

As the sun rose blood-red over the ancient tiles and bell towers, they were sitting on the tiny terrazzo of the Portoghesi's top floor, looking out, on one side, over *Via dell'Orso*—"Bear Street" sounded so much more intriguing in Italian—at its convergence with *Via dei Portoghesi;* and, on the other side, over the rooftops and cupolas of the *Antica Città,* the Ancient City. The Neapolitan woman who was bent on serving them endless cappuccino and orange juice met all their requests with a smile.

They'd given up trying to control their intake and consigned themselves to her abundant hospitality. At seven a.m. they had the terrace entirely to themselves.

"I just remembered something you said before I fell asleep last night," Emily frowned. "Something about his telephone being tapped? Who would do that?"

"You mentioned he was gathering evidence to link Jesus Christ with Augustus. Some people, myself included, would consider that insinuation sacrilegious and blasphemous. It's obvious his every move was being scrutinized. His last words haunt me... 'Tell Father Ryan...find memory in the ashes of Jasius...in the Gesù.' Jasius was the Roman word for Jesus."

She searched Ryan's eyes. "What he said makes no sense to me," she said. "Or maybe it almost does. Monsignor Isaac was searching for two things he believed to be crucial to definitively proving his revolutionary thesis. One of them had to do with ashes."

"The ashes of Jesus?"

She laughed. "Hardly the Jesus you and I know. If that Jesus was crucified, buried, rose from the dead on the third day—then ascended into heaven, I don't see any room for ashes there, do you?"

Ryan was even more puzzled. "That's what I've been baffled by ever since I heard the words. Whose ashes was he seeking then?"

"The ashes of Augustus," she said. "Monsignor Isaac was searching for the golden urn in which the emperor's ashes were placed before it was buried in the Mausoleum of Augustus. Livia, his wife, had presided over the burning of the emperor's body for three days and two nights in the presence of members of the senate. It was even rumored that Livia paid the senator Numerius Atticus to say that he had seen the spirit of Augustus ascending into heaven."

"Like Jesus' Ascension?" Ryan became introspective.

"Exactly. In ancient times, ascension symbolized that a deceased ruler was of divine origin. Livia wanted Augustus' divinity to be remembered for posterity."

"Why do you think Augustus meant so much to Isaac? What was he on to?"

She took her time answering. Then she repeated what she had said before. "He believed he'd discovered sort of a forgotten link between Jesus and Augustus. Some truth that had been known to Constantine, but had been lost to the general public before—and since."

"What do you think it was?"

She was unwilling to meet his eyes. "All I can tell you is that Isaac probably died for it."

Link between Jesus and Augustus. The troubling words kept playing in Ryan's mind. He recalled the enigmatic relic he had once seen as a young cleric while visiting Aachen Cathedral in Germany. He'd been unsettled by what he had witnessed there and had decided the best course of action was to add it to his mental catalog of the mysteries of the Church, and let it go. The object in question was the grand Cross of Lothair, an ornate tenth-century golden cross richly encrusted with jewels and still being used to lead sacred processions like the one he had attended.

But the strange thing was that a magnificent cameo of the Emperor Augustus with a crown and holding the royal Roman eagle scepter, reportedly carved during the time of Christ, graced the center of this holy cross. When he asked his Jesuit superior about the riddle of a Roman emperor honored in this way, the response had shocked and confused him.

"The cameo of Augustus on the cross was without doubt meant to indicate that the emperor was the earthly representative of the almighty power of God."

The memory thickened his cloud of confusion.

Ryan forced his mind to return to the present. "You said the monsignor was after two things. What was the other one?"

"The second thing that Isaac was seeking was the coin that I discovered two weeks ago. He was convinced historical references to it would be proved accurate by an archaeologist getting lucky someday, and—"

"—And that archaeologist turned out to be you," Ryan interjected. "I have reason to believe that Monsignor Isaac thought his research was of vital importance for the origins of Christianity, and as a result there were some dangerous implications for the institutional Church and its headquarters at the Vatican." Ryan's tone was somber.

How could this recently discovered coin be so valuable that a highly-placed circle within the Jesuit Order was willing to kill to protect it? By now they'd concluded that it was indeed a Jesuit matter—the only reason Ryan could imagine why he'd been summoned so abruptly by Pimental. Since Monsignor Isaac was a Jesuit, it stood to reason that anything related to his research would continue to be controlled by the Society of St. Ignatius to which Ryan had dedicated his earthly existence.

The aureus had to be some kind of threat to the welfare of the Church itself, and, hard as it was to fathom, it appeared that the Jesuits would stop at nothing—even if it meant resorting to the sin of lethal violence.

But what could that threat be? Ryan's gentle interrogations little by little led Emily to reveal the details she had been hiding. She drew, crudely, on the white paper tablecloth, her memory of what Fatall told her was inscribed on her coin. "*Divus filius divi*"—"god and son of god"—embossed across from the name "Jasius Augustus."

Emily continued, "In 42 B.C., Augustus had broken ground in Rome for the *Templum Divi Iuli*—the temple of the divine Julius, after he'd lobbied the Senate to declare his adopted father, Julius Caesar, a god. That made him, of course, effectively the son of a god—the title that was, in fact, the new Emperor Augustus' exact objective. But he tired of being called son of god and preferred Jasius—Jesus—who Virgil referred to as 'Father Jasius, from whom our race descended' and was usually depicted as a wise man with a beard."

Ryan's eyes grew large. "Just like the depictions of Jesus."

Emily noted his discomfort. "Heard enough? Should I stop?"

"Are you kidding?" Ryan said. "Tell me everything."

"You're a glutton for punishment," she smiled. "Legend has it that Josephus himself had come into possession of an Augustan aureus when he was summoned to Caesarea by the Judean authorities to amend his historical work-in-progress, *The Antiquities of the Jews*. When Harel, my graduate student, found the coin on the wine krater, my imagination didn't have to stretch far to conclude it was most likely the very aureus that had belonged to Josephus."

Between the two inscriptions she drew a rough sketch of the emperor's head. "Although it was shadowed with age," she said, "I could clearly make out that the head of Augustus was wearing a crown—with twelve spikes."

Ryan was puzzled. "Like the rays of the sun?"

Emily's grin showed her approval. "Precisely like the rayed crown worn by Apollo the sun god—and reminiscent of the solar disc, reflecting the zodiac, worn by Horus as the re-born sun on the ceiling of the Hathor Temple where I met Monsignor Isaac."

"Horus?" Ryan wasn't sure he'd heard her correctly. What he couldn't see at first because it made no sense was what she'd just drawn beneath Augustus' head.

Noticing his frown, Emily explained. "It's the Greek letters *chi* and *rho,* found together on Constantine's military standard, the labarum."

"I've seen the *Chi-Rho* above the main altar of nearly every Catholic church I've visited since I was a kid. But it represents the first two letters of 'Christ'—*xristos* in Greek."

"You're right," Emily agreed. "But *xristos* is an ancient word, meaning 'the anointed' or 'awaited' one; and it actually derives from Chronos, the god of Time. It goes back at least as far as Homer, who was said to have lived during the eighth century B.C."

"Meaning the same as 'The Redeemer' or 'Messiah'?"

"Exactly." She smiled. "Christ wasn't Jesus' last name; it was his epithet, signifying his sacred status."

"Jesus the Christ."

"The labarum *Chi-Rho* can be found in depictions of Apollo on vases, friezes, and statuary hundreds of years before Augustus. Plato referred to it in the *Timaeus*."

"You're going to say it's just another example of Augustus confiscating a symbol and applying it to himself."

"How did you guess?" Emily's eyes were much brighter than they should have been after their restless night. Now she was feverishly drawing another circle on the tablecloth. "I didn't get a clear view of what the reverse of the coin depicted," she said. "It was so encrusted I hesitated to scrape it for fear of damaging the original image. But Fatall, the low-life antiquities dealer that Luke took it to, polished it to its original luster. Here's what I could force out of him." She finished sketching and moved her hand so Ryan could see what she'd drawn.

It looked like a loaf of bread crossed at an angle with a fish.

"Loaves and fishes? Like the miracle Jesus performed?" Ryan tried to understand.

"Symbols of Ceres, the goddess of agriculture," Emily responded, "and Neptune, god of the sea—to signify that the most august emperor was the source of all sustenance, of life itself."

"Couldn't the church fathers have come up with *one thing*

that was truly original?"

Emily laughed. "One thing I've learned: there's nothing original under the sun god. Really, someone should set the record straight about the early church fathers' plagiarism."

Her laugh was contagious and Ryan found himself laughing with her, releasing their exhaustion in perfect sync.

Emily sobered. "Right now all I want is to get my coin back and go on with my career. It's beginning to look like the shortest distance to that goal lies through a labyrinth that you've been firmly planted in the middle of."

"Which makes me, what, the Minotaur?"

"Now there's an image!"

"It's beginning to look like you'll get your coin when I get Ariadne's gold thread, that allowed Theseus to find his way out," he said, serious again.

She took a deep breath. "Are we crazy?" She looked at him, for the first time revealing a shade of doubt.

"Is that a trick question?" he asked.

"And what *about* your vow of obedience?"

"I'm American enough to believe a sacred vow should not be twisted to evil ends. I also believe that whoever took Monsignor Isaac's life—and nearly ours—is pursuing evil, not good—no matter how they might rationalize or justify it to themselves."

"And you aim to get to the bottom of it? Like an old-fashioned private eye on a mission."

"Look who's talking! I was ordained only two years ago, but I've been studying the early church for nearly a decade. Now my vow of obedience threatens to scuttle all my research or any chance for answers."

"Let me ask you a question," Emily said, as if it had just occurred to her. "Did you take your vows to the church or to the Jesuit Order?"

Ryan was stumped. He'd never felt the need to ask that, or to imagine the two entities as separable. Now he realized it was a question he did not want to answer, could not answer until he found out who had murdered Isaac and why.

He would simply put the question on hold, and his vow on pause.

"Besides obedience, what were your other vows?" Emily asked, as though she'd thought better of pressing her original query.

"Poverty and chastity."

At the word "chastity," she looked away. After a pause, she added, "Well, I hope 'poverty' won't keep you from helping me follow the money."

XXVII/27
Istituto per le Opere de Religione

Concerned that the gunman in the Cinquecento might be patrolling Antico Centro to complete his deadly mission, Emily and Ryan stayed in the shadows of the time-worn buildings as they headed away from the hotel. Before they left the Portoghesi Ryan had allowed Emily to trim back his full head of wavy brown hair and darken it with a bottle of black coloring they had purchased across the street. She tied her own shoulder-length red locks into a tight bun, and used the dye to darken her eyebrows.

They made a stop at the market, and by the time they approached Piazza della Rotonda their transformation was complete. Ryan was wearing an Italian soccer t-shirt, Georgetown baseball cap, with patches of short dark hair peeking out here and there; Emily wore a v-neck Gucci turquoise pullover and leather hat that completely covered her bright-colored mane.

Despite their disguises, they neared the Vatican Bank with trepidation. They lost no time in finding the stone seat carved into the bullet-riddled side of the fountain where they'd kept vigil last night watching the stainless steel door until they'd realized Giammo was unlikely to exit. Then gunfire had erupted from the errant Cinquecento. Both of them now reached the conclusion that the steel door led to some kind of underpass that had allowed the bishop to escape. The question was, *Where had he taken the coin?*

Today, though, there was no reason to linger outside. Using the revolving door they entered the Vatican bank's main lobby, happy to see the place was crowded. Most of the clients were elderly women well-dressed in black, no doubt hoping that what they deposited with the Holy Spirit would enjoy more security than that offered by secular banks riding the downward-spiraling Italian economy. Everyone believed that, despite dire warnings from the Holy See to the contrary, the Vatican economy would not fail even when the entire global economy failed.

A quick look over the lobby made it clear there were no stairwells leading directly from it, only a single red-lit exit that was clearly marked and not to be opened except in the case of emergency. At the counter, they headed for the shortest line, and waited together for the complicated banking transactions of the pilgrims and residents in front of them. Twenty minutes later they'd reached the teller's cage.

Emily pulled out a wad of traveler's checks that widened the eyes of both the banker and Ryan. "I'd like to change 10,000 new shekels into euros," she began. Her voice fell to a whisper, as she opened her bag to reveal dozens of similar wads. "And I'm wondering if I can rent a safe deposit box."

The clerk looked put upon by the double request, and for a moment froze.

"I'm already a little nervous," Emily told him, with a childlike giggle. "Please don't draw attention to me."

The clerk instantly adjusted his demeanor, and began inspecting the wad of checks she'd pushed beneath the glass-protected grill. "*Certo*," he said. "Let me make the exchange first; then someone will take you to the boxes."

Ten minutes later, escorted by a uniformed guard and led by an assistant manager, Ryan followed Emily to a security elevator, which took them to the basement. From there they walked down a steep flight of stairs into the bowels of the ancient building. Despite the relatively modern wooden paneling and marble floor, some pungent subterranean sewage leaked through the walls to create a distinctly unpleasant atmosphere that the manager's look seemed to apologize for. Out of the corner of his eye, Ryan spotted a men's room that said, *Bagno—Impiegati Soltanto,* Toilet—Employees Only.

"Sweetie, I'm so sorry," he burst out, exaggerating his American accent and affecting a distressed look. "I have to excuse myself."

Emily's Italian sounded apologetic. "My husband," she said to the assistant manager, "gets nauseous easily."

The manager looked from her to Ryan to the Guard, trying to decide on the best course of action. Finally he shrugged, and nodded in the direction of the rest room they'd just passed. He indicated for the guard and Emily to continue with him, while Ryan doubled back and ducked into the marked door.

Just as Ryan hoped, the door led to a hallway and the hallway offered three choices: *Uomini, Donne,* and a door marked *Servizi.* He knew he had only a few minutes, and without hesitation entered the service door. The air was even mustier than that of the rest of the basement and it didn't take long to find another door, marked *Uscità,* "The exit," that led to a staircase. Going through it he found himself on a landing. Surely the stainless steel door leading to the piazza would be found at the top of these stairs, but he didn't have time to explore both directions so he descended into the darkness.

With the small flashlight he'd picked up at the market that morning, he illuminated the rapidly darkening stairs. He estimated fifty steps or so before ducking his head to enter a narrow alcove and found himself face to face with an ornate door that was tightly locked.

He looked at it, dazzled. Framed in elaborate wood and ivory carvings, the door appeared to be solid gold. A quick examination indicated that security had been digitalized. Instead of the skeleton keyhole he expected, what he found was a card slot like those used in hotels. Adjacent to the slot he found, not the Papal Insignia he might have anticipated, but the letters, IHS, stylized within a solar disc—identical to the image above the main altar of the Gesù.

The trigram was composed of the amalgamated Greek letters, *iota, eta,* and *sigma,* inscribed upon a radiant burst of golden light. It was the official symbol of his Society, the Society of Jesus—the Jesuits. The letters were the first three of the Greek word *IHSUS,* Jesus. Adding the cross above the middle letter, the Society of Jesus had adopted the trigram as its emblem and proudly carried it on their missions throughout the world.

The trigram also stood for, variously, *In Hoc Signo (Vinces),* "In this sign you will conquer," *Jesus Hominum Salvator,* "Jesus the Savior of Mankind," and, in Ignatius Loyola's native

Spanish, *Jesus Hijo Sacro,* "Jesus, Divine Son"—all praising the name of Jesus, to which the founder of the Society had pledged its entire existence.

Ryan checked his watch and realized he had to hurry. Running up the steps he quickly returned to the exit door by which he'd entered the staircase.

It was locked.

Once the usual ritual exchange of safety-deposit keys had been accomplished, Emily found herself alone inside the vault room where, after checking the walls for hidden cameras, she made as much noise as she could opening the box she'd been assigned, rustling wads of traveler's checks in and out of the box, then noisily shutting the metal container again and reinserting it into its mausoleum-like compartment. She hoped to hell Ryan would be waiting for her on the other side when she finished.

But he wasn't.

Greeting her with a concerned look on their faces were only the assistant manager and the security guard.

"Where is your husband?" the manager demanded.

"He didn't return from the bathroom?"

The man shook his head. "We will have to sound the alarm until he is found."

"I'm so sorry about this," Emily said. "Please don't sound the alarm." She hesitated, as if embarrassed.

But it was too late. The alarm was wailing through the building, sending everyone inside scurrying for the exits.

"The smell...didn't agree with him," she tried to explain above the din. "I'm sure he just left the bank instead of coming back and risking another attack."

The two men looked at each other, and gestured to her.

"Follow me," the guard said. The assistant manager hurried upstairs to manage the turmoil in the main lobby.

The guard took her by the elbow and escorted her up the stairs into the security office, where she faced a bank of old-fashioned black & white monitors that were supposed to be scanned by a second guard who quickly hid his magazine as they entered. Nearly every inch of the bank's interior was covered by the screens—as well as the piazza directly in front of it.

The guards scanned the monitors, one by one, Emily's eyes running ahead of theirs. *What in the world would they do if one of the cameras caught him snooping?*

Emily's heart almost stopped as one of the monitors focused on Ryan, who was trying a door that was obviously locked. It was all too apparent he was in a stairwell frantically searching for an exit. The guards hadn't yet spotted him on the surveillance system. *What can I do?* She'd always been adept at finding creative ways to work through awkward situations but now images of being thrown into a dreary Italian prison flew through her mind.

She let her open purse fall noisily to the floor. The guards were momentarily distracted as they reached down to help retrieve the rolls of bills that flew out in all directions, carefully scanning the purse's contents at the same time. They were even more diverted by the sight of Emily's cleavage as she leaned over to collect her belongings.

The camera exposing Ryan had temporarily progressed to other views in its circuit.

Ryan had no choice but to try the steel door at the top of the stairs. On it he noted the same IHS insignia, this one a miniature of the other, directly above the cardkey slot. Gingerly, he turned the handle, and pushed. To his dismay, it too was locked. There was no exit.

He felt like a caged animal desperately searching for an

escape. *Let's hope Pimental never finds out about this or I'll be awarded that ten-year project of deciphering ancient graffiti in the underworld, with insects and ghosts as company.*

The old monitors switched from one view of the bank interior to the other. Emily had broken into a cold sweat. She knew it wouldn't be long before the camera in Ryan's vicinity would again reveal his intrusion into forbidden territory.

By now, the sound of the alarms had shifted from a loud cacophony to a monotonous drone.

The guard who had escorted her into the security office announced in brisk Italian that he was going downstairs to look for the missing husband and that the seated guard was to remain in place and continue to watch for Ryan on the monitors.

Emily spoke up. "He must have gotten lost, taken the wrong door by mistake. He doesn't read Italian very well. I'll come with you and help you look." And before the guard could protest, she was on his heels as he flew out the door. The seated guard leaned forward in his chair, his attention riveted on the monitors.

Emily's semi-captive status had instantly changed to that of sharing the joint mission of finding an errant husband. She moved in unison with the guard as they clamored down the stairs and through the door leading to the hallway where Ryan had disappeared.

She thought she recognized the door where she spotted Ryan on the monitor. "Maybe he got confused and went through this one."

The guard pushed open the door marked *"Uscità"* and a white-faced Ryan practically fell into his arms.

Ryan blurted, "Honey, I'm sorry…I thought this was the door to the toilet…I got locked in…" In a flash, the guard expertly pulled Ryan's arms behind his back and snapped on the handcuffs.

XXVIII/28
Keys to the Kingdom

The second guard was summoned to escort the handcuffed Ryan upstairs to the security office. The other grabbed Emily gruffly by the elbow again to haul her upstairs behind Ryan and his captor. The faces of the two guards showed they were relishing the break in their boring routine and their newfound level of authority.

Once the door was shut and locked, the guards pushed Ryan and Emily into the only chairs. "We will hear your husband's story from the beginning, please."

In English, for the next half hour, Ryan told and retold his story of how he'd lost his way to the toilet. Finally tiring of the tale, the guards looked at each other uncertainly and held a brief muffled conference on the other side of the room. A decision seemed to be made and the senior guard unlocked the handcuffs and called the assistant manager.

After allowing Emily to retrieve what she'd deposited, the three men looked more than relieved to escort them to the doors and watched them exit the bank, as though to make sure they were gone for good.

"Did you at least find a tunnel?" Emily looked at Ryan as they walked along Rome's bustling streets in search of a quiet café where they could collect themselves.

"I'm sure I found its entrance. My theory is that Giammo escaped through a tunnel, though God knows leading to where. The door's not going to do us much good without the keys."

They spent the afternoon in an umbrellaed restaurant with Wi-Fi, Ryan poring over tourist maps of the catacombs, Emily lost in her Droid. They were weary by the time the setting sun made the lighting difficult. They ordered plates of antipasti, pasta, exquisitely fresh and crisp *cetrioli,* "cucumbers," and a *mezzo-litro* of *vino bianco* to help them unwind.

After their mutual debriefing was complete, Emily's smile was playful. "We may not have to go down there, after all," she announced, an air of mischief in her tone. "I found Giammo's home address."

"Why didn't you tell me earlier?" Ryan said, signaling for the bill.

"I was hungry."

As they made their way toward the upscale address on *Via Tritone,* Emily explained that she'd gotten through to Commander Kahane in Jerusalem and had convinced him to use his police connections to find Giammo's landline in a reverse directory. They were equally surprised that Bishop Giammo lived at a civilian address rather than in one of Rome's many Jesuit rectories. No doubt to give him more flexibility with his comings and goings, Ryan surmised.

Ryan and Emily arrived at *numero 3* in time to witness a

KENNETH JOHN ATCHITY

convoy of fire trucks standing before the building, their hoses dowsing the remaining flames on the top floor. A body was being carted toward an ambulance on a portable gurney.

Ryan acted promptly, approaching one of the firemen manning the gurney and catching his eye. "I'm a priest," he said. "Let me offer him absolution."

The fireman scanned Ryan's attire skeptically. But these days nothing surprised him. The way things were going, the clergy would be wearing spandex jogging shorts next. "I warn you, Father," he responded, his voice weary. "The body is charred horribly."

But Ryan had already donned his stole and was crossing himself, preparatory to the ritual he was about to perform. Warning Emily to look away, he pulled the cloth down that was covering the head—and took a deep breath as he peered into the hideously burned face. "I absolve you," he spoke the ancient words in Latin—the keys that unlocked the kingdom of heaven, passed by Jesus directly to St. Peter, *"Ego te absolvo"*...and made the sign of the cross as he completed the formula, *"in nomine Patris, et Filii, et Spiritus Sancti."* Out of the corner of his eye, as Ryan signed the cross on the corpse's forehead, lips, and heart, he noticed that the firemen had taken off their hats.

"It was His Excellency, the Jesuit Bishop Giammo," one of them said with respect.

Ryan nodded at the man, whose clothes had been completely burned away by the fire.

"Even the fire crew knew him," Emily whispered.

For the first time he saw fear in her eyes. He walked Emily out of earshot. "There aren't more than a handful of Jesuit bishops in the world," he said. "Whoever was behind all this was willing to do anything necessary to cover his tracks. Obviously it goes much higher than Giammo."

"I've got to find my goddammed coin," Emily said, pushing her way toward the massive wooden door that led into the building's inner courtyard.

"Signorina!" one of the firemen shouted after her.

"She was his neighbor," Ryan explained, surprised at the ease with which the fib had sprung to his lips. "She will need comfort after this. Was...her place damaged?"

The fireman shook his head. "The only damage was to the bishop's flat. Lucky we got here quickly," he said.

A few more white lies later, they'd found their way into Giammo's penthouse to discover that the fire, though still smoldering, was now under control. Only the main room was destroyed—those adjacent seemed only smoke-damaged by the blaze. Ryan told the inspector in command of the scene that he was "the bishop's confessor," and must find his ring, which was not on his body. The inspector nodded his permission for Ryan to stay, but told him to touch nothing. The police were en route to begin a formal investigation.

"What's taking them so long to get here?" Ryan asked the man, intent on making conversation after he'd nodded to Emily.

She had disappeared into one of the rooms, wondering how it could be that Giammo didn't escape the fire. *Was he drugged, or*—chills ran up and down her body at the thought—*was he already dead?*

"The bishop is gone," the man shrugged. "What could be the hurry now?"

Somehow it sounded more ominous in Italian.

Emily entered a private study as elaborate as any she'd seen or imagined. Balconies on both sides of the enormous room offered stunning vistas of Rome and Vatican City. Leather-bound books in a dozen languages colored the walnut shelves like a venerable rainbow of knowledge. She tried to picture Giammo sitting at the Napoleonic era desk with its multi-hued intaglio, but envisioned herself seated there instead.

She moved to the desk, scouring its surface, noticing the framed photographs of Giammo with the hierarchy of the Church and Italian politicians. Then she opened drawer after drawer—progressively more and more upset with not finding what she was looking for. But persistence was her profession.

In a small central drawer, she discovered a set of three plastic card keys on a gold chain. One of the cards was silver, and she remembered the silver door shining in Piazza della Rotonda in the middle of the night. Both the silver card, and a matching gold one, bore the Jesuit insignia, "IHS," surrounded by a sunburst.

The third key was white and embossed with the papal insignia, a gold and silver key crossed and intertwined with a red-ribbed anchor, beneath the three-layered papal crown known as the *triregnum*. Its edges were different from the other two cards, though Emily had no idea why. She slipped the cards into the back pocket of her jeans.

Minutes later Ryan and Emily exited the building through a side door leading from the courtyard into a tiny service alley.

"I take it you didn't have any luck," Ryan said, judging from her down-turned lips.

"I didn't find the coin." She reached into her back pocket, pulled out the three plastic cards. "But I did find these." She held open her palm.

Ryan recognized the white card with the papal insignia. "It's a computer access card, allowing entrance into the Vatican cyber library and archives. Thanks to the generosity of IBM, nearly the entire collection is now online." He pulled his own card from his billfold. She looked at it. Then he studied the other two cards. "Your little theft has saved us a lot of digging," he said. At her frown, he added, "These have to be the keys to the underground. If we make it through alive, the passage might even connect with the Vatican Archives."

"And hopefully my aureus," Emily added.

Determination outweighing their fear, they made plans for a descent into the passageway Ryan had discovered in the bank's basement. At a tiny hardware store, they purchased two serious flashlights, extra batteries, a thermos, and a backpack. At the corner café, they chose a half dozen *panini* and had them wrapped to go.

Finding a slingshot was a bigger challenge. But Rome, like New York, was a place where everything could be found if you "asked around." Within an hour they'd located a toy store near Ponte Sesto. Emily refused to tell Ryan why she felt she needed the primitive weapon. He kept them both amused with his guesses: "You're afraid of rats, and think we might find them in the tunnels. You're afraid of small cars and want to shoot their drivers before they shoot us. You've got a David complex, and you see me as Goliath. No, wait, I've got it— you're afraid we might get stuck down there and that I might convert you to your childhood faith out of boredom."

This last one made her cock her eyebrow. "Now you're losing it," she laughed.

To settle their nerves, and to wait till the streets were as clear as they ever get in Rome, they chose a little piazza nearly bereft of tourists and camped out at a trattoria populated only by locals.

Their talk wandered at first but inevitably arrived where it started, with Ryan speculating about Monsignor Isaac's research on Jesus and Augustus. He was on edge from what Emily had been telling him. *To believe Emily would be to suggest the Bible can't be relied on at all. Could two billion people, me included, have been so deceived for so long?*

When Emily quoted them from memory, Ryan was all too familiar with the lines of Virgil's Fourth Eclogue:

> *The last Great Era foretold by the Sibyl*
> *Of Cumae is now upon us. The Cycle begins anew.*
> *Now returns Saturn's Golden Age, now appears*
> *The Immaculate Virgin. Now descends*
> *From Heaven a divine Nativity…*
> *Haste the glorious birth, usher in the reign*
> *Of thy Apollo…this glorious Coming.*
> *The great months shall then begin to roll.*
> *After this, whatever vestige of Original Sin*
> *Remains, shall be swept away from earth*
> *Forever, and the Son of God shall be*
> *Proclaimed the Prince of Peace.*

Ryan didn't need to tell her that the verses were written no later than 39 B.C. and even as early as 42 B.C.—decades before the alleged birth of the biblical Jesus. The early church fathers wanted their followers to believe that the Prince of Peace the Roman poet referred to was Jesus of Nazareth, so the Middle Ages honored the poet as "St. Virgil," a lay prophet who had *foreseen* the coming of Christ.

She told Ryan what he already knew—that the verses of

the Eclogue actually referred to Augustus. Virgil was clearly writing a disguised political commercial.

Virgil composed Rome's great epic, *The Aeneid,* between 29 and 19 B.C. In the epic's vision of the future of Rome, Aeneas's guide, the Sibyl, tells him of:

> *Augustus, promis'd oft, and long foretold,*
> *that Saturn rul'd of old;*
> *Born to restore a better age of gold.*

She continued, "Other verses in *The Aeneid* substantiate the identity of the long-expected virgin-born Messiah that Virgil referred to covertly in the Eclogue: 'Augustus Caesar… brings a Golden Age; he shall restore old Saturn's scepter to our Latin land.'"

The quotes from Virgil reminded Emily of Isaac. She remembered the still night under the desert stars listening enrapt to the Jesuit scholar as he recreated the past and told her of Augustus' infatuation with Egyptian mythology. "Where do you get all these stories?" Emily had asked. "Or do you just make them up?"

The monsignor's eyes were twinkling as he replied. "What makes you think history isn't made up?"

Isaac's tale about Augustus' commissioning *The Aeneid* was one of her favorites:

XXIX/29
Audience with the Emperor

27 B.C.

For all his casual imperial gossip-mongering, the revered poet Publius Vergilius Mario, more commonly known as Virgil, had never spoken face to face with the Son of God. Augustus' trusted counselor, Gaius Cilnius Maecenas, made sure of that. Until today.

Virgil's heart was beating more rapidly than he could ever remember as he followed Maecenas through the marble-lined festive room of Augustus' sprawling villa on the Palatine Hill. They were heading for the room's smallest doorway, with a single slab of white marble as overhead support. The poet was startled to find himself comparing it to the simple chutes from which wild beasts issued into the arena.

"It would be wise for you to listen more than speak," Maecenas whispered as the Praetorian Guard who'd greeted them at the entrance to the villa ushered them toward the door. "And leave business details to me."

They were in in a stark cell bereft of all ornament. It took a few moments for Virgil's eyes to adjust to the relative dark of this room, illuminated only by a single shaft of sunlight that seemed orchestrated to the sole purpose of highlighting the curly-haired young man in the austere linen tunic who rose from his lotus position on a folding chair that looked like it had been salvaged from a military tent after a long field campaign.

Which indeed it had been, and brought here all the way from North Africa.

"We have come to see the emperor," Virgil blurted out, before Maecenas could clear his throat.

The young man chuckled genially. "And here you have found him." The answer came in impeccable Attic Greek. With an almost imperceptible nod of his head he dismissed the artisan who was etching a drawing of a tree with heart-shaped leaves on the wall of the sparse room. Then he gestured for the two visitors to be seated, indicating a hard wooden bench along the wall.

As Virgil's eyes adjusted to the gloom, he realized he was in the famous private quarters of Augustus, the title recently awarded him by the Senate, meaning "venerable." The curly-haired youth who greeted them was the god-man himself, the ruler of the world from Gibraltar to the Crimea.

The poet fell to his knees, eliciting another chuckle from Augustus.

The emperor nodded to Virgil to take a seat. "We have too little time and too much work to do." Augustus offered a plate of red figs, cheese, lettuce, and coarse bread, but both visitors hurriedly declined. Virgil had heard that the no-longer-bellicose emperor strove to live as a vegetarian now, and to abstain from wine and women.

Maecenas drew a breath of relief. No offense where none's intended, he hoped. If the emperor had wanted ceremony, they wouldn't be meeting in his private chambers. After years as Augustus' trusted adviser, Maecenas' imperial function was to supervise the artistic output of the finest poets in the empire in order to turn their verses to his emperor's own advantage.

Virgil noticed that Maecenas had taken out a quill and was preparing to make notes, and the seriousness of the moment registered full force. If his patron was planning to record the meeting, no doubt in that newfangled fast-writing he'd invented, then something important must be in the offing.

"You know how much the emperor loved your Fourth Eclogue," Augustus said. "That was good work. Of course it still perturbs him that you couldn't mention him by name while Antony was still squandering his manhood and political coin on that Egyptian whore. Bad enough that he had Cicero dispatched for calling the emperor 'the God-sent child.' Your Augustus would have deeply regretted to see your head nailed to the Senate podium next to his."

"Why don't we publish a new edition, sire? I can then name you—I mean, the emperor—openly."

Augustus shook his head. "The emperor has bigger things in mind for you. But, yes, the time has indeed come to be more open about the significance of his imperial power.

"And for monarchy to sustain itself," Augustus continued, "in the atmosphere created by our republican history, it must be based firmly on the myths associated with kings in every tradition. Augustus has been the *son* of god long enough." He gave the poet a conspiratorial look.

Virgil nodded, understanding why the epithet *filius divi,* "son of god," once so important to Augustus, might be getting old now that he had conquered more of the world than his adopted father Julius—known to the whole world now as the "Father God"—could even have imagined. It was time for an advancement of Augustus' status.

Though he couldn't be positive where this preamble was

going, Virgil could guess. The emperor wanted another poem.

The god-man looked thoughtful. "What the emperor requires now is verse that reaches out from *urbem* to *orbem,* which will be read, and recited, and performed, and remembered forever by all educated citizens not merely here in the capital, but throughout the empire and for all time."

Virgil's breath stopped. Every cell in his body tingled with anticipation.

"He has chosen you from all others because your skill and technique are strongest, your civic insight into our character clearest, your vision of our imperium most compelling, your dactylic hexameters the closest our Romans have come to the immortal cadences of great Homer."

"Thank you, sire. I am flattered—"

A glance made it clear his response was not required. "And for one more reason. Augustus knows you're not a man of faith—"

Virgil started to protest, but caught Maecenas' look and remained silent.

"You are, like the emperor himself, enough of a skeptic to recognize that just as much as all roads lead to Rome, so all religions lead to the same universal principles that should govern moral behavior."

The poet's appraisal of the emperor's intelligence rose to a new height. Could it be true that Augustus' perspective on the pantheon of gods that occupied the daily life of the city was like his own? That the traditions divinities stood for was far more important than how they appeared to differ on the surface?

"There is only one god worth worshipping," Augustus was saying. "But he is nothing like the gods that have surrounded us up till now." He paused, as if to consider whether to proceed along this line or get back to business. "Anyway," he sighed, "The emperor brought you here today to command you to write the definitive Roman epic, one that will rival Homer's *Iliad*, one that will eclipse Apollonius of Rhodes' tale of the Golden Fleece, and transcend anything any Roman has written before. An epic that the children of our children's children will recite in schools; one that will stir their blood to reverence and appreciation for what their ancestors have done to make them first citizens of the world."

Virgil's look of attention rivaled that of a gladiator about to enter the arena.

The emperor noted it with approval. "Of course Gaius Maecenas here will take care of your everyday needs. The emperor would like the work completed well in advance of a major planetary conjunction his astrologers have designated as the most propitious time for him to present the Roman people with the new divine mythology of his personal cult." Augustus' stare was piercing. "Augustus especially appreciated the lines in your eclogue concerning his father's divinity being proclaimed by the comet. The subtle way you alluded to Julius entering heaven as a star is particularly pleasing. It's a pity you hadn't thought to mention that the comet also signified Augustus' ushering in a new Golden Age. The emperor supposes he must be magnanimous in such matters." His sigh belied his words.

Should I be grateful, or apologize? Virgil wondered.

Augustus continued. "The predicted conjunction will herald the emperor's ceremonial nativity as the birth of a god—his apotheosis. The court astrologers will 'correct' this date to coincide with the Sibylline Prophecy foretelling the birth of the Messiah."

Virgil's face dare not betray his reaction. *By Jove, even the calendar isn't safe from this man's reach!*

"I'm certain you're aware that Jupiter is associated with kingly birth and Venus with fertility. The heavenly bodies will appear in conjunction as a single brilliant star, a sign of the emperor's second coming, this time as a god. Augustus will reintroduce the Centennial Games to mark the occasion and will mint special coinage. Maecenas will provide all the details in the next few weeks. You will have an unlimited staff of researchers and editors to support you in your task. But don't be concerned—the emperor wants you to continue as you have, following your own instincts. You will be well paid with gold—more than you could ever use. And you will receive a one-time recognition bonus of ten *aurei,* the gold coin King Herod is planning to mint in Judea, if you complete your magnum opus by the end of twenty-four months."

Virgil's mind was boggled. Gold! The fortune the emperor was designating for him was enormous. He blanched to realize he had absolutely no idea what he would do with that kind of fortune. *But I trust the ingenuity of the human mind to think of something,* he hastily assured himself. "I am overwhelmed with the emperor's confidence and generosity," he said, directing his statement at both men.

"The business portion of this meeting is over," Maecenas said. "Let us move to the creative considerations."

Augustus gave a slight nod to Maecenas. The emperor relaxed visibly. His eyes shone with an intensity Virgil had heard about but never witnessed first-hand. "Now, as you undertake this mission the emperor wants you to write freely, following your own vision of the past and future greatness of Rome. He knows you won't hesitate to throw in a little romance, but please nothing salacious, no explicit sexuality— unless of course it's a military rape described for the sake of dramatic impact or historical accuracy."

Virgil nodded his understanding. He much preferred romance to sex anyway.

"Several years ago, the allusion to Augustus in your Eclogue as the Prince of Peace, initiating a new Golden Age of Saturn, was precisely on point," the emperor reiterated. "The emperor applauded it! But now that peace is no longer just a dream and a promise but has been achieved, there's no longer any reason for indirection. You are to present the history of Rome in such a way that all characters and events foreshadow Augustus as the adopted son of his beloved uncle who the Senate declared to be a god. And, since he hardly knew his natural father, Gaius, let's just say he was born of a virgin, in the tradition of sun gods. And let us refer to her from now on as *Theotokos,* "God-bearer," he added. "That will give pause to everyone who views her monuments." Augustus' eyes got misty, and then he recited the perfect hexameters in the gruff voice he reserved for public appearances:

> *Augustus promis'd oft, and long foretold*
> *Sent to the realm that Saturn rul'd of old.*
> *Born to restore a better age of gold.*

The emperor looked at Maecenas. The creative spark in Augustus' eyes warned Virgil that the emperor was personally invested in these particular lines. Augustus Caesar would be the centerpiece, the awaited one, the anointed one, the savior of the world, the Messiah, the reborn Apollo, god and son of god, whose destiny it was to bring the Roman world through blood and sweat and tears to its fated greatness. His poem would make the emperor eternal.

Virgil fought to suppress a frown. He forced his attention back to Augustus' words:

"And when my priests and I have finished redacting the prophetic Sibylline Books, I shall order all of them destroyed except the re-authorized four scrolls that will be gilded and installed in the annex of the new temple I will build for Apollo in the Forum. Please, if you don't mind, insert into the story the oracle that wrote the books, the Cumaean Sibyl—as prominently as possible. Make her somehow the authorized gate to ultimate knowledge or her cave the transition by which the hero experiences the underworld. When the time comes, Maecenas will arrange free pass for you to inspect the progress of the new editions," he added graciously. "You'll see that they'll be brought into conformity with the official biography, as though even the Sibyl's original meeting with King Tarquin prophesied the coming of Augustus."

Virgil knew the story well. This brawny woman was believed to be the supreme oracle, the quintessence of prophecy. According to the ancient legend, the poetess-prophet came up from her cave in Cumae to Tarquin's royal compound near the site of what would later be Rome.

With her she carried nine books recording the future of Rome and offered them to the King for a price that was so astonishing he turned her down flat. Right before his eyes the sibyl set fire to three of the books. A year later she returned, offering him the remaining six for twice the price she'd originally demanded for the nine. Despite the sleepless nights she'd caused him the King refused her offer again, so she burned three more.

After another year had gone by, one in which the King many times wished he'd had a preview of the future, she returned a final time with the remaining three. Though her price was twice what she demanded for the six, he paid it to her without further protest and sent her away.

Some say the king—or was it Apollo? Virgil couldn't remember—cursed her, once the books were safely in his keeping. He wished her eternal life, which the Sybil accepted; but without adding that she would never grow old.

Meanwhile, back at the best and worst audience of his life, Virgil's face was slowly becoming an iron mask, the result of the most painful acting he'd ever achieved.

The poet laureate-designate well knew Augustus' practice of recasting ancient religions to include his coming in their traditional prophetic literature. Egomania coupled with absolute power could indeed change the world—but not necessarily for the better. *Why doesn't he just write the cursed thing himself?* Virgil fumed—silently.

As though reading his troubadour's mind, Augustus pulled another papyrus sheet from his tunic. "The emperor has jotted down a few other ideas," he said. "And a verse or two—if you can decipher the shorthand. But he leaves it all to your good judgment, having no doubt that your work will certainly please him."

The meeting was over. The Praetorian Guard was waiting at the doorway, no doubt summoned by a secret signal.

Still in a daze, Virgil let himself be whisked out of the Palatine villa, with parting words from Maecenas assuring him, "I'll meet up with you later. We'll review the details." Virgil's eyes fell on the papyrus, where Augustus' distinctive cursive had recorded the lines he had recited. Farther down he could just make out the sketchy words to mean, "Augustus Caesar... brings a Golden Age; he shall restore old Saturn's scepter to our Latin land." The poet rolled his eyes. And hoped to Hades that his Praetorian escort hadn't noticed.

The heat of his first quinarius burning a hole in his palm, Virgil would return to his Rome apartment and drape every single mirror. He was no longer a self-created genius. He had just become the best-paid propagandist in the world—for better or worse, a high-priced courtesan.

XXX/30
Catacombs

Ryan chuckled at Virgil as a highly paid courtesan. As they abandoned the small piazza where they'd kept vigil, Emily found herself laughing with him. "I'm going to miss Isaac's stories. I can hardly believe he's gone forever from our lives."

The backfire of a *motocicletta* brought them back to the present. Their heads turned to scan the tiny streets for signs of red Vespas or Cinquecentos. But the pair arrived back at the Piazza della Rotonda without incident, and made sure to remain in the shadows of the Pantheon while they did their reconnaissance.

By now it was nearly three in the morning and the piazza was eerily vacant. Ryan's attention was drawn to the street lights that gleamed off the surface of the silver door.

Emily noticed the direction of his glance. "Not only are they spotlighted," she said. "But both the main entrance and our door are covered by surveillance cameras."

"We'll have to hope whoever's monitoring them has fallen asleep."

"Hold up a minute." She was reaching into her knapsack, her limber arm making it look easy. Seconds later, she had the slingshot in hand and was preparing it, reaching down to the pavement for the fragments created by the bullets.

"Planning on shooting pigeons?" he asked her. "Or wandering friars?"

She ignored him and loaded the first marble fragment. Her aim was dead center. Both her shots zinged to their targets in rapid succession. The silence of the night was broken only by plunks from the street lamps imploding in near-simultaneous succession. The front of the bank went dark, rendering the surveillance cameras useless. Emily tucked the slingshot back into her knapsack, and motioned for him to follow her.

"That's quite a skill you've got." Ryan was wide-eyed. "Remind me never to pick a fight with you."

"Thanks," she said. My cousins taught me the fine art of sling shooting when we were kids. We'd have contests to see who could knock over the most tin cans." She laughed. "Just do as I say, and you'll be fine."

They were relieved to discover that the silver key opened the stainless steel door. Before anyone entered the empty piazza, they'd made their way inside the pitch-dark stairwell.

Ryan switched on his flashlight, gesturing for her to follow. Emily put her hand on his shoulder to steady herself as they descended. In two minutes they reached the smaller door in the exit staircase he'd described to her with the three interlinked letters that formed the insignia of the Society of Jesus, "IHS."

But Ryan was frowning. "I knew something was bothering me," he said.

"What is it?"

"The Jesuit insignia. This door was carved by Ghiberti, but the Society was founded by Ignatius Loyola in 1534. Ghiberti died the previous century."

"Maybe Ignatius Loyola got the idea from Ghiberti. Your Society's insignia, after all, is another ancient symbol—the symbol of the healing sun."

The comment struck home. *Like everything else*, Ryan thought, *even the Jesuit insignia wasn't unique?*

What must have been the original lock had been replaced with a modern card slot, the gold workmanship so carefully matched that only the slightly brighter coloration bore witness to its relative modernity. Emily reached into her jeans and pulled out the cards. The gold card slipped easily into the groove; a tiny light blinked green; and the door opened smoothly on its hinges as though it had just been lubricated.

They entered the dark tunnel to face a nearly overwhelming rush of fetid air redolent with tufa and decay. They closed the door behind them and carefully made their way down the irregular steps carved from stone more than two millennia ago. Five minutes went by and Ryan judged they were now moving beneath the ancient Campus Martius.

"Volcanic," Emily remarked, as their nostrils flared at the acrid odor of sulphur.

Ryan noticed the ruins of an altar at the foot of the narrow shaft she was pointing to, its sides blackened. He also noticed it had iron rungs fixed into one of its sides, climbing all the way toward the surface. "Looks like an emergency exit," he said.

"Or entrance." She studied the rungs. "It's probably topped by a manhole cover," she said.

Ryan noticed that the iron rungs were worn with millennia. The ingenuity of the classical Romans never ceased to surprise him.

In the next half hour or so, with the illumination from both their flashlights dancing against the ancient pavement and walls, they passed rows and rows of indecipherable inscriptions on niches that were randomly empty, sealed, or crammed with skulls or skeletons. They were in a catacomb. Sometimes the passageway was so narrow they had to turn sideways to get through. The inscriptions were in a language neither of them could decipher. Emily announced that it must be Etruscan, the culture preceding the Romans. But as they continued, they began to recognize Greek letters, then ancient Roman script.

One particularly hideous side corridor was lined with shriveled mummies hanging on hooks and dressed in funeral and wedding garb, just like those Emily had once seen in the catacomb of the Capuchins in Palermo. Ryan guessed from their clothing that this "new" corridor had been populated during the early Renaissance.

The main corridor they were following turned toward the right, and at the same time seemed to be descending; the starkness of the walls on both sides suggested more ancient times. Ryan drew Emily's attention to a small fresco of an amply-endowed woman who was standing on a snake and holding a suckling child to her bare breast, while another serpent coiled around her arm. "Obviously an early Christian icon, before the Puritans set the norm for public display," he joked.

"It's not the Virgin Mary," Emily said, "though it *is* a virgin mother. It's actually Bona Dea, the Roman goddess of fertility, healing, virginity—and of women in general. Her foot on the snake indicates her power over the phallus. She, in turn, was modeled after Isis holding Horus with the serpent of wisdom at her feet. Later Augustus allowed this antique goddess to be identified with the cult of his mother Maia, who was said to have lain with a serpent in the temple to be impregnated with the son of Apollo—and bore Augustus Caesar." She explained that the image of Bona Dea was found on many early Republican coins.

Ryan shook his head. The more he learned about the past, the more he had to reconsider the present. Obviously studying the early church fathers was not enough; he'd have to become a comparative anthropologist—and take a good course in art history of the ancient world—before it was all over. "These catacombs are pre-Christian, or—"

Emily nodded. "Both pre-Christian and Christian," she answered. "Romans hid here during threatened invasions, especially during the Civil Wars."

"So you're saying that early Christians took over the imagery they found in these Roman burial chambers and adopted it as their own? The way the Roman Empire took over the Republic's images? And before that the way the early Romans copied from the Egyptians and the Greeks?"

"I'll make a comparatist out of you yet," Emily said.

Was she toying with him? "It's odd that we haven't seen a single image of Jesus crucified," he pointed out.

"Maybe he wasn't," she laughed, moving so quickly that he had to hurry to catch up. They walked for another twenty minutes in the ancient corridor, chilled by the even cooler, drier air that better preserved both the bones and the art. "The tunnel is descending to pass under the river," Emily said.

"I've never seen a catacomb with so many of its inhabitants intact and on display. Obviously this one hasn't been open to the public—if it ever was."

"Maybe it's been concealed and locked since the time of Ghiberti," Emily offered.

"It's weird that all the corridors we've passed appear to be dead ends."

"Yeah, either natural or cemented. Whoever's still using this wants it secure." Emily had stopped to illuminate another image: The sun god, with a halo of spikes like the ones on her aureus, driving his chariot across the sky, the image surrounded by a grape vine. Beneath it in crude lettering, she traced the words, *Christus Apollo filius:* "Christ Apollo, the son."

Ryan expressed no surprise at this one. "I know, I know—

the early fathers of the church frequently referred to Jesus as Apollo."

"Of course they did. That's in my doctoral thesis, too. It's typical of absolute rulers to identify with the sun god. The vine is the symbol of Dionysus, the wine god, who was ritually torn apart and descended into Hades. Augustus had statues of himself crowned with the vine cast by artisans that used Greek statues of Apollo as models."

"Jesus *was* the son of God, after all," Ryan said, remembering how odd it was to think that English confused Christ's solar virtues, as the bringer of light to dispel the darkness, with his divine filial status. Son = sun.

"God and Son of God, the mysteries of the Trinity."

"It certainly is a mystery," she replied, "one of the ancient mysteries. One powerful enough to reach out and touch the two of us—and bring us together in this bizarre quest. The progenitor, the generated, and the energy flowing between them. Remember the words—*divus filius divi*—inscribed on my aureus?"

"But those words apply to Jesus—how did they come to be on an Augustan aureus?"

"Because they were being applied to Augustus at that time—years before Jesus was reputed to be born."

At one point they felt sure they must be directly beneath the Tiber. The ceiling of the passageway was beaded with moisture, and artwork had been nearly absent from the walls for several hundred yards. "It's a natural air conditioning system," Ryan thought out loud. "Just enough moisture to mitigate the dryness throughout the rest of the tunnel."

As they proceeded, the decline gave way to an incline and

they surmised they'd crossed beneath the river and were now on the other side. And the inscriptions resumed, one ancient image succeeding another along the walls highlighted by their

flashes: the phoenix rising from the ashes; Apollo carrying a lamb on his shoulders with the word *xristos* carved beneath him; the "XP" monogram of Christ and Chronos with the Greek letters alpha and omega, signifying "the beginning and the end."

Ryan had learned that when the XP was carved on a tombstone it meant a Christian was buried there.

Though they still saw no depictions of the crucifixion of Christ, the symbol of the fish was everywhere. Throughout Christianity, to the present day, the fish was a symbol of Christ, who promised to make his apostles, "fishers of men." Emily told him that the fish was actually an ancient Egyptian symbol, adopted by the Pythagoreans—the figure formed by the intersection of two circles, when the circumference of one touches the center of the other.

"What do the two circles represent?" Ryan asked.

"The lower one represents animal nature, the higher, divine. We humans are the fish—the conjunction of the two natures."

Ryan had been taught that the Greek word for fish, *ixthys,*

Latin *ichthus,* was an acronym for *Iesus Christos Theòu Uiòs Sotèr*—"Jesus Christ, Son of God, Savior."

He did not want to hear as Emily explained that Augustus had ordered the very same image and the very same words, *Theòu Uiòs Sotèr,* carved on the facades of his own cult temples. His mind was in turmoil.

More modern elaborate frescoes depicted Jesus walking on the water, Jesus raising Lazarus, Jesus entering Jerusalem on the back of a donkey—"another symbol of the intersection of the two natures," Emily said. They estimated those to be post-Constantine, fourth or fifth century. Earlier, simpler drawings, some of them quite crude, showed doves, symbols of peace and of the love flowing between the son and the father; and anchors, symbolizing the soul's final harbor in heaven. Emily reminded him that Augustus had replaced the eagle with the dove at the outset of the Pax Romana, the Roman Peace.

Ryan nodded but said nothing.

She had to admit she was impressed with the extent of the young priest's knowledge, though incomplete, of her chosen field of iconography. At one point she took his hand. "It's almost like I've been making this pilgrimage with another Monsignor Isaac," she whispered, giving his hand a squeeze then taking hers away before he could respond.

"Thanks a lot," he quipped. "I'll certainly feel as old as he was if I keep hanging out with you." He chuckled, but was troubled by her touch and relieved when she let go.

One image brought him to a dead stop. "What is this?" he asked her.

Emily looked over his shoulder at a crude drawing of a figure that looked like the young Augustus being lashed with a whip. She recognized it from one of Isaac's lectures. "It's an image of the suffering *imperator,*" she said, "willingly accepting pain for his people."

Ryan's frown eclipsed the need for words.

They'd stopped to rest. Checking their watches, they were surprised to discover that they'd been traversing the underground necropolis for less than two hours. It felt like an entire day.

The odor of the strong espresso, as Ryan unscrewed the lid of the thermos he'd taken from his knapsack, was revivifying.

"Ah, you do know how to please a girl," Emily said. Was that a tad of flirtation she heard in her own voice? Then she tasted the brandy in the coffee and made no effort to restrain her smile.

"Well, you certainly don't make it too hard for me," he cautiously teased back.

"At least I'm a cheap date," she said, smiling again. Then, before he could respond, she added. "The art in this catacomb is so well-preserved. I've never seen anything like it."

Ryan welcomed her change of conversation. He told her that he'd been thinking the same thing. Ryan's voice turned serious. He looked her straight in the eyes. "What do you know about all this that you're not telling me?"

"What do you mean?"

"I mean I think you're holding something back. Your explanations of all the icons seem to be leading me somewhere you've been to already. You're stopping yourself from completing sentences. You know more than you're letting on."

She looked away, as if to dismiss his words. "I've spent my life studying the representations of myths, remember? How a myth is the matrix that is transformed from culture to culture, but basically remains essentially the same."

"You also spent the last few years in regular contact with Monsignor Isaac."

She looked back at him. "Yeah? So?"

"So I think you know what he was up to, and I want to

know what it is. Why is this aureus so important, and why did you think he'd want to see it immediately?"

"If I told you that," she said, "I'd have to kill you."

"Very funny." He could sense her mind wrestling with something. "Apparently you'd have to stand in line," he added.

"I will tell you everything when I put together all the missing pieces of the puzzle."

"Why not now?"

"Honestly? Because you'll think I'm crazy."

"I've pretty much thought that since the minute you nearly ran me down." His eyes twinkled. "You're no crazier than I am. I disobeyed a direct order from my superior and abandoned my designated research to investigate what it was that Isaac knew that's been attracting murderers."

"If I let out his theory before I can present absolute evidence to prove it you'd laugh me to death. And I'd also be the laughingstock of iconography. I'd be hounded out of academia and into the backwaters of fringe scholarship for the rest of my life." She paused. Her gray eyes grew dark. "I can't—I won't take that chance. I need to dot every i and cross every t."

"Then at least give me a hint," he said, topping off their cups. "There's enough espresso left for another cup each."

"I hope the brandy settled to the bottom." Emily reached for the cup, took a deep breath, and began another of Isaac's stories.

XXXI/31

Ἐν Τούτῳ Νίκα
In Hoc Signo, Vinces
In this sign you will conquer...

312 A.D.

Today was not a good day for Emperor Constantine. Today the legions he'd led in triumph against the Franks, Picts, and so many other enemies in far-flung parts of Europe and the Middle East, were facing their greatest challenge of all, and in their own backyard: a force, nearly twice their size, of fellow Romans led by his brother-in-law and co-emperor Maxentius.

On top of that, Constantine's legions were dead on their feet, grumbling to the edge of mutiny because he'd moved them away from Malborghetto where they could *inhale* Rome's intoxicating odors of food, sex, and circus blood wafting from behind the closed gates of the Prima Porta.

Now they were encamped a few leagues north of the city where Maxentius, proclaiming as his own the imperium that Constantine had won only six years earlier by old-fashioned military acclamation, was supposedly readying for their attack.

The October breeze bore hints of winter from the north, but the pleasant weather was only making his men more anxious and restless, still frazzled from their forced march down the Adriatic coast.

Truly Constantine could not have predicted that his

brother-in-law would take the offensive. Now his scouts were reporting from all directions, not only confirming that Maxentius was on the move, but also estimating that his brother-in-law's force was closer to 120,000 than to 75,000—against Constantine's dilapidated 50,000!

The prospect facing him today was daunting. The meager remnant of his army were bone-weary infantrymen all too ready to end their campaigns in the arms of the wives and whores of Rome—expecting to confront fresh troops whose bellies were sated, lusts satisfied, and purses primed for the reward and spoil promised by Maxentius.

Where was his mother, Helena, when he needed her? With Maxentius now positioned where the Milvian Bridge crossed the Tiber—situated between Constantine and his troops and Rome—he knew he was facing his personal Rubicon, a moment as auspicious for its impact on his place in history as it was on the future of the empire itself. And as for his beloved *mater*—for all he knew she could probably be found on her hands and knees in a temple in Judea scratching around like a chicken for another rusty nail or splinter of the "true Cross."

And then there was that infernal stone bridge that had appeared to him in last night's bizarre dream. She would have known what to make of it and either confirm or invalidate his interpretation. In the dream, he was standing on the Milvian Bridge, his eyes fixed on the sun, staring at the sphere fearlessly in the way that only an eagle-like emperor could do. As the shining golden disc came into focus, he saw that Sol invictus—the unconquerable sun he worshiped—was mounted at the head of each legion's pennant. Within the dazzling disc itself Greek and Latin letters began to appear, *Εν Τούτω Νίκα, in hoc signo vinces,* "In this sign you will conquer."

Then, like letters formed from lightning bolts, those words gave way to others. Constantine had awakened to find he'd scribbled on the papyrus next to his cot, "XP" and "IHS." "XP" he understood, the first letters of *Xristos,* "the Anointed One" that his mother was claiming to be the only god.

He dispatched a message to Helena, who would know how to decipher the other insignia, one unfamiliar to him. She would have undoubtedly told him that the dream was important, and had something earth-shattering to relay to him from her god Jasius. Although he wasn't superstitious, Constantine had agreed to convert to the secret religion of the *Xristos* mostly because he respected its abstemious values, adhered to by his revered imperial predecessor Octavian Augustus; but also because it would get her off his back.

It occurred to him that he was facing a true crisis of faith. Not that his amorphous religious faith had anything to do with it; he understood now that his men's faith in victory was their only hope. He sent for his aide de camp to deliver an order to his faltering legions.

"Tell the men we will engage Maxentius at the bridge when the sun is halfway across the afternoon sky. Between now and then, each legion must build a fire and melt down the golden eagles on their standards. Then, command each *aquilifer,* 'eagle-bearer,' to create a cross that loops into a ✸ from the melted gold"—he drew the figure carefully on a blank piece of papyrus—"and mount the symbol at the standard's tip."

Constantine continued. "A vision came to me last night. Tell them their emperor, who loves them, is assured that with this sign of *Sol invictus* on our side we are ourselves invincible."

His paltry army marched into the jaws of death carrying the newly-fashioned labarum standards, each sporting the *Chi-Rho.* They pushed the enemy troops to the river. Then Maxentius fatefully decided to retreat and regroup in the city—where he should have stayed in the first place. Constantine instantly employed the partially-destroyed bridge to his advantage, and turned the bottleneck into an abattoir. Maxentius' troops were routed, or slaughtered. He himself—poor, dear, deceitful brother-in-law—drowned in the Tiber trying to escape. His characteristically craven behavior—and his head raised on a spear point to receive the spittle of the Roman mob—only enhanced Constantine's triumphant procession into the Eternal City that was now his and his alone.

A response from his mother had arrived instructing him to fill out the rest of the piece he somehow hadn't recognized: I H S U S, "Iesus." Together the three scribbled initials and the *Chi-Rho* monogram added up to the Greek cult name of Jasius Xristos, the man-god she worshipped—the rediscovered *divus filius divi,* God and Son of God, who had led her only son into his greatest victory. He would persuade the Senate to give his mother the title of *augusta* as soon as the consolidation of the empire was completed.

From this time forward the labarum would bear the ⚴ symbol, which the emperor also ordered restored to imperial coinage in honor of the original Augustus.

Constantine the Great, as he was henceforth known, would build a new Rome on the seven hills overlooking the Bosporus, creating it in his own image and likeness; and give the new eastern capital his name: Constantinople, "the City of Constantine." Mindful of Herod's gesture of gratitude to the first Caesar Augustus in building the temple in Caesarea, Constantine consecrated the cathedral of his new metropolis to Jasius Augustus, the one god he'd learned to rely on, his mother's god.

He would clarify, codify, and perpetuate the original Julian-Augustan cult based on the principles of *clementia,* "mercy and tolerance," universality, and resurrection. Now that he thought about it he might even lay the foundation for the cult's transromanization, turning it into the ultimate worldwide moral system by removing Augustus' name from it and calling it, simply, *Christian*. After all, emperor worship was becoming unpopular.

The final gift Emperor Constantine could offer Helena, on his deathbed in Nicomedia, was to submit formally to the baptismal sacrament he'd accepted in spirit years ago. Lord knows, it'd be excellent to believe that his bloody sins were forgiven in eternity. By that time his saintly mother's and now his own chosen religion, the religion of *Jasius Christus,* "Jesus the Awaited One," had become the official religion of the empire.

The Emperor Constantine's last will and testament recorded the crowning grace note of his mother's legacy. His body would be placed in a sarcophagus flanked on both sides by six standing tombs containing the relics of the twelve apostles. For all eternity, Constantine the Great, *O.M., Optimus Maximus,* "the Best and the Greatest," would be positioned like the Christ the son god, Jasius Augustus, in the center of his personal zodiac.

XXXII / 32
A.R.S.I.

Ryan had studied the most important ancient sources for the legendary account of Constantine's sign in the sky. None of them captured the drama like Isaac's tale as she retold it. "I'd have loved to be your student."

"I got all my best stories from the dearly departed monsignor."

Ryan was confused by the direction the tale had taken at the end. "You're saying that Constantine saw Christianity as a cult going back to the founding days of the Roman Empire?"

Emily nodded. "He spent the rest of his life reestablishing the cult in its original form, worshiping the true founder of Christianity, Jasius Augustus."

"And you expect me to believe all this?"

"I knew you'd find it hard to accept," she said, looking at him solemnly, "although you should know from your study of the Fathers that it wasn't called 'Christianity' until Constantine's last years." She watched him roll his eyes.

"I get it," he joked. "Constantine and Helena were the first Jesuits."

"Something like that," she said. "Think about it, the emblem on your coat of arms is the sign in the sky Constantine witnessed. If you're lucky—and we're not gunned down by an ecclesiastical sniper in a helicopter—I'll tell you another story."

"Ever a woman of mystery." Ryan plucked up the courage to look directly into her eyes as he stood up. "We'd better move on now before we're discovered. I know you'll tell me everything when you're ready. Right now, the secrets of the Vatican await us."

She took the hand he offered, holding onto it a few moments longer than necessary as she got to her feet. "You're assuming that's where this catacomb leads."

Ryan nodded. "I think the tunnel is an escape route. The icons make me think we're directly beneath the ancient cemetery under Via Cornelia, where St. Peter was crucified upside down. Let's hope to God we find what we're looking for so we aren't next in line."

Reenergized by the caffeine, they moved swiftly into the darkness. Ryan was lost in thought trying to piece together Emily's story of Constantine's re-confirmation of an ancient Roman faith with accounts he had read in the early Church Fathers. Her version of history didn't seem to fit with the Fathers' accounts, not to mention that of the New Testament. But he had to admit their accounts were so contradictory and even bellicose that it wasn't easy to characterize them one way or the other.

He and Emily were moving even more quickly now, sensing that the end of their underground trek was near. A clanging alarm suddenly rang somewhere in the distance, echoing so eerily through the cavernous tunnel that neither of them could tell whether it came from in front of them or behind. They couldn't be sure but they thought they also heard the distant sound of running footsteps.

"Oh my God," Emily muttered to herself, "we're toast." When they stopped to listen the sound of footsteps faded away.

They increased their pace to a sprint; and, just as the alarm muted as abruptly as it had sounded, they came to the end of the tunnel. It was marked by another golden door, twin to the one they'd entered beneath the bank. They hastily tried the gold key card again and were both relieved and anxious to find that the door opened easily, as though it, too, had been recently serviced.

A small corridor, graced with a vivid bas-relief of the Cumaean Sibyl as a beautiful young woman seemingly by the same ingenious hand that had painted her in the Sistine Chapel, led to a more modern silver door, like the one at the bank.

"This corridor must have been extremely important for Michelangelo to work where he knew very few eyes would ever appreciate his art," Ryan's whisper betrayed awe as Emily hastened to keep pace with him.

The letters ARSI were inscribed on the silver door in institutional script with the "IHS" insignia carved beneath.

Emily looked at him. "ARSI?"

Ryan shook his head. "It's not the Vatican after all. I should have realized." He turned and hurriedly slipped the other plastic card into the slot. Again the door accommodated it, the mechanism betraying their trespass and setting their nerves on edge as it hissed again, automatically closing the door behind them.

She hurried behind him through the portal and up the short staircase wondering if he was going to answer the question. Though the dawn light from the side windows forced their eyes to adjust, Ryan recognized the place. "'ARSI' stands for *Archivum Romanum Societatis Jesu*—the 'Roman archives of the Jesuit Order,'" he said. "This room contains the records of the official business of the Jesuit Generalate in Rome."

They had infiltrated the Society's most hallowed ground.

The Vatican was indeed close—only a few hundred yards away. But they were in Borgo Santo Spirito, specifically in the faux-Grecian building tucked into the gardens behind the Jesuit Curia, in the shadow of St. Peter's dome. Ryan had attempted to visit the building during his first week at the College but had been told it was "closed indefinitely for restoration."

Upon entering this enigmatic chamber, Ryan shivered. Along with letters from the Generals of the Jesuit Order to the various provinces around the world, catalogues from all the provinces giving data on individual Jesuits, histories of the Society's activities, mission inventories, and Annual Letters, would be Monsignor Isaac's notes, and his own individual record waiting to be updated with silver stars—or black Xs.

Directly across the room from where they entered, Ryan could see another gold door. Emily was heading toward it, determined to complete her mission. "I don't know about you, but I'm beginning to feel a little like Alice in Wonderland. And this Alice needs to find a bathroom soon."

Ryan gave a wry smile as he paused to marvel at a double display case that contained the original manuscripts of *The Spiritual Exercises* of Ignatius of Loyola, the Society's founder; and, on the opposite side, *The Constitutions of the Society of Jesus,* both in Ignatius' own handwriting. Though the documents were youthful compared to the ancient secrets of the Vatican itself, Ryan was overcome with a fervent sense of reverence. He wondered why these precious documents were locked away from the scrutiny of pious pilgrims. This was the holograph of the man for whom he'd sacrificed a normal life. *What would Ignatius have to say about Isaac's work and the meaning of the Augustan aureus?* He also noticed there was no sign of restorations.

But as he dashed to catch up with Emily, Ryan's attention was caught by what looked like wooden shipping boxes in all stages of packing and transition. He stopped to examine one of them, noting that all were marked *"Ad Cumas, v.f.A."* "to Cumae"—whatever the following initials stood for he had no idea.

The box in front of him had not yet been sealed. He slid

the wooden top along its tight-fitting grooves. "Take a look," he said, the surprise in his voice compelling Emily to his side.

The box contained leather-bound books topped with printed-out computer text. Ryan quickly scanned the page headers – "Josephus," "An Audience with the Emperor," "The Sibylline Redaction," "Birth of God," flush left, and "Augustus Gospel/Isaac" flush right. His eyes widened as he realized they were looking at fifty pages or so of Monsignor Isaac's magnum opus. Ryan snatched the print-outs and tucked them into his backpack.

"Hurry!" Emily said. She was standing a few feet away, beside an ornately carved wooden screen, near the next gold door they assumed led to the Vatican Curia.

They could hear footsteps approaching from behind the door.

"They're onto us," Emily whispered.

Grabbing Ryan by his shirtsleeve, Emily pulled him behind the screen.

The gold door swung open.

Within yards of where Ryan and Emily stood concealed in the shadows, figures were scurrying in all directions. Two Swiss Guards entered the room, their walkie-talkies crackling to life. "All units accelerate search. Repeat: Accelerate search."

Finding the archive room apparently empty, the two defiant guards flopped down on the sixteenth-century Flemish tapestry chairs for an impromptu break. Sweat poured from the face of the stout senior guard. He offered a Marlboro to his novice partner, then lit his own and settled back in the delicate chair, ignoring the pounding footsteps of the other guards dutifully scampering past the door.

Ryan and Emily strained to listen, barely able to follow the Swiss-accented Italian.

They learned from the guards that only a few minutes ago Father Regis Schork had been replaced by the Argentine, Miguel Leontel, who had been elected the thirty-third superior general of the Society of Jesus. "The new Black Pope," the senior guard called him. "But no one here would ever openly call him that—unless you want to be thrown into the vault until you repent," he added.

"That's what the Jesuits themselves call him, so what's wrong with it?" the young guard said, confused.

"Only among themselves." The senior guard carelessly flicked an ash onto the thick pile carpet. He was just getting into stride and embarked on a lengthy monologue of Vatican-Jesuit politics, focusing on the newly-elected Black Pope who was rumored to oppose Pope Pius' arch-conservatism.

Emily stole a glance at her watch. Twenty-five minutes had elapsed since she and Ryan had hidden behind the screen and the discomfort in her bladder made it almost impossible to stand still.

The younger man, who'd been absentmindedly staring at the swirling rings of smoke, sat up suddenly. "Seems like this new man must be a real radical."

The senior guard ignored the interruption. He went on with his discourse. "Leontel really pisses off Pius because he embraces *all* religions. The gap that's existed between the Society of Jesus and the Papacy all these years could turn into a giant rupture."

Ryan and Emily's legs were stiffening, and were feeling the effects of standing motionless. To add to Ryan's discomfort, the espresso had found its way to his bladder as well. Emily was sure she was about to burst.

The stout officer slowly rose to his feet, and his colleague, whose eyes had glazed over, eagerly came back to life and jumped up to follow him. As far as he was concerned, the less he understood of all these goings-on the better; he was here only to serve the Holy See.

The two guards returned the way they came.

Ryan's face was ashen. "Holy Cow!" he sighed. "We'd have won at a game of Hide 'n Seek."

Emily laughed softly. "Yeah, or seeing how long we can hold our bladders."

As if in perfect sync their eyes moved from the wooden box that held Monsignor Isaac's pages to the nearby rest room. "Ladies first," Ryan said.

Emily sighed her gratitude as she moved to the *bagno*, leaving Ryan to exercise yoga control while he waited. He stared at the box of print-outs, where a section heading read, *"Hoc opus, hic labor est,"* "This is the work, that is the toil."

XXXIII/33
Requiem Aeternam
Eternal Rest

Emily and Ryan used the second card key to open the door, which was marked "A.S.A.V." "Let's hope they're off our trail," she whispered as they hurried through the portal before the door closed. They were in an antechamber with several small corridors leading left and right. They quickly traversed the long, dimly-lit mahogany-paneled corridor leading straight ahead and came to another gold door that accommodated the second card key.

Judging from the door-seals and the automated ducts, they were in what appeared to be an enormous air-regulated chamber. Row upon row of shelves and museum cases receded into the distance. The shelves were stacked to the ceiling with papyrus scrolls and codices. Emily felt as though she'd just entered the fabled Great Library of Alexandria. "This must be the Vatican Treasury." She sounded breathless. "I've never seen it before."

"I've visited the Vatican Treasury a number of times," Ryan said. "It's a tourist attraction, the mere tip of an iceberg to what the Vatican possesses. This isn't it. This is the *Archivum Segretum Apostolicum Vaticani*—A.S.A.V."

Emily translated: "Secret Archives of the Vatican Apostolate."

"C'mon, we'd better keep moving. Even with my high-level access I'd never be allowed in this room," Ryan said as they passed row upon row of shelving.

Emily paused to marvel at friezes on the walls and the brightly-colored ceiling frescoes, most of them documenting bequests to the Vatican from the kings and emperors of Europe. The lower walls, beneath the friezes, were lined with polished mahogany sliding file doors that made the room appear like some sort of gaudily-decorated imperial morgue.

"I'd gladly sacrifice two graduate assistants to snoop around in this room for a day or so. Too bad we're in a rush," Emily murmured.

"That's exactly why Paul V ordered it sealed back in the seventeenth century. For two hundred years no scholar was allowed to use it at all. Starting about a hundred years ago," Ryan said, "requests could be made in writing. You have to know the book is here to begin with, of course; no index has ever been published. I've heard there may be as many as 75,000 manuscripts and over one million volumes here—on over fifty miles of shelving."

He grabbed her arm to hurry her forward, but the ornate display cases that occupied the center of the chamber drew them like magnets. "This must also be the *Tesoro Segreto,* 'the secret treasury,'" Ryan speculated. "Artifacts they don't want to entrust to lowly clerics like myself, much less to the general public."

"Or don't want the public to know about," Emily said, "like my aureus. If I ever get my hands on it again I'll never let it out of my sight." She heaved a sigh as they pushed on.

A fragrant smell of pine wood penetrated their nostrils.

"The walls are lined with cedar," Ryan said as though reading her mind, "to preserve the manuscripts."

"Pretty old-fashioned, if you ask me," Emily said. She stopped at a utilitarian showcase, stooping to examine its lower shelves. Ryan barely avoided tripping over her. The dust-covered shelves were stacked high with Dead Sea scrolls from the "library of Qumran." The display top presented an array of Romano-Christian artifacts. She read their identifying tags: an Egyptian miter belonging to Mark Antony, consort of Cleopatra and first high priest of the Julian religion that worshiped Julius Caesar as a god; the solid-gold menorah from Jerusalem brought to Rome after the sack of the Temple in 70 A.D.; the Rothenberg casket containing the *lapis exillis* also known as the "stone of destiny"; the actual pharaonic flail given to Augustus by the Egyptian priests after his defeat of Antony

and Cleopatra that Emily had first taken note of in the carvings on the ceiling of the temple at Dendera; Augustus' ornate eagle-topped gold scepter; a red chasuble sewn entirely with gold thread and studded with precious stones, worn by Augustus as Pontifex Maximus.

"All that's missing is the Easter Bunny and the Holy Grail," Ryan commented. "And your coin."

"Here's another thing that's missing." She pointed to a circular ring on the velvet pad occupying the otherwise empty display case that was tagged as the "funeral urn of Octavian Augustus Caesar." Only a tiny archive photograph indicated what it looked like—but the photograph was too small to make out the inscription.

Emily's attention was drawn to a papal crown, the tiara. She indicated the legend on its tag. Ryan's face fell as he read the words *"coronus Augusti, Pontificis Maximi,"* Crown of Augustus, Pontifex Maximus.

They continued their brisk pace and Emily spoke in undertones telling what she'd learned about this crown from

Monsignor Isaac. "Although the rumor is that he wore the tiara on ceremonial occasions long before, it wasn't until 12 B.C. that Augustus allowed himself to be officially consecrated as Pontifex Maximus, the 'bridge-maker,' between men and gods, *urbem et orbem*."

Ryan stole a glance at her. He was beginning to see the shape of the jigsaw puzzle Emily's story hinted at and felt the hair on his arms stand up.

"Donning the triple tiara was the final expression of full imperium, assuming the powers of religion as well as state in one man. There was nothing left for Augustus to strive for, except eternal peace on earth—and ascending to join his father Julius in the afterworld. It was the crown he'd been waiting for."

Ryan's voice betrayed disillusionment. "If I didn't know better, I'd say Augustus' tiara is exactly the same as the ones worn by the popes."

"There you go being territorial again," Emily smiled.

"You're not going to tell me Augustus was the first pope," Ryan laughed. "I guess it makes sense that the popes would copy the design from the emperor of Rome."

"He wasn't the first and there's much more to it than that," Emily said enigmatically.

"Your evasiveness is frustrating," Ryan said. "Please just tell me what you're talking about." What they had witnessed in the tunnel, and the peril they were in now, was troubling him to the core. *What is it she knows that she won't share with me?*

There was something deeply disturbing about this section of the huge chamber as well. It was in turmoil, as though packers and movers had fled after a pitch battle, leaving behind a battleground of half-packed and sealed boxes.

Emily ignored his momentary flare of anger, her attention caught by a small red light high up on the wall—the active light on a closed circuit camera. "Oh my God, Ryan. We're being watched." She reached for her slingshot.

Ryan spotted the camera and grabbed her hand. "Forget it," he said. "We've got to find what we've come for and get out!"

"Hold on," she whispered, dropping his hand and darting away. "Look at this," she said, urgency in her voice and suddenly oblivious to the camera. She'd dashed to the other side of the aisle and was facing a wooden crate with four carrying handles. "Whatever's inside must be valuable. Crates with carrying handles mean only one thing: their cargo is delicate and priceless. We use them ourselves at the University when we transport precious artifacts."

Ryan was looking at the Styrofoam peanuts on the floor around the crate. "Whatever's in it," he said quietly, "was freshly packed, like the ones in the Jesuit archives."

Emily was pulling at the crate lid. "It's not sealed," she said. Ryan bent down to help her and together they succeeded in sliding the top along its tracks.

Ryan read the bold cursive on the top—*speco Cumae, v.f.A.*—the same inscription he found on the crate containing Isaac's printouts—when her whisper became an enthusiastic outburst.

"There it is!"

He was at her side in an instant, quick enough to glance at the clear plastic container that held the burnished aureus. Emily lifted it to the light to make sure.

"My coin!" Its brilliant patina momentarily dazzled her until she broke the thrall and came to her senses. "Let's get out of here!" They began to run toward the exit, but stopped short.

Three shadowy figures were blocking the doorway. The hush was broken by a booming voice. "Then we've all found what we've been seeking."

"You two have become an enormous pain in my ass." The voice from the other side of the chamber sounded disembodied. The powerful figure of Ramon Pimental, the Procurator General, glided toward them from the shadows, wearing the velvet slippers of his office that made no sound at all on the polished marble floor. Two darkly-clad men followed at his heels. One man's head was shaven; the other's body was so massive that Pimental appeared miniscule beside him.

Obviously not Jesuits, Ryan thought.

"With the ruckus around the General Meeting, don't you think I have better things to do with my time? Did you really think the keys to the kingdom were left in Bishop Giammo's office by accident?"

"You led us here?" Emily's disbelief was clear in her voice.

"I think you'd call it a last temptation," Pimental said, "one last test of your and Father Ryan's obstructive determination." He turned to Ryan. "We suspected your quest for the truth— despite all warnings to the contrary, and despite your vow of obedience—would end only when you found your way here. You're much like your benefactor, Isaac, you know. True to the principles of our Society, even beyond a fault. As upsetting to Holy Mother Church's purposes as that is, I have to acknowledge that in both of you."

"It's obvious," Ryan retorted, "that Holy Mother Church has been less than holy lately. Your thugs blocking the door affirm that. Was it you who was sponsoring Isaac's continued research?" Ryan tried to restrain the anger in his voice. "Against the Vatican's wishes?"

"It's not that simple," Pimental replied, "but basically, yes. We allowed—we ordered—him to continue. The Roman Curia wanted him to stop. He was too close to proving that the hypothesis he'd given his life to was in fact provable; and the new papal administration wasn't prepared to take a back seat to a revelation that could undermine its authority. It turned out, by happenstance, that this young lady stumbled on the ultimate proof before Isaac himself could put the last pieces of the puzzle together—though her evidence came too late for him to appreciate, or authenticate."

"I'm here," Emily bristled. "You don't have to refer to me in the third person."

Pimental turned to face her. "Your finding the aureus was your destiny. Your phone call to Monsignor Isaac was his fate. And it also made us realize, too late for the good monsignor, that we'd come to an irrevocable parting of the ways with the current Holy Father."

"We? Who is we?" Emily wanted to know.

"He's referring to the Society," Ryan said.

It was as though Pimental hadn't heard them. "I suppose His Holiness never really trusted in the truth, never really believed we would not so much prove it, but be able to demonstrate it convincingly, to the world. So, you see, you arrive at a most auspicious moment. The alert has been sounded, and we are in danger of imminent discovery before we complete today's little project." He broke into a wry smile that revealed a mouthful of perfectly white crowns.

Pimental gestured toward the packing cases, and Ryan realized the little project was removing precious manuscripts and treasures from the Vatican while the Pope was away on a visit to the United States.

"The time for decisive action is at hand," Pimental continued as if to himself. "Nothing can possibly alter the course of events."

"What danger are you talking about?" Ryan asked. He'd noticed that Emily had followed Pimental's words with a look that betrayed her understanding was much greater than his. She was staring at the plastic container that held her aureus.

"Go ahead," Pimental prompted. "Open it. Take a good look. You won't be disappointed. The Society has been seeking the aureus for nearly four hundred years, since Ignatius himself came across evidence of its existence," he added. "Soon it will be time to reveal it to the world. Now that the moment we have waited for is at hand—the moment that will put us in position to restore the true faith—you two loose cannons, like Monsignor Isaac, dare to threaten the careful balance we've struggled for so long to maintain. And you—" as if on cue, Pimental's men lunged forward a step "—have made our task doubly onerous, by destroying Isaac's lifetime's work."

"What are you talking about?" Ryan asked, eyeing the men.

"We know it was you who went to the Pontifical Institute and tried to access his computer files."

Ryan's face was defiant. "I wanted to know why he had to die."

"The files were set to self-erase if anyone tried to access them," Pimental said, the fire in his eyes betraying his anger. He stepped toward Ryan, the unholy pair moving with him. "For an old man he knew much more about the latest technology than by rights he should have." Seeing their frowns, Pimental proceeded. "I know you don't fully understand. How could you? I'm speaking elliptically, in riddles, as I must while we are in this place so vital to the Holy See. I'm afraid you'll have to put the pieces together in the time you have left."

"What do you mean?" Ryan demanded, utterly confused. Then he noticed the look of comprehension on Emily's face.

"It's about Augustus," she said as much as asked, "and Jesus, isn't it?"

The expression on Pimental's face was enough to confirm

her question, only to further mystify Ryan. He knew clearly by now that some kind of close connection between Augustus and Jesus Christ lay concealed at the heart of the maze he'd stumbled into that day in the confessional at Gesù.

Before Ryan could open his mouth with his questions, Pimental reacted to a distant noise. "You were a little later than I expected," he said. "You should begin with the transcripts you borrowed from the Archives." He nodded at Ryan's knapsack. At Ryan's guilty look, he added: "Of course we have every inch of that room under surveillance. You don't think the crate was left in your path by another accident, do you?"

Emily stared at them as though they'd both lost their minds.

"They're all we've found so far of Isaac's work. Please try not to damage them as you read if you don't mind. I won't make that an order," Pimental said pointedly to Ryan. "We've tested your respect for the Vatican. I don't have the heart to test your respect for the Society of Jesus." He moved to the door with his henchmen lumbering behind; then turned to smile at them. "Manage your time. You'll have at least ten minutes," he said, "before you lose consciousness."

Emily sprung toward him, as though to attack but thought better of it. "What are you talking about?"

But Pimental and his men were already standing in front of the doorway that led back to the Archives. "The chamber's atmosphere control recycles every night to protect the contents. Today's recycling begins momentarily, removing all the air within the treasury to prevent toxin accumulation." He wrinkled his nose at the vestigial odor of tobacco that lingered from the errant guards. "Later, purified air is reinserted into the system—alas, a bit late for you both to appreciate." His chuckle was sinister, and yet somehow playful at the same time.

"Congratulations on your work. Until we meet again at

the entrance to hell." He made the sign of the cross, then deftly slid his gold card through the lock mechanism. "*Requiem aeternam dona nobis, Domine,* 'Eternal rest grant unto them, O Lord.'" With that, the grim trio glided through the portal as the gold door shut behind them with a pneumatic hiss that sounded a troubling tone of finality.

They were hermetically sealed into the secret archives. Emily's attempt to use the card key was met only with a flashing red light. She jiggled the door in vain. All thoughts of investigations evaporated. A loud clunk signaled the startup of the extraction fans. In the thick-walled vault, deprived of oxygen, they would face slow and certain suffocation.

XXXIV/34
Lion's Den

Hours earlier, a repentant Lucas Adashek stood before the burnt-out ruins of Bishop Giammo's once-magnificent flat on Via Tritone. Firemen and metropolitan police were fingerprinting the interior of the bishop's car.

Preempted by fate from confronting the man he'd sold his soul to, the shabby diplomat was desperate to pick up the trail of the woman he'd betrayed. When he overheard talk of a Vatican official arriving to retrieve something from the bishop's study, Adashek thought nothing of pulling diplomatic rank—and the offer of Chesterfields—to get an exhausted inspector to admit that a set of important Vatican keys were found to be missing from the bishop's desk.

"How do you know they're missing?" he asked the inspector. The inspector laughingly told him that the Curia official nearly went berserk when the keys weren't found with the cadaver either. "Or if they were, they were melted indistinguishably into the poor man's bones."

"What were the keys to?"

"Judging from the official's reaction, they must have been the fuckin' keys to the Pope's private treasury."

For the longest minutes of their lives, Emily and Ryan had frantically searched the entire perimeter of the chamber to the accompaniment of the high-pitched whine of the extraction system. They discovered another locked gold door at the other side of the chamber that they presumed lead into the Vatican and leaned against it breathless and fatigued.

"I'm certain we'd be better off making our escape through the Vatican. It'll be shorter and safer. If only we could find some kind of lever to pry open the goddamned door." Emily's voice was on the edge of panic.

Almost before she'd finished uttering the words, they lunged for the case containing Augustus' golden scepter. "This is our best chance," Ryan said as he tore open the doors and grabbed the priceless artifact. It was nearly three feet long.

Their limbs were aching from oxygen deprivation, but Ryan managed to wedge the end of the scepter into the thin crack beside the lock mechanism. With both hands on the gold lever, they pulled with all their might. Nothing. They pulled the scepter toward them again, using every ounce of their strength. This time the implement bent like a flimsy spoon. Ryan's disappointed sigh came out as a soft wheeze.

They collapsed to the floor exhausted, their remaining vitality sucked straight into the ducts. The doorframe now sported a small dent—the pitiful extent of their efforts. The golden door itself remained resolutely intact.

Emily's sun-drenched face had turned ashen. She was gasping for air. Beads of perspiration covered her skin as she moved close to Ryan's side.

As suffocation seemed more and more certain, neither could deny the attraction between them and the regrets it left them with though they acknowledged it only with unspoken looks.

"I truly hope we meet on the other side," Ryan said, firmly placing his hand over hers, "though I fear I will be long consigned to the Purgatory reserved for doubters of the faith."

She squeezed his hand. "It's not your faith in God that's failed you. It's your faith in the infallibility of the Holy Roman Catholic Church as an institution worthy of your unquestioned obedience."

"One thing we agreed on," he admitted, his voice growing weaker, "was that organized religion was going to destroy us all."

Emily freed her hand and wiped away a tear. She held up the plastic case containing her aureus, determined to examine the coin with her last breath.

Ryan watched her, his heart filled with a hollowness he had never before experienced. And with that, something gnawed at the fringes of his consciousness.

They were lightheaded and fighting to breathe.

"Oh my God," Ryan rasped. "I just figured it out. Setting the file to self-erase makes no sense unless Isaac made a copy!"

Ryan's revelation hardly registered with Emily, who was now close to unconsciousness. There was a resounding clank as her aureus fell to the marble floor.

But from the direction of the Vatican an alarm chime began ringing and with it what Ryan thought might be the sound of running footsteps.

Ryan moaned and feebly thumped the door.

Emily's eyes flickered open and then closed.

By hook and crook, Luke Adashek, with a Swiss Guard in tow who wasn't quite sure whether he was accompanying or pursuing him, had found his way to the wall that separated the public Vatican treasury from the private. The only entrance from one to the other was a door displaying blinking red lights. At the sound of the moan and the muffled beating on the door, he demanded that the door be opened, but was told by the guard that opening it was impossible while the air was being removed during the recycling process. Only air entering the chamber, when the recycling ended, would trigger the mechanism.

Before the surprised guard could gather his senses, Adashek ran to a red wall box, broke its glass with his elbow, pulled out a fire ax, and, ignoring the solid metal door, hacked into the cedar wall. The guard stopped short in surprise, even as Adashek managed to create a gash in the precious wood paneling large enough to let air whoosh into the near-vacuum on the other side. "Emily! Goddamit, where are you?"

On the other side, the blast of fresh air rushed above them as they lay next to each other. Ryan raised himself on an elbow and gently shook her, hoping the gush of air wasn't too late.

Through her fog, Emily recognized the voice.

Adashek's axe wielding became more frenzied. "Please, Emily, answer me!" he yelled. The guard, recovering, launched himself forward, but not before Adashek took another wild swing.

"We're here, you miserable wretch," she choked out—just as the ax crashed through the wall beside her and a fierce blast of air whistled through the gash.

The lights on the golden door went green, and it opened so abruptly that it slammed into the guard. Stunned by its impact, he slumped to the marble floor. Ryan, pulling the dazed Emily along by the hand, staggered over the crumpled guard and stared at Adashek as though he were Superman incarnate. Emily weakly leaned against Ryan. Both were panting for breath.

"Just get out!" Adashek, breathless, screamed.

"I have to go back for my aureus," she rasped and turned unsteadily to reenter the vault that was now filling with outside air. Ryan caught her as she stumbled toward the door—just as it hissed shut.

"Tell me this nightmare isn't happening!" She pounded the door with her fists as a burst of anger-charged adrenalin surged through her. Sobbing, she collapsed against it and crumpled to the floor.

Adashek pleaded with Ryan. "Get her out of here before we're surrounded by Vigilanza. I'll stay and deal with the consequences. It's the least I can do."

Ryan's heart went out to Emily as he helped her to her feet. "How did you find us?" he breathed to Adashek.

"I went to Giammo's to warn him that Emily would try to retrieve the aureus and that if any harm came to her the entire incident would make international headlines. But then I learned of Giammo's death and that you'd taken the treasury keys. The Vatican authorities were going berserk and it became obvious you were in immediate danger of losing your lives," he spewed out the words as she glared at him. "I may be a thief, but I couldn't live with myself being an accessory to murder."

Adashek looked around. "Get out of here. Now. I'll delay the guards."

Ryan grabbed Emily's arm. She struggled to free herself, but stopped at the sound of footsteps approaching from inside the vault.

"Thank you," Ryan responded. "We owe you."

"Owe you? Why don't you come with us so I can strangle you myself?" Emily's voice rose, her ire flaring.

"These people are ruthless—they'll stop at nothing, including murder. Go!"

Now they could hear the guards clambering through hallways from all directions.

Adashek tossed Ryan a set of keys. "My rented BMW is parked on Via Pfeiffer off Borgo Santo Spirito."

Ryan nodded. He knew the street.

Alarms were echoing in their ears as Ryan and Emily, leaving Adashek behind, staggered through the public treasury to the exit that looked least trafficked.

To Ryan's surprise, the door opened onto a corridor he recognized as the hall leading to Pimental's Vatican office. A private tour group was leaving the Museum and moving toward the exit doors on Viale Vaticano. "Thank God we're incognito," Emily said, urging Ryan toward the mostly American tourists. "We'll blend right in."

Ryan started to follow her lead, but then pulled back. "This exit is too obvious. They'll be waiting for us," he warned. He remembered the door at the far end of the hall, through which he'd left the unpleasant interview with the Procurator General to await Giammo in the Belvedere courtyard.

As they rushed down the dimly-lit steps they passed the portal marked *Tesoro,* "Treasury," and Ryan understood that the little door had been Bishop Giammo's private gateway to the Vatican secret treasury, the Jesuit Archives, the catacombs, and the bank across from the Pantheon.

They ran right by it, continuing down the dark stairs.

Under the trellis outside, Ryan pulled his Roman collar from the knapsack and underwent a reverse transformation. Handing Emily the backpack and asking her to follow a few steps behind him, Father Ryan braved the Belvedere Courtyard. Just as he'd hoped, the guards were preoccupied with the alarms. They were hunting for the renegade diplomat, not for a priest.

"What's going on?" he asked one of them.

"Father, you should be leaving now. The Museum is closing. *Subito,*" he added, "Immediately."

Ryan nodded at him, flashed his Vatican identification badge, and gestured for Emily to catch up. "The tour is over," he said loud enough for the guard to hear. "We have to leave."

The guard pointed toward the nearest private exit and hurried off in pursuit of bigger fish.

In the crush and confusion of hundreds leaving the compound, they managed to slip easily into the back streets leading toward Via Pfeiffer. The sirens from arriving Italian police, *carabinieri,* echoed along Via della Conciliazione as they clicked the key chain to identify the refuge of Adashek's rented BMW.

"I can't believe we went through all that and came out without the aureus," Emily said.

"We came out with our lives. At least for now."

"Shall we hide out in the hotel?"

"No. Whatever's going on, they'll have a dragnet out for us, official or unofficial. The desk has my passport information. It's time to get to the heart of it. I want to know why my superiors are trying so hard to kill me—both of us. And, on what I thought was my last breath, I think I realized where to find the answer."

"What do you mean?"

This time it was Ryan's expression that was enigmatic. "The memory, the ashes," he said.

XXXV/35
Pulvis es
Thou art dust

W hen Ryan started the BMW's ignition, it was all too
apparent that he knew little or nothing about driving a
manual shift.

"Let me," Emily said, pushing him into the passenger's
seat. "I was raised driving sticks. Besides, now you *have* to tell
me where we're going." She operated the gears as though she
were born to it, and angrily pulled out of the parallel space in
which Adashek had parked his rental car, managing to bang
both the back and front bumpers for good measure.

Ryan saw she'd done it on purpose, and laughed, then
sobered. "We're paying a visit to the Gesù," he said.

"Do we have time for visits?" she asked, checking the
rearview mirror. "My vote is that we need to go into hiding
until we figure out how to get the aureus back."

"I think I know where Monsignor Isaac's research is,"
Ryan answered. "It's clear that they only found a part of it—
the pages I borrowed from the Archives. If we find his backup,
we hold the entire secret in our hands."

"All I want is my aureus," she said, her brow wrinkled.
They had reached the end of Via della Conciliazione. "Which
way?"

He gave her directions, as best he, an inveterate pedestrian,
could, to the Jesuit mother church he had always approached
on foot.

At one point, Ryan grabbed her shoulder. "It's a red light!" he shouted. "Stop!"

"What? And get us killed?" Emily continued through the intersection amidst the crush of cars that hadn't even slowed down at the signal. "Do as the Romans do," she said.

Ryan's head was turned to see if they were being followed.

"Don't worry," she said. "I don't think they arrest people for going through lights here."

"That's not what I'm worried about. I'm just hoping we're not being tailed. Somehow it seems all too easy that we got away."

"Easy? Are you joking? Luke axed a hole in a Vatican wall and set off every alarm in the kingdom! And I left my aureus behind! Where's the easy?"

But Ryan was thinking, and couldn't dismiss the sense that they were far from being in the clear. "We just have to check out my hunch. It's what Monsignor Isaac would have wanted us to do."

"So what's the hunch? I have a right to know."

"If I told you, and I was wrong, you'll never stop laughing at me," he said, echoing her words. "Trust me."

Emily's response was to accelerate into another pack of vehicles, slip around in front of a delivery van, then take a sudden right into an alley that connected with the Piazza del Gesù. "You've got five minutes," she said, as she pulled the BMW up in front of the church.

Ryan quickly found his way to the familiar door. Within a few moments he was inside the sacristy, where solemn mahogany cabinets and chests of drawers harbored the vestments and sacred implements of the Catholic liturgy. Ignoring the drawers that held the variously colored stoles he normally donned to begin his priestly duties, he headed for the cabinet where he knew the chalices, altar bells, and patens were stored.

He wasn't sure what he was looking for. Monsignor Isaac died on Ash Wednesday, just after receiving the Holy Ashes that were the devout Catholic's annual reminder of mortality: *Memento, homo, pulvis es et in pulverem reverteris*, "Remember, man, that dust thou art and unto dust thou shalt return."

Monsignor Isaac's last words were that Father Ryan should somehow connect his memory with the ashes of Jasius in the Gesù. What could that mean?

The ashes the celebrant employed for this annual ritual were smudged with his thumb into the shape of the cross onto the forehead of each member of the congregation, who would wear them in the outside world in witness to his pride in being Catholic.

The ceremonial ashes were created by the burning of palm leaves used on the previous year's Palm Sunday, the Sunday before Easter to celebrate the imminent triumph of the redeemer—of the god-man who would die, on Good Friday, for the sins of humanity and rise from the dead on Easter Sunday. Some of the ashes were retained from year to year to symbolize the eternal continuity of the liturgy.

Ryan retrieved the key to the mahogany cabinet from the cooler that held the sacramental wine. The cabinet's top shelf was packed tight with chalices, used to hold the wine during the celebration of the Mass.

The bottom shelf displayed an assortment of containers, including altar bells and censers but also other implements Ryan didn't recognize. On his knees to inspect them one by one, he was about to admit the absurdity of his hunch when his heart suddenly picked up a beat as he was lifting the very last ciborium on the bottom shelf. The other heavy goblets had each exhibited a familiar heft from the weight of the unconsecrated hosts they held. This last one was so light it nearly flew out of his grasp as he lifted it. The unexpected motion knocked the vessel's top off, and it jangled to the floor with a clang that resonated throughout the wooden sacristy.

And revealed its contents: last year's held-over ashes.

Ryan paused to listen in case the clang of the lid on the marble floor would lead to his being discovered. But no one came.

He carefully set the ciborium on the top of the adjacent garment chest. The goblet contained only an inch or so of last year's ashes, the rest having been disbursed to the foreheads of the faithful. Feeling more than a little silly, Ryan stuck his finger into the black powder and poked around.

Then he felt it.

Something strange about the bottom of the metal vessel. It moved at his touch.

It wasn't the bottom of the ciborium that was moving, but something else. Ryan gingerly lifted out a small glassine envelope that was hidden beneath the ashes.

It appeared to be more ashes, but these were much lighter in color and contained—small pieces—of bone?

He noticed the tiny slip of paper taped to the envelope, bearing a few words written in cursive: "Ashes of Jasius Augustus." There could be no doubt it was Monsignor Isaac's handwriting.

"Memory in the ashes of Jasius." Isaac's last words flashed through Ryan's mind. *So, he did manage to find them...* There was no time to pause and consider the significance of what he was holding in his hands. He felt around inside the envelope until his fingers made contact with something small and hard. His fingernail caught its edge, and retrieved it through the dust.

When he carefully brushed the ashes off, Ryan recognized what he had found. It was a flash-drive, the kind of portable memory stick for computers that people carried around on their key chains, in their cameras, or even on their Swiss Army knives. The adrenalin rushed through his veins again as he realized he was holding, in its own exquisitely up-to-date vessel, the magnum opus of Monsignor Oscar Isaac.

XXXVI/36
Ash Wednesday

The news Monsignor Isaac had just received from the Procurator General, Ramon Pimental, was certainly the anomaly in today's schedule. It was not an everyday event to be told that Holy Mother Church considered its faithful servant to be imminently dispensable, and may have ordered a hit on you. Nor was it hum-drum news that the Society of Jesus would be providing him with clerical bodyguards starting first thing tomorrow morning.

It was the latter news that bothered him more than the former. Isaac valued his privacy, not because he didn't enjoy human interaction but because solitude was the only state of being in which his thinking remained clear. He'd much rather be working away, privately, on his all-consuming project.

In any case he had the rest of this memorable day to himself. The new "protective regime" would not commence until tomorrow morning when his guards would begin shadowing him everywhere he went and every moment of his days and nights.

Today was still his to spend as he alone willed to spend it. As Monsignor Isaac completed his visit to the desktop in his book-lined cubicle at the Pontifical Institute, he'd already decided how he would fill the rest of his last twenty-four hours as a free man.

He would do exactly as he had done on Ash Wednesday for the past thirty years. He would receive the ritual ashes at

Gesù. Then he would enjoy his favorite meal of succulent *carciofi alla romana* and *funghi trifolati* at his favorite trattoria.

His love for fine dining baffled those who knew him, if only because his willowy frame showed no sign of it.

Outside the Pontifical Institute, a glance at the darkening sky led him to open his umbrella and shift the books he'd chosen for his post-prandial studies to his left hand. He thanked the Lord his job was not to save the world, or even to understand it; his job was only to seek the truth. Despite the warning from Pimental, Isaac would, as much as humanly possible, continue to go about his destined work. In a world rife with insanity, what else should a logical man do?

Well, he could take precautions, Isaac thought to himself. Which is why he had rigged the desktop computer. He had no idea what was going on in the Vatican, but his instincts told him it wasn't as simple as the Procurator General had led him to believe. Isaac understood why His Holiness might feel threatened by the results of his research.

He also understood why the Society would tell him to continue his work and assure him of both financial support and physical protection.

The two powers, Holy Mother Church and Society of Jesus, were often at odds, and it made sense that they would be on the momentous matter raised by the revelation his finished narrative would support. He didn't for a moment believe that Pimental or the Society of Jesus cared one whit for his personal safety. It wasn't about *him,* but about ecclesiastical forces swirling high above his head.

He had waited long enough for the American, Father Ryan McKeown, to reach conclusions about the life of Jesus that would lead him back to request the mentorship he'd professed to desire. Now that he had the ashes, Isaac was contemplating how best to arrange a clandestine meeting with young Ryan. The thought of his research falling into the wrong hands and, God forbid, perishing, sent a chill down Isaac's spine that had nothing to do with the rain that was now pouring in abundance from the Roman sky.

If the wrong eyes attempted to read his computer files, they would be disappointed.

As little as he knew the American priest, his instincts told him that Ryan would stop at nothing to find the truth. Which, indeed, had been the reason he'd arranged for the younger colleague to study in Rome.

Despite the rain, the main doors of the Gesù remained wide open, beckoning the faithful, however few and far between they were these days.

Monsignor Isaac would take refuge with the sparse congregation and receive the blessed ashes that reminded all the devout of their short time on this good earth.

After the brief ceremony he would say his office in the emptying church. And when he was certain the sacristy was empty as well, he would remove the flash-drive from the pocket of his cassock and conceal it where his unknown enemies could not possibly find it until a year had gone by and it was time to distribute the palm ashes again. If they found it at all, they would, of course, think his hiding place was comical. Then they would remember that an eccentric sense of humor had long been Isaac's signature.

XXXVII/37
L'Autostrada del Sole

Emily and Ryan were racing down the "Motorway of the Sun," marked on maps as the A-1, and barely took notice of the volcanic mountains, hillside castles, ancient vineyards, olive orchards, and three thousand years of history along the way.

Emily liked the speed. Even traveling at 140 kilometers per hour, cars were whizzing by and leaving them far behind.

They had remained silent until they were well away from the *Centro Antico,* heading toward the cultural wasteland that lined the beltway surrounding the greater metropolis that was modern Rome. Emily had been duly impressed by Ryan's discovery, and pointed out that hiding the memory stick in the glassine envelope of enigmatic ashes was characteristic of Isaac's unfathomable sense of humor.

Ryan's attention was divided between keeping an eye on the GPS they'd just discovered on the BMW's dash so they wouldn't make a wrong turn, and thinking about Isaac and what he'd gotten them into. "We need to stop," he said, indicating a nondescript Agip gas station at a nondescript intersection of two nondescript suburban *viali.*

Emily looked at the gauge. "The tank's nearly full," she said. Then she saw what had caught his attention.

The Agip offered a cafeteria—and "Wi-Fi."

"I need to make sure this is what we think it is," Ryan said simply. "Park. We'll get something to eat." He brandished the flash drive. "We need to figure out what Isaac was really up to so we can get ourselves off this rollercoaster ride."

While Emily purchased food for the road, Ryan managed to load the Gesù flash drive into the station's one available desktop computer. "Yes!" he mouthed to her as she approached with the provisions.

Reading over his shoulder as he scanned through the contents of the drive, her eyes filled with tears as she read the title of Isaac's thesis, *Messiah Matrix*. It was now painfully obvious that Isaac's unraveling the mystery at the heart of Christianity represented too great a threat to the Vatican Curia.

Mindful of time, they slowed down their reading only enough to confirm that Isaac believed the Apostle Paul was not a Roman soldier at all, as tradition had it, but Greek. "And not just any Greek," Emily commented. "That's why the DNA test was so important."

Isaac wrote that he believed Paul might have been, in actuality, a well-known Neo-Pythagorean philosopher, Apollonius of Samos who taught in Rome at the time of Augustus and was a frequent guest to the emperor's home on the Palatine Hill.

"Where was he going with this?" Ryan thought aloud, pulling his attention away from the screen. "I'm confused."

"Page down," Emily said.

Both Paul and the Pythagorean Apollonius traveled from Ephesus to Corinth to Rome, both preached asceticism in food and drink—both were vegetarians; both insisted that the highest lifestyle was that of the single person pursuing only enlightenment and awakening of the god within. Both were credited with miracles.

"Isaac was identifying them one by one, that's it!" The excitement in Emily's voice surprised even herself.

"Identifying who?" Ryan said.

"The Apostles." She looked at him. "He was determined to buttress his theory by figuring out the identity of each of the original twelve Apostles—and of Paul, who came along after—in terms of the Augustan cult. It's clear from what he says here that he was certain Augustus had designated a dozen of his pontiffs as *Augustales,* to spread the rubrics of his cult throughout the empire. They, in turn, appointed successors."

The look on Ryan's face showed that he was forcing himself to acknowledge what Emily was saying, what Isaac was up to, where all this was leading. He'd read somewhere that all mythified leaders had twelve followers, going back to basic sun god worship, the twelve rowers of the boat of Ra, and the houses of the zodiac. And even why there are twelve members of the jury. "You're talking about the relationship between Augustus and Jesus again, is that it?"

Emily nodded.

"Then there's no other way. We have to proceed to Cumae," he said, looking down at the text before him.

"What did you find?"

"V.f.a.," Ryan said. "The initials on all the crates, along with *speco Cumae.* 'To the Cumaean cave.'"

"That's where they're taking my aureus!"

"Among other things," Ryan agreed.

"And what is v.f.a.?"

He pointed at the header on the screen: *"Vera fides Augusti,* "The true faith of Augustus."

Emily's face lit up.

"So the cult of Augustus, reinstated by Constantine, is somehow alive today? In the Roman Catholic Church." Ryan answered his own question, staring out the window as they reached the far suburbs of Rome.

"Yes," Emily said. "The Roman empire survived through its founder's mythology."

Ryan spotted a sign for the A-1. "Up ahead," he said. "Right lane."

Emily down-shifted for the turn, and before he knew it they were heading south toward Napoli.

"Yes, I'm sure that's it," she finally answered. "I just need to understand the dynamics of it all. Not to mention how we ended up caught between the Jesuits and the Holy See."

"Well, it certainly explains the first popes' embracing the ancient title Pontifex Maximus—not to mention the pontiff's triple crown or the continued use of Latin even in the Vatican ATMs. If this mysterious relationship between Jesus and Augustus is true, as Isaac believed, why doesn't everyone know it? Why did this knowledge go underground?"

Emily's look showed she'd asked herself—or Monsignor Isaac—the same questions. "To begin with," she finally said, "other emperors may have wanted that knowledge forgotten or at least ignored."

"Why?"

"Because *they* themselves wanted to be worshipped as gods. So they tried to eradicate not just 'Christians,' as we now call them, but all cults that weren't directly associated with their own honor. It could be that simple."

Again they drove in silence. Finally, somewhere north of Naples, they approached an overpass hosting another AGIP rest stop cafeteria, this one straddling both sides of the highway. "Let's pull in here," Ryan said, studying the GPS screen. "We'll need a good map. The GPS confirms what I learned researching Cumae when I was trying to determine why he was down there so often. It's good that Isaac goes into so much detail about the location. It's not easy to find. Way off the beaten path."

"You can't get there from here?" Emily smiled, as she down-shifted and pulled off the road.

"Doesn't even look like you can get there from there."

"Do you remember the last words we heard before Pimental slammed the door to the vault behind him?" Ryan asked her. It was less than a half hour later as they left the rest stop and were walking back to the parked BMW. Ryan was carrying a plastic bag containing wine and several maps they found in the Auto-Stop's magazine section.

"Something about meeting us at the gate of hell?" Emily tried to remember the exact words.

Ryan pushed the unlock button. "That's what Virgil called the Sibyl's cave at Cumae," he said.

Emily frowned. "I don't get it," she said. "Why were they shipping everything there?"

"Whether Pimental is expecting us or not, I have a feeling we'd have ended up there one way or another," was his only answer. "They were probably planning to ship us along with the crates. Why didn't you tell me what Monsignor Isaac's theory was all about earlier?"

"We only met three days ago, remember?" she teased. She saw that he was waiting for her to answer his question. "Very simple," she sighed. "Until I had proof to show you—and the world—how could I possibly tell you? It's too preposterous. You wouldn't have believed me."

Ryan took a deep breath. "Monsignor Isaac and Bishop

Giammo have been murdered, and you and I may have narrowly missed joining them on the other side. At this point I'm prepared to believe almost anything."

As Emily drove toward the distant mountains, Ryan pored over the maps and travel guides. "It's all very vague here," he commented, after checking the third guidebook. "No clear directions. No time-of-year suggestions. No schedule of opening and closing times. Virgil was clearer about the layout of the cave than Michelin is."

"Looks like we'll just have to follow our noses," Emily said.

"Yeah. Look where that's gotten us so far."

XXXVIII/38
Hell on Earth

It wasn't just Virgil who identified The Bay of Naples as hell on earth. The infernal reputation of the lowlands between Vesuvius and Solfatara and the Bay of Naples went back as far as the Greek mariners who first sailed into, then occupied the area. Known originally as the Phlegraean Fields, the area was long famous for being covered alternately with low-hanging clouds and sulfuric vapors rising from vents in the volcanic earth.

Not until emperors like Tiberius and Hadrian built villas throughout the sweep of its magnificent vistas from Vesuvius to Sorrento to the islands of Capri and Ischia—did the area become a holiday destination for wealthy tourists, ancient and present day. Aside from the sheer beauty of the view, the greatest attraction was the volcanic thermal springs. Heedless of uprooting angry gods, the domesticated emperors found cures for their venereal ailments in the mud, sulfuric waters, and steam baths of the area. Two *stufe,* one known as Purgatory and the other as Hell, were used as natural saunas for the inhalation of these sulfurous vapors, which were considered to be specifically beneficial for respiratory illnesses.

Ryan, deeply submerged in his thoughts, couldn't appreciate the natural wonders of the area. He was disoriented by the Augustan theory as presented by Isaac's research and Emily's overview. He couldn't make sense of the Paul/Apollonius of Samos parallel, for example. How could "the founding father of the Christian church," as St. Paul was often called, have actually been a pagan philosopher in attendance upon an emperor of Rome? None of it made sense, but only echoed the doubts surrounding his studies of the early sacred texts.

Of course he now understood why Monsignor Isaac was so intent on checking the DNA of "St. Paul's" remains, and also why he was ordered by the Vatican to cease and desist. Some of what Pimental said was falling into place. The Vatican would never want any piece of such research to reach the public eye. The whole monolith of the past two thousand years of sanctioned belief would begin to crumble stone by stone, pebble by pebble if Jesus were somehow shown to be a mythical persona of Augustus. Or if the twelve apostles were nothing more than a new iteration of the universally-worshiped zodiac.

Ryan was so lost in thought by the time they'd reached the coastal foothills northwest of Naples that they almost missed their turnoff. Fortunately Emily had her eye on the GPS screen. "Isn't this where we get off?" she asked as they zoomed past a sign for "Pozzuoli."

"Yes. Exit here." Ryan brought his mind back to the present. "I'm sorry. I was thinking."

"Aureus for your thoughts," she quipped.

From the off ramp they turned right toward the Bay of Naples, navigating by map and GPS from one obscure byway to another until they were on SS162 heading for Varcaturo and Cuma. Somehow they managed to take a spur that linked them to the ancient Via Domitiana and followed it along breathtaking vistas of the Bay studded with sailboats and realized they'd gone the wrong way again. Emily made a U-turn, and they doubled back to Via Ariete and took the tiny road seaward. "Here!" Ryan said, as they reached a side road that led to the south, away from the red-tile-roofed houses that dotted the coastal plane. After only a few hundred yards, the pavement gave way to a gravel road full of nasty ruts.

"You were right. Not very tourist-friendly," Emily commented, flinching as the right wheel encountered the first hole. She down-shifted the BMW.

The narrow road began to descend toward the distant sea and after only a kilometer or so gave way to dirt—a rutted country road snaking its way between steepening cliffs on one side and dark forest on the other.

"Are we sure this is right?" Emily checked the GPS. Its arrow was dancing like a spinning top, crazily changing directions as she maneuvered from one curve to another. There was no road name displayed beneath the arrow.

Ryan looked up from the best map. "Would you call this a dotted line? Because that's what I'm reading here."

She grunted as the left tires lurched through another pothole. "Feels like a dotted line to me."

"Whoa. I just saw the fine print. 'Four-wheel drive recommended.' Didn't notice it before."

"I'm used to driving jeeps through trackless desert. We'll be fine. But with any luck at all Luke will have a lot of explaining to do when he returns his rental car with ruined tires and suspension."

Ryan looked up from the map and laughed.

Emily started to laugh too but as they rounded yet another steep hairpin turn she slammed the brakes on. The BMW skidded on the loose surface and Ryan was thrown forward, his head hitting the sun visor as the car crunched to a stop. Then he saw the wiry countryman standing directly in their path staring at them as though they'd just landed from Mars.

The man, who looked to be in his thirties, carried a lamb over his shoulders. He was roughly garbed like shepherds portrayed in landscape paintings through the centuries. The lamb was fast asleep, oblivious to the fact that the BMW had missed hitting them by inches. "He came out of nowhere," she apologized as Ryan rubbed his forehead. "Are you okay?"

"I'm fine," he said. "Just glad I was wearing my seatbelt."

The shepherd meanwhile stood at Ryan's window. Ryan pushed the button to roll it down. "*Va bene?*" he asked. *"Fatto malo?"*

The shepherd released a spate of Italian so distorted by his country dialect that they could make out barely the gist of it: assuring them that he wasn't hurt, thank you; was happy they weren't either; and was mightily curious about what the two of them thought they were doing in this off-the-beaten-path.

Ryan explained they were heading for the cave at Cumae, but it took several attempts to get his message across. Either the man was dense, had no idea what Ryan was talking about, or was unable to believe his ears.

"*E questa la dritta via?*" Ryan heard his own words and recognized that he was quoting the opening lines of Dante's *Inferno:*

> *Nel mezzo del camin della nostra vita*
> *Mi ritrovai in una selva oscura*
> *Perche la dritta via era smarrita.*

> In the middle of the path of my life
> I found myself in dark woods
> Because the right path was lost.

"Did you ask him if we can get there from here?" Emily's voice took on the tone that every woman's voice took on when the man she's with is doing a botched job of asking for directions.

The *paisano,* meanwhile, had calmed down, but was still looking at them earnestly and shaking his head.

"He's saying the road used to go there, but it's too dangerous to use anymore. He's insisting we turn back."

"Well, that's par for the course." Emily put the car into gear and began to inch forward, even though the terrain ahead looked like it had been left behind two centuries ago.

The shepherd became even more agitated. "You cannot go there," he called after them. "It is closed."

"Now he speaks English?" Ryan looked back as the BMW gained speed.

The shepherd stood stock still in the road, watching them intently.

Emily kept it under twenty, sometimes slowing to a crawl as she navigated the deteriorating road.

"Why is everyone we run into trying to stop us?" Ryan realized he'd spoken his thought out loud. He'd been inspired by his Jesuit mentors to believe that the pursuit of truth was the highest calling of the intellect. He recognized that Emily's attitude and training were identical. He'd already become accustomed to thinking out loud with this fiery, attractive woman who invested her entire life in uncovering the secrets of the past—their destinies growing ever more closely intertwined in pursuit of the mystery that had brought them together.

The road had narrowed even further and was now winding downward at a progressively steep angle. Ryan's train of thought was derailed by Emily's shout.

"Oh my God, we're slipping!"

They'd reached the onset of another hairpin curve and Emily was riding the pedal as they approached it. The tires weren't holding on the thick layer of loose gravel.

"Pull the wheel to the right!" Ryan shouted.

"What do you think I'm doing!" Emily fought to control the wheel, but the BMW had consigned itself to obeying the laws of gravity and was heading not into the curve but toward the precipice on the far side of the road. They were out of control and heading straight for the drop-off, Emily vainly pumping the brakes and cursing while the sickening sound of the tires told them they weren't going to stop. Fortunately or not, there was no abutment and they were soon rushing down a bramble-studded rocky slope—Emily still fighting to maintain some semblance of guidance even though their destiny seemed to be a group of jagged rocks on the shore below. She swerved to avoid a boulder.

A prayer involuntarily slipped from Ryan's lips. "God save us…"

"Forget God!" Emily yelled. "Help me with this wheel! The oleander bush!"

Ryan leaned over and helped her yank the wheel to the right, with a combined final exercise of sheer muscular determination, they managed to correct the car's course away from the rocks. The BMW ploughed straight into the massive bush and slammed to an abrupt stop. Both airbags exploded. Emily and Ryan looked at each other like pierced bugs perched unexpectedly on separate pincushions.

"Are you okay?" she asked, struggling to breathe beneath the press of the bag.

Ryan moved his mouth away from the bag that was still squashing against his head. "Too early to tell," he said. "How are you?"

She was wriggling out from under the bag, jamming her shoulder against the door to force it open. She managed to get out, shook herself to check for broken bones, then made her way to the other side and tugged against the passenger door.

"It's locked," Ryan finally said. "Let me open it." He moved his right arm beneath the bag, found a button, and pushed. It wasn't the door lock; it was the passenger window. Emily reached over it and pulled at the lock manually. Together they forced the door open. She helped him exit by pushing the bag toward the cracked window. It was a clumsy exit, and they suddenly found themselves entangled, on the ground, their faces mere inches apart, Ryan's weight pressing down on Emily.

Ryan breathed heavily, unsure of what to say. He was feeling things he hadn't felt for years, things he wasn't supposed to be feeling.

"Are you coming on to me, Father McKeown?" Emily finally teased, to break the tension.

"Pardon me." Eyes askance, he climbed off her hurriedly, careful to keep his hands away from private areas of her body. She took the hand he offered, and they were on their feet, studying each other for injuries.

"Well, that happened," Emily laughed.

"I think we're okay," Ryan said awkwardly. "Though your friend's car is a mess." The BMW's windshield was shattered. But its steely strength had saved their lives.

"Serves the bastard right. What are you doing?" Emily asked.

Ryan was reaching back into the car. "Retrieving our maps, and the knapsack. We'll continue on foot."

But the sky had other plans. In the few moments it had taken for them to leave the road and careen down the hill, a thunderhead had descended on the little canyon like a dark shadow. Lightning struck a few feet up the slope. "When it rains it pours." Emily hugged herself against the sudden chill. The thunder carried with it the sharp scent of ozone. The rumbling accelerated to such a harsh crack she covered her ears.

"Get in." Ryan was already pulling the back door open. She climbed in, and reached back for his hand to pull him in after her. Despite the claustrophobia of the back seat—with the air bags forming a virtual wall in front—they were grateful for the shelter. The rain pounded on the roof of the car, the heavy thunder and lightning continuing for at least an hour before the storm settled into a more sustainable siege of steady rain and a breeze that swayed the car gently.

Once they'd adjusted themselves so they were comfortably apart, Emily dug into the bottom of the knapsack to retrieve the half bottle of wine they'd purchased at the auto-stop, "in case we're in need of medication." Her Swiss Army knife was equipped with a corkscrew. The medication was welcome, though they had to take turns sipping from the bottle.

Ryan loved the rain, loved hearing it on the roof of the car, watching it sweep the sides and dance with the mist, the cracks in the windshield just big enough to allow the smell of ozone—all of which was accentuated perfectly by the robust red wine, and the calm excitement of simply being with this remarkable woman.

And the rain showed no sign of abating.

By the time they'd finished the bottle and eaten some biscotti, the sun had already set. The weariness of their adventures weighed on their shoulders and Emily laid her head back on the well-upholstered seat. Before she could say a word, her eyes had closed and she was breathing deeply. Ryan watched her sleeping, her face relaxing from its intensity, and recognized this as one of the most unforgettable moments of his life. His last memory, before sleep worked its contagious magic on him, was that he could be content forever watching this woman sleeping in the rain. If this was the gate of hell Pimental was talking about, maybe heaven was overrated.

XXXIX/39

Introibo ad Altare Dei
I shall go unto the altar of God

They were awakened rudely and instantly by the deep chopping sound they both mistook for the return of the thunderstorm. But the sun was shining brightly. Emily's head had somehow managed to be resting on Ryan's shoulder. She sat up, her face flushing. Ryan hoped she wouldn't notice his body's reaction to her proximity and turned to roll down his window. Realizing that wouldn't work with the ignition off, he opened the door instead—in time to see the black helicopter throbbing directly overhead.

Emily scrambled out of the car behind him. "Think they're after us?"

His attention had been caught by the insignia on the craft's fuselage, that of the Society of Jesus: IHS. Her question didn't seem that off the mark. But as the chopper passed above them Ryan caught a glimpse of the pilot, whose eyes were intent on the horizon as he leaned on the joystick in a gradual decrease of altitude that was clearly unrelated to their camouflaged refuge among the oleanders. "I don't think they saw us," he said. "They must be going to the cave."

They'd wolfed down the last of the espresso and biscotti and were heading on foot in the wake of the black chopper. As they trudged along the road, now made doubly treacherous by mud and water-filled holes of indeterminate depth, they couldn't help but pause from time to time to take in the magnificent early morning vista of mist rolling off the water and toward the slopes of the volcanic mountains behind them. The air was tinged with a slight smell of sulfur and pine, and they realized some of the mist was sulfuric fumes.

With the uncertainty of every step, it felt natural that they were holding hands. Both were painfully aware of the charge between them but neither wanted to let go.

As they walked in silence for the next half-hour, Emily was mentally cursing her luck: *why did the most attractive, intriguing man she had ever met have to be utterly off-limits?*

Ryan, meanwhile, found himself in a state of inner turmoil. He had questioned many aspects of his self-willed vocation before, but never so strongly, and never the vow of chastity. Now every nerve in his body was tingling. He felt like he was in high school again, holding his dad's Riviera's door open for Carrie Catherine.

At one point, when a misstep caused them to stumble, bringing their bodies together, both somehow managed to recover and draw back—and continue without further contact.

The view of the Bay of Naples, with the sun now gleaming triumphant on the waves and the islands of Ischia and Capri in the distance, struck them to the heart. The grassy meadow was lined with ancient cypress trees. Almost like an apparition from the past, a bent-over figure in white emerged from the stately trees and headed in their direction.

"Maybe this is our Sibyl," Ryan said. "The one who asked to live forever, but forgot to ask that she not grow old?"

The ancient woman, limping along steadily with a gnarled walking stick, was within hailing distance now, but showed no signs of seeing them.

"Maybe she's blind," Ryan said.

As though she heard his words the woman began to speak in a voice hoarse as though from long disuse. The sound resonated in the little hollow between the cypress rows—and at first they couldn't understand a word she said.

"It must be Neapolitan, the old dialect." Emily knew that only a master linguistic historian could trace some of the older dialects to the Florentine-derived Italian that had been the primary linguistic currency in Italy since Dante polished it to its height of perfection.

"No, it's some kind of Greek!" Ryan recognized a few of the words, and remembered that the Greeks had conquered this part of Italy long before the city of Rome had been founded. "What I can make out sounds a lot like the Homeric dialect."

The woman was abreast of them now. She was entirely cloaked in white from head to toe, but enough of her face was visible for them to see a myriad of wrinkles around jet black eyes that had lost none of their intensity. She stopped and gave them a piercing look, then from the depths of her throat rattled out a few harsh words that almost seemed to rhyme.

"I have no idea what she's saying, but she sounds pissed," Emily remarked dryly.

"She's saying, 'If you know where you're going, why are you going there?' Somehow I got that very clearly."

The woman watched them talking, then in a sudden gesture that so surprised them they had no time to react, reached out with her ancient stick and whacked both of them on the shoulder, first Emily, then Ryan, croaking out another phrase. Then she turned and continued her walk up the road whence they'd come.

"What on earth was that?"

"Nonsense," Ryan said. "It sounded like, 'Avoid the fire or find the ice.'" He laughed, "Or, 'Find the river of ice.' I'm not quite sure."

They turned to watch her move away, mud clinging to the hem of her gown. She looked back at them again, and cried out, as Ryan translated, "Take the golden branch."

"What does that mean?" Emily asked.

"Probably nothing," Ryan replied. "But it sounds vaguely familiar."

"Maybe she's just nuts," Emily said.

A few moments later, the woman disappeared into the oak trees around the hairpin curve. She vanished like a mirage. *Did we actually see her,* Ryan thought, *or are we now hallucinating together? But that whack on the shoulder was no hallucination.*

Lost in thought, they continued down the road, which was now bordered with an ancient stone wall. The dirt gave way to the kind of pavement stones Ryan remembered seeing on the Appian Way outside Rome—deeply rutted by iron-wheeled wagons and chariots that had passed this way more than two thousand years ago.

He was resisting the temptation to reach for her hand again. He definitely had celibacy issues to deal with—and a pressing mystery to unravel that seemed intrinsically connected with the very foundation of his priesthood. His perplexing feelings for this woman must take a firm back seat.

They had progressed along the walled road only a hundred yards or so when it turned to reveal another postcard-perfect vista, this time of the ruins of Cumae against the backdrop of the wine-dark sea: the crumbled Greek temple complex long ago converted into a basilica and a Christian church; the formal processional leading up to the ancient ruins; and the entrance to the cave itself below the acropolis on a conical-shaped hill nearly obscured by overhanging vegetation. The processional was made of giant flagstones interspersed with hardy clumps of grass that had filled in where centuries had stolen stones away for more mundane purposes. They stood in silence, inhaled the crisp morning air, and knew that they would never forget the view before them.

"There it is," Ryan said. Below them was the formal entrance to the Sibyl's cave.

The moment was interrupted by the urgent throb of rotors. Neither had noticed the dark shadow of the Jesuit helicopter, which was now rising from behind the remains of the temple of Apollo. It reached altitude, then abruptly turned northeast, gained speed, and within minutes disappeared beyond the horizon.

XL/40
Cerberus

Looking to make sure no one was around to see them, they descended the broken processional staircase until they reached the formal apron in front of the cave's entrance. At first they didn't notice the elderly guard, who was seated to one side of the closed door that led to the cave. The man was fast asleep. Emily grabbed Ryan's arm, and lifted her finger for silence.

But the black-suited guard's eyes flickered open. He looked startled, then embarrassed, then as belligerent as a Rottweiler appraising the two bedraggled arrivals. *"Che cosa state facendo qui?"* he asked. "What are you doing here?" he barked the question. *"La cava é chiusa."* The cave is closed. He stood to block the entry, his hand reaching toward his sidearm as he bellowed that the site had been closed to the public for over a year. At their interrogation, he snarled something about earthquake damage—that it was dangerous inside and was under repair.

Emily flashed her archaeological credentials, and explained to the man that she was working on a project that involved the Israeli and Italian governments and had been given permission by the Superintendent of Monuments to visit the cave. Ryan was impressed by her facility for spinning a tale. She had only one day, she added, to complete her visit.

At first the guard was adamant. He knew nothing about her mission. The Superintendent of Monuments, he told them, had no jurisdiction here.

They realized what a formidable obstacle they were up against, and Emily tried flirtatiousness. The disappointment in her eyes made it look like she was on the verge of tears. Gaze lingering on her arms, the man looked her over, took in the beauty that lurked beneath the scratched-up exterior, and was now listening attentively. "Could you at least tell us what you know about the cave?" she pleaded.

Ryan had lived in Italy long enough to know that, along with Emily's charms, the fifty euros he folded into his palm as he reached for the guard's hand might seal the deal. It did. The euros disappeared so quickly Emily never saw them. The guard instantly relaxed and gave them a friendly smile, his gun hand returned to his side.

Suddenly he couldn't stop talking, eager to answer their questions. He told them he'd been guarding the cave since the fifties, when at the age of twenty he'd taken over from his father.

Ryan thought they had won over the man's trust, and asked him the question that was burning in both their minds: Had he ever met a Monsignor Oscar Isaac? An instant of suspicion crossed the guard's face, but it was soon overcome with the pride of ego and the pressure of isolation.

"The poor man," he said, crossing his heart. "He was a good friend. He died before he could finish his work here. That's why the cave was sealed," he added, and then grimaced at his careless divulgence.

Ryan exchanged a glance with Emily. Her face told him that she too had noticed the discrepancy in his story. He proceeded to confirm the rumor that the monsignor had been directing a secret excavation project of some sort. When they asked him what Isaac was looking for, he told them he didn't know. On being pressed, he admitted that the cave used to be under the jurisdiction of the Italian government but that for a while now it had been taken over by *i Gesùiti*—the Jesuits. How did he know that? Because that's what was written on his paychecks, he told them. They laughed.

"Why would the Jesuits take over a cave?" Ryan wanted to know.

The man rubbed his fingers together, the simple gesture to indicate that the Society had the money to keep the ruins from falling back into oblivion, while the bankrupt government did not.

When Ryan asked him when he last saw the monsignor, the guard hesitated but finally told them he encountered Isaac just two days before he was run down in Centro Antico. Something obviously troubled him about the memory. When he asked Isaac what he was up to, the guard reported, the monsignor told him the same thing he always said when he came to work at the site: that he was merely "serving the will of the *dominus verus,* the true Lord. But somehow something was troubling him that day," the man finished.

"So Isaac's 'finds' combined with what he knew about the Sibyl led to his death?" Ryan asked Emily, not stopping to edit his words.

Suddenly the guard realized he'd talked way too much already, well beyond fifty euros worth. "As I told you, this place is closed," he barked, circling back to his original tone of voice. "You must leave at once."

Ryan had taken a few steps back from the entrance, ignoring the guard's command, his eyes fixed on the hillside above the caves. His nose wrinkled as he tried to identify the faint odor he was detecting.

"*Vai via,*" the guard's voice rose. "*Subito!*" Angry now, he pointed down the road. They would leave now or he would call the *polizia* to escort them out. He held up his walkie-talkie for emphasis.

"*Va bene*, we're sorry to have upset you," Ryan said hurriedly, drawing a questioning glance from Emily. "We will leave. Thank you for talking to us."

The guard was mollified, and dropped his voice. "The walk back to the autostrada will take no more than two hours. From there you can call for assistance to tow your vehicle."

"Very strange that he knew about our car," Emily said as they walked down the road the way they had come. "What's really going on here—and why did you suddenly agree to leave so readily?"

"I saw something. Let's wait till we're clear of him."

"What did you see?"

"First I smelled it. A whiff of frankincense, or at least I thought that's what it was."

"You'd be the authority on incense."

He ignored the comment. "Then I saw it rising from the hill above the cave, beyond the temple."

"And your point is?"

"That there must be another way in—from the hilltop, where the incense came from."

Emily looked thoughtful. "Well, Isaac always told me there was more than one way to get into and out of the cave," she said.

"What did he say exactly?"

She paused a moment to bring the memory back. "He said the way in was by earth, or heaven, or hell."

"Easy to get in," Ryan nodded. "Hard to get out."

They'd reached a bend in the road and could see the guard. He was back in his original position, and already nodding off again.

"Follow me," Ryan said, as he turned perpendicular from the road, and headed into the tall grass toward the conical hill above the cave.

Their zigzag climb was arduous for the first hundred yards, but eased a great deal when they joined the ruins of the sacred road halfway up the hill that seemed to rise to a sanctuary at the top.

"The Temple of Jupiter. This must be the 'heaven' Isaac was talking about." Ryan remembered what he'd read in the printouts.

An hour later, making better time thanks to the stone roadbed, they'd completed the circuit of the cone-shaped hill and were looking down from the apex. Before them stood the ruins of the Temple of Zeus-Jupiter, the planet and god identified with Augustus, its once mighty roof now open to the sky, its cornices inhabited by swallows instead of gods. The crumbled ruins beneath were mostly indistinguishable blocks of marble. But among them Emily pointed out a half dozen or so broken statues of Jasius, the Trojan ancestor of Rome referred to by Virgil—the personal *lar familiaris,* "protective spirit," of Octavian's family. In the year Augustus announced his census of the entire world, he also ordered that the little statues of his genius—his guardian spirit—be posted at every intersection of Rome.

"A few remain in place to this day," Ryan said. "I've seen them." He recognized the bearded figure as identical to one he passed on his daily hike down to Gesù from the College.

"I first saw them in the Capitoline museum, if I recall," Emily said, "on my first trip to Rome."

They were exhausted from the climb and slumped to the ground to catch their breath. In the distance they could see Monte di Procida and the islands in the Bay through the gathering mist. Not more than a few minutes had passed when

Ryan whispered, "There it is again. Take a look."

They were now looking down on wisps of incense rising from a hidden crevice that seemed to originate near the base of a crumbling ancient staircase. They began their descent and made their way carefully toward it. Though the guard was probably still napping, the threat of his handgun was a vivid reminder to move with extreme caution to avoid a rock-fall that would alert him. They reached the lip of the hill, now fully shielded from the piazza below, and sat on the last step to reconnoiter.

They squinted until they again spotted the tiny wisp of smoke. It appeared to be rising from a leaf-covered stone among the jumble of broken masonry. Then Emily smelled the acrid aroma of the frankincense, mixed with something else. "What's that other smell?" she asked.

"Myrrh," Ryan replied, his nostrils flaring, his memory taking him back to early mornings in his adolescence where, as an altar boy, he filled the censer with the colorful mixed crystals before lighting them during the Consecration. "It has to be an opening," Ryan said. "And that's unmistakably liturgical incense."

They worked together to rake away centuries of rotted leaves; and finally reached what must have been intended as a circular air vent, its ancient grate so rusted it was nearly disintegrated. "An oculus," Ryan identified it, "a miniature version of the great circular window in the Pantheon. I can just make out what looks like a dirt floor several feet below."

"The question is can we fit through it?" The opening appeared to be less than half a meter in diameter. Emily squeezed through easily, released her grip and let herself fall into the unknown.

Ryan heard the thump of her impact on the ground. "Are you okay?" he whispered.

"Fine." Emily's faint reply was not quite convincing.

Ryan negotiated the squeeze and let out what sounded very much like a curse as his clothes snagged on the rusty grate. A second later he landed clumsily by her side on the floor of the cave.

For a moment they lay dazed on the dirt floor, both by the fall and by the sudden dimness. "We're in!" Emily was grinning like a hunter settling into a blind. "But we'll never get out that way. We must have dropped eight feet!"

The noise they'd made was considerable, but they heard no footsteps approaching to check on their unquiet and unauthorized entry.

Ryan was struck silent, for the moment, by the single fact that he was standing in the steps of the fabled Aeneas, hero of Virgil's *Aeneid,* the survivor of Troy, who came to this cave to plead with the ancient Sibyl to allow him access to hell. In the underworld Virgil's hero would make contact with the shade of his father Anchises in order to learn the exact location where he was destined to found the city of Rome.

Little by little Emily's eyes adjusted to the gloom punctuated by the shaft of light that emanated from the oculus and by votive candles that flickered from niches carved into the sides of the cave, about eight feet apart. "I don't see any sign of recent earthquake damage, do you?"

"Somebody's using this place," Ryan said. "Those candles need to be replaced daily."

Emily was taking in their surroundings, marveling at the long, straight tunnel flanked by a series of geometrically perfect and identical apertures, mirroring each other on opposite sides of the corridor that seemed to recede downward to infinity.

At first glance, Ryan thought, the corridor appeared to be fashioned in the shape of a woman's vulva. He looked away from Emily in embarrassment at the thought.

It was as if they stood in front of a mirror faced with mirrors. Nearly as far as they could see, a progression of identical "mouths" opened to side caves facing each other on both sides of the main antrum. Carved out of volcanic stone, the cavern appeared to be a trapezoidal passageway nearly three hundred feet long.

"It's Virgil's thousand mouths," Ryan said, wrinkling his nose.

Then Emily recognized it too, the obtrusive biting odor of a Gaulois cigarette.

"Actually, when you count them yourself there are only one hundred," said the voice emerging from the shadows.

XLI/41

Resurrexit sicut dixit
He has risen, as He said

"Let me be your *cicerone* from here," Bishop Giammo continued. "Actually you're very close to being on time, according to our estimation. Let's hurry along." The bishop smiled to see Emily's face turn white. "No, dear, I'm not a ghost," he added.

"You expected us!" Ryan accused.

"Follow the gold." Giammo smiled.

"We thought you were dead!" Emily sputtered.

"As you can see, I'm very much alive," Giammo said. "The blackened body you saw in front of my apartment on Via Tritone belonged to the unfortunate man who became somewhat of an embarrassment after failing in his appointed task."

"The task of killing us at the Pantheon?" Emily retorted.

"The same task he succeeded at," Ryan added, "in front of Gesù when he gunned down the man who killed Monsignor Isaac?"

Bishop Giammo motioned for Ryan to follow. "Yes, the very same man. We tracked him down to ask him who had commissioned him. Unfortunately, someone else got to him first. It was left to us to honor him in death as we would honor any brave soldier, even when he has ultimately failed on a mission that should never have been authorized."

Ryan could barely speak from shock. Was this really the

Society to which he had pledged his life? He'd done more than his share of reading about political, social, economic, even moral abuses associated with the history of the Jesuit Order. He knew that many of the allegations were spun of jealousy, misunderstanding, and just plain spite. But there were enough of them for him to conclude where there's smoke there's fire. The residue of unease left by these revelations had been fanned by the last week's adventures into a flame of suspicion.

Researching the true history of the Society of Jesus was a project for another day. He needed some answers, now. "Isn't it about time to tell us what this is all about? Where are we going?" he demanded.

Giammo turned; his voice was gentle. "It's not like you still have control over your goings," he said. "But Ms. Scelba is going to retrieve her coin. And you are going to receive answers to questions you never even thought of asking."

They followed the resurrected bishop through what he termed "the public areas of the cave," moving along the progressively smaller trapezoidal mouths toward the far recesses of the central corridor. Like the guide he'd promised to be, Giammo related to them some of the details Monsignor Isaac had recorded about his discoveries: that the Sibylline verses preserved by Augustus, though pagan and much more ancient in origin, were incorporated into the early Gospels and were the foundation of the Book of Revelations.

As Ryan well knew, the oracles became of great interest to scholars investigating the sources of the early Christian Church, and therefore would naturally have been of keen interest to Monsignor Isaac. "If only he'd lived long enough to read the actual manuscripts," Giammo commented.

Ryan thought he detected a nuance of regret in the bishop's otherwise flat and businesslike tone.

As Emily listened, Ryan watched her face for signs of how much she already knew. She didn't look surprised when Giammo said, "You must know that Octavian had a revised version of the Sibyl's oracles written to fit his new personal divine status as son of god and god before proceeding to have the original copies burned."

"Augustus was greatly influenced," Emily added, "by Pythagorean views of what virtue and moral behavior ought to be to create an environment of peace and prosperity for everyone in the worldwide empire."

Giammo looked at her with approval. "Yes, we know it well, as you shall see. Only it wasn't just Pythagorean."

Near the end of the tunnel, they reached the pedestal of an enormous golden statue. Emily gasped in astonishment.

"What is it?" Ryan reached instinctively for her hand, and then stopped himself.

"From everything I've studied, it has to be an absolutely perfect copy—of the colossal statue of Augustus at Caesarea."

The statue before them was bearded, and at once he understood: it was extraordinarily similar to the bearded *lares* they'd just observed among the ruins of the Temple of Jupiter like the figure he passed every day on his walk to Gesù. Giammo listened approvingly as Emily explained that the great statue forged on King Herod the Great's orders to celebrate the dedication of the temple in Caesarea had indeed been based on the cult statues that Augustus ordered erected in every household and in every district of Rome, and throughout the empire. Augustus didn't want to be worshiped as his mere mortal self, but as Jasius—as the divine avatar of the predecessor-founder of Rome, ancestor of Aeneas, namesake of the titan Iasius.

Giammo smiled at her. "You are correct. Except what you see before you is not a copy at all—it is the original. Pillaged from Caesarea by Herod's enemies, but recovered from Damascus by Constantine's mother, Helena, and brought to Rome when her son agreed to work with her to restore the ancient cult of Augustus. When we decided to close the cave to the public to protect us from the announcement that is to come, we transported it from its secret crypt in Gesù to its present position."

"I thought it was the true cross that Helena went to recover." Ryan looked perplexed.

"She pretty much recovered whatever she ran into," Giammo chuckled. "She was an archaeological vacuum cleaner."

Emily drew Ryan's attention to the symbol of the simple Roman cross, engraved in the foliate capital above the statue's head. "It's identical to the base I found in the ruins of Caesarea," she whispered, breathless with excitement.

"Yes, the capital here is a facsimile," Giammo interrupted, "modeled on the one you found in the ruins. The cross, symbolizing the four corners of the world as well as the conjunction of physical and spiritual, was once the mark of the Roman legions. As early as 52 B.C. Julius Caesar himself adopted it to his standards—and his coinage—after vanquishing the followers of the Gallic god Hesus and assimilating their symbolism."

"And according to Monsignor Isaac," Ryan interjected, "it came to stand for Rome's domination of the known world. I'd sure like to see the evidence of all this."

Giammo paused and smiled faintly at Ryan's consternation then led them through a narrow opening on the right side of the giant statue. With every step they took, the ominous feeling inside him increased.

The information he had been learning about the Roman cross had a sobering effect on him. Now Ryan found himself staring at gold leaf inscriptions—the words written with no spaces between them like an endless ribbon—that decorated the ancient marble pavement beneath their feet.

"If you can make out the words, you may recognize them from the pagan-Christian historian and church father Lactantius," Giammo told him.

Ryan knew that Lactantius' *Divine Institutes,* written in the fourth century under the patronage of Constantine, included substantial portions of the Sibylline Books that seemed to be prophesying the Christian Jesus Christ. Without waiting for Giammo, Ryan translated the words into English in the tones of a litany he'd spent a lifetime reciting:

He shall walk on the waves, He shall release men from disease. He shall raise the dead…

With five loaves at the same time, and with two fishes,
He shall satisfy five thousand men in the wilderness;
And afterwards taking all the fragments that remain,
He shall fill twelve baskets to the hope of many.

…and He shall wear the crown of thorns…And the veil of the temple shall be rent, and at midday there shall be dark vast night for three hours.

And after sleeping three days, He shall put an end to the fate of death; and then, releasing Himself from the dead, He shall come to light, first showing to the called ones the beginning of the resurrection.

Ryan thought he recognized the verses as direct translations from Lactantius, but Giammo corrected him. "The text you read," he said, "was only *quoted* by Lactantius and came from the Sibylline Verses that Augustus adjusted to create the image of himself as Jasius—his divine incarnation. That imperial redaction," Giammo added, "was probably finished by 10 B.C., around the same time that Augustus caused his cult statues to be erected throughout the empire, and at the same time that King Herod offered the temple to Augustus' cult in Caesarea."

"What are you saying? That Augustus claimed to have performed marvels like those associated with Jesus?" Ryan couldn't restrain his curiosity, yet dreaded the answer.

"I'm saying that the oracles as edited by Augustus were fashioned to make it appear that Jasius, Augustus' divine persona, performed those mythical deeds."

As they walked through the grotto, the gravel beneath their feet had given way to highly-polished marble. Carried on a breeze that made Emily shiver, the smell of incense became stronger now, wafting toward them in a pungent wave that overwhelmed the fumes of the Gaulois, which Giammo carefully crushed out in a marble *portacenere*. "We're approaching the inner chamber of the Sibyl, the true holy of holies," he said, "where she pronounced her oracles and wrote them on oak leaves that flew on the wind throughout the cave. This is where legend says Aeneas met the prophetess and persuaded her to lead him to the gate of the underworld."

They had reached the last of the mouths and stared at what appeared at first to be a blank wall at the end of the diminishing corridor. Ryan's fear gave way to awe. Carved into the base of the wall was what he recognized as the ancient throne of the Sibyl herself. The smoke of the incense was now visible and appeared to be rising from the fissure in the floor next to the wall.

A rumbling sound startled them but Giammo, who had pressed his hand against the wall, seemed not to notice as the ground beneath them trembled. The wall he had pressed, directly behind the Sibyl's throne, began to open—the odor of incense intensifying—until the massive stone partition revealed itself to be an entry into another subterranean cavity. An eerie flickering light poured into the Sibyl's chamber, throwing them into gargoyle-like shadows and contorting the face of their guide so it took on a diabolical aspect.

"*Introibo ad altare Dei,* I shall go unto the altar of God." In ancient ecclesiastical Latin, the voice was intoning the opening words of the sacred Mass of the Roman Catholic Church.

The familiarity of the respondent's voice startled Ryan. *Ad Deum qui laetificat juventutem meum,* Ryan echoed to himself automatically, "to God who gives joy to my youth."

At first they didn't notice a flight of steps descending sharply into a recessed chamber whence the incense—and the Latin prayers—arose. With a mixture of excitement and trepidation, they followed Giammo down the ancient steps.

An enormous Alpha and Omega—the first and last letters of Apollo's name—were carved in gold mosaic above an obsidian altar before which a celebrant was slowly swinging the censer.

"He's wearing the tiara," Ryan whispered, his gaze fixed on the celebrant. Then his eyes moved, to confirm that the acolyte assisting in this secret Mass was in fact none other than the Procurator Ramon Pimental. *He must have arrived in the helicopter,* Ryan thought, looking at Emily to see if she had recognized him. The blood rushed through their veins at the scene before them.

Pimental caught Ryan's glance, this time without the anger

Ryan had seen flashing from his eyes on their last encounter. Instead the look, no less intense than before, was one of understanding, sympathy, and approval.

"Oh my God," Emily said, pulling at Ryan's jacket, her attention riveted on the priest.

"It's the one who tried to kill us!"

At that moment, the hallowed sacerdotal words, *"Dominus vobiscum,"* "the Lord be with you," were intoned by the celebrant as he turned to spread his arms in blessing to his visitors.

"Et cum spiritu tuo," "and with your spirit," Ryan, Pimental, and Giammo answered automatically. Emily joined them without thinking, her childhood indoctrination surfacing.

But Ryan was fixated on the celebrant. His jaw dropped when he realized the priest wearing the tiara was the Father General of his Society, the newly-elected "Black Pope"— Miguel Leontel.

"You are in the inner circle," Giammo whispered.

Without expression, Father Leontel offered his ring hand to Ryan and Emily. Emily stared at the ring with curiosity, but Ryan fell to his knees and leaned forward to kiss what looked to be identical to the one worn by the pope to signify his possession of St. Peter's power to loose and to seal the gates of heaven.

Still on his knees, Ryan was frozen in place. What was the Jesuit Father General doing with a papal ring? Ryan felt as if he'd been transported into a Fellini film, visiting an underground of the surreal. As Ryan examined the ring, he became conscious that Pimental and Giammo were studying his every move.

Giammo signaled for Ryan to rise from his knees. Ryan rose and bowed again to the mysterious ring. Giammo looked relieved. Ryan did his best to hide his emotions. *The audacity of*

Leontel!

"You will understand all in due time, my son. *Pazienza!*" Giammo said, answering his unspoken questions.

The ceremony continued. To the chiming of altar bells held by acolyte Pimental, the sacred host, the wafer of unleavened bread, was consecrated and thereby transformed into the body of the Christ.

Leontel genuflected, then turned to raise the host for the elite congregation to worship.

Emily gasped. It wasn't the host he raised. It was her aureus. She started to speak, but Giammo's look returned her to silence.

Her eyes never left it as Leontel began to intone the ancient words over the golden chalice: *"Hic est enim calyx sanguinis mei, novi et aeterni testamenti, qui pro vobis et pro multis effundetur in remissionem peccatorum.* 'This is the chalice of my blood, of the new and eternal testament, that for many shall be shed for the remission of sin.'"

Emily and Ryan stared at the chalice, finally recognizing it beyond doubt when Father Leontel held it up for all to worship the consecrated wine that was now, by the power of the Sacrament of the Eucharist, supposedly transubstantiated into the blood of the Christ. It was the same goblet they had seen a photo of in the Secret Archives. Obviously it had been transported, perhaps with the celebrant himself, to this secret place. The pictures of miracles engraved on the cup made it clear that this ancient vessel was the funeral urn that once contained the mortal remains of Octavian Augustus Caesar himself who, according to eye witnesses at his cremation ceremony, "on the third day rose from the ashes and ascended into heaven."

The celebrant slowly rotated the chalice for all to read the ancient inscriptions burnished into the gold. Emily recognized on the band that bordered the images of miracles the same inscription found on the temple at Caesarea: *Jasio Augusto Divus Filius Divi Caesar Imperator Pontifex Maximus,* "To Jesus Augustus God and Son of God Emperor and Supreme Pontiff." And between the words *Jasio* and *Augusto* Ryan saw the *Chi-Rho* monogram from the labarum, ☧, in the exact same style as on Emily's aureus.

Ryan's eyes took in the other inscription: "*Hoc est enim corpus meum,*" the sacred words of the Consecration, "This is my body."

Leontel looked at them. "Yes, my children," he said, "Augustus himself, Jasius Augustus, was the true *christos,* the awaited one, the anointed one, a god born on earth of a virgin to return the Golden Age. Now, forever, like Horus, Prometheus, Orpheus, Dionysius, Attis, and Mithras before him he gives his blood for his people to make possible with his all-seeing love, a peace that will truly be eternal. Approach to receive the true Blessed Sacrament."

Ryan's mind raced over the implications of what he was hearing. If what the Black Pope was saying were true the lives of a billion Catholics worldwide would never be the same. They would be forced to reexamine the very foundations of their faith. They would, each and every one, experience what he had been experiencing. Was the Christian world ready for this knowledge, or was the matrix of religious conviction too deeply embedded in the minds and hearts, if not the very genes, of believers?

Emily's mind took a different perspective. *Jasius Augustus may have been the Christ, the awaited one, but he was born of a normal pregnancy and was a murderous tyrant in his younger years. How can*

they be so deluded, except by the human need to sanctify remarkable leaders? If not based on the wide-eyed truth, their plan could end up by replacing the myth of the biblical Jesus with another fairytale.

Pimental and Giammo crossed themselves reverently, and held out their hands. Pimental placed a host in each of them, with the words, *"Corpus Augusti Christi,"* "Body of Augustus the Christ." Responding, "Amen," they accepted the host and placed it on their tongues. It was Ryan's turn. In a daze, he followed suit, his mind more on Emily than on this strange iteration of the ancient liturgy. Why would she be receiving the Holy Sacrament?

He watched with dread as she held out her hands. But what Leontel offered her was not the host. It was the aureus.

"Christus Augustus," he said.

"Amen," Emily said, her hands trembling as she felt the weight of the coin in her palm again. *Why in the world would they give this to me?*

In the depths of this secret place, at a moment in time he could never have imagined, Ryan looked on in awe. Emily had recovered her aureus; her mentor had somehow obtained the ashes of Augustus but the data he had planned to make public had cost him his life. *Will Emily and I experience the same fate?*

XLII/42
Ordination

The ceremony ended. Father Leontel's eyes were fixed on Ryan. "My son, will you complete Monsignor Isaac's work for us?" he asked. Before Ryan could answer, Leontel reached forward to put a finger on his lips. "This is the most important decision of your life," he said, in a voice that captured the gentle tones of paternal concern. "Please allow yourself sufficient time to deliberate."

"Wait a minute," Emily said, her eyes demanding. "I have as much right as he does to take part in Isaac's research."

Leontel looked at her tenderly before answering. "You were correct about the aureus. It is your destiny. You will embrace your destiny, as I have ordered, when your work is completed."

"What the hell is that supposed to mean?" she asked.

"Now," he smiled, ignoring her question, "I must return to Rome." Without another word, he turned, nodded to Pimental, and followed Giammo toward the mouth of the cave.

Pimental ushered them to a tabernacle hidden behind the ceremonial altar, where they watched him secure the gold goblet in its velvet pouch. He then turned to them with a sad smile and said, "Welcome to the gates of hell."

"You've got some nerve welcoming us when you tried to

murder us!" Emily said.

Pimental took a seat in a large upholstered armchair and motioned for them to be seated on the small red velvet seats in front of him. "Murder? You are mistaken, my child. We merely wished to demonstrate that we are not to be trifled with. You would have ended up here regardless, perhaps with a fearsome headache from oxygen deprivation—but with a lot less trouble in the end."

"No thanks to you!"

But Pimental could see that Emily was torn between her anger and her fascination with the polished aureus. "Though one thousand were struck," he said, "to complement the symbolism of the Sibyl's thousand mouths from which she predicted the coming of Jasius Augustus, your aureus is the first that has been found since the nineteenth century—and the one that turned up then has disappeared. Ignatius Loyola's private discovery that the aureus existed, though he never found one, changed his life—and history."

Ryan came closer and Emily allowed him to examine both surfaces of the newly-polished coin.

On one side was the bearded image of Augustus, wearing the "crown of thorns"—the symbolic golden spiked crown worn by the god Apollo as he drove the sun's fiery chariot across the heavens. Ryan could see the resemblance between this face of Augustus and the common image of the thoughtful, bearded Jesus familiarly depicted on holy cards, statues, and paintings throughout the Catholic world. The words *Divus divi filius,* "God and Son of God," were inscribed to the left of Augustus' head, the words *Jasius Augustus* to the right. Beneath the emperor's head, joining the two phrases, was the *Chi-Rho* symbol.

He had to admit he himself was transfixed as she reacquainted him with the iconography on the reverse of the brightly shining aureus.

This side displayed the loaves and fishes, crossed and as if mounted on the simple Roman cross. The conjunction of the fish image of Neptune god of the deep and the loaf symbol of Ceres the goddess of grain signified the emperor's abundance, generosity, and power over land and sea throughout the four corners of the earth. When Fatall had described what he found on the reverse after the coin was cleaned, he failed to mention that beneath the cross were the initials *D.T.*, for *dominus terrae*, "Lord of the earth"—and "*O.M.*" short for *Optimus, Maximus*, "the best and supreme."

Emily's heart raced with having finally obtained the confirmation she needed to validate Isaac's theory.

It was now painfully clear to Ryan what Emily's—and Monsignor Isaac's—big secret was, and why she kept it from him until she could show him the proof.

Jesus—*Jasius*—was nothing more, or less, than the cult name for Augustus. It wasn't about "the relationship between Augustus and Jesus," after all.

They were saying that Jesus *was* Augustus. It was that simple.

Ryan fought to maintain his equilibrium. The evidence he was hearing from Emily and the Jesuits was all secular and scientific. No argument from the spirit had been presented, nothing that spoke to the feeling of just plain goodness he experienced when he swallowed the host, smelled the incense at Benediction, watched shafts of sunlight piercing through the stained glass, or heard the organ and the choir. *What about the Sermon on the Mount? Did that really come from Augustus? What about giving your cloak to some bastard who tried to steal it?* This didn't sound like

Roman imperial thinking to him. He could imagine Augustus espousing the first of Christ's two great commandments, "Thou must love the Lord thy God with thy whole mind, and thy whole heart, and thy whole strength," but couldn't imagine him practicing the second one, "Love thy neighbor as thy self."

Giammo reappeared pushing an ancient bronze cart with a steaming silver teapot, a pitcher of milk, and a plate of delicate pink cookies.

Ryan sipped his brew and devoured his cookies. They tasted faintly of roses. He dared not state his thoughts. They would no doubt have ready answers to them that he wasn't ready to confront.

A sickening realization sank in. If what they believed was true, if Jesus Christ was the cult name for Augustus Caesar, then he had consecrated his life to a mere mortal man, a man whose ambitious bid for immortality had succeeded—at least, for two thousand years so far. It took all of Ryan's self-discipline to break his deeply-conflicted reverie and turn his attention to Emily as she clasped the coin tightly in her hand.

He watched her closely, trying to read her mind. This brilliant woman was the quintessential scholar, determined to publish the proof of her discovery no matter what—and regardless of what it might mean to millions and millions of Catholics and Christians the world over, and regardless of the unnamed jeopardy he could feel the two of them were in. Ryan watched to see how Pimental would react to her appropriation of the artifact.

"Don't worry, my dear. It's only right that you keep it with you," Pimental said. "It's not like there's any place here to hide."

Was Ryan imagining it or did his tone sound ominous?

"You're damned right I'm keeping it with me," Emily retorted. "And I am *not* your dear!"

"It's time we know the whole truth," Ryan demanded of his superior. For the first time, he could not read the emotion in Emily's eyes.

Pimental smiled. "Yes, the time has come. I think your friend here knows more than I do. Why don't you ask her?"

Emily spontaneously reached for Ryan's hand, but quickly withdrew the gesture when she felt him flinch at her touch.

"Once again I am going to take a page out of Monsignor Isaac's repertoire, and tell the story as he did to me," she began.

XLIII / 43
The Sibylline Redaction

18 B.C.E.

The poet Virgil sat with other honored guests in a semi-circle around Emperor Augustus in the Temple of Apollo. There were playwrights and poets, soothsayers and astrologers, astronomers and sophists, philosophers and theologians from throughout the vast empire—all of who had gladly traded their autonomy for the pleasure of basking in imperial approval.

Priests of Serapis, Horus, and Osiris had made their way here from Egypt. Devotees of Mithra and Attis had traveled all the way from Phrygia; Talmudic scholars from Palestine; priests of Hesus from Gaul and the Druids; of Zarathustra/Zoroaster from Persia; of Dionysus Dendrites from Greece along with a full contingent from Plato's Academy to represent their allegiance to Socrates' *daemon*; devotees of Indra, Buddha, and Krishna from far-off India.

Virgil had heard about Augustus' propitious encounter with the immortal Sibyl of Cumae on the emperor's last birthday, known popularly as "the feast of the Nativity." The Sibyl had managed to be alone with him in the Forum at high noon when he asked her whether the world would ever see the birth of a greater man than he.

She had looked toward the heavens and seen a golden ring around the sun in the middle of which appeared a beautiful virgin holding a child to her bosom. The Sibyl pointed it out to

Augustus, and said to him, "This woman is the *Ara Coeli,* the Altar of Heaven. Her child is king of kings, the son of the Living God, born of the spotless virgin."

Augustus embraced the gift contained in her message: *He must be the holy child to whom she referred.*

The next day, he established an altar at the highest point of the Forum, and ordered a temple built to enshrine it as the Altar of Heaven with the inscription: "This is the altar of the Son of the Living God." On the same day he ordered that all temples dedicated to Julius Caesar, be called no longer *caesarea,* but henceforth *augustea;* and that all inscriptions be altered accordingly—in a single edict effectively fusing the cult of Julius with his own. The Centennial Games were ordered to be held on the anniversary of the propitious epiphany, once each century so no one could attend them twice.

As soon as the various papyrus manuscripts containing the sacred ancient myths had been gleaned of anything useful to the *augustan* cult, they would be destroyed.

Presiding officially over the unwieldy assemblage of sages was the emperor's current favorite "philosopher," Apollonius of Samos. Virgil was instinctively distrustful of the so-called mystic Pythagorean, barely eighteen years old, who Augustus had first encountered in the Middle East on his way back to Rome after the African campaign. Pol, as the emperor nicknamed him, was supposedly chairing this assembly, sitting in its center in the *asana* position he had imported from far-away India; but with Augustus in the room there could be no doubt about who the true presider was.

"We could say his father was a craftsman," one scribe was suggesting to Pol. "It's important to relate to the common people."

"The emperor's only true father, Julius, was a god," Augustus whispered to the Samian. "It was his earthly caretaker, Octavius, who was a craftsman."

"Krishna's father was a carpenter," one of the Indian sages close to Pol piped up.

"Then let's say the emperor's paternal caretaker was a carpenter, too." Augustus smiled as he addressed the impertinent visitor directly. "And have the emperor born in a stable among shepherds." His decision garnered applause from the Hindu and Mithra delegations who had reported to the assembly earlier that Salivahana, Krishna's avatar on earth, was born in a shepherd's cottage; that the Persian sun god Mithras was born in a cave at the winter solstice; and that the infant Zeus was hidden in a cave by Rhea and nurtured by shepherds.

Amid this colorfully international assembly, the high-pitched voice of Apollonius was now insisting that Augustus be called "the healer of all mankind," *iasos panton anthropon* in Greek, whose coming had been predicted by the Sibyl herself when she was still in her beauteous prime.

Augustus responded that the emperor preferred the simple Greek *soter,* "savior-messiah," currently inscribed on the pediments of his father Julius' statues throughout the world.

Virgil noticed knowing glances passed back and forth covertly among the assembled.

Augustus noted them as well, but bided his time, except to murmur to Pol, "They are wondering whether the emperor will also demand the title *theos,* 'god,' which usually stands next to *soter.* You will see he has no need to demand it now; they will offer it to him of their own accord when the time comes."

Virgil's mind flashed back to the fateful day of his private meeting with the emperor. His master was not content to be *huois theou, filius divi,* "*son* of god." He must *be himself* a god.

The poet Horace now rose to argue, in a voice creaking with age, that Augustus' mother's name be recorded as Maia, the name of the ancient Romans' chief goddess. Augustus' eyes caught Apollonius', giving his assent.

The priests of Horus rose to remind the emperor of his conquest of Egypt, and of his visits to the temples of the gods. They urged him to model his divine ascendancy more closely on the Osiris-Horus myth, which they claimed was the prototype of all "mother and child" motifs: every god was a manifestation of Ra, the sun god, the all-powerful eternal creator of all things, who gives life to mankind.

The emperor listened, remembering his defeat of Antony and Cleopatra. He nodded. "It shall be so, though we must draw from all cultures under our sway as well."

Then he gave another order to the scribes.

One of the eunuchs responsible for guarding the Vestal Virgins rose to speak. "For the senior disciple of Augustus the son of God, let's use Petrus, 'Peter'—'rock' in Greek—for the rock on which Rome was founded."

Virgil mused that the accelerating cacophony sounded like a wide-open auction of ideas:

"World tree—Roman cross—they're the same," said one of the Greek visiting scholars of iconography. "It symbolizes the infusion of the divine into the human…"

"Hercules at the tree of Hesperides, with apples and a snake—" was drowned out by a shouted reply from Apollonius: "No. Does not fit the emperor's story."

Augustus nodded his agreement.

"I understand, *dominus*," said the same Greek sage. "Then I suggest Hercules carrying his cross as he labors to the death for the sins of humanity?"

"Like Orpheus-Bacchus hanging from the cross," a member of Plato's Academy added pedantically.

"Yes! That element is acceptable," Pol replied.

"Sit next to Augustus." The emperor motioned to Virgil and indicated an empty space on the hardwood bench no one had dared occupy. "The emperor will enjoy your comments."

Virgil complied, and thereby became first-hand privy witness to the progression of circuses Augustus was planning to celebrate his ceremonial appearance as a living man-god, culminating with him donning the triple crown of Pontifex Maximus, High Priest of Rome. The audacity of his vision was astonishing.

"The emperor's mythic persona will endure longer than any ruler's ever before—far into the distant future, you will see," Augustus said as an aside to his confidant. "The emperor will no longer be merely the son of god, but a god himself in his own right, *divus filius divi,* god *and* son of god."

"I understand perfectly," the poet said quietly, as he signaled his acquiescence.

An artisan now approached the emperor with the cast of a small statue, which Virgil recognized from its beard as Jasius, the revered ancestor of both Rome and Troy. Augustus had specifically insisted that Jasius be mentioned in Virgil's epic, and the poet had just recently polished the lines from Book 3:

> *A land there is, Hesperia call'd of old,*
> *(The soil is fruitful, and the natives bold-*

Th' Oenotrians held it once,) by later fame
Now call'd Italia, from the leader's name.
Iasius [Jasius] there and Dardanus were born;
From thence we came, and thither must return.

When he brought his mind back to the present, Virgil overheard the emperor insisting that the beard "absolutely" must be retained on the statue. "The emperor's personal preference for being clean-shaven is not the point," he patiently explained. "His cult representation of his transcendent self should not be limited to his time-bound reality." With an encouraging smile he dismissed the artisan, who left, pocketing a royal purple pouch Virgil was all too familiar with.

As though reading his poet's mind, Augustus explained, "The emperor has ordered a thousand of these *lares* to be placed at every crossroads in the city."

Virgil was impressed. What had once been Augustus' personal *lar*—his household family god—would now be worshipped by all Romans.

"But, *domine*," he ventured to ask during a pause in the mill of activity, "Does the emperor really believe he can create a sacred text that will remain intact through time? Considering how fallible, not to mention willful, we humans are—and scribes are after all human. Every new copy that is made, not to mention every translation into every language spoken throughout the empire, is no more than yet another opportunity for changes to creep in, sometimes by accident, more often by design."

"Exactly," the emperor laughed, without attempting to conceal his pride. "At every turn, embellishments will occur; spellings will be miscopied; names will be blurred; identities will be mistaken; etymologies invented; interpretations will make the narratives the emperor is constructing closer in understanding to the translator's audience. Yet everyone will embrace the religion of the father god who died for his people and his beloved son—and equal god—who came to redeem them for their guilt. But they will combine it with the traditions they already know and understand. A populace who believes that a savior god walked on earth as they do and died for their individual sins as they can die to their own sins and rise again purified is a people united in their faith." Augustus' smile was unsettling.

Virgil recalled a widely accepted truth: that a myth survives by always changing, yet always remaining the same. He looked at the emperor with renewed admiration. This was, after all, the man who had conquered nation after nation, then assembled each nation's priests to rewrite its heritage to include prophetic references to his *adventus,* his "momentous coming." Virgil heard about the hieroglyphics commissioned for the ceiling of the Egyptian temple at Dendera that showed Octavius Augustus as the long-awaited and ultimate pharaoh-messiah, newborn Horus, come to save the people of the Nile from all future invaders.

Virgil cast his eyes to the floor. "*Domine,* a thought crossed my mind." He barely dared breathe as he waited for permission to proceed.

The emperor impassively turned toward him.

Virgil continued. "A cult that unites the people of the empire will undoubtedly help maintain peace, but there will always be those who might view the tenets of the emperor's new gospel as showing weakness—forgetting the younger Augustus who conquered so many tribes and lands. If I may suggest to the imperial majesty, perhaps it would create a more balanced image to add a line or two that demonstrates strength."

Augustus' face registered mild surprise. "Yes, yes, the emperor takes your point. Let us add a line that states something like, 'I come not only to bring peace but a sword.' That should redress the balance, and keep people wondering as well."

Apollonius had now centered the debate on the legend that the mother of Octavian, Maia, had fallen asleep in the temple of Apollo, whereupon she had been "visited in the night" by a sacred serpent. According to one of the Greek delegates, when she awoke she purified herself, somehow conscious that she had been intimate with the serpent. Ten months later she gave birth to Octavian—who, as a result, she considered to be the son of Pythian Apollo the serpent and sun god. Throughout his infancy, she placed Octavian's crib to face the rising sun.

The debate concluded when Apollonius ruled to delete reference to the serpent, but to say instead that Maia had been visited by the white dove—the symbol Augustus had chosen for the Pax Romana, the Peace of Rome. Augustus disagreed and ordered that the serpent be retained, "as the link to the earth that proves the emperor's sharing in all aspects of being."

Then Augustus held up his hand. "What is the decision?" he asked. "When the book has been enshrined, will it be ascribed to one editor or to more than one?"

Marcus Annaeus Seneca, known as "Seneca the Rhetorician," rose as self-appointed spokesman for editorial protocol. "If it be pleasing to the emperor," he addressed Apollonius but dared to look straight into Augustus' eyes, "we have concluded that the issue of authorship or editorship should remain mysterious, and that it should be made so by occasional intentional contradictions within the text itself. Nothing is more characteristic of enduring myth than its having many faces and multiple authors."

Nods and grunts of approval showed he spoke accurately for the assembly.

Augustus assented, and Pol added that a sacred text that

continued to evolve, from the seed being planted today, would be more effective than one that was smoothly homogeneous. The very process would keep the cult vigorous and self-perpetuating. The peace of Rome would live forever through the grace of the savior god, Jasius—the divine spirit of Augustus.

Seneca approached, and handed the emperor a small papyrus scroll. "Here, *domine,* the emperor will find the details we have gleaned from the best Egyptian astronomers. The findings will become useful for the emperor's selection of a prodigious star in the east that will herald the birth of his persona as ushering in a new Golden Age and becoming the cosmic bridge between heaven and earth. Perhaps the emperor could even plan the Centennial Games to coincide with this celestial event?"

The gleam in Augustus' eyes confirmed his assent. Seneca bowed to the emperor, ignored Pol, and sat down.

The emperor gestured to a waiting artisan to approach. The gold vessel the man held was ornately carved and, according to the proud craftsman, recorded on its sides the "miracles of Augustus." Virgil's eyebrows rose and the emperor turned to him to explain. "This solid gold vessel will eventually serve as urn for the imperial ashes," he said distantly, as though his mind were already in the beyond looking back at his mortality. "Before that day comes, before all the people, the emperor will drink from it the consecrated wine that will symbolize his blood spilled on behalf of all citizens of the Roman Empire."

He handed the goblet to the poet, who turned it slowly and marveled at the bas-relief all around the vessel—a design stunning in its simplicity, though it contained dozens of symbols that marked the character and power of Augustus' unprecedented reign. He also recognized the *Chi-Rho* emblem that he had seen on tombs dedicated to Chronos. He read the Latin words aloud, *Hoc est enim corpus meum.* "This is my body."

The emperor nodded. "It will contain the emperor's final remains, which the emperor has ordered to be collected and offered ceremonially to his father in heaven on behalf of the people of Rome."

For a brief moment, Virgil locked eyes with his emperor, who accepted the admiration he could read in them.

By late afternoon the assembly had fashioned the outline of the *Evangelium Augusti,* "the Gospel of Augustus," the newly-proclaimed religion of "Father and Son, Julius and Augustus." Apollonius, summarizing, pronounced that the myth would imitate ancient sun god myths and go like this: *The virgin-born anointed savior of mankind descended from heaven and manifested in human form; put an end to war and strife; instituted a policy of reform, graced by tolerance, mercy, forgiveness; conquered the animal that would drag us down (represented by the snake and the donkey) and instead adored the god within each person; performed miracles to attest to the power of the divine force; was betrayed and sacrificed by his countrymen; rose from the dead and then ascended to the heavens whence he came to sit at the right hand of his father, as Osiris ascended to the right hand of Ra—his revelation to be worshipped; his memory to be revered by all who aspired to the best that human nature is capable of.* And the beauty of it was that the cycle was reflected and repeated by the son in the name of his father, and could be repeated by anyone who imitated the Christ, *imitatio Christi.*

For the third time that day Virgil ventured an unsolicited opinion. "It is indeed wondrous, but there is something that makes me uneasy about the pattern, something imperfect," he whispered to his imperial patron. "Something that doesn't yet echo throughout the universe as the emperor intends it to."

"What do you mean?" Augustus pressed him to continue.

"*Three* is a more mythically resonant number," the poet offered. "It's the natural number. Beginning, middle, and end. Morning, noon, and night. Left, right, and center."

"I see," Augustus said, savoring the thought. "The principle of trinity. Heaven, earth, underworld."

"Yes," Virgil said. "Past, present, and future."

"Father, son and—" Augustus wrinkled his brow. "What is the third?"

"The cosmic *Logos*," Virgil suggested. "The Word used by the Stoics to signify the seed of the divine mind incarnate in every human being as well as the Utterance that creates the universe. The sound that creates light. The exchange of energy flowing between the father and son."

Augustus nodded. "The breath that passes between them. Their love for each other."

"The sacred spirit that unites them, whose breath enlivens the world." Virgil said.

"That shall be so," Augustus clapped his hands. "That is the completion of the sacred trinity. Father, Son, and Sacred Spirit! A triune God. We shall use the white dove to signify it."

The long day closed with Apollonius reading Augustus' imperial order that the updated Sibylline Books would be housed in a magnificent gold chest in the new Temple of Apollo that would be erected next to the emperor's Palatine villa. What better way to legitimize that he was not only the divine progeny of the powerful god Apollo but *was* the actual incarnation of the god, his avatar. He signaled for the attendants to pull back a purple curtain—and that very chest, still a work in progress, was displayed so the committee could appreciate its superior artistry.

Unlike the urn's miraculous Augustan subject matter, the case was decorated with images of his forebears: Jasius, Dardanus, Aeneas, Venus, Apollo, Jupiter-Zeus. A magnificent central diptych on one side presented Augustus himself driving the four-horse chariot of the sun god, a twelve-spiked halo crowning his head; and, on the other, the Cumaean Sibyl foretelling the coming Golden Age of Saturn-Chronos when the newly-born Roman sun god would bring a new day of universal peace.

The emperor gestured toward the thousands of scrolls that now lined the shelves on every wall, and addressed the gathering in Greek: "Let the pontiffs consign the rest of these to the flames—to make way for the enshrinement of the new and eternal testament of the true son of God."

When he repeated the command in Latin, *"novi et aeterni testamenti,"* Virgil cringed. An unbearable sorrow filled his heart as he, along with the redactors led by Apollonius, followed the pontiffs outside into the light rain to witness the bonfire on the steps of the temple.

Emperors burn books. Long after the last ember had died, the poet found himself still standing there, alone, tears streaking his face.

XLIV/44
The Gospel according to Augustus

Emily completed her tale and sat in silence, moved by her own story. No one spoke. Ryan noticed her eyes were glazed over as if she were in some kind of trance, which indeed she had been.

Finally Ryan touched her shoulder. "Are you all right?"

She startled. "I—I'm fine...really, I'm...sorry."

"You had me worried there for a second. As for your story, I have to say I found it deeply troubling. I really don't know what to believe."

She sighed and smiled wearily. "It was one of Isaac's favorites."

Ryan was shaking his head. "Among other things, didn't Virgil die in 19 B.C.? How could he possibly have been present at such an event?"

Pimental frowned. "In my last conversation with Isaac he told me he was working on evidence to suggest that Virgil's death was faked in 19 B.C., at the direct order of Augustus so that the poet could focus full time on his imperial responsibilities. Apparently Augustus had gotten wind that Virgil was using his new-found wealth to entertain and travel, neither activity serving the speedy completion of the awaited epic.

"Virgil chose the only way out: to suffer the indignity of the official announcement of his death accompanied by an imperial funeral, and subsequently spent the rest of his lonely life incognito. Whether history proves that to be true remains to be seen.

"But in any case Isaac was telescoping events that almost certainly occurred incrementally, between 18 and 7 B.C. He always claimed he was an adherent to a central dictum of Aristotle's aesthetics: the dramatist is allowed license in order to portray the greater truth beneath the superficial truth of 'mere facts.' For the sake of communicating the higher truth to his audience in a memorable way, he must be permitted to reshape events somewhat."

Up to this point Ryan had believed that Christ was actually crucified and actually rose from the dead, and surely that differentiated him from Augustus? But now his thoughts were mired in confusion. "There's something else I don't understand," Ryan said. "Why would you continue to worship, knowing the true basis of this religion?"

Pimental's expression showed that he expected the question. "The basic moral tenets Augustus adhered to in his later life—love, peace, compassion, discovering the divinity within us—lie not only at the heart of Christianity but of all religions. The combined wisdom of ten thousand years of human existence prevails regardless of the biography of the founder. Billions of people have been programmed with the *need* to believe in a savior. Our job is to fulfill that need. We revere that central faith itself, not the founder's ontological status. Can you imagine where the world would be without our spiritual guidance?"

Emily struggled to maintain her composure. *Yeah, I imagine it would be a lot better off, you arrogant jerk.*

Ryan could *not* imagine the mind-set Pimental was

revealing. There were too many contradictions left to resolve.

He remembered what the Jesuits had taught him in high school—that Julius Caesar, accused, as Jesus was, of being kinglike, walking across water, dying for his people in Pompey's theater—stabbed in the side by a man named Cassius Longinus, as Jesus was stabbed by a centurion—also named Longinus. It seemed that the lives of the Caesars and Jesus, at the very least, were strangely intertwined.

He snapped back to the present.

Emily was reminding them that the head of Augustus on the aureus was portrayed crowned with thorns that also symbolized the rays of the sun to combine the image of the emperor's self-sacrifice for his people with his ultimate triumph over all the adversity of animal nature on their behalf. "You can see why the discovery of the aureus would have been so important to Isaac."

"Yes," Pimental agreed. "Had he lived to see it, he would have forced us to reveal all we already knew. We had withheld much from the monsignor because we wanted him to confirm what we believed independently. Unfortunately he withheld much from us in the end," he added. "We have been unable to locate the bulk of his research. With your wiping out his computer files during your visit to the Pontifical Institute, we have only the pages you helped yourself to."

Ryan's face flushed.

"The Gospel according to Augustus, when it is presented properly as containing the essential spiritual elements of the world's religions, may well finally end the destructive power of warring fundamentalists," Pimental continued. "But to accomplish that it must be accepted by the world as the ultimate doctrine, not just embraced by an elite fringe. We needed as much proof as we could muster, and until you both came along Monsignor Isaac was our best hope."

Pimental went on to explain that when members of the Augustan sect made their way in numbers from the original cult-center of Caesarea to the capital city of Rome, they threatened the succeeding emperors' egos. Indeed their belief that every individual was a spark of the divine fire, and their simple grace and tolerance of the Augustales, by now known as "anointed ones" or "Christians," became such an anathema to Augustus' imperial successors that they sought to root it out in favor of their own personal worship.

Decadent emperors persecuted the cult mercilessly, and turned its most loyal practitioners into martyrs. Christians were hunted down and offered the option of worshiping the current emperor instead of Augustus, the true *pontifex* and *filius divi* for whom they originally made pilgrimage to the eternal city. When they refused, they were tortured, fed to the lions, and left to rot in the open. Their fellow Christians buried the martyred bodies underground in the catacombs.

The creation of these martyrs strengthened the cult, no longer associated directly with Augustus' name, far more than anything else might have strengthened it. Augustus' wisdom in letting his gospel evolve from culture to culture made it a reality worthy of the enmity of official Rome itself. He had failed only to foresee one thing: the venality of his successors.

Ryan was reeling. "How long have you known all this?"

"It has been known by the inner circle since the beginning," Pimental replied. "It has been lost and it has been found. A lieutenant of Ignatius Loyola himself was the first of us to gather evidence in an organized way; to continue his work, he established the Society of Jasius, a circle within the larger circle that was the Jesuits. This young lady here not only happened to discover the only known aureus left in existence, but she also is the first outsider to have pieced together the truth from Isaac's hints."

"And from my own excavations," she said.

Ryan looked at her, disappointment writ large in his eyes. *This* was the knowledge she'd been eking out to him. And he'd thought they had formed a real connection; that they could trust each other.

She returned his glance. "I told you that you wouldn't have believed me. I'm sorry." She reached for Ryan's hand. "You're right. I could have trusted you, could have let you deal with it your own way. But I needed your help and I—"

"—used me," Ryan said, pulling his hand away. Certainly that was the lesson of the day.

"I'm sorry I didn't tell you. I came close to it in the catacombs when I told you the story of Constantine. But when you didn't put it together then—"

"—You never gave me the benefit of the doubt. Obviously your priorities were clear."

Pimental ignored the heat building between them. "Thanks to our Society of Jasius, the record has never been clearer than it is to us now. Monsignor Isaac's work, corroborated by Emily's discovery, would have been the capping synthesis of systematic research and physical evidence we required before declaring the truth to the world and serving as its ecclesiastical custodians. Now we need to reconstruct his narrative first, then complete it."

Going back and forth in his mind, Ryan replayed Emily's story. Augustus had appointed himself the true bridge between heaven and earth, the *Pontifex Maximus* and the self-sacrificing hero that was, Ryan knew, a myth that ran back all the way to the very beginning of civilization.

Pimental interrupted Ryan's musing. He explained that Isaac had been working quite oblivious to the jockeying going on between the Vatican and the Society of Jesus regarding the Augustan revelation—until he stumbled across evidence that the urn containing Augustus' ashes was, in fact, not stolen from the imperial mausoleum as the "authorized" legend had it.

Monsignor Isaac confronted the Curia with his suspicion that, by the grace of Constantine and his august mother, the Vatican itself had taken the sacred ashes into its safekeeping. At that the monsignor was let in on one of the most treasured secrets in the history of the Roman Catholic Church. Indeed, he was told, the urn did in fact exist, and was hidden safely in the Secret Archives. Isaac was also informed, in no uncertain terms, that he was prohibited from publishing *anything* until the Holy See was ready to authorize it explicitly.

The Vatican, according to Pimental, agreed to temporarily entrust the sacred chalice to the monsignor so that he in turn, could entrust it to a top-secret lab in Munich.

Within months the lab determined that the ashes it contained were definitely those of Jasius Augustus—base-tested against the lock of Octavian's hair that had been preserved in its original reliquary by Constantine's mother Helena and given to Pope Sylvester after the Council of Nicaea. Isaac was assigned to return the urn to the safety of the Cumaean Cave following the DNA analysis.

"Isaac's discovery signaled to all of us in the Society of Jasius that the time was close for revealing the true identity of the Christ and that the restored *evangelium*—the new gospel—was clearly on the immediate horizon." Pimental frowned. He told Ryan and Emily that Monsignor Isaac had provided evidence that the Roman Catholic church was invented by an emperor well versed in the nature of humanity to enshrine, not a prophet nor even a god, but the principles of universal tolerance found in the heart of every great world religion.

The rumors of the Julian-Augustan origin of Christianity were used adroitly by the Jesuits through the centuries to prevent anxious popes, concerned only with maintaining personal power and control over the faithful, from repressing the Society altogether.

With Emily's discovery of the only extant aureus, there could be no further delay. Negotiations with Pius would soon be underway, and *must* succeed. If she were to publish her findings without the superstructure Isaac's narrative provided, she would overturn a plan that had been five hundred years in the making. The intention was not just to announce the Augustan faith, but to ensure its universal promulgation and acceptance.

When Pimental had finished, Ryan looked at Emily. "I think you'd better tell me everything you know, before I lose my mind. I need to understand what you understand," he asked.

"I could try to explain, but Isaac taught me that the best explanation in the world is most often a story. He said that life itself, when all is said and done, good or bad, comic or tragic, happy or sad, always comes down to nothing more—nor less—than a story."

LV/45
Birth of God

15 B.C.E.

On a chilly December morning Rome awakened to find the *lares* statues of Jasius Augustus in place at every street corner. Above them stood official placards sealed with the imperial crest inviting the populace to participate in "The Birth and Death of the Son of God" in Campus Martius.

Last night the light show at the circus had been dazzling—a repetition of the recent Super Nova created by some hitherto unknown pyrotechnics imported from the far borders of the empire had brought the crowd to its feet in a finale they would never forget. The very stars in the blue-dark December sky above the city had been eclipsed by the splendor that announced the coming of a new golden age—and a new savior who would link heaven with earth.

Today, the closing day of the Saturnalia, the streets were thronged with people. Everyone was wide awake with adrenaline, all heading in the same direction like a downhill stream and all carrying palms that were being distributed free on every street corner.

Having been jostled along with the crowd en route, Virgil was oblivious to the fine rain descending from an enormous thundercloud that had nearly turned mid-afternoon gloom to night. There were long lines at every street vendor's cart. He noticed that most people were wearing scapulars dangling around their necks, little squares of leather embossed in gold with the image of the bearded Augustus, his eyes raised to heaven. Concerned only with keeping his feet on the ground, Virgil arrived at the Campus Martius but realized he could see nothing in front of him; he simply wasn't tall enough.

What he *could* see was the enormous Attis-Mithra tree that must have been erected overnight, the tallest solstice pine Rome had ever seen. Brought from the mountains of Gaul, the giant tree was decorated with a thousand lanterns whose light brought a flickering man-made version of the daylight to the huddled crowds staring up at it in awe.

Putting aside all modesty and egalitarian spirit, Virgil reached up and took the hand of an imperial courtier who had spotted him in the crowd, saw through his plebeian disguise, and hoisted him onto the raised viewing platform reserved for Rome's privileged.

From his new vantage the poet could see legionnaires passing out endless loaves of golden bread stamped with the emperor's image, and *baccalà,* cod filets on skewers from the largesse of the imperial kitchens. Vendors were hawking commemorative medallions in the shape of the bearded Jasius, of the sacred winter tree, of the spiky solar crown, of the phoenix, of the winged sphinx, even of erect penises—symbols of the fertility god Priapus! Wine merchants dispensed wine in tiny tin cups that the plebs would treasure as long as they lived.

With all the merriment, the sun turned the scene dark to bright so perfectly gradually it was all but unnoticed. Virgil looked up to see the thundercloud had been, at least for the moment, vanquished by the sun's penetrating rays.

The solar disc now hanging low in the sky was transformed to a brilliant golden orb, when the fervor of the crowd's roar reached its crescendo. Virgil could see that the Campus Martius was being cleared by the legionnaires, the plebs pushed back to the circumference. The *adventus dei,* "advent of the god," he was about to witness seemed so much more vivid now than it had during the endless planning sessions three years earlier in the Temple of Apollo.

As the newly-installed red granite obelisk cast its mighty shadow near the bronze line marking the three o'clock point of the enormous sundial that was now cloaked with humanity, the air was pierced by imperial trumpets.

Two gargantuan slaves, their faces masked with chain mail, approached the Attis tree. Each bore a gold labrys—the ceremonial double-headed ax that Augustus had imported from Knossos.

The slaves faced the pine's mighty trunk, lifted the axes—and struck one blow after another. Virgil knew that this arboreal sacrifice of the tree of life used to be accompanied by the castration of a novice, a volunteer who would henceforth dedicate his existence as a eunuch to the worship of the god Attis—until Augustus' recent decree forbade the savage practice.

The trumpets' warnings rose to a higher and higher pitch. Suddenly the crowd cheered. The mighty tree was falling.

The opening in the circumference became even wider as the crowd pushed to get out of the way of the falling pine—its limbs already blazing from the tumbling lanterns.

The tree crashed into the pool that had been excavated for the purpose, precisely intersecting the dial at the very moment that the solar disc itself slipped toward the horizon.

The base of the fallen tree now pointed directly to a slab of marble, incised with the Roman cross, slightly raised above the pavement of the Campus.

The roar of the crowd was lost in the roar of the crackling pine as the leaping flames consumed it in one enormous bonfire. A mushroom cloud of smoke arose in the fetid air and once again the murky afternoon turned to semi-darkness.

The smell of resin and char assaulted Virgil's nostrils. He took a deep breath to store the memory.

When the trumpets quieted, three kings of vanquished territories—one African, one from Babylon, and one from the Caucasus—rose in all their finery and spoke in unison: "Where is he who has been born king of the Julii? We saw his star two solar cycles ago and have come to worship him with gifts of gold, frankincense, and myrrh."

A shout went up from the trumpeters: "He comes. Blessed be the lord and son of God, in the name of the Father from whom he issues."

Virgil realized the moment was unique. How many would ever again be present at the birth of a god?

As though by magic, at the exact point of the sundial, through the diminishing flames, a red rose-carpeted ramp was deployed across the smoking pool.

Six pontiffs were led in procession across the fire and water by Aemilius Lepidus, the legitimate Pontifex Maximus, who had been allowed to return from exile for this occasion. Lepidus carried the *securis*, the axe symbolic of his high office. All the priests were wearing the simple white tunics the plebs had been told the emperor himself wore in private. As they slowly approached, the pontiff sprinkled soil from all the nations Augustus ruled.

Out of the white smoke of the smoldering pine—forced to billow by the fans operated by Nubian slaves—the pontiffs entered the vacated surface of the Campus Martius. They spread palm leaves as they walked in advance of the ram-rod-straight man who rode on a miniature white horse behind them. Virgil remembered that Julius Caesar had imported the diminutive equines from Gaul. He also remembered that riding on the back of a horse too small for him symbolized the emperor's overcoming his animal nature.

He could see that one pontiff carried the *aspergillum,* the sprinkler that dispersed the holy water of Mother Tiber; another the *simpulum,* the scoop that signified the power of abundance and had been borrowed from Egyptian liturgy.

The billowing smoke added theatrical magic to the processional image that blazed a lifelong impression on the retinas of all who viewed it.

Virgil was startled to find himself brushing a tear from his eye. He didn't have to hear the shouted name to know who the upright rider was. He had to give Octavian Augustus accolades for understanding the art of spectacle as clearly as he understood the arts of politics and war.

The pontifical procession preceding the white horse consisted of the six pontiffs from ancient priestly colleges followed by six Vestal Virgins carrying baskets and with crosses pendent adorning their necks. Six senators followed the white horse. Two slaves of Attis brought up the rear.

The procession led Augustus clockwise in the circle. He was swaddled in white linen, symbol of death, and wore Apollo's gold crown—its thorn-like spikes symbolizing the rays of the sun.

As if on cue, the last vestiges of the Roman sun streamed through the clouds and struck the spikes like lightning bolts, throwing reflections back at the sky as though a bridge between heaven and earth was indeed being constructed before their eyes.

As the white horse traversed the first quarter of the sundial, the Vestals, from their baskets, passed out disc-shaped cookies with an infant stamped on one side and the sun on the other.

In the second quartile, the cookies they passed out to the crowd bore the image of a young man; in the third, of a warrior come of age.

Finally, as the horse, its pace slowing, moved through the final quarter of the dial and approached its starting place—just as the sun touched the horizon—the cookies being scattered to the crowd were in the form of the Egyptian cross, the ancient symbol of the four corners of the world, of communication between heaven and earth, spirit and matter, darkness and light, as well as of the sun king's self-sacrifice and death for his people. Stamped into the cookie's surface, were the initials "J.A." for "Jasius Augustus."

Now Augustus was dismounting. When his white linen gown was taken from him, he was revealed to be wearing nothing but a coarse loincloth. His face was clean-shaven, his well-muscled body gleaming with oil—the evening glow caught its highlights, making him appear youthfully godlike indeed.

One of the elder pontiffs removed the solar crown from Augustus' head and replaced it with a thorny wreath of *quercus ilex,* a sprig of the Holly oak bush found on the periphery of the Campus Martius and worn by heroes who struggled and suffered for Rome.

Another pontiff approached behind him.

Augustus knelt on one knee.

When he stretched his arms out as if to embrace the crowd the roar of approval and acclamation made the very earth tremble with the stamping of feet.

For this was the exact gesture that had been made to the plebs by his adopted father, Julius, before entering the Senate to be sacrificed for his people.

One of the slaves of Attis now approached with a ceremonial flail like the one carried by Osiris, the Egyptian god who was restored to life.

Quickly—causing the crowd to catch its collective breath—the slave whisked the flail across the emperor's gleaming back.

"Look what thou hath wrought," the pontiff taunted the hushed crowd.

Augustus did not flinch.

The slave stepped away.

The crowd gasped as a drop of the emperor's blood issued from under the thorny crown, which was now removed by the first pontiff.

"Hail, Lord of the Julii!" the pontiff declared in a penetrating tone. A spatter of uncertain applause issued from the crowd at the circumference of the Campus.

But their applause was cut short by the emperor's words, proclaimed in his flawless Greek: "My God, my God, why hast thou forsaken me?"

Virgil was astonished to hear the emperor speak in the first person. But he recognized the lines from *Prometheus Bound,* and admired Augustus' ingenuity of adapting them to his cult ceremony.

The pontiff faced the emperor. "Do you call yourself a god?" he demanded.

Augustus held his head high and replied. "I am the son of my father. What do you say I am?"

"A god! A god!" voices shouted from the crowd.

By now, the apotheosis reaching its climax, Augustus had positioned himself in the center of the raised marble slab.

"I am the Alpha and Omega," he intoned. "The first and the last, the beginning and the end."

The six senators came forward to surround him. The crowd screamed in warning as they saw that the senators were bearing ceremonial daggers.

As the senators mimed their onslaught, the figure of Augustus fell to the surface of the cruciform slab. One of the senators, Cassius Longinus, feigned a final blow to Augustus' side and the silence in the Campus was complete.

When the senators pulled back, Augustus lay on his back on the marble slab, his arms spread and somehow secured to the marble.

The two slaves of Attis lifted the slab and the crowd held its collective breath to see their emperor ritually crucified.

The raised marble was on a pivot and the slaves turned the apparently lifeless emperor through the four quartiles of the enormous sundial until all had witnessed his sacrifice.

Wracking sobs could be heard from all directions as the pontiffs bore the still body of Augustus to the pyre that was now revealed when the slaves pulled back the green and red cloth previously concealing it.

The slaves positioned Augustus' body on the pyre, and shrouded it with palms.

Holding a ceremonial torch, Lepidus touched its flame to the emperor's final resting place.

Suddenly, to the amazement of the crowd, fiery sprays positioned on the sides of the pyre, in alternate bursts of gold and imperial purple, spelled out the letters R—O—M—A on one side, and on the other the letters A—M - O—R: "Love—Rome"—the *christos soter,* the blessed awaited savior, who so loved his country he gave his life for it.

So dazzling was the display that the crowd was distracted from the fiercely burning pyre and the horror of the moment.

When the fireworks and flames died down, the palms that covered the emperor had been reduced to white ashes. The pontiffs fell to their knees, collected the powder in golden cups, and marked members of the plebs who had surged forward to receive on their foreheads a cross-shaped smudge of the sacred ashes.

The silence was broken when a sudden array of fireworks rose into the dark thunderclouds that had amassed above the Campus. A hundred Roman candles shot high into the sky— and burst to reveal first, an explosion that miraculously resembled a multi-pronged gold crown, then as it faded, a shimmering cloud of tiny glinting crosses falling to outstretched hands below—cherished keepsakes of this momentous day.

And when the last of the miniature symbols of their savior's death had been collected, all that remained was an eerie wailing that issued from the crowd as though it had reverted to animal nature.

But then a shout went up on one side of the Campus, and arms began pointing toward the dais on which Virgil was sitting. The poet looked toward the stairs leading up to the raised platform and was amazed to see Octavian Augustus standing there, a smile on his face, his arms extended to the crowd.

The entire mob jumped to their feet as one, and chanted, in a distillation of pure surprise and joy and relief, "Jasius Augustus! Jasius Augustus! Jasius Augustus!"

Augustus, ever the showman, had used the manhole opened for the purpose, crawled down the ancient volcanic shaft that had been laddered with iron rungs, leading from the pyre to a subterranean altar; and ascended from the catacomb via another ladder leading back to the surface, behind the stadium.

The crowd was still chanting when the second pontiff approached Augustus carrying the *triregnum*. He raised the tiara—the triple crown topped by the Roman cross—and read aloud the words that nearly gave the poet a heart attack.

After all, he himself had just recently written them, or at least polished them from the draft Augustus had recited to him in their first meeting:

> *Augustus, often promised, long foretold*
> *Arrived at the realm Saturn ruled of old*
> *Born to restore a better age of gold.*

One of the pontiffs was fastening a ceremonial beard on the emperor's face and placing the censer of the Pontifex in his hand.

Another pontiff draped a purple robe with gold embroidering on Augustus' shoulders. In a moment the emperor was transformed into the very image of the Jasius *lares* that had appeared overnight at the crossroads throughout the city.

The chief pontiff proclaimed, "Behold the son of god, true god and true man, sometime and always Imperator, now and forever our virtual Pontifex Maximus, who ascends to the heavens on the legions' cross to bring back fire to those of us lost in shadows below, who descends from the cross into darkness to restore light to those lost in night, who has brought *ad urbem et orbem,* 'to the city and the world,' a golden age of lasting peace."

A senator—it looked like the shameless sycophant Numerius Atticus—offered a gold cup to Augustus. Virgil recognized it as the same chalice he'd inspected in the Temple of Apollo, offered for his inspection by the emperor himself.

The crowd held its breath as Augustus raised his hand to the senator, as though to refuse the cup. Then he raised his arms to the crowd again, and looked toward the sunset:

> *I am the way, the truth, and the life:*
> *No man cometh unto the Father, but by me.*
> *I swear by Apollo the Physician*
> *That I will be from this day forward*
> *Servant of the servants of the empire,*
> *Servant of the servants of God.*

Servus servorum dei—the Latin words echoed among the buildings.

Augustus accepted the urn, raised it to the crowd, brought his lips to its brim and sipped. His lips were red from the strong wine as he flung the contents of the goblet toward the people standing witness in the circle. They strained forward for the honor of having the consecrated wine splash on their garments.

Aemilius Lepidus stood up and lifted a bronze megaphone to his lips.

"The most high God and Father has become visible as our Augustus, Caesar has fulfilled the hopes of earlier times; and whereas the birthday of our God Jasius Augustus has been for the entire world the beginning of the *evangelion,* 'a message of good news,' a gospel, concerning him, therefore let us reckon a new beginning from this date of his divine birth, and let this holy day mark the start of the new year, *anno domini,* year of the august god, and of a new Golden Age.'"

At Lepidus' nod, one of the pontiffs put a sponge on the stalk of a hyssop plant, dipped it into a jar of wine vinegar, and placed the sponge to Augustus' lips to symbolize the bitter taste of bearing responsibility for the people.

When Augustus had tasted the vinegar, he bowed his head and intoned in a melodic chant, "It has ended and it has begun. The eagles of war can rest. Let the doves of peace fly to the four corners of the earth."

A pontiff handed him the *vexillum legionis,* the standard of the Roman legion, this one of burnished gold, except for the ivory-inlaid dove that surmounted it in place of the traditional gold eagle.

Augustus accepted the newly transformed standard, and held it aloft for all to admire. "From this moment onward," his voice rose, "we shall all live *in nomine patris, et filii, et spiritus sancti,* in the name of this Father, and of this Son, and of their Sacred Spirit."

Augustus had fashioned a god in his own image and likeness.

At that moment thousands of white doves were loosed from the roofs of the buildings surrounding the Campus. The sky was darkened by the passing of their wings.

To his utter surprise, Virgil realized the hoarse screams deafening his ears were his own.

XLVI/46
Loaves and Fishes

When Emily finished, Ryan's eyes were wet with tears. Finally he returned to the present moment. "Are you telling me that such an event actually happened?"

"Isaac put it this way," Emily said. "Every single element of this story occurred—if not all at once, at least at one time or another. Telescoped events, remember?"

"The evidence is overwhelming," Pimental added. "We have assembled all of it here the best we could without Monsignor Isaac's guiding hand, in readiness for its proclamation to the world. You will see for yourself."

As Pimental opened the gilded cabinet to display the scapulars, the flail, even the cookie molds described in Isaac's story, Ryan could see the childlike gleam in Emily's eyes. For her, this was a dream come true. For him, it was the ultimate nightmare—a massive crisis of faith.

He had to admit the story she retold was compelling, even logically convincing. He also had to admit it filled him with a sense of peace, the same feeling he had previously experienced only in church.

What would it mean, though, for his—for millions of Catholics'—understanding of their Christian faith?

She'd reminded him, in the catacombs, that the word *chrestos* was Greek for "good," and that *christos* meant "the anointed" or "the awaited."

"Jesus Christ," therefore, would mean "Jesus the Good" or

"Jesus the Awaited One."

He'd also learned, from the few printed pages of Isaac's narrative he'd managed to peruse in the car, that both words, *chrestos* and *christos,* had long been applied to Augustus on monuments and in temples throughout the Greek parts of the empire.

But to accept the idea that Augustus was the true founder of Christianity; that he intentionally initiated the cult that later became the Roman Catholic Church, was a leap almost beyond imagining.

Almost.

Ryan's rapid mental sorting recognized that most of the places mentioned in the New Testament could not be identified in reality. Most of the persons were not mentioned in documents other than the gospels: Mary, the three kings, Lazarus, Judas, Barabbas, Nicodemus, Joseph of Arimathea, Mary Magdalene, even Peter. None were mentioned in documents of the first century. Legends had grown up around them, but these legends were based on the gospels themselves—circular evidence. And somehow not a single autograph of any of the four gospels had survived.

Something about Emily's story resonated with his deepest being, chilled him with the feeling that not only did it make sense, but it also moved him to the core.

Pimental continued. "At first the Vatican, persuaded and supported by the Society, had agreed to quietly finance Monsignor Isaac's work, enabling him to put together the puzzle one piece at a time. He was to collect all the corroborating artifacts here in Cumae, do his DNA tests on the ashes of Augustus and then to complete the process of writing the history of how Augustus' personal cult was formulated. Most importantly he was to refrain from publishing his discoveries until the Holy See granted him permission to do so.

Isaac was working to establish that Augustus' cult was rediscovered, researched, and restored three hundred years later by the Emperor Constantine and his mother, St. Helena into substantially the form taken by the Roman Catholic Church today."

"Are you saying that Constantine was aware that his mother's chosen religion was the religion of Augustus?" Ryan asked.

"Exactly that," Pimental said. "Her research in the Holy Land was very similar to Emily's—if, no doubt, much less scientific."

"So Constantine's sign in the sky, the first letters of *Christus*, referred to Jasius Augustus?" Ryan didn't need to hear the answer to know what it would be.

A distinct odor penetrated his nostrils, and he suddenly realized he was famished.

Pimental was ushering them toward the intoxicating smell—garlic and olive oil—and paused at a narrow door. "Your meal awaits you in the refectory."

As they entered the brick-walled room, they caught sight of Giammo, a cheerful purple and gold apron over his episcopal cassock, carrying a skillet—the source of the irresistible aroma—toward the simple wooden table. "Come in, *ragazzi*," he welcomed them. "You must be starving after a very trying day."

With a spatula that looked as ancient as the cave, he carefully removed the sautéed *branzino* and placed the boned filets onto their rashers. He turned back to the kitchen as Ryan and Emily seated themselves and quickly returned with two home-made baguettes and a carafe of white wine. "Fishes go better with loaves, isn't that what they always say?" He grinned. "*Mangiatene,* Help yourselves."

Giammo removed the apron and glanced at Pimental. "We'll return to join you for an after dinner drink." The two Jesuits left together, closing the door behind them.

Civil to the last drop of blood, Ryan thought, as he watched them leave.

Emily had pitched into her food, and gestured for Ryan to do the same. "No matter what," she said, "you must be starving. I know I am."

Without answering, Ryan wolfed down several garlicky bites, took a long swig of wine, then turned from his food and stared at the floor, sorting things out with his brain and with his heart alternately—as though he held a Rubik's cube in each hand.

Emily finally broke the silence. "Let me ask you a question," she said without preliminaries. "Is your faith in the principles of Christianity based on nothing more than the historical truth of the Gospel stories?"

"I don't know what my faith is based on." He tried to conceal his annoyance with her. "That's exactly the point, isn't it? I guess I never did." His voice had gone quiet, as though drained of energy. "If Jesus Christ did not really die on the cross, what have I dedicated my life to?"

"You dedicated your life to the principles symbolized by the Jesus story. The story of redemption and transformation. The manner in which those principles originated and were disseminated is irrelevant, isn't it?"

"Of course Christian values are fundamental," Ryan said. "But how can I rationalize my faith when it's becoming evident that the Jesus I've always believed in didn't really walk the earth?"

"Look at it this way. Augustan Christianity has endured

because of the foresight of its founder. Two hundred and sixty-six popes have handed down its principles from one to another for over two millennia. It's the values we believe in and build our lives around, not Jesus' photo i.d. Which, by the way, is missing."

"What do *you* believe in?" he wanted to know.

"I believe in the emperor's good intentions," she replied. "I believe in the morals he sought to enshrine in his cult." She held his gaze. "How could knowing that Augustus founded Christianity change anyone's view of the values his imperial cult embodied, values that deserve to be adhered to much more than the rules and rituals of today's overly-political Church?

"And what's so upsetting about accepting the teachings of the Church as the enduring legacy of a larger-than-life real man who began his career as a savage avenger against the enemies of his beloved adoptive father, then became a ruthless commander who conquered the known world, then finally went on to transform himself into a living god—even as he transformed Rome and the Mediterranean over a span of forty years into the mightiest and most peaceful empire the world has ever known? He truly lived up to his acclamation as Prince of Peace."

She continued her argument. "The militant Augustus was proclaimed in his own time the savior of mankind. His Pax Romana, the Peace of Rome that endured for over 200 years has been considered the longest period free of warfare in the history of Rome and of the world, but it was established with the sword as well as by proclamation," she concluded.

Yet, as much as it all made its own kind of uncanny sense, Ryan wasn't yet jumping onto the bandwagon. Could the thoughts and beliefs of a lifetime be so easily swept aside? What he was being asked to accept was, on the face of it, unbearable—his own crucifixion of doubt. His allegiance to

Roman Catholicism allowed discussion, even his persistent questioning; but it also demanded total acceptance of the final ruling from superior authority. And superior authority, as of the moment, still proclaimed that Jesus was actually born in a manger in Bethlehem, not in a distillation of ancient myths borrowed and crystallized by Augustus Caesar. There was no provision he knew of for the dilemma confronting him now.

His doubts had become dragons, threatening to devour his very faith in faith. He couldn't decide which was worse—to be trapped in this heretical cave, or to be trapped in his own tormented mind.

Ryan could well understand Emily's feelings. With the discovery of the aureus and all the knowledge that had led them to this point, her career was approaching an apex she could never have imagined.

The ramifications of it all were staggering. Even if the Catholic faithful could be made to accept it, the Protestant fundamentalists would go berserk.

But as disbelieving in this "crazy Augustan theory" as he would have liked to be, he had to admit that, if it were true, it made so many pieces suddenly fall into place, things which made no sense to him before: the inability of historians to pinpoint the "Christ" of the Church, or even to agree on the supposed "facts of his life"; the absence of contemporary sources reporting on the life of Jesus of Nazareth; the fact that most of Jesus' statements of wisdom predate him in Egyptian, Jewish, Buddhist, Greek, Roman or near-eastern sacred literature; the inexplicably rapid spread of Christianity throughout the world, in a time where the entire empire was required to honor Augustus as highest among its gods.

If what later became known as Christianity was in fact none other than the imperial cult of Augustus Caesar, "Jasius Augustus"—then the Roman Empire itself would have approved and spread that religion throughout the world. *Of course it would quickly go viral! Why wouldn't it?*

Ryan shook his head. It was becoming all too clear that Emily and Pimental were saying it was historically logical to accept that *Jasius Christus*, Jesus Christ, was simply the imperial cult's name for the deified Caesar Augustus, and that the early Church Fathers would later spin the manufactured mythology to create a literal biblical Jesus.

Emily could no longer contain herself. According to Isaac's notes, she told Ryan, the Sibylline Books that they were now viewing were in the original gold chest in which Augustus had ordered them to be enshrined. The priceless documents had been kept safe by "the Jesuits, the guardians of the ancient religion of Jasius Augustus." From time to time, as political circumstances dictated, the Jesuits had to secrete the artifacts away from the threatened eyes of the Curia—just as they had done again now.

Ryan was fairly certain that the Vatican Curia as well as the Jesuits had read Isaac's print-out containing the story of the Sibylline redaction. One of the chapters from Isaac's work left no doubt that Augustus had altered the ancient books to foreshadow his coming, adding elements gleaned from religions and myths throughout his empire. In effect, he'd written his own divine biography declaring himself the long-awaited Messiah, Redeemer, Healer of All Mankind, the Mighty God, Son of God, Son of Man, Savior, Prince of Peace, King of Kings.

"Are you sure you're really devastated?" Emily asked. "Or are you just dramatizing the intellectual shock of finally having all your questions and doubts laid to rest?"

Why is she being so harsh with me? Doesn't she know how hard this is?

She looked away from him, anguished that a wall had fallen between them.

They finished their loaves and fish in silence.

XLVII/47
Communion

Emily accepted a *limoncello*, Ryan a Cynar to quiet his nerves. Pimental and Giammo, as though to demonstrate the depth and breadth of the cave's wine cellar, chose to indulge in a 1935 Armagnac.

The circle of four sipped in silence until a question that had been gnawing at Ryan finally found voice. "I still don't understand why Monsignor Isaac had to be killed."

Pimental sipped his Armagnac and inhaled deeply. "That is indeed a critical question. The short answer is that he made the mistake of telling the Curia he had no intention of delaying publication of his work. He was not content to wait, probably fearing he might not live to see its publication before God took him. How right he was. The monsignor's decision to publish sealed his fate."

Ryan's throat tightened at the thought that the Vatican had issued the order for Isaac's murder. He was appalled at the callous calculation that ended the life of a devoted Jesuit scholar. *In the name of what higher cause?* "Surely they could have reasoned with him?"

Pimental let out a long sigh. "I believe every inducement was offered but to no avail. The good monsignor's intentions were, it seems, immovable."

Little by little Ryan and Emily drew more details from the two clerics. The Society had long blackmailed—Pimental preferred the word "pressured"—the Papacy with the threat of revealing the truth about the origins of Christianity. They thought they had reached agreement with Pope Pius that all would be revealed by the Vatican to the faithful "in the fullness of time," when the true revisionary Gospel had been recorded accurately, and presented with incontrovertible proof. That had been the mission of Monsignor Isaac.

As Isaac's research advanced, and his DNA tests supported the proof of Augustus' ashes and Paul's identity as a Greek from the island of Samos; and when Emily, a lay person not under ecclesiastical control, discovered the Augustan aureus; the time seemed to be arriving for the Society and the Vatican to make their stunning announcement to the world.

Pimental explained the Society's exuberant certitude that the moment of revelation, thanks to the instantaneous power of the Internet, would manifest the "Omega Point" that excommunicated Jesuit paleontologist-theologian-philosopher Pierre Teilhard de Chardin had prophesied in 1940. It would be the moment when through the universality and instantaneousness of communication all human beings could access all knowledge simultaneously, thereby becoming the very definition that the twelfth-century theologian Alain de Lille gave for God: "an intelligible sphere whose center is everywhere and whose circumference is nowhere."

The equation of humanity with divinity, Ryan knew, was not as strange as it would sound to the less informed communicants. After all, even the Book of Genesis testified that human beings were created in "the image and likeness" of the creator.

Pimental continued. "Augustus proclaimed himself 'the firstborn of god'—to instruct his Augustales, as the first members of his cult were called, that divinity rests within each of us."

Ryan looked thoughtful, and this time expressed what he

was remembering. "Something that Athanasius wrote sounds very like this: 'God became man that man might become God.'"

The Society widened the ecclesiastical gap by its insistence on "justice above religion" and increasing recognition and approbation of the moral truths found in the Osiris-Dionysian cults, in Buddhism, Hinduism, Jainism, Taoism—and Islam. Once again, as it had so many times in previous centuries the Papacy turned against the Jesuits and sought to repress the Augustan origins as an ill-conceived myth, with the exception of maintaining moral tenets that Jasius Augustus had embraced, including the golden rule, "to love thy neighbor as thyself."

It all comes down to who you consider to be your neighbor, Ryan thought.

When Isaac signaled that all was nearing readiness, and the first draft of the narrative had neared completion to accurately record the actual beginning of what over the centuries had become known as Christianity, the pope would make the announcement—and the golden age of peace and universal tolerance among all religions would be initiated via the Internet's proclamation of Jasius Augustus' vision.

That vision would be proclaimed as the "New Pax Romana." Giammo beamed.

"But power changes people," Pimental commented bitterly, "and infallible power changes even popes. We believe that Pius' papal vow to implement our plan was purely Machiavellian. He was meant to repay the Jesuits' political support by announcing the return of the Augustan Age but now it's obvious that he never intended to keep his word and risk threatening his hard-won position of power.

"Until news came to the Vatican Curia of Emily's discovery of the aureus, the new pope had resolutely ignored Monsignor Isaac's research."

"How did they find out about my discovery?" Emily wanted to know.

"We believe Monsignor Isaac's telephone may have been tapped by those at the Vatican determined to protect the pope at all costs," Giammo said.

Emily's face went ashen, but she gestured for Pimental to continue his explanation.

"If we hadn't managed to remove the aureus and Isaac's manuscript from papal hands we would have lost control of the situation forever."

Giammo gave Pimental an uneasy glance.

"You have been unwilling accomplices in this endeavor," Pimental continued, "but nevertheless we've succeeded in averting a disaster—Christianity's true founder consigned to eternal oblivion."

Pope Pius, in an attempt to justify himself, had announced to the Jesuits that he, from the infallible perspective of the throne of Pontifex Maximus, no longer believed that the world was prepared for the universal tolerance promoted by the Augustan religion.

The Jesuits' "Plan B," engineered by Ramon Pimental, was therefore now in effect. The lobbying of the College of Cardinals had begun once again; but this time there would be no bargains between lions and sheep. Argentine Miguel Leontel, S.J. would be the next Pope and, if Pius departed from the throne in a timely manner, he would be allowed to live out his natural lifespan in great luxury.

"And if Pius does not go timely?" Ryan wanted to know.

"If Pius does not go timely, well," Pimental smiled wryly, "practical measures will have to be contemplated." He looked to Giammo for confirmation, but Giammo looked away.

A private meeting had been called between the outgoing Black Pope, Father Schork, and Monsignor Isaac - arranged by

Procurator General Ramon Pimental. Monsignor Isaac was warned that the Roman Curia was no longer to be trusted. At the same time the Society assured the single-minded scholar that he was now under its utmost protection as well as its unlimited financial support.

He must hasten to complete the last piece of the narrative that had occupied him for nearly ten years and prepare the message for public consumption.

He would be duly honored as the designated finder and transcriber of the truth, the chronicler of the new evangelion. As Jerome had been given credit for producing the Vulgate version of the Bible, Isaac would forever be associated with the Gospel according to Augustus.

Schork told Monsignor Isaac that a twenty-four-hour detail of bodyguards would begin shadowing him the next morning.

Emily broke in. "But the next morning never came."

"And now?" Ryan asked, numb from attempting to assimilate the story he'd just been told. *Who could believe such a tale?*

But who could—who would—make it up?

Ryan looked back at Emily, but saw in her face that she was as upset as he was.

"Where do we go from here?" Ryan finally asked.

XLVIII/48
Midnight Visitor

Ryan lay in his damp but comfortable cell and listened to distant water gurgling somewhere beneath him. Incarcerated in a spiritual and intellectual parallax, he was experiencing a true existential crisis. He wondered whether Emily was able to sleep, wondered what she was thinking of all this, wondered if she was thinking of him right now. *How am I going to resolve this dilemma I face? How are we going to get out of the cave, with a twenty-four-hour guard outside the entrance?* It had become all too obvious that his Jesuit superiors would stop at nothing to fulfill their agenda.

He was finally about to nod off sometime after midnight, when he heard a rattling sound from the door. His eyes flew open in time to see the Procurator General letting himself into his room.

Pimental moved to the only chair; and sat down as if visiting a patient in a hospital. "I have come to answer your question, my son," his superior began, "to explain in detail why we are forced to choose this aggressive course of action."

"Explain?" Ryan frowned. "You mean justify and rationalize."

Pimental shrugged. "You know as well as anyone that if it accomplishes its intended purpose, today's rationalization is tomorrow's sacred history. Let me speak. I will let you decide what to make of what I have to say."

The more he'd heard, the less Ryan liked the situation he

had thrust himself into. But he held back and waited for Pimental to proceed. The least he could do was gather as much information as possible.

"Pope Pius's betrayal of the Society was the ultimate evidence that Holy Mother Church has lost her way. In a world characterized by too much fanaticism, the Holy Father cannot accept that she is no longer *prima inter pares*—'first among equals.'"

"When was the Church really *primus* in the world?" Ryan interrupted. "Did Israel, Arabia, India, China, Japan come into being only yesterday? Aren't we all a little too educated to continue confusing Europe with the world?"

As though Ryan had not spoken, Pimental proceeded. "The Church is indeed only one among equals—and we in the Society believe it is inhumane to dream of converting the entire world to Roman Catholicism, especially as it is now practiced, that is, arch-conservatively, self-protectively, and based on mistaken history."

"I'm not sure what you're saying," Ryan interrupted. "It sounds like you're talking in circles. How do you reconcile all this with papal infallibility? What about the doctrine of the Pontifex—that the Church is the *only* link God permits between heaven and earth? And that Simon Peter alone holds the keys to the kingdom. Pope Pius subscribes fully to this doctrine, and has done his best to bring us back to the original ways. Are you suggesting that faith now be left up to the individual? Doesn't that contradict Augustus' demand that everyone honor *him?* Excuse me for being more than a little confused."

"Augustus insisted that everyone honor the divinity within

themselves and it will be the Society's responsibility to guide all humanity to that point," Pimental replied. "What we know about Augustus and his cult tells us that the 'original ways' you're referring to aren't the original ones at all. Corruption of his ethos was rampant from the cult's inception.

"The personal example of Augustus' way of life initiated with our New Pax Romana, will spread throughout the nations via the Internet, and lead to the restructuring of all Christian religions under our direction—even some that are non-Christian—and the final establishment of world peace."

Ryan was stunned. He was well aware that the Jesuits assimilated into their thoughts and teachings the universal principles of the religions they encountered along the way. Jesuit philosophy often seemed more Buddhist than Catholic, more Hindu than Catholic, more Taoist than Catholic.

On one thing he knew for certain, religious fundamentalism had more often than not been a plague on the human race. More people had died in the name of religion than for any other cause, and it was way past time that such paradoxical horror should end.

Pimental's voice lowered. "There's more—something I've waited until now to divulge to you."

In heaven's name, what more could there possibly be? Ryan steeled himself.

"Pope Pius declared privately to Father Schork that he intends to initiate the last Holy War throughout the world—and that Piazza San Pietro will once again be flowing with the blood of martyrs. That is why he cannot afford anything like our Augustan revelation to affect the strength of his infallible authority."

At Ryan's look of horror, Pimental nodded. "Now maybe you understand why the Society prefers a more peaceful way to prepare for the second coming of Augustus that was prophesied by Suetonius in the halls of the senate almost two millennia ago."

Ryan sat paralyzed, the other side of his mind kicking in. If only it was his superiors, not the Holy Father, who were mad. The nightmare Pimental had outlined, if it really *was* the vision of the present Vatican Curia, would be the final straw, the final onslaught against humanity and world peace by organized religions. Either way it left him, the doubter, standing alone, on one side of the vast abyss that separated them, with the Procurator General currently sitting only a few feet away, on the other. *Should I speak or remain silent?* Finally he asked, "What must be done to stop this madness?"

Pimental ignored the question. "The basic difference between the Society and the Curia," the Procurator General said, "is that we trust in the strength of the human spirit and its ability to thrive on freedom, whereas the Vatican believes that freedom is dangerous and that the people are unable to deal with it. Freedom, trust in human nature, and communication are our best hope."

Ryan's stomach was churning. All this talk of freedom was coming from the most disciplined, hierarchically ordered chain of command in the world. Who, Pimental claimed, would be "directing" the Augustan revolution. How could the Procurator General promulgate such high ideals and then suggest doing away with Pope Pius to accomplish them?

Pimental reached forward, took Ryan's hand, and was not deterred when Ryan quickly pulled it away. "Your own pertinacity, my son, has led you to be chosen by our new Father General as Isaac's successor—to witness Emily's conclusion of his investigations, and to revise and complete— for seekers throughout the world—the New Testament according to our Lord, Jasius Augustus."

Ryan sat in bewildered silence, his mind racing. *Revise*

Isaac's entire opus? Me? How in the name of God did I get into this mess?

Pimental waited with a patient, almost paternal, smile on his lips.

Finally Ryan spoke. "And when it's done, you will—what?—assassinate the Holy Father? Disappear him? Poison him in his chambers? So that the conclave of Cardinals can convene to elect Father Leontel his successor?" Ryan turned away from Pimental and stared at the wall, not wanting to see what might be written in Pimental's eyes, afraid to hear his response.

"Pope Pius believes we're content to play out his new concord with Father Leontel: that if we promise to hold off the announcement during his lifetime, we will assume the Papacy, but only upon Pius' death. At that time, as far as Pius is concerned, we're free to reveal the true cult of Augustus and reinstate its universal glory."

Pimental said nothing further. He simply waited.

"I still find it morally unbearable that Isaac had to die."

"As do we, I assure you," Pimental said, placing his spatulate fingers together. "That is why we must be prepared to fight fire with fire. The Holy Father got word that the Monsignor was bent more on proving his theory than on obeying Vatican orders. Isaac simply knew too much and was spinning out of control. His elimination would allow the Vatican to harvest secretly the fruits of the Monsignor's labors before we realized what had occurred; and to thwart the Society of Jesus by removing our ace in the hole. We believe they may have the missing computer files."

Pimental's mention of the files that were resting safely in his Swiss Army knife made Ryan choose his next words carefully. "How exactly was he spinning out of control?" Ryan asked, not trusting his dark suspicion.

The Procurator watched Ryan as he responded. "Ms. Scelba coincidentally discovered the aureus, the Rosetta Stone of Isaac's entire theory that would corroborate his physical findings—if the good monsignor had come into possession of it, he would have never held back. He was a scholarly bulldog. From their point of view, he had to be silenced."

It took all the self-control Ryan possessed to contain his rage. This callous and twisted man seemed to take it for granted that serving God meant having people murdered. He was a fanatic exemplar of the horrors that organized religion had perpetrated.

And Ryan's suspicion had been right. Emily's voice message had been Isaac's death warrant. She must be suffering great remorse since she learned this.

With Isaac's work in the "safe" hands of the Vatican—or destroyed—the Society's ultimate plan would be stopped in its tracks. Ryan understood what Isaac had been facing, and that he and Emily were now caught within a conflict between the will of the Vatican and the will of the Society of Jesus. The ruthlessness that led to the death of Isaac was nothing but the tip of the iceberg.

Ryan tried to keep his voice level. "What about Emily? How does she fit into your plans?"

"Ultimately that remains to be seen," Pimental replied. "For the moment, she can still be useful. The scholarly publication of her findings, and of the significance of the coin, will corroborate the truth of our revelation. She will therefore work here and inspect everything we have collected with absolutely free access. We will hide nothing from her, and will make her comfortable until she has finished her definitive monograph—confirming all from a respected academic's viewpoint."

"She's agreed to this?" Ryan asked.

Pimental nodded.

"Then what?"

"Her work will be published simultaneous with your revision of Isaac's 'Gospel according to Augustus.' Since we haven't been able to restore Isaac's hard drive, with her help you will recreate its contents through both yours and Ms. Scelba's research. Your version of the narrative history will be written, and then translated into Latin and the major languages. You will be promoted to monsignor—eventually bishop, possibly General Counselor to the Society of Jasius—and hailed as a hero of the universal cult of Augustus." He laughed. "Maybe you become the youngest cardinal in history. Maybe even the second Augustan pope."

"All in exchange for keeping the secret of this coup d'état? What makes you think Emily will honor that secret?" Ryan flashed on the New Testament scene where Jesus was tempted on the mountaintop by Satan.

"Alas," Pimental sighed. "We can't afford the luxury of taking that chance. Until she can prove to us that she is trustworthy and until we have reshaped the Gospel as we want it to be released, she will remain here in the cave. She will enjoy the fruits of her publication until she earns the privilege of worshipping in the Chapel of Martyrs."

"The Chapel of Martyrs?"

"You will visit it before long. But remember, it was your own intrepid nature that brought us to this point. It's time for your decision."

Ryan assessed the situation, and rose to his feet.

His voice was flat, but convincing. He took a deep breath, and looked Pimental in the eye. "When I was ordained, I chose to serve, first, the Society of Jesus, then the good of the

Church, in that order. Although I never imagined the two would be at odds, I see no reason to revise that decision. Although I still have much to learn, I am honored with the trust you have placed in me. I have made my choice, and reaffirm my vows. I accept this challenge, and this cross." He paused. "This may very well be the final resolution of all my doubts."

With a smile of approval, Pimental stepped forward. The two men embraced.

XLIX/49
The Cumaean Library

Pimental escorted Ryan to a dry, well-regulated chamber that could have served as the library of a king. Its shelves were lined with the great works of the Roman tradition, many in their original scrolls. Ryan's eyes widened as he saw the names inscribed in several languages beneath the various shelves: *The Egyptian Book of the Dead,* Aurelius, Josephus, Constantinus, *Letters of Paul to Seneca, The Book of Peter, Preaching of Peter and Paul in Rome, Joseph's Flight into Egypt* by Arius Calpurnius Piso, *The Bhagavad-Gita, The Life of Apollonius,* Eusebius, Octavianus, Maecenas.

"These are copies from the Vatican Library." Ryan was in awe.

Pimental winked. "The copies are *in* the Vatican Library. These are the originals, here for transitional safekeeping."

"Transitional to what?" Ryan asked.

"Transitional to outgrowing their usefulness, and when you have created your *magnum opus,* they will be re-scanned, digitized, and secreted in a vault that, once locked, can't be unlocked for a hundred years. By then we anticipate the world will be—how should I put it?—less archaic in its thinking."

"You seem to have thought of everything." Ryan could hardly believe his ears. "You have what looks like the entire Gnostic library here." Ryan noticed identically-bound volumes that occupied three shelves.

Pimental explained. "Yes, all fifty-two manuscripts,

including *The Aprocryphon of James and of John, The Gospel According to Philip and to Thomas,* Marcion's *Gospel of the Lord,* the *Sophia of Jesus Christ...* All had been hidden at Nag Hammadi in Upper Egypt until they were rediscovered and brought to our library here by Monsignor Isaac."

Ryan noted the cot at one end of the room, his eyes showing recognition.

"Yes, it's your very own," Pimental said, "transported from the College." He paused, smiled. "You are right. We do try to think of everything. Please, make yourself comfortable in your somewhat upgraded cell. There's still time to get some sleep tonight."

There could be no question of Pimental's madness. Ryan gave him a glance he hoped would be one of complicity. He noticed that his photos were already on the writing desk along with his laptop. Pimental had turned to leave. "Where's Emily now?" Ryan asked.

"Giammo has escorted her to a library room of her own." Pimental paused, then winked again. "Hers *are* copies."

"One more thing I still don't understand," Ryan said. "Why did Constantine drop Augustus' name and call the cult Christianity?"

"The Emperor Constantine believed the god who intervened with the ✳ symbol that omened his astonishing victory was none other than *Jasius Christus,* Jesus Christ. He was insightful enough to realize that contemporary human nature would not allow it to endure with an emperor's name." Pimental's smile was engaging.

In the days that followed, Ryan established a routine. Exercise for a half hour upon arising, work at the desk until two p.m.

laboring over Isaac's manuscript, which he read only from the memory stick without loading it onto the computer's hard drive; then a search through the ample shelves to corroborate the monsignor's scholarship. The text of each church father Ryan now read through new eyes. He had to admit that they made more sense in light of the Augustan paradigm.

Every time he heard a sound outside the door, Ryan pulled the portable drive out of the machine and concealed it. He wondered what would happen if Pimental realized he already possessed Isaac's work, but he certainly wasn't taking any chances until he'd gotten to the end of his quest for the entire truth.

The two young Americans were allowed to meet in the private dining room for a late repast—their only substantial meal of the day—and to compare notes. Their computers' Internet access and email functions had been permanently disabled.

Ryan began meticulously comparing the densely written text of Matthew's Gospel with the surviving Sibylline oracles that had been preserved since the time of Augustus. He was pretty much convinced that the so-called Matthew text was bogus—at best, it was a poorly rendered copy of the oracles combined with other ancient texts.

As he read the ancient codices with trembling hands, Ryan could begin to visualize how Augustus had adopted traditional writings to reflect his own divine biography, and to predict himself—in language borrowed from several cultures including the Jewish Talmud—as the long-awaited Messiah. Ryan's eyes were opened as he pieced together how much of Biblical text resembled Augustus' handiwork and how the process of assimilation and distortion that led from Augustan cult to Christianity had come about. And that it subsequently spread all over the empire for almost 300 years until Constantine restored it closer to Augustus' original vision and gave, at the Council of Nicaea, his official blessing to the now-completely-assimilated cult of Jesus Christ.

Meanwhile Emily had researched the history of the word "Jesus" beginning with the Egyptian *Iusu* or *Iusa* as an epithet of Horus, the Hebrew *Yehoshua* which underwent a spelling change into the Aramaic *Yeshua* or *Joshua,* meaning "Jahweh saves"; the ancient Attic Greek *iasos,* "healer," from *Iaso,* goddess of healing; the Koine Greek used at the time the New Testament was written, *Iesous;* the Gallic *Hesus;* and the ancient Roman, *Iasus*—and saw that *Iasius*—or Jasius as it was spelled after the letter J was invented centuries later—was an amalgamation cleverly forged to enhance Augustus' stature in as many cultures as possible, especially in Rome where the divine Father Jasius was believed to be the god who founded the Eternal City. The final westernized version, *Jesus,* was simply the last in a long line of etymological progressions.

Little by little they were understanding how the Augustan editors had blended together ancient multi-national texts along with Hebrew and Greek sacred writings into the Gospels of the Augustan cult—exactly as Virgil, under Augustus' vigilant patronage, had woven previous epics like Homer's *Iliad* and *Odyssey* and Apollonius of Rhodes' *Argonautica* with Roman, Italian, and Greek oral tradition to form the marvelous imperial tapestry of *The Aeneid.*

"I have to admit that everything I'm reading in Isaac's narrative," Ryan said, "is making it all more and more persuasive."

"You sound disappointed." Emily tried to read his eyes. *Had Ryan been won over to the truth?* She decided to give Ryan her notes. "I'd love to review yours too—I'll show you mine, if you show me yours." She smiled mischievously.

L/50
Return of the Dragon

By the time they met again for their afternoon repast, Ryan had finished studying Emily's notes. "I have to admit I wasn't prepared to face everything I read in your notes, and Isaac's research really hit me between the eyes." He hadn't touched his food. "It's going to take a while for all of this to settle in, but I'm fast becoming a believer."

Emily was relieved but knew he needed time to think things through. They consumed their simple meal of bread, cheese, and olives in silence while Ryan's thoughts churned.

As she finished the last few bites of food on her plate she glanced across at Ryan. "There's more you might want to know."

"I don't think anything will surprise me now." The hint of a smile belied his solemn tone. "Go ahead, enlighten me."

"Isaac told me about a gold-glass roundel that was uncovered at Masada." Emily sipped the last of her wine. "It featured the image of the bearded Augustus and the inscription, *Bibe sacramento Iasio Augusto,*" "Drink the sacramental Jasius Augustus."

Ryan looked at her with amazement. "What is gold-glass?"

"It's a process the Romans probably learned from the Egyptians. Mixing gold into glass as you blow it, so the finished product goes from clear to red."

"Red like blood..." Ryan muttered, more to himself than her.

"*Sacramentum* was the name given to the oath Augustus ordered that his legionnaires take before being initiated into active duty. His cult turned it from a military to a religious term."

"Hold on a minute," Ryan interrupted. "Am I understanding you right? You're saying the Holy Sacrament of the Eucharist, drinking the wine that has been transubstantiated into the sacred blood of Christ, was initiated by Jasius Augustus?"

"Well not exactly," Emily nodded. "It was a practice the Greek Mystery cults adopted from the Egyptians before them."

"My God, even the Holy Eucharist?"

"Yes, even that. So now you see why it's even more important to get the hell out of this cave and spread this information freely around the world."

God help us, Ryan thought. "That's assuming we *can* make it out of here alive," he said.

For almost the entire first week of their scholarly confinement, they saw no more of the errant Procurator General. They threw all their energy into filling in the gaps in Isaac's narrative, debating with each other over their research. Together they were closing in on the mysterious details of the truth that the Jesuits had consistently championed—and that the Vatican was currently intent on hiding from the world.

Their hands often touched during their lively discussions, recreating a palpable chemistry that both tried to ignore.

During one of their afternoon repasts they were sitting side by side going over Emily's notes when suddenly the deep drone of the generator that had been part of the daily background soundscape began to falter and finally grind to a halt. The single light bulb overhead flickered for a few moments and then left them in total darkness.

"What, they didn't pay the power bill?" Emily said.

Ryan realized as they clumsily moved apart he had been more focused on the clean smell of soap on Emily's skin than on her research notes.

They could hear their own breathing and a very faint tap-tap-tapping sound in the distance, as if someone was working with tools.

"Must be someone trying to fix the generator," Ryan said.

Emily sighed. "Now what?" She was increasingly uneasy in the pitch black, and reached for Ryan's hand.

"We sure won't be playing charades," Ryan joked.

"At least there are votive candles in the corridor. Maybe now's a good time to take our daily constitutional. I could use a good stretch." She tugged at his hand.

"Sounds like a plan."

They began slowly walking toward the door and had taken only a few steps when Emily stumbled into the refectory cart and nearly lost her balance.

"Jesus! What bozo left that there!"

"I suggest you mind your language around here, young lady—at least until we determine whether 'Jesus' is the best choice of expletives or not."

They proceeded cautiously, feeling their way, until they reached the dimly lit corridor. The soft glow of the votives cast eerie shadows from the multiple mouths of the passageway, and the only sound that could be heard was their footsteps and the incessant tap-tap-tapping.

"Why don't we find the oculus and get some fresh air?" Emily suggested. "We might even see some sun. I've been feeling like a bat down here."

Walking toward the Sybil's throne they noticed that the

retractable wall was standing ajar. The fragrant smell of incense filled their nostrils and reminded them of the heretical ritual in which they had been compelled to participate upon their arrival to this dark underworld.

Emily looked toward Ryan wondering if they dare trespass down the rock-hewn staircase. Ryan started to move away but curiosity drew her slowly into the dim recess. Ryan hesitantly followed. The barest glimmer of candlelight guided them as they softly made their way downward into the sacrosanct chamber.

Emily was on the last step when she thought she heard her name spoken in a soft murmur, as if in a prayer. She gasped when she stepped into the chamber and witnessed the Procurator General sipping from Augustus' golden chalice; his lips were so red that, for a split second, she thought it might not be wine at all that he was drinking.

Pimental turned toward them and hurriedly wiped his lips on an embroidered white linen napkin. His elongated shadow stretched into the gloom.

"We didn't realize you had returned," Emily offered.

Pimental ignored her comment. "May I inquire why you have entered this sacred chamber uninvited?" A menacing undertone lurked beneath the disciplined voice.

Ryan spoke over Emily's shoulder. "We were in the refectory when the lights went out and saw the...well, we decided to—"

"—to trespass," Pimental interrupted, his tone betrayed irritation. "One of your characteristic vices. I really must insist that you ask permission before entering this most sacred chamber."

"I am to blame," Emily stammered. "My curiosity got the better of me. We saw the candlelight and followed it down the stairwell."

Pimental cleared his throat. "There is no harm done, my children," his voice once again under control. "But please return to your quarters for the present. You will be summoned to meet in the refectory when the lights return. I'm sure there is much to discuss."

Later, over a simple meal of bread, cheese, and red wine Pimental spent hours with Ryan and Emily being updated on their progress, nodding affably first at Ryan, then Emily, as they shared details they had discovered—careful to exclude information they'd gleaned only from those sections of Isaac's narrative that the Society had not seen, in the drive Ryan had carefully kept hidden.

The long sessions became regular after that, the most intense hours Ryan had ever spent—so intense they paid no attention to what they were eating or drinking. After one such session, Pimental excused himself to retire and they realized it was eight o'clock. They'd been talking for six hours. They noticed a slight shuffle in his walk as he moved toward the door, a misguided man of God weary from the heavy burden he was carrying.

Then Emily turned to confront Ryan. "Despite what you've said about getting out of here, I'm aware of the choice you've made," she said. "I can't blame you. And I'm also well aware that your Society will never let me leave this cave to reveal its pending revolution."

"How are you so sure of all this?" Ryan reached for her hand.

Despite the electricity she felt in his touch, she withdrew her hand. "It's the only thing that makes sense," she said. "The only way they'd give a firebrand like me access—the only way they'd trust a doubting Thomas like you." Her sense of humor seemed to return. "And on top of that, I heard every word that you and Pimental said that night in your cell."

Ryan's face showed his surprise.

"There was a fissure in the wall."

Ryan smiled. "If you know me so well," he said, "then you'd know what I'm about to do." He rose and moved toward her.

She stood up to face him.

He opened his arms to embrace her; she lifted her face to his. It seemed inevitable that it had come to this. The attraction between them was too powerful; the temptation to play with fire had become irresistible.

But the sound of Giammo's muffled footsteps moving toward them aborted the moment. They separated just as he entered.

"I must clear the table," Giammo said, feeling the tension that laced the room. It was his routine polite way of telling them it was bedtime.

"We were just leaving," Emily said, her head reeling from what had almost happened. "What do we do now," she whispered to Ryan, whose hand reached for hers in the corridor, the spark again arcing between them.

"We escape."

Their plotting occupied the evenings' "nightcap meetings," after Pimental retired. The key to their plan was based on the fact that both of them had heard distant water rushing beneath the floors of their original cells, but could not hear it from their studies, which were on the same side of the cave as the oracle's throne. "There must be a stream beneath us," Emily said.

"Isaac wrote that the cave was surrounded *on all sides* by water, and that leaving it by the secret stream would cause it to collapse upon itself."

"Yikes," Emily said. "What do you think that means?"

"Legends long before Virgil told of the underground river of Styx or Phlegraean," Ryan replied. "I've been reading the geographer Strabo, too, who says the same thing. The warm stream must be the source of the hot baths the place has been known for since prehistory."

"Too hot to be swimmable?"

"Hopefully less hot as it moves underground," Ryan said, uncertainty in his voice. "Otherwise we'll end up looking like a couple of lobsters."

XLI/51
Final Confession

On the appointed morning, shoes and napkins tied around their necks, feet clad only in socks to avoid noise, and with Ryan's backpack in place, they were to rendezvous in front of Emily's study at exactly four a.m. No one would be expecting them in their usual places at the refectory table before eight. By that time, they planned to be long gone.

But plans have a way of going awry.

Emily stood outside her door, worried about encountering a random pass-by by Giammo. But four-fifteen came and went with no sign of Ryan. Just as she was reopening the door again to retreat to the safety of her lodgings, Ryan rounded the corner.

"You wore your collar," Emily noted, trying to conceal the disappointment in her voice. Then she noticed how upset he looked. "What's wrong? You almost gave me a heart attack. Problem with your alarm?"

"I've got the ashes of course, but—the memory stick is missing," he said simply.

"What do you mean it's missing?"

"I left it under the desktop in my library," he said. "I've been hiding it there for several days, after I used it. I went for it this morning, and it's not there."

"You must have misplaced it," she said. "Let's go look together. We can't leave without it," she added. "Not after all this."

Ryan led the way back to his door, opened it, and turned on the lights.

Emily scanned the room as she would a new archaeological site, trying to see what was truly there and not what she expected to see, just the way her mother had taught her when she was very young.

Ryan went back to the computer, searched again beneath it. No luck. Checked in the drive port, and of course it was not there.

Emily was on hands and knees examining the marble pavement beneath Ryan's desk, and beneath his cot. "Did you lock the room when you were in the refectory?"

Ryan admitted, sheepishly, that he never locked the room, even when he was sleeping. "Pimental must have known about the stick, or Giammo."

"One of them took it while we were eating. When was the last time you saw it?"

"That's just it," Ryan said. "I got it ready last night, wrapped it with foil, and put it back under the computer so I could grab it this morning."

Emily shuddered, glad that she had always locked her room before she went to bed. "Obviously you had another visitor during the night. You must be a sound sleeper."

"Never mind my sleeping habits," Ryan said. "We can't leave without it, can we?"

"What choice do we have?"

"How many times did you read it?" he asked.

"Twice," she said. "You were hogging it most of the time, remember. How many times did you read it?"

"At least three times," he said.

"Then we have a choice. We either take our chances and remain until we find it, or we get the hell out of here now and rely on our joint memory to reconstruct it together."

"We can't stay," he said. "It's clear they knew we kept it hidden from them. There's no way we can be trusted at this point."

"And we know they prefer forgiving the dying to forgiving the living."

In the days that preceded the planned escape, they'd reread every word they could find about Cumae in the scrolls and codices—and every word of Monsignor Isaac's "The Gospel according to Augustus." Giving up on the historians and church fathers, Ryan had finally turned back to Book VI of *The Aeneid,* and followed Isaac's written tips to search beneath the epic's symbolism for clues to the way out.

Until he read Isaac's reminder, he had completely forgotten that the exact way in which the Sibyl led Virgil's hero into the underworld was only vaguely described in the epic. Arguably the actual entrance into Hades was not through the Cumaean cave at all but through some other entrance, near a lake known as Avernus to the Romans—"birdless," because the fumes issuing from it, lethal for birds, ensured that none could be found nearby. If there was another entrance, there was an exit to be found somewhere.

Ryan doubted that this piece of avian literary trivia would be useful. And where were he and Emily going to find a "golden bough" that would light the way through the darkness back to the light of the sun? *At least we still have our flashlights,* he thought, *to substitute for Virgil's "shining branch."*

Each day, too, leading up to this morning, they'd taken a foray during their walk into different alcoves of the cave. Leaving via the main entrance was out of the question. Not only was the guard posted outside, but an iron gate had been lowered between the inner cavern and the sealed mouth of the cave. Though their shared research all pointed to there being a secret outlet, Ryan and Emily couldn't help but worry when he repeated Virgil's dire comment that, "*Facilis descensus Averno,*" "the way down was easy," but the way up, "*Hoc opus, hic labor est,*" was "the difficult part."

Pimental had promised they would visit the Chapel of Martyrs eventually. They'd finally stumbled onto its entrance on their own a day earlier when they discovered that the columnar arch directly opposite the Sibyl's chamber led to a kind of bulkhead with a passageway on each side they had not yet explored. The odor of sulfur grew stronger as they hiked to the end of the corridor—only to find it most intense at the gold door blocking their path. The secret opening had to be through the chapel.

They'd looked at each other. Emily reached into the back pocket of her jeans and pulled out the key card that had permitted them entrance to the secret catacomb. She turned for confirmation to Ryan, who gave her a shrug. Why not? The key had worked everywhere else.

Here it did not.

Ryan held his hand out and Emily, rolling her eyes, handed it to him.

He gave it a try. No luck.

"What do we do now?" she whispered. "Let me see if I have a hairpin." She reached into her pouch.

But Ryan had another idea. He still held the plastic card with the papal coat of arms. Instead of inserting it into the security device as they'd both done repeatedly, he slipped it into the crack between the tongue of the lock and the door—the way police demonstrate a house-breaker's easiest trick.

And it worked. The card slipped down the tongue of the lock. They heard a click, and the door opened into what could only be the chapel Pimental told them about.

"It's too easy," Ryan said.

"Don't look a gift horse in the mouth," Emily replied, starting to enter.

But Ryan pulled her back. "Every gift horse we've run into so far has been a Trojan horse. We'll see it when the time comes," he said. "Now let's just make sure we aren't caught here."

"At least we know we can get in," Emily said.

The morning of the escape, still agitated from the loss of the memory stick, they faced the chapel door again.

"Visa or MasterCard?" Emily asked.

Ryan chuckled as she used her American Express gold card. He followed her in. The scent of sulfur assailed their nostrils as they entered, and the chapel was warmer than the rest of the cavern. They froze at a noise that sounded like the scraping of steel against stone, but it immediately stopped and they assumed it was only the door closing.

The votive lamps were lit in here as well as in the cavern itself—casting, Ryan thought, an almost hellish hue on their surroundings. He felt like Dante walking into the Inferno.

Both sides of the long marble aisle that faced them were lined with a breathtaking array of red porphyry sarcophagi that looked exactly like the ones Michelangelo sculpted in Florence's Cappella dei Medici. In gold-embossed letters, the marble sepulchers proudly proclaimed their occupants. Ryan and Emily found it hard to believe their eyes as they read the names: Alaric, Constantinus Magnus, Galileo Galilei, Leonardo da Vinci, Michelangelo Buonarroti, Napoleon Bonaparte, Andrej Niemojewski and onward as far as they could see—

facing, on the opposite side—Ignatius Loyola, S.J., Francesco Borgia, S.J., Francis Xavier, S.J., Pierre Teilhard de Chardin, S.J.

They took no further time to pause as they moved through the crypt toward the far side, until Ryan stopped to note the gilded inscription on the wall above the tombs that provided the key to their question about this particular assembly: *Defensores fidei verae,* "Defenders of the true faith," he translated. On the wall opposite Emily read, *Testimoni Augusto,* "Witnesses to Augustus."

"I guess this is all the evidence we need that at least the belief in Augustus goes way back," Ryan mused. "Do you think it's really possible, as Pimental suggests, that the Society of Jesus was formed to protect the knowledge of Christianity's true origins?"

"I think that's what Pimental was trying to tell us," Emily answered. "But I don't understand what we're seeing here. How can these be tombs? Maybe they're just monuments. Aren't most of these bodies buried elsewhere?"

"I was thinking the same thing," Ryan said. "Father Manuel is buried in a side chapel of Gesù. I used to pass what I thought was his final resting place every day."

"Napoleon is buried in Les Invalids in Paris," Emily said.

"And Michelangelo in Florence," Ryan added.

They both stopped when they reached the last few tombs that had inscriptions—with a few as yet un-inscribed. Suddenly Emily gasped, and fell to her knees.

Ryan reached for her instinctively, and then saw the inscription she was staring at: "Msgr Oscar Isaac, S.J."

"He's here," she said, in a whisper, as she reached forward and touched the cold marble.

"Yes," a voice from the shadows agreed. Giammo, a smock covering his clerical gabardine, stepped in front of them, chisel in hand. He pointed to the next tomb, and then wiped away, with the sleeve of his cassock, the curls of fresh-carved gold from the inscription, until the letters came clear:

"Emily Scelba, Ph.D."

"And so would you be shortly, my dear," Giammo said. "Safe for all eternity here among the elect, the *cognoscenti*—those who know the truth about Augustus."

She showed no surprise and gave him a withering look. "So it ends up being publish *and* perish with you guys, is that it?"

Ryan admired her bravado.

Giammo, smiling at her joke, confirmed that the elite entombed in the Chapel of Martyrs were initiates, like themselves, to the true faith of Augustus—many of them preeminent Jesuits, from the time of St. Ignatius, who had long honored the Augustan cult.

The initiates had refurbished the hidden parts of the cave, where they preserved the artifacts of the true faith in readiness for this day. The Jesuits had faithfully sought out, and brought here for eternal rest, the remains of those who died believing *in nomine patris, et filii, et spiritus sancti*—"in the name of Father Julius, his beloved son Augustus, and the *logos*, the spirit of peace and love that flows between them."

In front of Isaac's tomb Giammo reaffirmed in no uncertain terms that Isaac had been condemned not by the Jesuits but by the Vatican Curia. Following the Curia's directions, he admitted that he himself had given the order, but only because he was led to believe that the Vatican's decision had been condoned by the Black Pope.

He had been told at the time that Isaac was on the verge of

publishing his work on the Internet, though he now doubted that was true. Only recently had he learned that the Curia had betrayed him as well as the entire Society of Jesus. The phone call inciting him to murder was counterfeit; it had not been known to Father Schork at all.

Emily's expression showed no sympathy. "Either way," she accused, "Monsignor Isaac was doomed."

The elder Jesuit rushed on to explain the sequence of events. Under Pius XIII, the conservative Vatican Curia became increasingly uncomfortable with the possibility that the Christian faithful would move from their current dogmatic orthodoxy toward an embrace of moral principles that were the same for all humanity: "love and compassion, patience, tolerance, forgiveness, contentment, a sense of responsibility, a sense of harmony, which brings happiness to both self and others."

Emily looked at Ryan. "Where have I heard those words before?" she asked.

"They're the words of the Dalai Lama," Ryan said. "I memorized them when I studied meditation with Eknath Easwaran." He turned to Giammo. "But what you've just said makes no sense. Surely the Church supports love and compassion and all those other principles?"

Giammo shook his head. "While the Roman Catholic Church may pay lip service to such ideals the reality can be quite the opposite, as you've witnessed yourself."

"So how does all this tie in with Augustus?" Emily glared at Giammo.

"The Dalai Lama shares the same faith Augustus sought to instill: the one the emperor had learned from Apollonius of Samos and that Teilhard prophesied would someday again be made universal by the worldwide web of knowledge and communication. Isaac's Albanian assassin of course had no idea of all this." Giammo's tone was halfway between apology and bewilderment. "He was nothing more than a gun for hire."

"Or he would've been buried right here with the others, is that it?" Emily commented. "And speaking of guns for hire isn't that a gun I see in the folds of your cassock?"

Giammo continued as if he hadn't heard her. "I had no idea what I'd perpetrated until a day later, when I heard that the assassin I commissioned had been executed by a man on a red Vespa in front of Gesù."

"Where I gave him the last rites," Ryan said.

Giammo nodded. "But let me finish," he said. "When the connection was made between the Albanian and Father Isaac, I realized that the gunman was a Vatican hire, who removed the assassin so he would never talk—and that I had been deceived.

"I reported my suspicions to the Procurator General. We hurried to evacuate the artifacts remaining in the Jesuit archives as well as in the underground secret treasury adjacent to them. Because I, obviously, had become a marked man who stood between the Curia and its deeds, my death in the fire was contrived so that I could continue functioning for the good of the Society. But underground."

"Your own little witness-protection plan," Emily said. "How convenient for you not to have to face the consequences of your actions. I guess that's the difference between being an individual and being a member of an order." She looked pointedly at Ryan.

"Believe me, Miss Scelba, I am facing the consequences in my own way," Giammo replied, then fell silent.

"Why are you admitting all this now?" Ryan asked Giammo, letting Emily's jibe slip by.

"What doth it profit a man," the bishop said, "if he gain the whole world but suffer the loss of his immortal soul?" quoting the words of Augustus recorded in Matthew's Gospel, words that Ignatius Loyola lived by. "What they have asked me to do next is more than I can contemplate. Chiseling your name, my dear, I realized it has gone too far, and I can no longer rationalize that the end justifies the means. I'm afraid the Society has unwittingly imitated the errors of the papacy." He shrugged, as though apologizing for the history of the world. "I needed you to know as much of the truth as I do," Giammo said, "in case your own fates allow you to escape."

Ryan and Emily exchanged a glance.

"One way or another, we are going to escape," Ryan said. "You can depend on that."

"*Buona fortuna,*" Giammo said. "Keep your wits about you, and may you go with the Son of God."

The bishop turned his back on them and headed for the entrance to the chapel. He stopped there and looked back. "The Jesuits believe, no matter how over-zealous their leadership may have become," he said, "that the public announcement by Father Leontel that Augustus and Jesus were one and the same, along with his proclamation of the moral principles Jasius Augustus meant to purvey to the world, will break down all the old structures that are in danger of falling anyway—and make way for a new era of peace.

"People will realize that divinity lies not in heavenly or earthly gods but in the immortal god within each one of us. I hope so. I would like to believe it too; but I admit to you now that I have my doubts. Not about the truth, but about its purveyors. The order may not be ready to allow freedom, anymore than the Vatican. Exchanging one totalitarian rule for another would be pathetic."

"What about the truth?" Ryan demanded. "Where does that figure into the equation? And who are we to decide what humanity is capable of?"

"The truth," Giammo said, "is what I have spent my

lifetime serving. But what *is* truth? Is it in the details or in the essence?"

On that enigmatic note, he was already walking out of the chapel.

At the portal, the bishop stopped, turned back for a moment, reached into his pocket, and pulled out a small object that flashed even in the dim light of the chapel. "I almost forgot," he said. "I've read enough of this to know it's better off in your hands than in anyone else's. Guard it with your lives until the truth must come to light. You should have about half an hour before anyone notices you are missing. Make the most of it. I've always believed this chamber has a secret exit, though I've never managed to find it myself." He placed the foil-wrapped object on a candle niche.

He smiled and turned toward the door. "I hope you are blessed with divine guidance."

"Is that what I think it is?" Emily asked nervously, moving close to Ryan.

He walked toward the niche and retrieved the portable drive, placing it safely into his travel pouch. "Let's not waste any time finding the way out," he said. "We're going to need all the divine guidance we can get."

His words were punctuated with the resounding clash of metal on stone. What looked to be a steel-enforced firewall had clanged into place at the chapel entrance, shutting them inside. The echoing gave way to an eerie dead silence.

Emily jostled Ryan with her arm. "What *is* it with us and entombment?"

LII/52
Exeunt omnes.

"Entombment is getting old, is what it is," Ryan replied. "He didn't sound the alarm—or try to stop us. Maybe he really did have a change of heart."

The red votive lights, embedded in the wall niches, seemed indeed to illuminate the antechamber to hell.

"Yeah, silly me to think for a moment that a ten-ton iron door would hold us back."

"We weren't going to leave that way," Ryan said. "We came in that way. He had to have known that."

"I see what you mean," Emily said. "It doesn't add up, does it? He believes that the way out is somewhere in this room. After all, he gave us back the stick. But I don't mind admitting that seeing my name on that tomb was alarming. What if we don't find a way out? What if this is just another set up?" Emily shuddered and instinctively reached for Ryan in the near-dark, pulling him toward her.

He could see her eyes shining up at his in the flicker of the red lamps. He started to speak but she cautioned him with a finger to his lips.

Her slight touch was all that was necessary to ignite the circuit between them—and the next thing he knew he was crushing her body to his in a passionate embrace, an all-consuming kiss that made him feel more alive than he ever remembered feeling. It was as if he had freed his soul from captivity and consigned it to her sweet welcome—all thoughts of vows obliterated in a dimension of blissful rightness he could never have imagined even in church.

Their kiss was explosive, enduring, ardent and bore the intensity of the moment and the power of eternity.

How could he have thought this place was Hell? He was holding an angel, and would never let go.

Emily was responding with equal intensity, so dazed that she had to remind herself to keep breathing. Was this really a priest making her so weak at the knees?

They had never in their lives experienced such profound unity, as though their very beings had been forged into one.

Emily finally broke away. "Why did I do that? I—I'm sorry," she stammered.

"I'm not," Ryan whispered huskily. "I may have lived my whole life around a lie. At least now I still have something real to live for."

What sounded like a gunshot rang out on the other side of the steel door, the metal resonating like a gong.

"Omigod—sounds like Giammo did have a gun after all. Someone will have heard that shot," Emily whispered. "We've got to get out now!"

"He must have ended his life. God rest his soul. But you're right we've got to escape this hellhole—and fast. Do you still smell the sulfur?"

Emily sniffed the air. "Yes, as a matter of fact. It's even stronger now than when we entered the chapel."

"That's because the air is shut in with us. Which means—"

"—wherever it's coming from, it's not coming from the entrance. I still have my flashlight," she said, reaching into her hip pack and removing the compact LED they'd purchased in Rome before entering the catacombs.

With the light's guidance they scanned the way to the far end of the cavern—to the wall opposite the now-sealed firewall entrance.

On both sides nearly every inch of the long cavern walls were hidden behind the marble sepulchers. But at the far end opposite the entrance, the wall was unobstructed. Emily's beam revealed the surface was decorated with a perfectly-preserved Roman fresco, like the ones she'd marveled at in Pompeii and Herculaneum, only this one was much freer of the ravages of time.

But Ryan was looking at the architecture rather than the fresco. The walls were grooved on both sides and the top was outlined by an architrave raised above the surface of the surrounding masonry, as though it were a portal. "Maybe this is a door," he said.

Emily shook her head. "See any hinges? It's not a door. I've seen almost the exact configuration in Egypt, in a temple near Luxor. It's what Egyptologists refer to as a false door, a symbolic portal through which the *ka,* the departing soul, can come and go. Like this one, they often have sunken panels carved into them, giving it the appearance of a paneled wooden door."

"Seems strange to go to all the trouble of making a false door," Ryan said as he turned his attention to the fresco. "But this image is familiar—it's the tree of life." He was admiring the Roman artist's ability to depict this ancient symbol in both its full complexity and simplicity at one and the same time. Despite the centuries that passed since its creation, the tree's branches remained the darkest green he'd ever seen. The heart-shaped leaves shone with such vivid colors that it took a moment to realize that the branches were teeming with life: birds, animals, insects, flowers, figs, oranges—all positioned among the branches issuing from the straight trunk. The roots of the tree penetrated the dark brown soil depicted beneath it; its crest pierced a full golden moon.

"The tree is the prototype of the cross," Emily said. "Planted at the navel of the earth, it stretches its branches to embrace the horizon and its roots to bridge heaven and hell."

Suddenly a distant bell rang in Ryan's memory. "The way up and the way down," he said, "are the same thing."

"What?"

"A fragment from Heraclitus, an ancient Greek philosopher. He meant that the shaman, because he knows where the world tree stands, has access to both heaven and hell. He crawls down its roots to the underground, up its branches to heaven."

"Like Jesus on the cross," Emily said.

Ryan ignored her. "I'm convinced this wall is a real portal. He stepped back for a better perspective. "See how the mortar is raked around the edges of the *door?*"

Emily sighed in exasperation, then watched with horror as Ryan ran at the masonry—only to bash his shoulder. He winced.

"Now do you believe me?"

"Okay, okay," he said, rubbing his shoulder.

"Look, one of its branches is gold." Emily had returned her gaze to the fresco and was running her fingers across the brightly shining branch that seemed to be three-dimensional. It was pointing inward, toward what appeared to be the opposite side of the wall.

"The golden bough," Ryan said to himself out loud. "Remember the golden branch the old woman said not to forget—and that the Sibyl told Aeneas would lead him out of Hades?" He pressed his ear against the wall. "Come here," he motioned. "Do you hear it?"

Emily stood next to him, following his gesture. "Water. I can hear running water like I heard the first night in that damp cell."

"There must be a secret switch around here that will prove to you this wall *is* a door. We just have to find it."

"You've seen too many movies," Emily teased. I've spent my life as an archaeologist without finding a single secret switch."

"Then we'll have to break through. Trust me on this—it's the way out." Ryan looked around the chamber for a tool.

Their eyes, at the same moment, fixed on the sepulcher where Giammo had been carving Emily's name. It was at a slight angle from the wall, not yet in its permanent position.

"You've got to be kidding," she said. "We'd never be able to move it."

"We have no choice." Ryan had positioned himself at the end closer to the wall.

Emily, grumbling, moved to the other end.

To their astonishment the sepulcher swung about easily, and they had to cling to it to maintain their balance. It was on rollers.

"I don't believe we're doing this," Emily said. "In seconds, they aligned the sepulcher with the wall fresco.

"Wait," Ryan said. "The napkins."

They raised the napkins to cover nose and mouth. With a final glance at each other, they heaved the improvised battering ram toward the false door.

The weighty tomb roared across the thirty feet of marble pavement toward the grooved wall, gaining momentum as they pushed.

It slammed into the tree of life with enormous force—and a resounding roar.

The ancient masonry gave way from the impact—and they were nearly overwhelmed by the influx of pungent fumes.

LIII/53
Inferno

The next few seconds' cascade of events passed in a single terrifying blur. Holding onto the sepulcher, Ryan and Emily fought to stay on their feet as the marble projectile careened through the wall—falling masonry narrowly missing them—and, like a roller coaster, instantly dipped in a stomach-wrenching forty-five degree angle to race down the fume-filled incline on the other side of the cavern.

The screeching noise of the marble tomb against uncarved rock was nerve-grating—but even more horrendous was the deafening rumble made by the collapse of the vaulted chamber behind them. Their rupture of the wall had triggered an implosion that buried the Chapel of the Martyrs, maybe even the entire Cave.

The surface beneath was slippery now and it was impossible to stay on their feet as the momentum increased. Not daring to let go, they allowed themselves to be dragged downward through the gaseous chamber.

Suddenly, with an enormous splash of nearly scalding sulfuric water, they were plunged into a subterranean river. The sepulcher that had been their salvation dropped like a stone into the river, creating a vacuum that dragged them into the depths of the infernal stream—and suddenly the heat was replaced by cool, then by cold, water.

Stay deep, Ryan screamed silently to Emily.

Fortunately, Emily didn't need to be warned. She'd been

nearly shocked unconscious by the near-scalding water and was determined to swim as deep as she could for as long as she could hold her breath. Somehow the depths of the river moved faster than the surface.

Like pieces of debris they were swept along, barely able to use their limbs to steady their progress.

Emily's analytical thinking was impaired by the cold. She couldn't decide what she should do next, not that she had much choice.

Ryan was moving with slow and deliberate strokes, stilling his mind, which he knew would give him twice as much time underwater than before he'd mastered the technique.

Emily had her own special trick learned from years of scuba diving. She swallowed hard, knowing it would delay her need to breathe.

Ryan was freezing; he could feel his hands going numb from the iciness of the stream. His need for air had become so powerful it now filled his mind.

Emily had reached her limit. She had run out of breath but she determinedly ignored her need to surface.

And lost consciousness.

A moment later, as rudely as the river had welcomed them into its hot and cold embrace, it unceremoniously ejected them. They were flung facedown onto a slab of stone deeply overgrown with moss that somewhat broke the force of their impact. Shaking his head free of water Ryan pushed himself unsteadily to his feet. "Are you okay?" he asked, his voice cracking.

There was no answer. His heart sank as he knelt and turned Emily's body to face him, carefully removing the napkin from around her mouth. *Don't let her be dead,* he prayed to whatever god ruled in this hell. *No. Not after all this. Not after…*

Her face was a color he'd never seen before, blue from the

numbing cold, and blotched red by the scorching heat. A finger on her carotid indicated the blood was still pumping through her body, but she wasn't breathing. He'd never taken a course in cardiopulmonary resuscitation, but he suddenly realized he should have left her face down. *Oh my God,* he thought, *I've killed her.*

Ryan rolled her over, straddled her back, and pumped against her ribs with both hands.

Nothing.

He pumped again, and, blinking away tears, focused his entire being on willing her to breathe.

Water spewed from her mouth. Ryan said a silent prayer as he turned her over, held her nose, and put his mouth on hers in an attempt at artificial resuscitation.

As he deeply inhaled his next breath, Emily's chest heaved. She sputtered, "Can't get enough of me, hunh, Father Ryan?"

As if he'd been caught by a nun in his fourth-grade class kissing a girl in the locker room, he hurriedly and awkwardly clambered off her. She lay motionless for a few seconds, stabilizing from the shock of nearly drowning.

An enormous relief swept over him even as she continued to taunt him.

"Or were you trying to take advantage of me, is that it?" she said. The energy and humor returning to her voice was the sweetest sound in the world—in the underworld.

"I thought you'd drowned," he said, shrugging his shoulders in an attempt at nonchalance. "I was trying to revive you." Then, at the memory of their kiss in the chapel, Ryan's mind shut down.

She gave him the eye, and then looked serious. "Thank you," she said, and poked him. "I was pulling your chain. I'm a good swimmer—but not nearly good enough to battle the River Styx."

A great sense of urgency forced Ryan to focus his attention back to the underground torrent they'd escaped. Only a couple of yards wide, the stream with the split personality jogged sharply to the right at the foot of the mossy bank, explaining why they'd been ejected.

Emily saw they were in a concave room about twenty feet in diameter. Its walls had been carved with figures that looked more ancient than the Roman era. Ryan pointed to the alpha and omega that identified the inscriptions as ancient Greek. Unfortunately most of the lettering was too worn and dim to be readable.

They were struggling to keep their footing on the slippery moss, wondering why they could see at all until they realized the surface of their Styx was a constant flow of natural incandescence—appearing like a living, neon "L."

"Do you think the Sibyl's cave was destroyed?" Emily asked.

"Well, the chapel was sealed shut, that's for sure. There's a good chance we're being pursued right now by some trigger-happy zealot, so we'd better get out of this hell-hole—and fast!" Ryan couldn't help but shiver.

With the help of the incandescence and his fingers, he began feeling his way around the walls of the antechamber.

Emily was doing the same on the opposite side. "I found an opening," she yelled.

"Me too."

She turned to see he was standing on the other side of the chamber, directly opposite her. "Which one do we try?" She couldn't hide the anxiety in her voice. The last thing she wanted was another slippery chute into boiling water.

"This one," Ryan was saying. He could see, deep within the tunnel, a faint light. "This is it, I'm sure—it's the two white doves the Sibyl told Aeneas would guide his way back to the earth."

Emily was at his side. He pointed it out to her: two faded white images above the fissure. They looked to the other side, to see that the birds over that opening were painted black.

"You won that round," she said. "That means you get to go first!"

Three yards or so inside the narrow tunnel, Emily, who followed so close behind him Ryan could feel her breath on the back of his neck, pointed to a camel frescoed on the narrowest point in the fissure. "It is harder for a queen to leave her kingdom," she intoned, "than for a blind man to thread a camel's hair through the eye of a needle."

"What? Another plagiarism?" Ryan asked.

"Monsignor Isaac translated it for me from the wall of the Dendera temple, in Egypt. Something Cleopatra may have told Antony when he invited her to Rome with him."

"And you believed him? How did you know it wasn't one of his lame jokes?"

Before she could answer, Ryan found himself lodged in the narrow passage. He couldn't move. "I'm stuck," he said. "I can't even go backwards."

"Take off your clothes," Emily said, a giggle in her voice.

"Watch your mouth, young lady." Ryan made his voice its sternest.

"No, but seriously—don't take this personally." With admirable dexterity she swept her leg into a kick that pushed him free.

He watched Emily slip through the spot with inches to spare.

The light was brighter now. Moving more quickly, they

soon entered a large grotto that, at first glance, looked like an underground temple. The river entered the chamber to their right and was abruptly diverted by a wedged cross of hand-hewn stone that sent half of it careening to the left, half to the right.

Fumes were rising from the right fork. Emily leaned down to test the water on the left. "It's cold as ice," she said. The horizontal wedge was designed to divide the water vertically.

"Amazing." Ryan marveled at the perspicacity of the ancient engineers. How did they even know there was an underground river, much less figure out how to divide cold from hot? He realized they must be directly beneath the imperial thermal baths that were built by Hadrian to catch the fumes.

He took the napkin down from his mouth, and gestured for Emily to do the same. "It's not poisonous at all. The fumes are actually good for us," he said.

"If you enjoy rotten eggs!" Emily kept hers intact against her mouth.

"I'm getting used to it. That smell might be healthy. I just remembered reading in the guidebook that the emperors came here specifically to bathe in sulfuric waters."

"Yeah, but they're all dead now," Emily shot back.

The large ceremonial room they were standing in was lit from a triangular aperture, centered in the inaccessibly high ceiling. The walls circling the chamber were penetrated by numerous artificial tunnels excavated into the volcanic rock—too many to explore which one might lead them out. The walls were covered with religious artistry depicting a judgment of the dead.

At the visual convergence of the sweeping fresco, Ryan recognized the two enthroned gods as Hades and Persephone, the ancient Greek king and queen of the underworld. The two gods were handing out judgments in exchange for offerings from the tormented souls beseeching them.

"Wonder what we'd have to offer them to get out of here?" Emily asked.

"They're not our gods," Ryan replied. "We'll get out of here on our own volition." He paused, then added: "I think I know this place. It's the 'oracle of the dead' visited by Odysseus on his return from Troy. A king came here for a prophecy and wasn't happy with the vibes the Sibyl gave him so she was forced to move to a hidden place nearby."

"The Cumaean cave?" Emily guessed.

"Must be."

Almost directly opposite the crossed wedge construction, they spotted two sets of stairs that led straight into the chamber wall. One staircase was positioned at the point where the fiery river of sulfur disappeared into the far wall of the chamber; the other, where the icy stream moved through a tunnel near where they stood. Each staircase had six identical steps rising about six feet before ending at the blank wall. The staircases were about twenty feet apart—roughly the radius of the cavern.

"Now that's interesting," Ryan said.

"His and hers braining devices?" Emily quipped. "In case we get a bad prophecy from the king there, we just run up the stairs at the same time and slam our foreheads into the wall."

"The sulfur's getting to you," Ryan laughed. "Let's check them out."

"You take the hot road, I'll take the cold," Emily said, moving toward the staircase by the icy stream.

Ryan moved toward the other staircase, trying to keep his breaths shallow. The fumes rising off the incandescent surface of the river of heat were increasing in density.

By now they'd each ascended a staircase. They placed their fingers on the walls, feeling for tell-tale bumps or crevices. They shook their heads. Nothing.

"Maybe it's like your golden bough," Emily said. "Maybe the artwork will tell us. She studied the depictions on the wall above her staircase. "Over here it's a ram standing guard at a gate," she said. "Doesn't ring a bell with me." Then she recalled the image of the Pharaoh Augustus in the Egyptian temple, his head crowned with the horns of a ram. But what had that to do with the Cumaean cave? "What about yours?" she asked.

"Believe it or not," he said, "It's an elephant. Also in a gate. Doesn't make much sense, either. Wonder why we'd find an elephant in Italy."

"Don't forget Hannibal," she said. "He crossed the Alps with elephants and found the Romans had already imported a number of the behemoths from previous forays against North Africa. Julius Caesar's first coins depicted elephants on one side."

"Wait a minute." Ryan was studying Emily's ram. "Horn," he said, "and ivory."

"Hunh?"

"At the end of Book VI of Virgil's *Aeneid,* Aeneas finds himself forced to choose between two gates that will lead him back to the surface. They were known as 'the gate of horn' and the 'gate of ivory.'"

"What was the meaning?"

"Virgil's narrator says that one of the gates, the gate of ivory, was the way by which false dreams and spirits found their way from the underground up into the air of day."

"And the gate of horn?" Emily asked.

"That way was for real dreams and true visions to reach the

upper world. If what we have experienced is true"—Emily had placed the flat of her palm on the image of the ram—"we would exit through the gate of horn and-"

"Oh my God," Emily cried, trying to keep her equilibrium as her hand still flat on the wall began to shift. "It's moving! The wall is moving!"

Ryan hurried down his staircase and rushed up behind her just in time to witness a narrow portion of the wall silently opening before them on a pivot as precociously ingenious as the crossed wedges that separated the hot from cold water.

"Probably designed by Strabo." Emily shot Ryan a glance, "like the swivel door on the Great Pyramid he built to keep Roman tourists out. But this is definitely a first for me."

They rushed through the opening into a chamber flooded with light, their eyes struggling to adjust to the dazzling brightness.

They turned to watch the exquisitely balanced pivoting wall segment move back into place. There was no artwork on this side. Ryan imitated Emily's palm pressure that had opened it for them. But the door would not budge.

"Looks like we're committed," Ryan said. "We can't go back."

"At least not from here," Emily agreed.

Guided by the flood of daylight, they moved up a narrow ramp that had been paved with marble. Much of the surface, though, was crumbling from age and they had to scramble to keep their footing, more than once falling to hands and knees.

When they reached the top, they were thrilled to see the light of day but disappointed to find themselves in a rectangular space about twenty feet wide—with an opening the height of a man at each end. The room appeared to be an observation post, with a slit in the stone wall about six inches in height and six feet in length that allowed the first inhabitants of these caves to view the external world. As they approached the slit, Ryan and Emily took a deep breath of the cool sea air that filtered through the opening.

"How beautiful!" Emily said. "A lake that flows into the Bay."

Ryan studied the vista before them. Indeed they were looking down at a shoal-water lagoon, the size of which, he guessed, was appreciably affected by the tides from the Bay of Naples. He could see a small boat heading off the Bay into the tiny strait that connected it with the lake. "It's Aornos," he announced. "The Romans called it Lake Avernus. We must be southeast of Cumae."

"I remember you told me about it. I forgot what Virgil had to say."

"He said an entrance to hell was here, where the birds fear to fly."

"What I'd prefer even more than literary exegesis," Emily said, "is finding the goddam exit."

Ryan was studying the lake below them, which had just cleared of haze and sparkled in the morning sun.

"What are you looking for?" she asked, drawing closer to the slit in the wall to peer out with him.

"Birds," he replied.

The air beneath them was, in fact, dense with birds: gulls, terns, sea hawks, cranes, wheeling in the breeze.

"There!" Emily shouted. "Look, to the right. There's vapor coming out of the cliffside—and not a bird nearby."

Ryan looked in the direction she was pointing and could just make out an aperture from which the fumes arose, secreted behind a bramble of bushes. "You're right," he said. "That must be it. The place the Sibyl described to Aeneas, a gash in the cliff covered with protective growth."

"So we go to the right again," Emily said. "Let's just hope this tunnel connects to it." Without waiting for Ryan, she moved toward the opening.

As the Sibyl predicted, the way down and up was indeed laborious. They descended on the rocky path studded with jagged outcroppings for nearly fifty feet before the narrow tunnel abruptly started to climb. The incline, through a corridor that was no more than two feet at the widest, ascended what Ryan estimated was at least three hundred feet before they heard a sudden rush of water and were assaulted at the same moment by the thickest sulfur fumes they'd encountered so far. Both of them re-tightened the napkins around their mouths.

"I just hope to hell we don't have to swim out of here in boiling water," Emily complained.

"Look," Ryan said, indicating a shaft of sunlight just ahead of them. "This corridor runs parallel to the river. I think we can walk out."

"If we don't gag to death from your dead egg health cure first," Emily said moving quickly up the now more gradual slope. They were converging with the underground river, following the reek of sulfur and the increasing light. Ryan moved after her toward the crack in the ancient fortress from which light was beckoning them.

But when they arrived at the exit, their relief was short-lived. The sulfurous stream shared the same fissure and there was no way out except through the fuming water, whose surface was only inches from the roof of the orifice. On top of that, they could see through the narrow gap that the stream's entrance into the lake was shielded by the brambles—dotted by some kind of dark red berry. And the brambles were chock full of thorns.

"Looks like we dive," Ryan said, shaking his head. "I'm sorry."

"Why would you bring a nice girl like me to a place like this?" Emily whined.

Then, without a word, she took a deep breath and dove into the churning water.

Ryan followed in a heartbeat, suddenly remembering something.

Emily was finding out for herself what he was remembering. No matter how deeply she dove, the water was no cooler. She was burning up inside, and knew it was only a matter of time before the intense heat stopped her heart.

What Ryan had remembered was that the two layers of the river divided inside the Temple of the King of the Dead. The icy stream exited somewhere else, or plunged deeper into the earth. He forced himself into meditation as he swam, but his technique wasn't nearly strong enough and he feared that he would open his mouth and scream. He gritted his teeth and forced his lips shut.

Seconds later they both felt the water around them cooling. They could see light at the surface of the water and knew they had made it into Lake Avernus, where the shoal waters countered the sulfurous current that swept them to freedom.

The water was now lukewarm. Emily surfaced first, ripped off her napkin mask, and shook her head in the cool breeze. "We made it," she shouted. "Ryan, where are you?"

Ryan popped up ten yards farther into the lake, took the sweetest breath of his life and turned to look for her. "That's it!" he yelled. "We're free!"

The thunder of rotors overhead made them look up. The giant black helicopter with the Jesuit insignia on its fuselage was flying over the hill they had just exited.

"Dive!" Ryan shouted.

"You've gotta be kidding," Emily said.

But they both plunged back into the depths of the lake, holding their breaths till they calculated the chopper had passed.

When they surfaced, they could see the helicopter moving toward Cumae—no doubt to search them out and to investigate the status of the cave that their rude departure had caused to collapse.

Emily smiled at Ryan. "Your face looks like a baked clam."

"Look who's talking." Ryan laughed.

Before them, on the placid lake, the fishing boat they'd spied from the cliff observation point was moving toward them.

LIV/54
Purgatorio

If the boatman wondered why two fully-clothed Americans—one a priest—were swimming in Lake Avernus, he didn't ask. He took them to a nearby café, where they warmed up with cups of latte, and learned that the man had given up computers for fishing, which had been his family's occupation for over a century. The sound of the sea was preferable to the sound of clicking keyboards and agitated clients. As it turned out, the boatman's cousin was the mechanic.

They bounced along in the mechanic's vintage pick-up to find the crippled BMW. He towed the car to his shop, where he promised to remove the airbags and improvise a plastic windshield.

They were waiting in the café, nibbling sandwiches with their coffee when their tense reprieve was interrupted by the sound of chopper rotors.

"My God," Emily gasped, her latte splashing over the table as she slammed her cup down. "They must've followed us—let's get out of here!"

Ryan grabbed her arm as she rose from her seat. "No, wait. They couldn't have trailed us here—it's not possible. They're probably just scouring the area."

"Are you sure? It seems like there are Jesuits everywhere, like the all-seeing eye of God—only these eyes aren't exactly benevolent." She sat back down and anxiously gazed skyward.

"I hope you're right."

They remained immobile while the chopper continued to circle the little village. After several minutes the noise of the rotors became weaker and then disappeared altogether.

"We'll be lucky if we get out of here in one piece." Ryan spoke first. "They've got to be mad as hornets."

"Yeah, and with deadlier stings."

By sunset, they were on the road back to Rome in the dented but functional BMW, hoping they had escaped unobserved and debating where they were going to hide out until they'd made up their minds about what to do with the rest of their lives.

Emily pulled her aureus from her hip pack. "You can't imagine how hot this got in that water! I'm afraid Augustus' face is permanently tattooed on my butt."

Ryan burst out laughing. "You've been branded as an Augustalis."

Despite their relief at being free of the cave, the tension between them seemed to increase by the kilometer. At one point, when Emily touched his hand Ryan had drawn back, hoping she wouldn't notice.

She did. She was filled with consternation. *Was this the same man with whom she had exchanged the most passionate kiss of her life?*

"I don't think we should go back to Rome. They'll be looking for us."

"You can count on that," Emily frowned. "Looks like Giammo is no longer among the living. But Pimental, if he survived the cave-in, will be on the war path."

Except for Emily's coin and the flash drive, all the evidence of the Jasius Augustus cult—oracles, urn, the printed out pages of Isaac's manuscript—would remain safely buried for the time being deep in the ancient cave.

If Christianity, as it was presently understood and variously practiced, was the legacy by which the Roman Empire survived its fall, why not leave well enough alone? "Never underestimate determined Jesuits," Ryan said. "We could head for Bologna. I know a little pensione there next to the bell tower of San Petronio."

But Emily was sensing the distance growing between them. She realized she could not stand spending the night in the same room as this man with his obvious ambivalence. "I've got to get back to my work," she finally said, doing her best to hide her disappointment. "I think it's safer if we split up. You can drop me at the airport and I'll stand by for the next flight to Tel Aviv."

He looked at her, noticed both her hands were holding the wheel so tightly her knuckles were white. "After all this," he said, "you'd leave, just like that, to finish your article?"

"Is there a fairy tale ending to our story I'm missing? You're the prince who kissed the frightened maiden in the cave. What do you suggest?"

Ryan bristled. "I suggest we need time to talk, to sort things out."

What is he talking about? Where did my romantic hero go?

"I'm not sure revealing the truth is the right thing to do. Maybe it's better to leave things as they were before you found the aureus. Maybe His Holiness is correct. He is infallible, after all." Ryan tried to make the last comment convincing, but it somehow rang hollow even to him.

"Infallible, hunh? Boy, would I love to be infallible like that. It's a self-serving doctrine that covers for organized thuggery if you ask me."

"Maybe the faithful aren't strong enough to handle the

knowledge that the God-man we've worshipped for two millennia was the most powerful emperor in history."

"Don't you understand yet that with Jesus being revealed as the deified Augustus Caesar and part of the trinity that began with Julius, no one can claim any longer that Jesus Christ didn't exist historically, because no mortal or immortal had a more real and tangible historical presence! Christians will finally have a reason to rejoice, even to triumph." She paused. "The real question I'm getting here is, are *you* strong enough to handle it? Because if you're not, how are you qualified to make that decision for others?"

"You sound angry," he said, not answering her question. *But she's absolutely right,* he thought. *I have no idea how to respond to that charge, at least not at the moment. This is all happening too fast.*

Emily took a deep breath and realized he was right. "I guess I am angry. Why did the most interesting man I've run into in my life have to be not only a Hamlet, but a goddamned priest?"

Ryan laughed, but it was a rueful laugh. "I haven't forgotten what it felt like back there in the cave," he said, prying one of her hands from the wheel and holding it in his. "If it's any consolation, I've been thinking part of me would like nothing better than to leave the priesthood and spend the rest of my life exploring caves with you."

Emily looked away from him, trying to conceal the tear that, of its own volition, had rolled down her cheek. She couldn't brush it away because her free hand was in Ryan's and she didn't want to take it back. "And the other part of you?" she asked.

"The other part of me clearly must see things through to the end." He shrugged, and took his hand away.

"What is the end?"

"I don't know," he said. "I wish I knew. I always believed my foremost duty as a Jesuit was to Jesus Christ's transcendent truth—a truth I swore to pursue and protect. If all we have learned is true, I must decide whether to reveal it or not; whether people are ready to receive it, or not."

"Don't you understand that the transcendent truth of Jesus Christ is inside every man, woman, and child?" She was getting more agitated with every word he spoke. "And what about me," she asked. "Am I supposed to sit on what I know and await your Holiness' decision? Who appointed you Pope? What about what's happened between us? Suddenly I'm on my own, is that it? Is that something you *decide* by yourself?"

Their eyes locked momentarily. "There's much to sort out—"

"Well, do what you have to do," she interrupted him. "But what I want to know is how do you sort out powerful emotions? Is that in one of your secret Jesuit manuals?"

Ryan had no answer. He stuck a finger into his Roman collar and ran it around, as though it were choking him. He found himself perspiring.

Emily, for her part, reached across and struck him on the shoulder with her fist.

"Ouch!" he said.

But she had turned to stare out the plastic window at a highway that suddenly looked to her as though it were leading to the dark side of the moon.

Silence filled the car again, the awful, tangible chemistry of strong personalities and strong emotions expanding into every available cubic centimeter. And neither of them could find the words to break the palpable tension.

LV/55
Paradiso

For the past two weeks Emily had steeled her mind to focus on her profession, the mainstay of her life, the bedrock of her mental stimulation and stability. Her hormones had never led her toward happiness. It just wasn't in the cards. No more time wasted on school-girl crushes on unattainable Hamlets who couldn't decide whether they should be men or monks. Not a stray thought allowed, at least during her waking hours, to distract her from her determined path as she put the final touches on the scholarly article she knew would take her career to a new level. That it might also change the world for billions of people, she decided, was simply not within the purview of her academic competence.

Based on a précis she'd sent by email to the *Journal of Classical Archaeology,* the article had already been formally invited by the editors. They urged her to take her time, to present her evidence and arguments with full annotation and illustration.

But ever since she'd returned to the Caesarea site, Emily's pace had been more feverish than measured. She'd been delighted to see the enormous, and obscenely expensive crane and bulldozer that Luke had funded and to hear Harel and David's report on the progress of the refitting.

The battered barge was not only as good as it had been before the storm; it was now beyond state of the art, fitted with diving bell, backup oxygen generators, and storm-proof buoys that would keep it afloat even through the Apocalypse. Adashek had found a way to make his guilt constructive, hoping she would discover another aureus. At his own personal expense, he'd arranged for a magnetometer survey of the area to rediscover the wreck's location. Her students had retrieved hundreds of artifacts from the ancient wreck, but so far not another aureus. She would see to it herself that her precious coin would be safely secured in a unique display at Yale's Beinecke when she was done examining it for her paper. Oh, yes, and she'd not forgotten to leave a voice mail for Jamil Fatall telling him to retrieve the antique diamond and emerald necklace from under the fez mounted just outside his door, where she'd concealed it for safe keeping during her recent visit to Jerusalem.

Despite her certainty, which she kept to herself, that another aureus would not be found, she'd even cheerfully agreed to Adashek's self-invitation to pay her a visit tomorrow afternoon. "You can update me on your progress," he said, "and maybe we can have dinner at that quaint place we ate at last time."

"Sure," she agreed. "Why not?" Her career was all that mattered to her now. This man, only recently her mortal enemy, had transformed himself into an essential asset. Bygones could be bygones.

If that was a rationalization, well, she would make the most of it.

Despite her iron will, Emily tossed and turned throughout the night—and it wasn't just the humidity. She awakened at five a.m. to stick her head under the cold-water faucet and brush some sense back into her tangled hair. She looked with distaste at the wrinkled knot of sheets. *That's my life,* she decided. *Gold on one side, barnacle shit on the other.*

In her wildest dreams, she would never have imagined that she could be this distraught on the eve of the greatest turning point of her already-precocious career. Maybe that was just life: Every ray of sunlight attracted clouds. She was intent only on documenting her discovery, and what she believed it proved. She thanked God she didn't feel responsible for any political or theological repercussions from her findings. As an academic focused only on pursuing the truth, that was not her job. As far as she was concerned, let the devil take the hindmost.

Slipping into her sleeveless khaki shirt, Emily tied her red hair deftly into a no-nonsense ponytail. She was garbed to face the workday, and she focused, despite her nagging heart, on making herself feel invulnerable.

She skipped breakfast and headed across the nearly constructed boardwalk toward the dock, pulling from her pouch the aureus as she had been doing each morning since her return to Caesarea.

The rosy fingers of dawn that greeted her were heralds of the sun—the eternal, faithful, and dependable sun—just rising above the low mountains to the east. Its first rays glanced off the coin and highlighted the pronged crown that sat regally on the head of the Emperor Jasius Augustus.

She rubbed the surface for good luck, then tucked the coin safely back in her pouch.

When she looked up, she could see the figure moving toward her on the beach.

Damn, he's early—way too early. She realized that, despite her rationalizations and determination, she wasn't, after all, really looking forward to seeing Luke Adashek today.

Then she studied the figure more closely. Something was wrong with this image. There was no hesitation in the walk.

The outline was much slimmer than Luke's.

She stood still, her heart skipping a beat.

At that moment, the sun appeared above the horizon and revealed it was, instead, Ryan McKeown.

Heading straight for her, lifting his hand in greeting.

Emily was too startled to respond, too surprised to move.

"What happened to your collar?" It was, stupidly, all she could think to ask when Ryan was within earshot.

"I left it in the sacristy," was his answer. "I won't be needing it anymore."

She couldn't help teasing him. "And why is that, Father Ryan? What conclusions have you reached?"

He looked back at her as though he had long prepared himself for this question. "I loved you from the moment I first saw you. When you left, it was as though part of me left with you. I don't sleep. I don't eat. I can't stop thinking about you, and I want you in every way a man can want a woman."

Tears streamed down her face. "I didn't dare hope...But what about your vow of celibacy?"

"Left in the sacristy with my collar," he said. "I've come to realize that sexual intimacy is a way for devoted couples to merge their divinity and experience oneness. Seen in this light enforced celibacy dishonors that which is sacred." Ryan looked down for a moment, struggling to maintain his composure. "It's also the greatest expression of love between two people." Ryan held her gaze. "Do you think you could love me?"

"Oh, Ryan," Emily replied. "Come here and kiss me."

Under the fiery light of the Mediterranean sun, they approached each other slowly, embracing the lightning that reignited as they melted into each other's arms.

LVI/56
Ite, Missa est.
Go, the Mass is ended.

"I told you I was a survivor." The sentence was completed before Emily and Ryan could identify the voice.

Ten days after Ryan had arrived so unexpectedly, they were sitting on the seawall watching Harel and David completing the day's inventory of artifacts. The man behind the voice circled into their vision before they could turn around.

It was Bishop Giuseppe Giammo who, except for his Israeli khaki, looked none the worse for his supposed suicide.

"We thought you were dead," Emily blurted, at the same time noting the concern in Ryan's eyes and feeling his arm moving protectively around her shoulder.

"Someone did indeed pass away rather abruptly," Giammo replied, this time allowing himself a smile. "Only I'm afraid it was my late superior. I suddenly came to the realization that my usefulness may not have been outgrown."

"You killed Pimental?" Ryan could not believe his ears.

"Let's just say I helped relieve him of his earthly responsibilities," the Jesuit bishop said. "But, to be precise, no, I didn't kill him. I just indisposed him with the very hard handle of a Luger."

"But we heard a gunshot," Emily said.

"That is correct," Giammo admitted. "The Luger discharged accidentally when it impacted on Pimental's skull. Scared the Holy-you-know-what out of me. I pulled him out of sight and went to get my things intending to come get you. But all hell broke loose with your handiwork and I prayed you would somehow survive. He was, alas, crushed under tons of rubble. I was lucky to get out with my own life."

"So you were able to just walk out?" Ryan asked.

"I waited for the debris and dust to settle, then ran like my ass was on fire." They both laughed out loud. "The front entrance of the cave was almost completely blocked by fallen rock, but I managed to pick my way through and unlock the gate. I didn't see the guard—he must have run off. When I heard later that a fishing boat picked up two people, I was satisfied you had safely escaped. I had things of my own to deal with."

"I'll bet," Ryan said.

"I'm here because I'd like to compensate for my sins by helping you in any way I possibly can."

"I'm surprised the Holy See *allowed* you to survive," Emily commented.

"I secured my freedom my own way," Giammo said. "That's why I borrowed Isaac's flash drive that morning."

"You made a copy?"

Giammo nodded. "And I wrote a letter to the press to be opened in the event of my demise. In addition I felt compelled to expose to the Society the devious scheme Pimental and Leontel had been cooking up to usurp Pope Pius. I think we'll be hearing rumors of a new black pope soon."

"So you didn't buy in to a new age of Jesuits ruling Christianity?" Emily asked.

"No, my dear," he answered. "I believe too much in individuality—people like you two, who pursue what is right, and when they discover it, stand behind it. That's the world we need to live in, not another one where individuals are told what to believe."

Ryan hesitated, and then held out his hand. "All right, then. Welcome to the Funny Farm."

The romantic mood of the last few days was rudely shattered as they begrudgingly gave Giammo the attention he demanded. It was true they faced an enormous dilemma. It was true they had no idea how to handle it. So it was also true they could use an ally who understood the workings of the world, and was fully aware of the decisions and jeopardy they now faced.

As unlikely as it seemed to both of them, who could play the role of guardian angel more effectively than the rogue bishop that had served as their Virgil in their descent into the inferno?

With Emily's help and Giammo's critique Ryan completed Isaac's narration, smoothing out the roughs, filling in the blanks. Giammo admitted he'd uploaded the flash drive to HushMail.com that morning in the cave, as a "precautionary backup."

At the same time Emily polished her article.

When they were satisfied, the three of them faced the tribunal: David and Harel. Emily knew they would be the ultimate devils' advocates, not allowing their professor and her new boyfriend to get away without answering every single question. She had introduced them to Ryan and Giammo as the "Dotter of I's" and the "Crosser of T's," epithets the graduate students had accepted with loyal appreciation.

Needless to say, Ryan's appearance on the scene had turned the camp upside down. Emily managed to disarm the adolescent meltdown that might have occurred by preemptively confessing that she'd met this man on her trip to Rome, and that he was her lover—so butt-the-hell-out and live with it. From that moment onward, they'd kept their sharp tongues to themselves and eyed Ryan with curiosity, jealousy, and respect. They did not know that he was a recently self-defrocked Jesuit priest.

The dynamic duo, filled with self-importance that they alone of the students enlisted for this fall's dig had been chosen by their leader for the honor, listened to Emily's and Ryan's presentations with full attention, taking notes at every possible discrepancy.

How did the cult spread from Judea to Rome? they wanted to know.

"We don't yet know all the particulars," Emily admitted. "But Augustus predicted it would evolve as it traveled, and it was a long distance in those days. We will continue our excavations between here and Rome until we've solved the puzzle."

The answer more than satisfied them, especially when she assured them they would be coming along.

"Keep in mind that I'm announcing my identification as preliminary, as a theory begging for corroboration, correction, or contradiction. This is just the beginning," Emily said.

"Who's this bloke?" Harel finally dared to ask out loud, indicating Giammo, who had remained uncharacteristically silent through it all.

Giammo laughed. "I'm the bloke who's going to cover their asses and make sure they survive the public announcements to come."

Aided by Ryan's objective editing, Emily's final draft was officially accepted by the *Journal.*

It would be published on the day of an official public announcement, and the release of Ryan's narrative. Weeks of behind-the-scenes negotiations by Giammo with Pimental's successor led to assurances from the Society of Jasius that Pius XIII would serve the remainder of his reign undisturbed, but would forego any further gestures that might weaken the Society's Augustan agenda.

They would release the lifework of Monsignor Oscar Isaac, S.J. at a highly-selective press conference in the meeting hall of Gesù, the Jesuit mother church in Rome, the capital city of Christendom.

At the last minute, however, Giammo, from a safe place outside Rome, contacted Ryan by cell phone. Word had leaked out about the press conference, and the Gesù was suddenly rife with warring factions headed by the panel that had released Ryan from his vows. "Plan B," Giammo said. "We need a less politicized environment so I've arranged for the announcement to be made in New York City, heart of the world's news services. I'll meet you there."

So, though neither of them could have foreseen it, the joint statement that rocked the world was made across from Saks on Fifth Avenue, in the venerable—and overflowing—Cathedral of St. Patrick. Although every V.I.P. imaginable had pressured the Archdiocese to attend, the protocol had been negotiated by Giammo and breached no exceptions. Only working members of the international press corps would be allowed.

News of the impending announcement had attracted an angry mob of protesters gathered outside the cathedral, chanting, "Satan's allies spreading lies!" and wielding placards, "Burn in Hell, Sinners!" "Blasphemers!" "Heretics!" and "My

Jesus Lives!"

Surrounded by officers of the New York Police Department in full riot gear, Ryan and Emily were escorted into the sanctuary from the sacristy, accompanied by the new black pope Nelson Lowry, S.J., and His Eminence Donald Cardinal Griffin. Bishop Giuseppe Giammo, in full episcopal regalia, served as their acolyte and bodyguard. The chanting and angry cries from the protesters became a muffled grumble as the heavy doors were locked tight behind the little entourage.

"Ladies and gentlemen of the press," Father Lowry began in the clipped tones of a man who was used to having his orders followed without question, "we have reached at last the Omega Point prophesied by our beloved Pierre Teilhard de Chardin. The Internet has made possible the dissemination of truth throughout the world, influencing even yourselves," he added. That caused a rueful laugh from the journalists assembled from nearly every nation of the earth.

"Abraham Lincoln once said, 'You can fool all of the people some of the time, and some of the people all of the time, but you cannot fool all of the people all of the time.' In our modern world of instant access, when the word goes out to all nations, it is the *same* word and it reaches all nations simultaneously."

A round of hearty applause greeted him, which Emily and Ryan thought surprising from this particular assembly whose daily work was so often preempted nowadays by the tweets of amateurs.

"Through the remarkable work of recently departed Monsignor Oscar Isaac, further developed and completed by the two remarkable people you see seated with us at the altar," Father Lowry continued, "we are here to make an extraordinary announcement about the foundation of the world's oldest and largest Christian religion. But I leave that announcement to the man and woman who have done most to make it possible. I ask only that you open your hearts as well as your minds, and hold your questions until the end."

The Superior General then introduced Ryan McKeown as a former Jesuit priest who had taken the "new order" vows of lay service to the Society of Jasius. Brows wrinkled at his pronunciation of the name. Lowry did not need to mention that the vows did not include celibacy. Ryan was openly holding Emily's hand.

Emily and Ryan had prepared a PowerPoint time line chart from Isaac's research, comparing Augustan history with events described in the Bible. Ryan made the signal for the lights to be lowered. He found his breath catching in his throat, and was sure, as he mounted the marble steps, that his mouth would remain frozen shut. Then he glanced back at Emily. Their eyes met. Ryan felt the electric jolt he first experienced when she'd stumbled into him that long ago night in Rome. And his stage fright gave way to sheer joy.

The light beam from the projector streamed across the immense cathedral and several sections of the chart appeared across the wide screen. The moment had come to reveal their findings to the world. There was an audible collective intake of breath as the assembled reporters read the first few entries on the chart.

Ryan spoke without faltering as he read through the overview of Augustan history that the chart compared, side by side, with "Biblical history."

The Roman Empire had declined, but it had not disappeared.

The highest ideals of its founder and Pontifex Maximus may have waxed and waned through the turbulence of history, but they were clearly still alive today.

As Ryan spoke, a stunned silence permeated the baffled assembly.

"Wait a minute!" A female reporter from *Corriere della Sera,* a crucifix dangling from her neck, broke the lull. "Are you saying that Jesus didn't really exist and that we should worship the Emperor Augustus instead? That the Holy Bible is a lie?"

Other angry shouts joined hers.

The puzzled faces of the world press gave Ryan the opening he needed to summarize what he and Emily had discovered:

The origins of the Church's moral structure were Egyptian, Julian, Roman, and Latin—not just exclusively Jewish, Palestinian, and Aramaic/Greek.

The Church was built upon the ideals and moral verities espoused by the triumphant Octavian Augustus Caesar—Conqueror, Counselor, Prince of Peace, King of Kings, Messiah.

It took several pleas from Ryan for the uproar to subside so he could continue.

"We are not suggesting that Augustus was holy or that you should worship him—it would be pointless today to create a new god as Augustus felt he had to do to found his universal cult..." Ryan sighed. "Let me start at the beginning and summarize the background to this extraordinary revelation."

The gathering of reporters settled uneasily back in the benches waiting expectantly.

"Many thousands of years ago a myth developed that spread throughout all the countries of the Mediterranean, and even to India and beyond. The most likely source of the myth was the birthplace of civilization, Upper Egypt, and it became the foundation of many of the world's religions: the worship of the sun god.

"The ubiquitous story of the sun god went something like

this: A star on the horizon heralds his birth; he is born of a virgin in a humble dwelling in December; he grows to become a powerful and life-giving teacher; he performs miracles at the height of his powers; he heals the sick and raises the dead; is persecuted; declines and dies a painful death; and rises from the dead to prove to his followers he is indeed a god; finally he ascends into heaven to sit at the right hand of his father.

"Sound familiar? The stories in the Holy Bible are based on these and many other ancient myths.

"In preparation for Augustus' deification, the great intellectuals of his empire were ordered to compose his sacred biography, incorporating many of the usual elements of the sun god myth, like Sirius being considered the herald of the sun's birth each morning. Using astronomical charts, Augustus' astrologers proclaimed Augustus' forthcoming apotheosis—his birth as a god—with a conjunction of Jupiter and Venus that occurred in 17 B.C.—the 'bright star of the east' heralding his coming mentioned in the New Testament that appeared on December 25 of that year. Two years later, in 15 B.C., Augustus' birth as a god took place as 'predicted.' That was how the mystical belief in the sun as the divine savior of humankind was transformed into the persona of a literal savior—Jasius Augustus."

Ripples of protest echoed across the cathedral.

"Are you saying Jesus Christ is nothing but a myth?" demanded the reporter from The Christian Science Monitor.

"Nothing but a myth?" Ryan replied. "Myths have always been more serious than history in human lives. But I understand your surprise. Please hear me out. I too was filled with consternation when I first learned about this hidden history. If I may continue..."

The commotion gradually subsided, and he could see curiosity written on their faces as he continued. "Augustus' posthumous glory outshines that of all other deified rulers because of Herod's unprecedented loyalty to the mighty emperor to whom he owed his life as well as his kingdom. Herod was allowed to live upon transferring his allegiance from Augustus' defeated rival, Antony.

"As a direct consequence, Herod made his kingdom the original and main seat of Augustus' cult, and the city of Caesarea with its great temple to Augustus was built in his honor.

"Augustus was worshipped throughout Judea under many titles, including 'Messiah,' *Divus Filius,* 'Son of God,' *Divus filius divi,* 'God and son of God,' *'Iasus'* or *'Jasius,'* English spelling 'Jesus.' The Greek title 'Christ,' meaning 'anointed one,' was originally inspired by the ancient Sanskrit 'KRST' and later symbolized by the first two Greek letters of the word 'Christ, Χριστός, XP,' which often appeared on Augustus' Judean and Roman coins." Ryan activated a slide to display the titles.

"After Augustus' death, the worship of Jesus Augustus continued throughout the empire, alongside other competing religions. With the passage of time the name Augustus was dropped and the deity of the new religion simply became known as Jesus Christ. 'Christianity,' a term unknown before the second century, became the official religion of the Roman Empire in the fourth century under the rule of Constantine. The mythological sun god origins were later abandoned in favor of a literal belief in their savior's divine biography.

"The common sense values of the original Augustan religion that became distorted by its original custodian, the Roman Catholic Church, were guarded through the centuries and espoused by the leaders of the Society of Jasius and its worldwide missionaries known as the Jesuits: Heed the light within. Love thy neighbor as thyself."

The murmur of the press rose to a roar as ushers began passing among them copies of Ryan's "Gospel according to Augustus" and offprints of Emily's article "The Transformation of Augustan into Christian Iconography and Its Historical and Ecclesiastical Ramifications."

An agitated voice from the back of the cathedral bellowed, "What about the apostles Matthew, Mark, Luke and John? Are you saying they didn't exist either?"

"I'm not saying Jesus didn't exist." Ryan looked helplessly over at Emily. "I'm saying the man we've all called Jesus was Jesus Augustus."

As the roar continued in the crowd, he gestured for Emily to join him at the pulpit.

She had none of his trepidation. The figure she cut, in a green silk dress that accentuated her every breath, caught the audience's attention and held them spellbound. The press fell silent, awaiting her response.

"The worship of Jesus Christ," she began, "was created intentionally by the Emperor Jasius Augustus, otherwise known to the world as Octavian Caesar Augustus. He attached the ancient name of Rome's esteemed forefather, 'Jasius,' to his honorific to underline his mythical connection to the founding of Rome, the Eternal City, the city sacred to the god within all Roman citizens."

She went on, in ten minutes so packed with information that several pens ran out of ink, to describe her finding of the aureus, its provenance, and why it was minted by King Herod the Great.

She referred them to the offprints they'd just received, where photographs presented both sides of the coin. She parsed for them the meaning of the loaf and fish, the *Chi-Rho*, and the cross. She elaborated on the construction of the cult temple by King Herod in Caesarea in 6 B.C., its bearded golden statue, its inscribed dedication to Jasius Augustus, and how the shifting of the calendar occurred with the Latin Sacred College removing fifteen years so that 15 B.C., Augustus' birth as a god, his sacred nativity, became 1 A.D., *anno domini,* the "year of our Lord."

The question and answer period was chaos, at least until Bishop Giammo brought it to order. It lasted nearly three hours. By the time the cathedral had been emptied out and the doors closed, both Ryan and Emily were hoarse.

Giammo dragged them to Sardi's, plying them with food and drink until the first newspapers began arriving, starting with *Corriere della Sera* at one a.m. Its headline read:

Gesù-Augusto—Lo Stesso? "Jesus, Augustus—One and the Same?"

Finally the early edition of the New York Times was delivered to their table:

ROMAN CATHOLIC CHURCH FOUNDED BY JASIUS AUGUSTUS CAESAR?

The Daily News put it more succinctly:

EMPEROR JESUS!

LVII/57
My Father's Business

The ten years that followed were a rollercoaster ride. Outcry, from fanatical adherents to the old-fashioned religions, took every form of violence known to human nature, from rocks through front windows to mob demonstrations.

Since the revelation of the New Gospel according to Augustus in St. Patrick's, and their quiet wedding there a few weeks later blessed by the new Superior General, Ryan's and Emily's lives had been an unending blur of activity: interviews, travel, more interviews, research, more travel, publication, and serving as advisors to the ecumenical movement that had swept the planet. Millions of people left literalist beliefs behind in favor of heartfelt communication of the universal moral principles found within the human soul that the emperor had desired all nations to adhere to.

August Isaac McKeown had accompanied his parents throughout their endless odysseys, along with Bishop Giuseppe Giammo who had become both his guardian and his nanny.

Three more years went by and August had reached the age of confirmation, and the fanatics were out in force again.

Throngs of fundamentalist demonstrators assembled since dawn, their vehemence escalating, were shoving against the NYPD mob control squad and trying to get past the barricades on East 51st Street.

Their malice was directed toward the leafy serenity of nature known as Greenacre Temple, the newly-opened meeting place of the Augustan Universalists. The media simply called them "Unis."

The reverberation of the twenty-five-foot waterfall gracing the entry of Greenacre was drowned out by the cacophony of enraged shouts from across the street:

"God punishes blasphemers!"

"Burn, Heretics, Burn!"

Some were singing the hymn, "Give Me That Old Time Religion!" punctuated by loud cries of "Don't try to take our sweet Jesus away!"

Inside Ryan and Emily stood amidst the expectant crowd that had gained entry through a tight security system requiring each person to wear an invitational badge and pass through x-ray scanning. They were waiting under the temple's centerpiece for their thirteen-year-old son, August and his guardian, the bishop.

A clear quartz obelisk towered above them topped with an orb of gold glass that enshrined the ashes of Augustus in their golden chalice saved by Giammo from the cave.

Why aren't they back yet? Emily scanned the crowd.

Today thirteen-year-old August was to give the presentation at Greenacre's opening ceremony. His reputation had spread throughout the city and his speech was to commence on the hour, at noon—yet he was nowhere to be seen.

"You worry too much." Ryan caressed his wife's face.

"Of course I worry," Emily replied. "I'm his mother. That's my job." Her weak smile barely disguised her anxiety. "Where are they? The presentation begins in fifteen minutes and Giuseppe swore they'd meet us here by now."

"You wait here," Ryan said. "I'll go check to see if they're anywhere in sight outside."

Emily squeezed his hand. "Okay. I'll wait here for you."

The shouts from the volatile throng across the street penetrated the glass walls of Greenacre, creating a muffled din in the otherwise peaceful interior. *Those people are out for blood,* she thought. The recent death threat letters against her family confirmed that. She couldn't control the shudder that ran through her body; August was small and slight for his age, easy prey for such a rabid mob. *Please let him be okay.*

The place was standing room only. Had it not been for the fact that the usher recognized him from countless newspaper photos, Ryan himself might have been turned back from squeezing through the crowd.

Then two things happened at the same instant.

He caught sight of Giammo, still wearing, beneath his black serge jacket, the tuxedo t-shirt that had put August into gales of laughter this morning.

And he heard the sound of his son's voice.

Giammo spotted Ryan, and gestured for him to join him. He had secured a position on the periphery of the circle the crowd formed around the diminutive figure with the shock of red hair that Ryan could now see had to be his son.

The look on Giammo's face was that of avuncular, if not paternal, pride.

"I've got to get Emily," Ryan whispered. "She's waiting for us over there under the obelisk."

"I'll get her," Giammo said. "You stay here. Listen to your beloved son, in whom you will be well-pleased," he added, with a glimmer of merriment in his eye. Without pausing for argument, the bishop negotiated his way toward the obelisk.

Ryan focused his attention on his son's voice. He inserted himself into the gathering—men and women of all ages, races, economic status, and former creeds—and finally found an opening among them. He noticed both David and Harel, Emily's former graduate students, were among the crowd and, from the other side of the circle a rumpled Luke Adashek gave him an embarrassed look that said, "I didn't expect this to be so big or I would have bought a new suit."

Sitting on the steps leading to the speaker's platform with the adults circling him, August was radiant and collected.

All eyes were riveted on him, and, as Ryan picked up his son's words, he understood why.

"We are all one. Sacred are the humble in spirit who recognize the soul that unites us and have the courage to turn vision into reality, first of all in their own lives.

"It makes no difference what we call the One. Sacred are the teachers and artists, corporate leaders and entrepreneurs, politicians and activists, parents and custodians, who nurture our dream of a better world at the expense of their own.

"The light dwells within us all. You are the temple, and the spirit is reborn within you. Sacred are they who strive for its simple perfection knowing they will never reach it but finding excellence and peace along the way.

"The light is eternal. Socrates, Akhenaton, Julius Caesar, Joan of Arc, Mahatma Gandhi, Martin Luther King—all were slain because the world they lived in was not ready for their vision of its perfection. Sacred are they who dare to see, share what they see, and to lead us with their foresight without heed for their personal welfare.

"As we acknowledge the light, we achieve our destiny. We *become* the light. Sacred are they who sacrifice their lives for the life of vision. For vision of a better life will never die so long as leaders like you are ready to offer up body and spirit in its name.

"The light will move us if only we open ourselves to its

power. Sacred are they who open to the light. For they find the awaited one, the Christ, within themselves.

"When we open ourselves to the light, we become the answer to our own prayers. Sacred are they who turn prayer into action for the good of all.

"The light is the life of man. Sacred are the peacemakers, for they shall be called the sons and daughters of God."

Ryan sensed his wife's presence before he felt her touch. She clasped his hand, and stood with tears in her eyes, captivated, as were all the others, by the remarkable son they had brought into the world. They were, indeed, well pleased in him. For Ryan's part, he was filled with the spirit he could only describe as "holiness," his pursuit of oneness with creation that led him on his long journey through the priesthood to the true discovery of the Christ within, its true source, here being evoked—not by an actual man dying on an actual cross—but by the truth of his son's words.

Finally August allowed his eyes to catch theirs. *Why were you concerned?* the brilliant young eyes seemed to say, *Don't you know I must be about the emperor's business?*

Before our eyes human life lies squalidly oppressed
In the sand by the weight of religion.—Lucretius, *On the Nature of Things*

I believe there is an important distinction... between religion and spirituality. Religion I take to be concerned with belief in the claims to salvation of one faith tradition or another—an aspect of which

is acceptance of some form of metaphysical or philosophical reality, including perhaps an idea of heaven or hell. Connected with this are religious teachings or dogma, ritual, prayers, and so on. Spirituality I take to be concerned with those qualities of the human spirit—such as love and compassion, patience, tolerance, forgiveness, contentment, a sense of responsibility, a sense of harmony, which brings happiness to both self and others. —Dalai Lama

The chart that Ryan and Emily prepared for the press conference at St. Peter's in New York:

Actual History	Mythical/Biblical History
64 B.C.—Year of alleged miraculous conception by Atia (aka Maia), mother of Augustus Caesar	Mary (Maia) is visited by the Holy Ghost and has an immaculate conception. Note: Augustus' astrologers wove alleged miraculous conception of Octavian's mother, Maia, into the story that has come down to us in the Bible in which Mary is told "…that holy thing which shall be born of thee shall be called the son of God." Luke 1:35
Sept 23, 63 B.C.—Actual birth of Octavian, later called Augustus. Decree issued by senate to slay all male children because "a king was born!"	Church fathers later incorporated this decree into a fictional history in which Herod was named as the perpetrator: Matthew 2:16-18, "Then Herod, when he was mocked of the wise men, was exceedingly wroth and sent forth, and slew all the children that were born in Bethlehem."
44 B.C.—Octavian is named "Son of God"	Jesus is named "Son of God."
39 B.C.—Herod pledges his allegiance to Octavian following Marc Antony's defeat at Actium.	
31 B.C.—Octavian became	Jesus' titles include "Messiah,"

"Augustus." His titles include "Messiah," "Christ," "Lord," "Savior of the World."	"Christ," "Lord," "Savior."
28 B.C.—Senate acknowledges Augustus as the Sebastos, or Sacro-sanct (sacred, holy)	Jesus is acknowledged as holy.
27 B.C.—Augustus became the first Emperor of Rome, is worshiped as Son of God.	Jesus is worshipped as Son of God.
25-13 B.C.—Herod the Great builds city of Caesarea and dedicates it to Augustus. Creates cult seat for Jasius (Jesus) Augustus in Judea.	The setting for Jesus' life is Judea.
17 B.C.—Starting on December 25th close conjunction of Jupiter and Venus, stationary over Judea for five days. Used by Augustus' astrologers to predict the coming "birth" of Augustus as the Messiah two years later, in 15 B.C.	Matthew 2:9 states, "...and, lo, the star, which they saw in the east, went before them, till it came and stood over where the young child was."
15 B.C.—Augustus' Apotheosis, timed to depict him as the long-awaited Messiah, Lord of the World, Prince of Peace. From this time forward, the worship of Augustus as the Son of God became official religion of Rome. Henceforth he holds	"Birth of Jesus Christ: Note: Calendar was later adjusted by the Latin Sacred College by sinking fifteen years from the Roman calendar in order to make Augustus' apotheosis correspond with prophecy of Cumaean Sibyl of the coming of a Divine Being. Apotheosis

the title, Jasius-Augustus—Jesus Augustus.	of Augustus and the 'birth' of Jesus Christ are one and the same event. The year 15 B.C. thus became year 1 A.D.
15 B.C.-14 A.D.—Augustus' heavenly character attested by miracle of his touch, sufficient to cure deformity or disease.	Mark 6:56: "And wherever he came, in villages, cities, or country, they laid the sick in the market places, and besought him that they might touch even the fringe of his garment; and as many as touched it were made well."
12 B.C.—Jasius Augustus became Pontifex Maximus, the predecessor to today's Pontifex Maximus of the Holy Roman Catholic Church—the Pope.	
12 B.C.—Herod revives the panageia of Jasius—the Olympic Games, named Caesar's Games by Herod. Herod mints coins honoring Augustus bearing the XP (chi rho) symbol for Christ. (Christ, Christos, is the Greek equivalent of the Hebrew Messiah and means "the anointed one.")	Matthew 16: 15-16. "He said unto them, 'But who do you say I am?' Simon Peter replied, 'You are the Christ, the Son of the Living God.'"
37-4 B.C.—Reign of Herod the Great. The historical event relating to deaths of all male children actually	Matthew 2:16 "Then Herod, when he saw that he was mocked of the wise men, was exceeding wroth, and sent

occurred in 63 B.C. in relation to Octavian's birth; the order was issued by the Senate. Church Fathers later incorporated this fact into a fictional history in which Herod was wrongly named as the perpetrator of this decree in the 'Holy Bible.'	forth, and slew all the children that were in Bethlehem, and in all the coasts thereof, from two years old and under..."
4 B.C.—Death of King Herod the Great.	
2 B.C.—Augustus received the honored title, *Pater Patriae,* Father of His Country.	
1 A.D.—Year of Our Lord Augustus Caesar; Anno Domini: A.D.	Jesus' birth is traditionally said to be 1 A.D.
A.D. 6-7 Augustus orders a census in Syria, including Judea.	Luke 2:1—"And it came pass in those days, that there went out a decree from Caesar Augustus, that all the world should be taxed." In Biblical account, Jesus' nativity occurs during this census.
14 A.D.—Manilius, *Astronomica,* 1, 7-10 "...Augustus, thyself a god...who awaiteth his place in Heaven with the Father [Julius Caesar]..."	Mark 16: 19, "So then after the Lord had spoken unto them, he was received up into heaven, and sat on the right hand of God."
Aug. 29, 14 A.D.—Jasius Augustus' death and	"Crucifixion, death and ascension to heaven" of Jesus

ascension to heaven. The noble Roman senator, Numerius Atticus, took oath that he witnessed Augustus' spirit ascending into the sky.	Christ. Between Jesus' birth (Jasius Augustus' apotheosis, his birth as a god) and Augustus' death, equals thirty years, the approximate life span of the Biblical "Jesus Christ."
14-24 A.D.—By the time the Jasius Augustus religion left Judea and spread through Greece and back to Rome the name 'Augustus' had been dropped in favor of the 'cult of Jasius (Jesus).' Since it was not a threat to the current ruling emperors the Roman authorities eventually allowed it to flourish throughout the empire.	The New Testament of the Bible tells the story of Jesus Augustus veiled in myth and allegory, thus concealing its original Augustan origin.

The Lothair Cross, as depicted on the front cover and described in Chapter 26, is used in processions at Aachen Cathedral and is on display in the Aachen Treasury. It dates from the late 10th century and is believed to have been donated by Emperor Otto III (993-1002). In the center is a cameo of the Emperor Augustus, carved from sardonyx around the time of Augustus' apotheosis—his birth as a god. Normally an image of Christ goes on this spot on a cross, but it may be that Otto wished to fuse the symbolism of Roman emperor and Christ, a combination he represented as Holy Roman Emperor. Or perhaps he knew that Augustus and Christ were one and the same personage.

www.messiahmatrix.com

Acknowledgements

In one of my first books, *Homer's Iliad: The Shield of Memory,* based on my Yale doctoral dissertation "The Song and Shield of Memory," I argued that the epic poem chanted by the Homeric bards was the ultimate protection a society had against repeating the horrors of its own history. Enshrining the errors—and glories—of the past was this *mnemonic* shield by which listeners in the present could live a better life.

I believe that Augustus Caesar, pained by his bloody triumphs that laid the foundation for the Pax Romana, might well have desired to create a more lasting monument even than the roads and aqueducts that still span the Mediterrean region today.

This novel is based on the premise that his monuments, "more lasting than bronze" (to lift a line from his poet Horace), included not only Virgil's great epic, *The Aeneid,* but also the Roman Catholic Church in which I was raised that holds sway two millennia later over the minds and hearts of billions of people.

What feels like a lifelong road that led to this vision of Rome was paved with the good offices of devoted partners, friends, editors, and readers, who gave me so many points and pointers I couldn't begin to acknowledge them all.

I'm grateful to the contributions, editorial and otherwise, of my publishers in Britain, Imprimatur Brittania, Chi-Li Wong, David Angsten, John Ballam, the late Ben Freedman, Katie McGee, Rick Rosenthal, R. J. Schork, Terry Stanfill, my

Yale mentor Lowry Nelson, Jr., and my late and great-hearted sister Andrea McKeown—all of them patient beyond the call of duty and even friendship.

Thanks, too, to the research of Margaret Morris, which, though I extended it, contradicted it, and went against and beyond it as the story illuminated the way, lay at the start of this quest to understand the parallels between Christianity and the cult of the Emperor Augustus.

The amulet depicted in chapter 43 is on the cover of Timothy Freke & Peter Gandy's *The Jesus Mysteries*.

Finally, my gratitude goes to my peerless wife Kayoko Mitsumatsu, whose patience, insight, and determination simply kept me going through it all.

—K.J.A. Rome, October 2011

About the Author

The author of *The Messiah Matrix*, Kenneth John Atchity, at the age of ten began instructions in the Latin language from a multi-lingual Jesuit mentor and went on to continue his study of Latin, and to commence studies in Homeric Greek and French, at the Jesuit high school, Rockhurst, in Kansas City, Missouri.

He won an Ignatian Scholarship to Georgetown University in Washington, D.C., where he enrolled in the Honors Program as a classics major and won the University's Virgilian Academy Silver Medal for his nationally-tested knowledge of Virgil's *Aeneid*.

At Georgetown, he added to his four years of high school Homeric Greek with studies of Attic and Koiné Greek as well as further studies in Homer and four more years of Latin. He spent his junior year summer at King's College, Cambridge.

Atchity received his Ph.D. from Yale in Comparative Literature, after adding Italian as his seventh language, focusing on the study of Dante under Harvard's Dante della Terza and Yale's Thomas Bergin. His dissertation, *Homer's Iliad: The Shield of Memory,* was awarded the Porter Prize, Yale Graduate School's highest academic honor. His mentors at Yale included Thomas Bergin, Thomas Greene, A. Bartlett Giamatti, Richard Ellmann, Eric Segal, and Lowry Nelson, Jr.

He was professor of literature and classics at Occidental College in Los Angeles, 1970-87, served as chairman of the comparative literature department, and as Fulbright Professor to the University of Bologna. His academic career included books on Homer and Italian literature, and dozens of academic articles and reviews. During his years at Occidental, Atchity was a frequent columnist for The Los Angeles Times Book Review, where he reviewed the novels of Umberto Eco, Doris Lessing, Gabriel Garcia-Marquez, Carlos Fuentes, and many others.

In a second career he represented writers of both fiction and nonfiction, accounting for numerous bestsellers and movies he produced for both television and big screen. In the tradition of Dominick Dunne, Sidney Sheldon, and Stephen Cannell he has drawn on his professional experience with storytelling to write *The Messiah Matrix*.

His writing, managing, and producing companies can be found at:

www.aeionline.com

www.thewriterslifeline.com

www.storymerchant.com

For more information about this novel, visit:

www.messiahmatrix.com